"Let Us Understand
One Another, Ensign Kirk,"
Spock Began . . .

"Threats pull no weight with me, and I shall not tolerate them. . . . I am ordering you to tell me who is responsible for your injuries."

But Kirk remained mute and immovable. In his prison days, he'd learned what it meant to keep a confidence. "I'm responsible for my own problems," he stated at last. "And I don't need a keeper! Keep your half-breed sentimentalities to yourself, Spock!" He started toward the door. . . . The Vulcan moved to stand between him and the door.

Half-breed. The word hung somewhere outside reality. . . .

Look for STAR TREK Fiction from Pocket Books

Star Trek: The Original Series

Star Trek: The Next Generation

KILLING TIME

DELLA VAN HISE

A STAR TREK® NOVEL

POCKET BOOKS

New York   London   Toronto   Sydney   Tokyo

This book is a work of fiction. Names, characters, places and incidents are either the product of the author's imagination or are used fictitiously. Any resemblance to actual events or locales or persons, living or dead, is entirely coincidental.

An *Original* Publication of POCKET BOOKS

POCKET BOOKS, a division of Simon & Schuster Inc.
1230 Avenue of the Americas, New York, NY 10020

This book is published by Pocket Books, a division of
Simon & Schuster Inc., under exclusive license from
Paramount Pictures.

ISBN: 0-671-70597-0

First Pocket Books printing July 1985

10 9 8 7

POCKET and colophon are registered trademarks of
Simon & Schuster Inc.

Printed in the U.S.A.

For Jim and Wendy and Diane

Acknowledgments

To:

Wendy for listening to hours of writing, re-writes, and so on, not to mention constant support & belief that it could work.

Jim for first saying, "You really should think about submitting *Killing Time* professionally."

Diane for support and for carrying on with the madness. We'll find that answer!

Gene Roddenberry for looking into the future to bring a vision to a world that needs visions desperately.

William Shatner & Leonard Nimoy for breathing life into two legends.

Anyone connected with STAR TREK for keeping that legend alive.

Mimi Panitch for putting the wheels into motion and for suggestions which made it all work.

Karen Haas for seeing everything through to its conclusion and for all the time and energy necessary to put all the pieces together.

Mom . . . for having the insight to set me down in front of an antiquated manual typewriter at an early age.

Cynthia . . . for perseverance above & beyond the call of duty, and for dealing calmly and warmly with a slightly edgy writer. It's appreciated more than you can know!

Chapter One

FOR THE THIRD consecutive night, Captain James T. Kirk awoke with a gasp of surprise and something akin to fear clinging to the side of his throat. He blinked once, then struggled to sit up, leaning against the head of the bed as his eyes scanned the dark room. Reality returned and his gaze settled on the chronometer. It was shortly after 3 A.M., Ship Standard Time, but he was wide awake and knew he would have little hope of getting back to sleep before the alarm demanded his attention at six.

Releasing the breath he'd been holding, he replayed the recurring dream in his mind, wondering why it should have disturbed him so deeply . . . and so often.

After discovering no logical explanation for its cause or its unprecedented effect on him, he tried passing it off to the fact that the *Enterprise* had been on routine patrol of the Romulan Neutral Zone for nearly two months—an inexcusably boring mission. But with Romulan Fleet activity increased for no apparent reason, he accepted the fact that he was bound to be a little edgy.

After another deep breath and a shake of his tousled hair, he slowly lowered himself back into the warm nest of covers, and closed his eyes; but as expected, he was only pretending to sleep when the First Shift duty alarm sounded less than three hours later.

Stifling a yawn, Kirk entered the Deck 5 turbolift to discover the ship's first officer studying him with a lifted eyebrow.

"Morning, Spock," Kirk said with a sheepish grin, wishing he'd taken the time for a cup of coffee before presenting himself publicly.

The Vulcan's head inclined in greeting. "Captain," he said formally. The doors closed and the lift began its familiar horizontal motion, but the Vulcan continued to study his friend. "Is everything all right, Captain?" he inquired presently.

"Just fine, Mister Spock," Kirk replied. "Why do you ask?" He wondered if his eyes were a trifle more red than they'd appeared in the mirror.

The eyebrow climbed higher beneath the long black bangs. "You seem . . . unusually distracted," Spock observed after a questioning moment of silence.

So much for dismissing the matter, Kirk thought. Spock's scrutiny was never escaped easily. "Would you believe me if I told you that the invincible Captain Kirk has insomnia?" he asked with a smile.

"Indeed," Spock murmured. Kirk was normally a very private individual; but now the hazel eyes seemed alight with a combination of embarrassment and mischief. The Vulcan decided not to mention that he himself had been having disturbing dreams for at least a week. "I trust you have not sought relief from Doctor McCoy?"

Kirk shook his head. "For a few hours of lost sleep?" But the twinkle left his eyes as a frown found its way to his face. "I don't know why it should bother me at all," he said, feeling some need to explain himself. "But . . . never mind, Spock," he added as the nocturnal images returned to haunt him. "It was . . . just a dream." Trying to change the subject, the smile returned to his face. "Another human shortcoming, eh, Spock?"

2

Something in Kirk's too-casual tone caused the Vulcan to look at him more closely. "Would you care to discuss the matter in more detail, Captain?" he asked, momentarily wondering why *he* didn't dismiss the subject as Kirk was attempting to do. Yet he realized that the captain's normal reservations concerning his personal life did not extend to him, just as he understood that the reverse was also true.

Kirk glanced up from where he'd been studying his boots, and felt the familiar telepathic door swing open between himself and the Vulcan. It was something which had formed between them over the years, something which had saved their lives countless times and made them brothers. He *did* want to discuss it, but only with Spock.

McCoy would, as the Vulcan was fond of pointing out, dispense a handful of pills and an hour of friendly advice; and though Kirk valued the doctor's friendship, he wasn't in the mood for a full battery of psychological tests to determine the cause of a simple recurring dream. He chanced a quick look at the Vulcan as a plan of action took shape in his mind.

"I haven't had breakfast yet," he began, finding an excuse he needed. "But . . . I'm sure *you* have, Mister Spock. After all," he continued with a broadening grin, "Vulcans never *ever* miss breakfast, right? You have to keep those thought-wheels well oiled and in perfect working order." He studied his first officer's lean frame. "And you never gain an ounce either!" he added with a look of mock-disgust, remembering McCoy's warnings to cut back on the meat and potatoes and settle for a salad once in awhile.

The Vulcan brow lowered as Spock observed his captain's nonchalant approach. "I have not eaten this morning," he stated in straightforward contrast to Kirk's roundabout endeavors, "and I would be pleased to join you. And we need not inform Doctor McCoy as to the menu."

3

"I'll have Scotty take over until we get up to the bridge," Kirk said, not finding it in himself to argue. After all, he rationalized, the *Enterprise* was doing nothing more than traveling back and forth at the border of the Neutral Zone—a mindless action which hardly required the captain *and* first officer's presence.

Lieutenant Jeremy Richardson sank slowly into the navigator's chair, studying the familiar star pattern which had all but plastered itself to his inner eye during the two weeks Chekov had been on leave. He glanced at Sulu, inclining his head toward the viewscreen.

"How much longer do you think we're going to be stuck with this assignment?" he asked, rubbing his eyes. "Did Kirk get on some admiral's nerves, or just manage to draw the short straw for this mission?"

Sulu grinned amiably, relaxing in the helmsman's chair. "Hell, Richardson," he said, elbowing the other lieutenant in the ribs, "if you'd *sleep* at night instead of trying to find the air-conditioning duct that leads to Yeoman Barrett's quarters, you might not find it so hard to get out of bed in the morning!"

Richardson shrugged as he mechanically checked the sensors, finding absolutely nothing out of the ordinary for what felt like the hundredth day in a row. He returned Sulu's smile and shook neatly trimmed brown hair back from handsomely tanned features. "Perseverance," he said knowingly, and winked. "Sooner or later, Barrett's bound to recognize my finer qualities and invite me out to dinner . . . a few drinks afterward . . . and then, who knows?"

Across the bridge, Uhura turned in her seat. "Isn't it supposed to be the other way around, Jerry?" she wondered. "Aren't *you* the one who is always praising the 'good old days'—when all a man had to do was flex his muscles to have women falling at his feet?" Her voice was a deep, teasing purr as she looked him up and down, pretending disinterest. "And aren't you the one who always said it was the man's place to ask the poor, frail female of the species to dance?"

Jerry shrugged at her teasing. "I *did* ask her," he said with exaggerated disappointment, then leaned back in the chair and fought off another encroaching yawn.

Sulu turned to Uhura and made a quick slicing motion across his throat. "She turned him down," he deduced with an easy chuckle. "Barrett's got a lot of promise. She knows a good thing when she sees it—and apparently she hasn't seen it yet."

Richardson swung the chair back toward the view screen and confirmed the ship's computer-designated course for the second time in less than a minute. "I'm giving her another chance," he said magnanimously. "And . . . if she doesn't decide within a week that I'm her knight in shining armor, there's always Lieutenant Masters or Nurse Drew . . . or even Yeoman S'Parva."

Sulu rolled his eyes in a gesture of long suffering. "S'Parva isn't exactly your type, is she, Jerry? Besides," he added, "she's a quadraped."

But Richardson only sighed romantically. "Rules were made to be broken, my friend, and anyway . . . I just thought we could be buddies, pals, chums." He put one hand dramatically over his heart, then leaned back in the chair. "I've never met another woman like our Yeoman S'Parva," he continued playfully, outlining an hour-glass motion with his hands. "A body like a goddess . . . and a face like an Irish setter!"

Sulu chuckled quietly. "Man's best friend?"

Jerry nodded, then ducked just in time to avoid being hit with the writing stylus which Uhura hurled at his head.

"Do you two have any idea what S'Parva would say if she heard that?" she asked, struggling to contain the laugh which had risen in her throat. "She'd probably throw you *both* up against the nearest bulkhead and teach you a lesson in respect. And if you were *very* lucky, Jerry, you might escape with nothing more than

5

a few broken bones and puncture wounds on your throat!''

Richardson's eyes closed in enhanced appreciation of the image. "Mmmm," he purred. "Sounds good to me." He winked at the communications officer. "Everybody needs a hobby, Uhura. Captain's orders."

Uhura turned back to her own station with a shake of her head. "I know you're not a bigot or a xenophobiac under that wolf's mask," she said, "so maybe I won't say anything to S'Parva if you stop prowling the corridors at night like some lovesick tomcat."

Jerry turned, gave a conspiratorial wink to Sulu, then rose to his feet in a graceful movement and slinked over to stand by Uhura's communications panel. He looked down into expectant brown eyes. "Meow?" he purred innocently, rubbing his cheek on the top of her chair.

Looking straight into the handsome face, the lieutenant depressed a button on the lighted panel.

"McCoy here," came the filtered response.

"Doctor McCoy," Uhura began, her eyes never leaving Richardson's face, "we seem to be having a problem with . . . vermin . . . on board the *Enterprise*. There's one very large tomcat up here who's just begging to be neutered. I thought you might want to send someone from the zoology department up here to put a net on him."

Jerry's jaw went slack as he stared down into the wide brown eyes which were as mischievous as his own. With a silent "Meow?" on his lips and a negative shake of his head, he turned and tiptoed back to his own post.

"What was that, Uhura?" McCoy's voice demanded after a long silence. "Are you sure the whole bridge hasn't got a bad case of cabin fever?" But the lightness of his tone belied any attempt at gruffness.

Uhura smiled knowingly in Richardson's direction. "Never mind, Doctor," she replied. "I think we have the problem in hand for the moment. But we'll call again if we need you."

"Right," McCoy agreed. The communication clicked off, then abruptly reactivated. "And don't fall asleep up there!"

Uhura smiled. "That may be the toughest order of the day, Leonard," she murmured, then switched off the intercom and glanced over to where Richardson had settled down quietly and was stifling another yawn. "Sweet dreams, Romeo," she teased.

Jerry shivered almost involuntarily. Dreams . . .

Kirk poked at the eggs on his plate with the tip of his fork, but it was blatantly obvious to Spock that the captain had little interest in the food.

"I don't know who I was, but . . . I wasn't who I was *supposed* to be." He laid the fork aside and took a healthy gulp of the reconstituted orange juice. "And that's not exactly right either," he continued, not quite looking at the Vulcan. "It was as if I was *still* James Kirk—the same James Kirk I've always been—but I wasn't in the right . . . *place*." He shook his head in frustration. "I can't explain it, Spock."

Spock eyed his friend carefully. "Dreams of alienation are not unusual," he pointed out. "In situations such as exist onboard starships, they are, in fact, extremely common." Taking a sip of the hot herb tea, he pushed his own plate of untouched food aside. He couldn't help remembering that he, too, had been experiencing dreams of alienation and displacement for nearly a full solar week; but something restrained him from mentioning it. "In your dream, Captain," he continued cautiously, "was it as if you were . . . not how you would normally envision yourself to be?"

Kirk frowned thoughtfully, then glanced up as his open palm slapped the table. "That's exactly it!" he exclaimed, then lowered his voice as he noticed a young yeoman at the next table cast a quick look in his direction. He leaned closer to the Vulcan, feeling vaguely ridiculous for the outburst, but somehow closer to the solution. "I was on the *Enterprise*—but it wasn't even the *Enterprise*—at least not like *I* know her," he added as an afterthought. "And . . . I kept seeing you." At last, he looked up. "But you were different, too, Spock," he stated emphatically. "I'm not sure, but . . . I think you were the captain."

He shuddered internally, as the haunting quality of the dreams sharpened. He thought he saw a faint smile come to the young yeoman's face as she stood and quickly left the dining area, but he no longer cared. At least it might alleviate her boredom. "And I didn't know who *I* was." He shrugged uncomfortably. "I must've been an ensign or something, because I remember trying to think of some way to approach you—to tell you that things weren't the way they're supposed to be."

He grinned without looking up, and took another swallow of the orange juice, tasting it for the first time. It only strengthened his resolve to put in a formal request to Admiral Nogura for *fresh* orange juice at the next opportunity. "And I also remember thinking that you would never believe me. After all," he added as the smile broadened, "you were the ship's captain—and a Vulcan! What chance would a lowly human ensign have of trying to inform the Vulcan commander that he (meaning me!) was supposed to be the captain?" He laughed aloud, feeling some of the tension ebb away just in the act of telling Spock about the absurdity of it all.

The Vulcan leaned forward, and their eyes met across the table. "Jim," he murmured in a tone suddenly deep and foreboding, "I also dreamed."

Kirk swallowed the lump of nervousness which rose in his throat, but he could only stare mutely at his first officer. Guiltily, he looked around to see if the yeoman was still eavesdropping. *Bad enough that the captain's having delusions of anything but grandeur,* he thought. *But if Spock buckles . . .* He let the thought drift into silence.

The Vulcan steepled his fingers in front of him. "At

first, I believed the dreams were attributable to the somewhat uneventful mission currently assigned to the *Enterprise*. However, I am no longer convinced that such is the case."

Kirk looked at his friend for a long time, their eyes holding them together. "What did you dream, Spock?" he asked, forcing his tone to remain neutral. But he didn't need to hear the answer; it was clearly inscribed in the dark eyes, carved in the angular features, written in the almost tangible conviction with which the Vulcan spoke.

One eyebrow arched, and it seemed for a moment as if the first officer might surrender to the human urge of shrugging. He did not. "I do not believe it is worth concerning yourself, Captain," he said as if attempting to dismiss his own statement. Somehow, it sounded far less logical in reality than it had in his own thoughts. "We have observed in the past that our minds have developed a telepathic rapport of sorts. Perhaps I was merely receiving fragments of your dreams, thereby—"

"Spock," Kirk interrupted with an exasperated sigh. He reached across the table, resting his fingers lightly on his friend's arm. "I know it's an inconvenience to your Vulcan logic to have this link with a human, but just *tell* me!" But the gentle smile robbed the words of any harsh implications.

After a moment, Spock nodded almost imperceptibly and took a deep breath. "I dreamed that you were an ensign," he stated, "and that I was . . . captain of the *Enterprise*."

Kirk leaned heavily back in the chair, letting his hand fall back to his side. He could think of nothing to say.

"Perhaps we should inform Doctor McCoy," Spock suggested. "Since Vulcans do not normally dream whatsoever, and since our dreams *do* bear remarkable similarity . . ." His voice drifted into silence.

Kirk glanced at the chronometer on the wall, then nodded. "You're probably right," he agreed. "As a precautionary measure, we probably should tell Bones. But . . ." He put one hand to his forehead, sensing a headache struggling to break through. "Just keep it to yourself today, Spock. I'm going to talk to a few other people and see what I can come up with first."

Spock's head inclined in acknowledgment, and he rose from the chair as Kirk stood and followed him toward the door.

Once inside the lift, Kirk tried to shake the feeling of uneasiness with a deep breath. His success was marginal. But when the double doors opened to reveal the familiar refuge of the bridge, he stepped back, smiling deceptively at Spock's apparent confusion. "After you . . . *Captain* Spock," he offered graciously.

The Vulcan turned, both brows climbing in a moment of surprise. "Illogical," he noted, but nonetheless stepped onto the bridge first. "Captain, I need not point out that it would be irrational to base rank solely on the basis of dreams—regardless of the fact that I would, no doubt, make an excellent commander."

Kirk shrugged, scrutinizing his first officer discreetly. "Maybe," he conceded, stepping onto the bridge and pulling the professional air of command into place. But he couldn't resist one final urge. "But keep in mind that I'd make one hell of a lousy ensign, Spock!"

The Vulcan stopped, meeting Kirk's eyes warmly. "Of that," he readily agreed, "I have no doubt."

Cold and blue, it swallowed him, and he thought of being engulfed by the sky back on Terra. Iowa farm sky. Crisp and blue and winter-cold. Scent of corn and hay in the fields. Autumn breeze tugging hungrily at his clothes and hair. Thunderheads talking among themselves on the horizon.

He rolled twice, effortlessly, floating, then broke the surface of the pool and side-stroked to the ladder. Overhead, the fiberflex board seemed to hum, calling him back. For a long time, he merely relaxed against the smooth sides of the pool, letting thought come and go without recording it consciously. But gradually reality intruded and he considered the day's events.

Five officers approached—four of whom admitted to dreams. *Nothing conclusive,* he told himself. *Everybody dreams. Period. Drop it, Kirk. Stop looking for Klingons under every latrine.* He floated out into the pool, letting the water buoy him up. *Or if you're really that worried about it, go have a brandy with Bones and—*

But before his mind could complete the train of thought, a familiar high-pitched whistle sounded on the communications panel.

Can't even be bored without interruptions, he thought with a vigorous shake of his dripping head. He backstroked over to the edge of the pool, hoisted himself up onto the deck, and strode over to the wall.

"Kirk here," he said. "Unless it's a full-scale red alert, Spock, I've got a hundred thousand gallons of water on hold."

"Unfortunately, Captain," the Vulcan's voice replied, "I can offer nothing quite so . . . intriguing at the moment."

Even three decks away, Kirk thought he could detect the amusement in the Vulcan's tone. "What is it, Spock?" he asked more lightly.

"Lieutenant Uhura has just received a Class A Priority Transmission from Starfleet Command," Spock responded. There was a momentary pause, then: "The message is manually coded. I believe that requires your personal attention in the Com Lab?"

Kirk smiled at the question in the Vulcan's voice, and at the gentle efficiency behind that question. But beyond that, he felt a peculiar tightness settle in the pit of his stomach. Manually coded messages were almost unheard of. Manually coded messages meant hours of painstaking transcription. Manually coded messages were a pain in the—

He quickly clamped down on the intruding thoughts. Anything was better than boredom. But as he looked at the pool, a deep sigh escaped his lips. "Pipe it down to the lab, Spock," he ordered, gazing at the high-dive board which was still slightly vibrating from his first—and apparently last—plunge of the day.

"Affirmative, Captain," the Vulcan responded. "Spock out."

Kirk chanced one final look at the board, the pool, and the sky-blue water. For a moment, he thought of home again; but the hum of starship's engines reminded him that *this* was home *now*. He turned away, content with that knowledge, and thumbed the switch which would activate the hot blow-dryers hidden in the bulkheads. A cubicle came down from the ceiling on silent rollers, surrounding him with a privacy which wasn't necessary. Then, after grabbing a towel from the heated compartment on the wall and rubbing it briskly over his head, he quickly dressed, pulling the gold command tunic neatly back into place—and, with it, the responsibilities.

Four hours later—at precisely the end of the day's official duty shift, Kirk sat alone in the Com Lab, staring at the single slip of paper before him. Scrawled, scratched and practically illegible, the message was nonetheless clear—but hardly worthy of a manually coded transmission status.

Rubbing tired eyes, he switched off the computer terminal, erased all coding programs pertinent to the message, then rose from the tiny desk and stretched tired muscles. He looked at the message again, then folded the paper and slipped it into the palm of his hand.

"Damn!" he swore, and stalked out into the deserted corridor.

Chapter Two

YEOMAN S'PARVA PLACED the dinner tray on the table, sat down carefully in a chair which was somehow too small for her bulky frame, and stared at the food, picking gingerly at the egg rolls and won ton on the edge of the platter. Across the dining room, she noticed a few heads turn in her direction—most of them male, she noted. Muted conversation buzzed noisily in her ear, and she heard her name mentioned more than once. Turning a little more toward the wall, she found herself feeling self-conscious despite the fact that she was far from being the only non-Terran in the room. Psychically, she sensed a Denevan, an Andorian, two Rigelians and a Deltan. Logically, the Deltan female should have been the center of attention, she told herself, remembering her psyche studies of the compelling women who were required to take a celibacy oath before accepting starship assignment. But at least the Deltans were humanoid, she thought.

Carefully, she nibbled at the food, wondering what new rumors were making the rounds concerning her placement on a starship. Even though Katellans had been in Starfleet for years, she realized with a certain amount of pride that she was the first of her race to achieve a position onboard a starship. She smiled to herself, and absently licked at the morsel of shrimp which had accidentally dropped from the egg roll and onto her left paw. Then, realizing what she'd done, she made a mental note to be more cautious. *Old habits die hard,* she thought. After a few more delicate bites, she laid the egg roll aside, picking up the knife and fork. Inconvenient though the implements were, she accepted that they were a necessity—at least until her peers grew accustomed to her canine physiology. And yet, she realized that Katellans weren't *that* different from their human counterparts. Already, she had mastered walking upright—which, she had realized, was actually quite convenient. And the rest would come soon enough. Within a week, the control panel and equipment in her department would be completely refurbished—to accommodate both bipeds and quadrupeds. She looked at her hands, at the fork she had learned to hold with some amount of practice. Three longer fingers and a thumb distinguishable from its human counterpart only by the soft fur. Yes, the rest would follow.

"Hi!" a voice said as another steaming dinner tray seemed to appear on the table next to her own. "How's life down in the psyche lab?"

She jolted, gasped, then quickly recovered her composure, grateful that the facial fur concealed any tint of embarrassment which might otherwise have found its way to her cheeks. She looked up from her reverie to discover Jerry Richardson sitting across the table, a boyish grin playing in the deep brown eyes.

"Didn't mean to startle you," he apologized, grabbing an egg roll and unashamedly stuffing it into his mouth. "Just thought you looked lonely sitting over here all by yourself."

After the initial astonishment, S'Parva felt herself relaxing. She managed a smile. "Thanks, Jerry," she said quietly. "Guess I'm a bit nervous tonight."

Richardson shrugged, downing the remainder of the egg roll and reaching for the container of chocolate milk on the corner of the tray. "No reason to be," he said between swallows. "You seem to be doing just fine—at least from the reports I hear."

S'Parva leaned closer, her voice hushed. "It's not the work, Jerry," she relinquished somewhat hesitantly. "It's . . . well . . ." She sighed deeply, broad shoulders rising and falling in the blue V-necked sweater-tunic which had been especially designed for her. Even in that way, she was different, she thought. But Jerry didn't seem to notice—just as he didn't seem to notice that she was a foot taller than he was, or that she could snap his neck with one quick movement. And there was something compelling about that innocence, she realized. Something which allowed her to think of him as *K'tauma*—friend, companion, teacher, little brother. "It's something . . ." But she fell into silence. There were no words in Katellan or Terran to describe the feeling.

Presently, Richardson looked up, thin brows narrowing suspiciously. He set the milk aside. "You're not worried about the little remodeling job down in the lab, are you?"

Again, S'Parva shrugged, whiskered brows twitching slightly. "I dunno," she admitted with a sheepish smile. "It just seems like a hell of a lot of trouble—for one person!"

Jerry laughed, stabbed a fried shrimp with the salad fork, and popped it into his mouth. "Don't look at it that way, S'Parva," he said easily. "The Katellans aren't the only quadraped race in the Fleet; the refurb on the control panels down there is long overdue." He grinned broadly, munching down another shrimp and following it with something which vaguely resembled a french fry. "And besides—even if those changes *were* just for you, take it as a nice comment on your service record. Starfleet doesn't authorize that kind of alteration unless they think you're worth keeping on the payroll."

S'Parva considered that, and forced herself to relax. "Thanks, Jerry," she said with a grin. "Sometimes I just need to be reminded of things like that." After another moment, she picked up the fork again, holding it almost casually in one hand. It still felt damned uncomfortable, but bearable. She speared a clam, placed it in her mouth, and chewed absently as she continued studying Richardson from across the table.

For a human, she thought, he was handsome. And there was no denying the rapport they shared. She wondered if part of it was attributable to the fact that he was one of the only men on the *Enterprise* who didn't seem to have trouble just talking with her, spending time with her. Richardson was neither nervous nor cautious in her presence, wasn't always tripping over himself pretending *not* to notice their differences. He merely accepted them as she accepted his; and there was something about his casual demeanor which served to set her at ease as well. She smiled to herself, then realized abruptly that the young lieutenant was watching her quite closely, a faint smile tugging the corners of his lips.

"It works both ways, you know," he said warmly.

Her brows twitched; she wondered if he knew it was a Katellan trait signaling chagrin. "What works both ways?" she asked innocently.

Richardson shrugged. "The telepathy," he ventured as if discussing nothing more important than the schematics of a food processor. "*You* know what *I'm* thinking and . . ." He let the sentence trail off.

For a moment, S'Parva could think of nothing to say. Humans could be so damned open, so easy to read. Then, with a gentle laugh, she nodded agreement. But as she continued to look at the young man, her eyes narrowed curiously. "You look beat," she said, only then noticing the red-rimmed eyes and slouched posture. "Don't tell me the captain's got you sweeping the bridge as a cure for boredom."

Richardson drew back, lips tightening as he looked away. "No," he said, voice suddenly clipped. "Just . . ." He shook his head. "Nothing."

Briefly, S'Parva wondered if she had somehow insulted her friend; for no sooner had she spoken than she felt an uncharacteristic distance between them. It hurt. She leaned across the table, touching his hand almost without thinking. "Sorry," she murmured. "I didn't mean to—"

But Richardson shook his head, silencing her with a gentle smile. A pink hue had risen to color his face. "No, no," he quickly said. "You haven't violated any human tribal taboo, S'Parva. It's just that I've been having a little trouble sleeping these past few nights." He grinned. "And the captain's been greedy—doing his own sweeping: the bridge, the officers' lounge, the gym. And rumor has it that he's going to scrub the hangar deck with what they used to call a toothbrush."

S'Parva smiled, grateful that it was as simple as that. The door opened again. Easily. "He's quite a man, isn't he?" she asked.

Richardson nodded, taking a deep breath. "Captain Kirk's one of a kind," he stated. "I've been on three different starships on this tour of duty, and he's the best of them all."

S'Parva considered that. The knowledge wasn't anything she hadn't suspected. "Last I heard," she offered, "there was quite a waiting list just to get stationed on this ship."

Pushing the now-empty plate aside, Richardson grinned. "Did you specifically apply for the *Enterprise?*"

S'Parva shook her head. "I was assigned," she replied, feeling a sense of pride in that realization, which she hadn't recognized before. *Assigned—to the best ship in the Fleet.* Internally, she felt something settle—like a weight which had been off-balance for a long time. She looked up, and noticed that she'd completely finished the meal—without the self-consciousness which had been with her for the past month. She took another deep breath, leaned back in the chair, and shook her head in mild amazement.

"You're something else, Jerry," she said with a laugh. "For a human, you're really something else."

The lieutenant shrugged as a devilish grin took

shape. "Who told?" he asked, then yawned unexpectedly.

S'Parva lifted one brow with an admonishing glance. "You really should come down to the psyche lab, Jerry," she suggested. "We do most of our so-called 'business' during times like these. The crew gets bored and all sorts of symptoms start cropping up—such as insomnia?"

Richardson glanced around the room—almost nervously, S'Parva noted. She wondered what she'd said wrong—again.

"And dreams?" Richardson asked at last.

S'Parva's eyes widened. The fourteenth complaint today.

Kirk stared at the tri-level chessboard without really seeing it, and absently moved the white queen one level higher.

Eyebrow arching, Spock leaned back. "A most unwise move, Captain," he observed, easily detecting Kirk's uncharacteristic lack of concentration. Without trying, the Vulcan had won his third consecutive game.

Kirk shook his head with a sigh, remembering the slip of paper in the top drawer, the dreams. "Distracted, I guess," he ventured, meeting his first officer's eyes and forcing an unfelt smile. He inhaled deeply, then leaned back in the chair and folded his hands neatly behind his head, stretching. "I don't mean to keep whipping a dead horse, Spock," he began, "but . . . from what I've found out—about the dreams—it's starting to give me the willies."

The Vulcan stared mutely at his captain. "What would it profit to administer punishment to a deceased lifeform, Captain?" he wondered, attempting to lighten the heavy mood which had settled on Kirk during the course of the day. "And precisely what are the . . . willies?"

Kirk's smile broadened. "The creeps, Mister

Spock," he clarified. "The crawls. The shivers. The boogey-man blues."

The eyebrow slowly lowered. "Of course, Captain," Spock replied, as if the entire matter was suddenly explained.

With a shrug, Kirk rose from the chair, moving into the living area of his quarters. He looked at the dresser for a moment, then impulsively yanked open a drawer and seized a plaid flannel shirt. After hastily removing the gold command tunic and tossing it across the room into the laundry disposal, he slipped into the civilian attire and began buttoning the shirt. He had to put command temporarily aside, and the braid on his sleeve was a constant reminder that that was never easy to do.

"C'mon, Spock," he urged, walking toward the door and tipping the white chess king over onto its side. "Let's take a walk. Maybe I just need some distance from everything."

The Vulcan's head tilted in curiosity. The ship's patrol was so utterly routine that he wasn't particularly surprised to see Kirk's nature asserting itself. The captain was the type of man who was always on the move, always seeking new adventures—and usually involved in dangerous excitement. In a moment of admitted illogic, Spock questioned the mentality of Command for sending the *Enterprise* to patrol the Neutral Zone in the first place. Surely, he thought, it would have been more reasonable to assign such a mission to a Scout class vessel. The *Enterprise* was, after all, the most efficient ship in the Fleet; and the Vulcan couldn't help wondering if the reasoning behind their current patrol was more complicated than anyone had been led to believe. And there was the matter of the manually coded transmission. But he rose from the chair and followed his friend. Kirk would tell him—*when* and *if* the time was right. But as he passed by the chessboard, he reached out and impulsively righted the white king.

"What's the matter, Spock?" Kirk asked, face suddenly alight with mischief as he stood waiting by the now open door. "Afraid I'll have you court-martialed for insubordination because you beat me in another game of chess?"

The Vulcan merely shook his head as he fell in step alongside his captain, and they ventured into the corridor. "Hardly," he replied. "I merely thought it inappropriate to abandon the match so early in the evening. Your unorthodox approach to chess will doubtlessly assert itself later and you will discover some method of defeating me with an illogical and unpredictable move." He squared broad shoulders, innocently looking straight ahead as they approached the lift. "I am merely offering you that opportunity, Captain."

Kirk grinned. "In other words, Spock," he surmised, "you're generously giving me one final chance to humiliate myself."

"Captain!" Spock replied indignantly.

Kirk suppressed a laugh as they reached the lift. He thumbed the button, waiting for the doors to open. "You know, Spock," he mused. "Sometimes I wonder about you. Sometimes I think you're the ship's resident guardian angel—and other times I'm convinced you're the devil in disguise."

The Vulcan stared straight ahead, face expressionless. "Folklore *is* sometimes based in fact, Captain," he replied enigmatically.

For a long time, they simply walked, visiting areas of the ship which were normally removed from the world of command. Finally as if by intuition, Kirk stopped in front of a large door, looked at it as if deciding whether or not to enter, then finally depressed the lock mechanism and urged the Vulcan along with a quick nod of his head. Spock followed, somewhat reticently.

"C'mon," Kirk prompted with a grin. "Stop acting like a cat who's afraid of getting his feet wet."

Spock remained stubbornly standing outside the door. "Captain," he protested, "it is a biological fact that Vulcans are sensitive to high humidity. The gardens—"

But before he could complete the sentence, Kirk seized him by one arm and dragged him forward with a laugh. "Live a little, Spock," he suggested. "And that's an order."

The Vulcan sighed, and slowly followed Kirk into the room. For a reason he couldn't pinpoint, Spock felt uneasy—as if this area of the ship was suddenly alien, dangerous. He lifted both brows at the illogical consideration, and took a moment to look around. Nothing out of the ordinary, yet the feeling persisted— as if ghostly eyes followed them. He swept the thought away. Illogical. Unacceptable behavior—particularly for a Vulcan. Reality seemed unstable. The brows rose higher, and though Kirk seemed oblivious to the sudden ethereal change, Spock couldn't deny its existence. Somehow, he felt himself altered, alien even to his own mind. But he continued following, nonetheless. Kirk's instincts were always good, he told himself.

Once inside the lush green gardens, Kirk felt some of the uneasiness leave him. He thought for a brief instant that he detected a hesitation in Spock, but when he turned to glance over his shoulder, it was to see the Vulcan standing close at his side. He dismissed the sensation, passing it off to mundane distractions and tedium as his eyes settled on the "world" before him.

The maze paths which ran throughout this Earth-like area of the ship gave the illusion of five miles of hiking trails in a natural environment. Kirk attempted to divorce himself from the fact that it was merely an impression—carefully designed by the builders of the *Enterprise* to promote a feeling of "home." The room itself was approximately a hundred yards deep and seventy-five yards wide, almost overgrown with thousands of plants—flowers and small trees from a thou-

21

sand different worlds. It was always spring here, the air fresh and clean. Even the air-conditioning vents had been designed to provide the illusion of a gentle breeze; and the domed ceiling spoke of a clear blue Terran sky, complete with clouds and occasional rainbows. When ship's night began to fall, a pseudo-sunset adorned the high ceiling, its purples, pinks and oranges all but obliterating the reality that one was still aboard a starship at least five light-years from the nearest Class M planet.

Forcing himself to ignore his own tensions, Kirk slipped into the Earth fantasy as he began walking along the central maze path—which would, he recalled, eventually lead to the deepest portion of the garden. As he looked up to see the Vulcan at his side, he couldn't help noticing that the gardens were having their effect even on Spock. The first officer seemed so much more relaxed and at peace here—even if somewhat distracted, Kirk noticed. For a moment, the human could almost envision his second in command swinging from a tree limb as he'd done once before—but not without the influence of spores to erase the normal Vulcan restraints. It was a soothing image, despite the fact that it was impossible. For an instant, Kirk wondered what would eventually become of his friend—of the two of them, where they would be in another twenty years. For himself, he suspected he'd still find some way of manipulating the stars, chasing adventure through the dark regions of time and space. But for Spock . . . His mind traveled back in time—to Vulcan. To a day when Spock had been prepared to marry . . . and disaster had resulted. Unbonded now, the Vulcan was walking a tightrope between life and death; for without the deep mental rapport necessary to establish a bonding, Spock would die in the blood fever of pon farr.

Despite the heat of the gardens, Kirk shivered, walking a little faster toward the central portion of the room. Surely, he told himself, Spock wouldn't die. Surely, he told himself, there would be someone with whom the Vulcan could bond, someone who could walk the path with him, balance him, love him.

For a long time, Kirk considered that. He wondered if the Vulcan knew what he was thinking, decided that it didn't matter. He would have said it aloud—*had* said it aloud countless times. He smiled to himself. No secrets, he'd once told Spock. And the Vulcan had agreed. He closed his eyes, and attempted to put the frightening thought of the future in the back of his mind. It would take care of itself—somehow.

At last reaching the central portion of the gardens, Kirk took a moment to study his surroundings. Six large trees which vaguely resembled weeping willows grew in a circle approximately thirty yards in diameter. Branches like arms hung to the ground, sweeping against the grassy floor of the gardens.

Entering the circle of trees, Kirk took a deep breath of fresh air, and moved to one of the old stone benches which had begun to sport a healthy growth of mildew. He sat down slowly, then leaned back until he felt the cold moisture of the stone seep through his shirt and onto his shoulder blades. It was good in a way he couldn't describe—good in the same way a memory of childhood was good. It brought back recollections of sneaking off to the park on a warm May afternoon when he *should* have been in school. He closed his eyes, enjoying the fantasy, the memories . . . the illusions which existed only in the past. But when he opened his eyes again, it was to see Spock still standing, looking down at him questioningly. There was concern—and possibly Vulcan worry—written in the black eyes.

Kirk held the penetrating gaze for a moment, then managed a smile when he saw the Vulcan soften. "Live a little, Spock," he said again, indicating a nearby bench with a nod of his head. "Didn't you ever go out and roll in the grass when you were a kid?"

The arched brow spoke volumes for the Vulcan's childhood.

"No . . ." Kirk decided. "I guess not." He rolled

23

into a sitting position, feeling the nervousness and depression return despite the momentary external façade. He knew the Vulcan could see through his masks. "Sit down," he said more seriously. "I need a wailing wall, Spock."

The Vulcan might have considered responding in the customary, teasing way, but the idea left him as he observed the unusual tension in the familiar hazel eyes. Perhaps Kirk *had* felt the difference, the ghostly quality of their surroundings. He settled for a neutral approach. "This mission should not last much longer, Jim," he ventured, feeling suddenly inadequate to deal with Kirk's frustrations as he searched for something positive to say. "We are scheduled for shore leave in less than a month." He paused as if hearing the clipped tone of his own voice; perhaps teasing with this human *was* the only solution. "And I believe Altair has always been one of your favorites, has it not?"

Kirk shook his head, then felt the angry butterflies warring in his stomach again. "Altair . . ." he mused. He looked closely at the Vulcan, then impulsively reached into the pocket of the plaid shirt to withdraw the crumpled piece of paper he'd hidden there earlier. He unfolded it, handing it to the Vulcan. "The transcript," he explained. "All leaves have been indefinitely postponed."

The Vulcan studied the paper carefully, committing its sparse contents to memory.

KIRK: YOUR CURRENT MISSION EXTENDED UNTIL FURTHER NOTIFICATION. THREE EAGLES LANDING ON THE BORDER MIGHT NEED FLIGHT INFORMATION. A TIMELY CONSIDERATION FOR *ENTERPRISE*—EAGLES FLY BY NIGHT.

Spock looked up, handed the paper back to Kirk. "Romulan activity," he surmised.

Kirk nodded. "Romulan activity, Mister Spock." Then, with a frustrated shake of his head, he rose and began to pace back and forth in the confines of the circle of trees. "From the sounds of that transmission, the upper echelons are getting more than a little worried," he continued. "But no one seems to be able to pinpoint *what* the Romulans are up to this time." He shrugged. "Command suspects it has something to do with an attempt to invade Federation planets bordering the Neutral Zone, but . . ." He stopped pacing long enough to rub his forehead as he sensed the prelude to another headache. "But that's nothing new," he realized, resuming the nervous pacing. "Besides, that's what battle cruisers were designed for. Starships are *supposed* to be for exploration and contact; battle cruisers were built to deal with invasions and attacks." He managed a smile, an uneasy laugh. "General rumor also has it that three additional starships are being sent to this sector as a precautionary measure. And if that doesn't mean somebody's got their rocks in a grinder, then I don't know what to think." He took a deep breath. "But as usual with Command, they aren't being very generous with their information."

Spock was silent for a long moment. "And you stated that Starfleet has no precise knowledge of what the Romulans are planning?"

Kirk shrugged, threw up his hands, then forced himself to sit by the Vulcan's side. "All they know is that the Romulan Fleet appears to be converging near the border of the Zone. Our intelligence forces inside the Empire got wind of something concerning a time travel experiment which has been going on over there for quite a while; but according to Admiral Komack's last general transmission, we lost contact with the agents before they could relay the specifics." He grimaced. "I don't think we have to ask what happened to them."

Spock glanced away, confirming Kirk's suspicions; but the Vulcan changed the subject. "Do you believe the dreams could have something to do with events inside the Romulan Empire?" he asked

Kirk felt something stir in his stomach.

"Since certain Romulans *are* telepathic," Spock

25

continued, "do you believe it possible that your dreams could have resulted from a temporary psychic link to someone inside the Empire?"

Kirk's brows narrowed thoughtfully. A possibility, sure. But random speculation—from Spock? "I dunno," he admitted. "Maybe I'm just getting paranoid in my old age." He laughed gently, trying to chase away the cold, black thing which seemed to be lingering at his shoulder. It had his own eyes, his features, his mind. But it felt alien.

Kirk was the only person on board to whom Spock could open up, and he valued that freedom. "If there are answers, we will find them, Jim," he ventured. "But . . . I believe it can wait until morning. You appear somewhat . . . fatigued?"

Men like Spock weren't standard issue. "Thanks, Spock," he murmured. "I don't know what the hell I'd do without you." He stood slowly, and turned to go.

The Vulcan rose to follow his captain, taking a moment to appreciate the easy rapport which was always there between them. "No doubt you would win at chess, Captain," he suggested as they began walking back toward the entrance of the gardens.

Kirk laughed, then turned to glance at the "sky" when he noticed that nightfall had begun. Muted colors melted into the domed sky, and he allowed himself the luxury of inhaling the cool fresh air into his lungs and holding it there.

"It's almost like being home, Spock," he said. "No Romulans except in Dad's exaggerated space-tales; no nightmares other than algebra . . ." He gave in to the fantasy for just a moment, then, recognizing the lethal danger of homesickness and melancholy, opened his eyes once again. "You know," he continued, "my father used to tell me that childhood itself was the only home a man could ever have." He laughed—somewhat nervously—and continued to look at the domed ceiling. For the briefest instant, he could almost envision cloudy dragons and white-fluffed unicorns.

Spock's eyes closed for just a moment. "Your father

was, no doubt, a remarkable man, Captain," he replied after a long silence. His own father had rarely spoken of such matters—and never of the stars. He started to speak again, but stopped abruptly when Kirk shook his head with a smile.

"Don't worry, Spock," the human replied. "I don't expect an answer." He took one last look at the dome; it was almost "night" now, and soon the stars would be visible through the transparent ceiling. He turned toward the door, determined to leave the melancholy behind. "I don't regret *any* of it," he said. "And who knows? Maybe we'll be laughing about this whole thing in some Altairian café in another month." He turned to look at the impassive expression on his friend's face as the double doors opened into the main corridor of the ship. "Well, at least *I'll* be laughing," he corrected.

An eyebrow climbed under sleek black bangs as they stepped into the hall and resumed the correct routine. The masks of captain and first officer fell into place.

"I would not be adverse to spending some time on Altair, Captain," Spock said unexpectedly. "I am told that the museums and library facilities are excellent."

Kirk laughed as he drew up to a halt in front of the turbolift doors. "I didn't know Altair *had* museums and libraries, Mister Spock!"

"Well, Jim," McCoy drawled, "there's not much I can do about it without running tests on all the people involved." He relaxed in the high-backed chair, placing his feet on the corner of an always-cluttered desk. "And as you probably know better than anyone else on board, dreams are just a way of letting off steam." The blue eyes studied Kirk carefully. "Since the conscious mind is theoretically too civilized—and too *scared,* I might add—to even *think* certain things, those things work themselves out in dreams." A warm smile came to his face. "It's probably just a coincidence that the people you talked to had disturbing dreams."

Kirk shook his head. "I don't think so, Bones," he said, refilling the two brandy snifters and passing one to the doctor. "All the people I talked to had the same *type* of dream."

McCoy glanced up lazily. Granted, he thought to himself, Kirk had a point. But his professional ethics compelled him to dig deeper before jumping to any irrational conclusions. For once, he mused, even Spock would've been proud of him. And he knew Kirk would respect those ethics as well. It would have been easy enough to run sample vid-scans, but the Surgeon General would want specifics—*facts,* which as yet didn't exist.

"Suppose you tell me about this dream again, Jim," he said, taking a sip of the brandy.

Resignedly, Kirk repeated the dream, concluding with a heavy sigh. "Maybe you're right," he ventured. "Maybe I *am* placing too much importance on it." He paused, staring at the desk, using it as a focal point. "Hell, Bones," he confessed, "I've thought about losing the *Enterprise,* and I can accept that it'll happen one day. Nobody stays this age forever." He grinned, almost shyly. "So . . . that's not what's bothering me. And I'm not insecure to the point that I would ever suspect Spock of trying to usurp my command." He laughed, then fell silent. "Am I?" he asked at last.

McCoy looked up, blue eyes narrowing curiously. "So maybe your mind was just playing out a fantasy," he suggested. "In the back of your thoughts, you've wondered what it would be like to serve under that stubbornly logical Vulcan. Your dreams just let you act it out—harmlessly," he added. He leaned forward in the chair, resting his elbows on the desk. "Off the record, Jim, I wouldn't be surprised to discover that half the crew has the same kind of daydreams. But since you're the only one on board who happens to out-rank Spock, the dreams are going to be more disturbing to you than anyone else." He shrugged amiably. "But it's a safe fantasy, Jim," he stressed. "You're just curious underneath that command pose of yours. After all, with a Vulcan captain, no decision could ever be biased—"

"Are you insinuating that mine are?" Kirk asked.

McCoy grinned. "Not at all, Jim," he said quietly. "All I'm saying is that Spock has a certain . . . mystique. It leads people to wonder what kind of commander he would make. It's as normal as fantasizing about anything else—and twice as secure. As you already know, Spock doesn't want command; he never has; and he never will. The two of you owe each other your lives a hundred times over, so you can put your subconscious to rest. Spock would never be the one to take command of the *Enterprise*—especially if that meant commanding *you* as part of the bargain!"

Before Kirk could think of a response, McCoy leaned forward, refilled the suddenly empty glasses, and continued. "Personally, I don't think there's anyone in Starfleet who *could* command you—admirals and such included. But sometimes your mind gets tired of playing 'Captain Kirk.' Deep inside, there's still a part of you that *needs* someone to look up to—and that person just happens to be your first officer in this case. When you go to sleep, the little boy in you needs someone to relate to—and that little boy automatically chooses Spock—sort of a big-brother figure for your dreams."

Kirk considered that, and felt some of the worry leave him. It made sense—was even logical. "Okay," he conceded. "As I've said before, you're probably right. But . . . your explanation still doesn't cover one thing."

McCoy waited.

"Spock," Kirk said at last, laying the single syllable in the air.

McCoy stared mutely at his captain, then raised both brows questioningly. "What about him?"

"He . . . had the exact same dream that I did. He was the captain, I was an ensign, and the *Enterprise* wasn't exactly the *Enterprise*."

McCoy reached instantly for a stack of computer

tapes which rested haphazardly on one corner of the desk. "You should've told me that to begin with," he grumbled with a smile. "It would've spared you my lecture on the psychological significance of dreams."

Kirk returned the smile. "Maybe I needed to hear it anyway, Bones," he suggested. "It got me out of doing my nightly paperwork and gave me a chance to mooch some of your brandy, too. Not a bad way to spend an hour."

"Whoever said that starship captains always take the most direct approach to a problem obviously never met you, Jim," the doctor replied, rising to his feet and moving into the anteroom of the office. "I'll want a list of the people you've talked with so far," he called through the open door. "In the meantime, I'll get some of my people on it, too. I want to interview everyone on this ship and get a percentage rate. If it's just a few isolated cases, then it's probably just psychological— stress, boredom, whatever." He reappeared in the main office carrying a hefty stack of computerized clipboards. "But if it turns out to be more than twenty-five percent of the crew . . ." His voice drifted off momentarily. "If it's *more* than that, Jim," he repeated, "we'll have to inform Starfleet Command; put in for shore leave at a starbase."

Kirk nodded. "Any speculations, Bones?" he asked hopefully.

"I'm a doctor," McCoy pointed out as one of the clipboards slipped from his arm and clattered to the floor, "not a dream merchant." He plopped the remaining portable computers onto the desk, thumbing the intercom to the outer offices. "Nurse Chapel, I want six lab techs in here before the echo dies!"

Kirk grinned at his friend's obvious enthusiasm. "Looks like you're going to be a dream merchant this week," he pointed out, and quickly found an excuse to leave, recognizing the doctor's need for professional privacy and space.

But as he walked down the corridor toward his quarters, he couldn't help looking over his shoulder just once. Something felt wrong . . . and he hoped it wasn't already too late.

Lieutenant Jeremy Richardson looked at the bed, feeling a shiver crawl along his spine. After adjusting the thermostat on the wall and dimming the lights, however, he crawled beneath the heavy covers and listened to the sound of his own breathing. For a moment, he thought he saw a shadow—a dark, nebulous form which moved and took shape by the bed. He closed his eyes, but the phantom worked its way behind the lids.

It smiled at him—his own smile.

It winked . . . with his own eyes.

Chapter Three

CAPTAIN JAMES T. KIRK awoke in the middle of a night which was blacker than usual, startled by a dream which slipped through the ethereal fingers of memory. It left him alone and irrefutably shaken inside himself; and though he tried to open weighted eyelids, he discovered himself paralyzed.

The images of the dream continued to move, like obscene specters in his mind, like information being fed into a computer not prepared to accept new programming. He fought, writhing under the disheveled covers until beads of sweat stood at prompt attention on his forehead.

Intellectually, he knew he was awake; yet the nightmare quality lingered, refusing to deliver him into the sanity of consciousness.

His mind was ripped from him, pulled into unseen hands, then reshaped to create another creature, an entirely different being. His muscles remained taut, as sails on a ship; and he found himself too frozen with horror to move or breathe. Memories which had once been pleasant were suddenly unreachable as his past disappeared down a long, black tunnel. Painful recollections took shape before his inner eye—women he had loved, women he had lost. A ship—*his*. All gone.

"S-Spock?" he cried out, hearing it as a scream in his mind, but as little more than a dry whisper suspended in reality. The Vulcan should be there . . . yet was not. The familiar link seemed obscure and distant, as if it no longer existed.

For a single terrifying moment, Spock was dead; and the human knew instinctively that he was alone with ghosts. In the past, the idea of solitude had never frightened him; but now, a sense of mindless, terrible loneliness came to dwell in him with a vengeance, wrenching a cry of anguish from his throat as his mind instinctively sought Spock's.

No . . . not dead. Not quite. He thought he could almost sense the mental rapport which had always been there before. But it too slipped away . . . and was gone.

Time cartwheeled.

Backward . . . Forward again.

Somewhere in the back of his conscious mind, the human chastised himself for the abrupt and unprecedented failure of his command pose; but as his eyes finally wrenched themselves open, he realized that it had been nothing more than a dream within a dream.

With a gasp, he caught himself wondering where he was, why he was trembling in fear, and why he had been mentally reaching out to a man whom he'd never personally met. And, most of all, he wondered why he should consider the *ShiKahr*'s Vulcan captain to be a friend.

Shaking the disorientation from his mind, he forced himself to start breathing again, and slowly fell back into the strange bed as the dream transmutated and became reality.

A quick glance at the other single bed confirmed that his roommate—a man who had been introduced to him less than twenty-four hours previously as Paul Donner—was still sound asleep, apparently untroubled by dreams.

33

With an effort, Kirk rose, stumbled into the small bathroom, and splashed cold water on his face until the discomfort alone chased the last shards of sleep from his mind. But the anger returned with a vengeance when he realized that he *wasn't* a starship captain, would *never* be a starship captain . . . and that the dreams were just another way the Talos Device kept coming back from his past to haunt him.

Yet even those memories which had always been so sharp and clear seemed distant now—more than a vision . . . less than a recollection. He told himself firmly that dreams of disorientation and bitterness were bound to linger for a while; he'd been drafted into active Starfleet duty less than six months ago, and only assigned to the VSS *ShiKahr* yesterday. He glanced suspiciously around the dimly lit quarters, ignoring the easy snoring from Donner, and trying to shake the feeling of alienation as he studied the unfamiliar surroundings. None of it felt right . . . but he had expected nothing more or less.

And he also accepted the fact that he did not *want* it to feel right. . . .

Cautious, hardened hazel eyes scanned the bedroom carefully, gave one last check on Donner's status, then traveled to the small bag of personal belongings he'd brought on board and tossed haphazardly into one corner. Moving back into the living area, he knelt by the bed, fumbled with the tattered suitcase, then withdrew two small items. With trembling hands, he lifted the syringe to the bathroom light, filled it with the last few drops from the ampoule, then turned the instrument toward his wrist. For a moment, something inside him rebelled; something warned that drug-induced acceptance of Fate might not be the answer he needed. But he swept the nagging thought aside when stray fragments of the dream returned to remind him of what he had lost . . . what he had never possessed.

She . . . silver woman-goddess. She.

Dead and buried.

He brought the hypo down against his bare wrist,

flinching only slightly when the high-pressure needle injected cold fluid into the vein with a hiss which reminded Kirk of a serpent.

Donner moved in his sleep at the sound, slapping at his round face as if chasing an imaginary fly or spider. Then, with a grunt of dismay, the powerful body rolled onto its stomach, and strong arms pulled a pillow over tousled hair as he slumped deeper into sleep.

As the drug entered his system, Kirk replaced the damning evidence back in the bottom of the suitcase and staggered unsteadily to the bed, barely drawing the covers over his chest before the dizziness took him. He realized with dismay that that had been the last dose of lidacin. On Earth, the drug had been easy to buy . . . but on a starship, it would be next to impossible.

As his eyes lowered, he bit his lip until pain intervened. *Sleep. She* would be there. But *only* there.

With a heavy sigh, Ensign Kirk surrendered to the effects of the drug, to a darkness populated by spirits and a more acceptable reality. He was no longer the man he had been all his life, no longer Captain James T. Kirk. Now he too was a specter, another ghost of a far-removed surreal reality. The James T. Kirk he had known was now nothing more than a dream, a psychic stranger who occasionally came to the ensign in nightmares to demand a rank and a ship which would never be his in this universe.

Captain James T. Kirk no longer existed as the Romulan flagship descended from hyperspace and slipped into orbit over its home world . . . more than twenty light-years away.

Captain Spock walked down the deserted "night" corridors, completing the daily inspection with routine precision. Everything was in order: fire control systems fully operational on Decks 4 through 11; low-level radiation leakage in engineering well within normal range; matter/anti-matter pods checked and serviced by Chief Engineer Scott; warp drive functioning properly; ship cruising at Warp One on routine patrol of Romulan Neutral Zone.

The Vulcan studied the checklist on the computerized clipboard, made the appropriate notations, then placed the instrument under one arm and turned to go back the way he'd come. But as he gazed down the long, empty corridor, he felt something cold close over him. Dizziness surrounded him; gravity was suddenly twice normal. The deck seemed closer to his head than his feet. He inhaled deeply, surprised at the uncharacteristic sensations of vertigo. With one hand, he quickly reached out, steadying himself against the bulkhead as his ears detected the too-loud clatter of the clipboard hitting the floor.

Reality wavered like a malcontent child throwing a tantrum; and for a single instant, the corridors were . . . *different*. Fully lit. Daytime. Greater curvature— as if he were suddenly on a deck closer to the center of the saucer-dome. Instead of the Vulcan inscriptions denoting deck levels and instructions, Terran English swam before his eyes.

He blinked to clear the absurdity; then, recalling the correct procedure to combat vertigo, sank to his knees and placed his head firmly against the wall, breathing deeply. The air was thicker—Earth-thick instead of Vulcan-thin.

Alone. Thee are alone, Spock. Thee are no longer my son.

He shook his head violently, trying to clear words which melted into his consciousness from a time in the past. Words his father had said to him when he'd accepted command of the *ShiKahr*. He'd denied it— instinctively. But Sarek had been correct. Somehow, whatever companion he'd once envisioned finding among the stars had escaped him. And yet, the actual memories of Vulcan—of his own past—were far less real, more comparable to images on a vid-screen than to actual memories. But it didn't hurt that way. Nature's way of making rejection easier to accept.

36

For an instant, nausea rose in his stomach, and he tasted the metallic salt of a madness he had not felt in years. Vulcan. T'Pring. Home and wife and family and expectations: gone. What remained? The stars—something T'Pring would have forbidden. Space—freedom. Isolation—acceptable . . . for a Vulcan. And Command—a different type of home altogether.

He took another deep breath, trying to stand. But before he could gain his feet, a face materialized before his mind's eye: firm features, tanned flesh, expressive hazel eyes, and a compelling human grin. Single lock of gold-bronze hair falling to the middle of a high forehead. Still . . . a stranger. A man who inhabited dreams.

T'hy'la? He wondered briefly if this human could be the companion, the friend, the brother. But . . . no. Images received during periods of physical—or mental—illness could not be considered accurate.

He closed his eyes once more, fought down the nausea, and slowly inched his way back up the wall. But his legs trembled violently as he clutched the bulkhead.

Through a long tunnel which had neither a beginning nor an end, he heard voices. His eyes opened; he followed the sound.

"Captain?"

A hand touched his shoulder—firm, strong, human.

"Captain? Are ye all right? Here, sit down and I'll get in a call tae Sickbay, Captain Spock."

The hand urged him gently toward the deck, but he resisted, shaking his head in negation. He blinked once more, and forced his eyes to focus. Engineer Scott looked back at him as the ethereal tunnel shortened and finally disappeared. The Vulcan took a deep, unsteady breath, and reality stabilized.

"That will not be necessary, Engineer," the captain replied, unconsciously moving back until the other man's hand fell away. He realized disjointedly that it was Scott who had brought him back—but . . . back

37

from *where?* He tasted a single moment of illogical resentment. "I am . . . quite well now."

Scott looked dubious. "Are ye sure, Captain?" he asked worriedly. "If you'll pardon my sayin' so, ye look like ye've just been around the galaxy at warp speed—without a spacesuit!"

Again, the Vulcan shook his head, and absently straightened the maroon command tunic. The silk fabric felt cold, he realized disjointedly. Cold and alien and out of place. He glanced around the corridor. All normal now. Proper curvature of halls. Vulcan inscriptions. Darkened night corridors. All completely normal.

"I shall . . . retire to my quarters, Engineer," he stated in a voice which left little room for disagreement. "You may carry on with your duties."

Scott stared blankly at the Vulcan commander. "With all due respect, Captain," he replied, "it's three in the mornin'. My duty shift ended four hours ago." He reached out as if to steady the Vulcan, then stopped when the captain stepped away, deliberately avoiding his touch. "At least let me see ye tae your quarters," he offered.

Finally, the Vulcan nodded. "Very well, Mister Scott." *Illogical to argue,* he thought, remembering just how concerned these unpredictable humans could be. He studied the engineer out the corner of his eye as they began to walk—quite slowly, he noted—down the corridor and toward the turboshaft. Upon reaching the lift, he turned, facing the other man. The engineer's face was compassionate, warm and friendly . . . but not the same face as in the persistent vision.

"I am really quite well now, Mister Scott," the Vulcan reassured the other man, feeling a sudden need to be alone. "Please do not trouble yourself further on my behalf."

After a long moment of silence, Scott nodded, and reluctantly stood aside, wondering if he would *ever* understand the Vulcan captain's stubbornness.

*   *   *

Ensign Jim Kirk hadn't been aboard the VSS *Shi-Kahr* two days before the first fight began. He stared at the young oaf who had been assigned as his roommate, and felt the anger rise with visible results to darken his cheeks.

"Look, Kirk," the haughty ensign said with a sarcastic grin, pressing his weight against Kirk to pin him to the corridor wall. "We don't want you here any more than you want to be here. So you'd better just get used to doing what you're told!"

Jim wrestled valiantly, but to no avail. Donner was at least thirty pounds heavier, six inches taller, and considerably more aggressive than Kirk had felt in a long time. What with the Dark Times on Earth, the sudden reinstatement of the military draft, and Romulan forces threatening to invade Alliance territory at any moment, a lot of the fight had gone out of him. But as he observed the open resentment on Donner's baby-round face, a spark of the old fire rekindled itself in his veins.

"Why don't you climb down off my back, Donner?" he asked coldly, lifting his knee in defiance, then grunting with pain when the other man's grip tightened painfully on his throat. "If we're going to be forced to live together," he continued in a choked voice, "then you'd better get used to it, too!"

The grip loosened somewhat as Donner's face loomed closer.

"I was here first, draft-dodger!" Donner reminded him arrogantly.

Kirk laughed despite the pain in his throat, his legs, his arms. His voice lowered to a deceptive purr. "So were the Neanderthals, Donner," he replied sarcastically. "But just remember one thing, soldier boy: I have no great love for Starfleet, for the Alliance, or for you and your goddamned superiority complex! I'll get out of here—even if it kills *both* of us in the process." A dangerous smile came to his lips. "Or maybe you'll just disappear in the middle of the night—just like your Neanderthal ancestors!"

Donner laughed aloud, then impulsively tossed the smaller man against the bulkhead as if discarding a soiled shirt.

"For a *little* son-of-a-bitch, you've got awfully *big* ideas!" The cold gray eyes hardened as Donner's hands attached themselves to the uniform collar of Kirk's shirt. "Now listen up, runt, and listen good. Your personnel records are no secret to anyone on board this ship. You were obviously given a choice between Starfleet and prison—and for some reason unknown to God or man, you chose the Fleet. So you're just going to have to live with that decision—or your butt's going to end up in the brig for the duration of this voyage. Clear?"

Kirk stared at the other ensign with cold, lethal hatred. Of all the possible roommates, he just *had* to get Donner. "Who died and made you God?" he asked pointedly.

But Donner only shrugged with a leering grin. "Security posting has certain advantages, Kirk," he pointed out with a seemingly innocent gesture. "You're just lucky Vulcan stepped into the government back on Terra, or you wouldn't have had *any* choice! You'd've been taken out and strung up from the nearest high-tension wires. But since you're here, and since the rest of us have to put up with you for the remainder of your little visit, you'd better get it drilled into that puny little head of yours that you're my personal slave? Understand, *runt?* You eat when I say so; you sleep where I tell you and you do whatever the hell I tell you to do!"

Kirk noticed out the corner of his eye that several other crewmembers were starting to stop and stare at the altercation, and he felt the hot rush of embarrassment rise in his face once more. But for a moment, the dreamlike quality washed over him, bringing dizziness and nausea, and he could only stare mutely at the other man until the solid reality of anger returned. He lowered his head, biting the inside of his mouth in a

40

last-ditch effort to wrestle his admittedly hot temper back under control. But it was a losing battle.

"I understand perfectly, Donner," he said in a voice which was oddly compliant. But he raised hazel eyes aflame with unconcealed hatred.

In the background, Kirk heard a few of the crewmembers giggle appreciatively.

That was his last conscious memory before Donner's doubled fist sent him spiraling down into the dark abysm of nightmares he had come to know so well. But even in that defeat, Kirk tasted an odd-flavored victory.

No one commanded him. No one owned him.

There were three additional fights that week; and when Ensign James Kirk failed to appear on duty for the fourth consecutive day, he received the written summons to report to the captain's quarters for disciplinary consultation. He did not go.

Chapter Four

LIEUTENANT COMMANDER MONTGOMERY Scott checked the matter/anti-matter pods methodically; though there were no fluctuations on the hand-held tricorder, something caused the hair to raise up on the back of his stocky neck. He shook his head, glancing around the engineering section. Nightshift had already come on; and three technicians remained busy at their posts. But one, Scott noticed, seemed unusually distracted. The engineer's bushy brows furrowed as he rechecked the critical balance between the matter and anti-matter . . . and received precisely the same readings as before.

Still . . . as long as he'd served on the *ShiKahr*, something felt out of place . . . *eerie*. Mentally, he shook himself, trying to chase away the feeling of paranoia. He looked at the technicians once again, wondering if they were even aware of his presence. Donnelly and Anderson appeared at ease—almost bored, in fact. But Reichert seemed downright itchy, the chief engineer thought.

Scott moved behind a jutting bulkhead and took a moment to secretly observe the man in question. He knew little about the ensign, other than the fact that he'd been on board for approximately six months; he seemed stable enough, and his work had always been above average. Never late for a shift, never sick . . . and he liked Scotch almost as much as his boss.

Scotty smiled to himself, but the amusement quickly faded when he saw Reichert blink, waver on his feet, and catch himself with one hand on the engineering panel which jutted out from the wall at waist level. The other technicians were positioned so that Reichert's actions went unobserved; Scott alone witnessed the incident—which seemed remarkably similar to the episode he'd seen Captain Spock battling the day before. But before he could move from his position to assist the technician, Reichert righted himself, glanced guiltily about, and continued with his work for a moment as if nothing at all had happened. Then he turned from the panel, and Scott thought briefly that his presence had been discovered.

But the young ensign merely walked past his hiding place, over to Donnelly and Anderson. He slapped Donnelly on the back. "Think I'll take a break, you guys," he said congenially. "Watch the flow-board for me?"

Donnelly smiled. "Sure thing, Carl." He walked to the other panel, then impulsively called over his shoulder, "Hey, Carl! Bring me a cup of coffee and a doughnut, will ya?"

Reichert stopped at the door, saluting mock-seriously. "Sure thing, Admiral," he replied, and quickly slipped into the corridor.

As soon as the ensign had gone, Scott moved out from the jutting bulkhead, feeling uncharacteristically guilty as he moved to stand over Donnelly's shoulder. He peered at the energy-flow panel which Reichert had been monitoring, and felt a deathly chill crawl into his stomach.

"Don't tell me yae don't *see* that, man!" he exclaimed. "The whole damned flow's bein' interrupted by somethin'."

Donnelly looked more closely at the panel and the digital readings. "Reichert said it was a panel malfunc-

43

tion," he explained, glancing curiously at his supervisor. "Said you knew about it—and that Anderson and I shouldn't mess with it." But his eyes suddenly widened as the connection came clear.

A feeling close to death gripped Scott's heart, and he jumped across the room, thumbing the communication switch. "Scott to bridge! Captain Spock respond!"

"Spock here," came the calm response.

"Captain!" Scott barked into the panel. "Ye've got tae shut down all nonessential power immediately!" He glanced nervously at Donnelly, at the pale face, the horrified eyes. "Turn off everything that's not absolutely critical to life support!"

Before he could even begin to explain the problem, he heard the order being given on the bridge, and a certain amount of pride swept through him with the knowledge that Spock—a Vulcan sworn to logic and precision—could trust him on such sparse knowledge.

"We've got a problem down here," the engineer continued, almost feeling the giant starship shutting down, going to sleep. "And a serious one at that, Captain."

"What is the nature of the problem, Mister Scott?" Spock's filtered voice wondered without alarm or emotion.

Scott swallowed hard, absently noting the cold sweat which had broken out like a rash on his forehead. "The flow-valve to the matter/anti-matter pods has been left open. We'll have to keep power to a minimum—and shut down the warp drive completely—until I can verify exactly where the problem's located."

There was a momentary silence, as if the Vulcan was thinking, then: "Is it not correct that the matter/anti-matter flow system is computer monitored at all times, Engineer, and that any discrepancy should have been noted in your routine check?"

Scott glanced at Donnelly again, sharing the tension with his young technician. "Aye, Captain. That's what

I'm tryin' tae tell yae! In order for this tae happen in the first place, it *had* tae be deliberate!" He shook his head, struggling with words which didn't want to come out past the sudden thickness of his own tongue. "Whoever did this made damned certain that it *wouldn't* show up on the tricorder scan." Unconsciously, he lowered his voice; it was a hefty accusation. "It's just a miracle o' the saints that we didna blow ourselves into atoms! Ten more minutes and . . ." His voice drifted off.

Again, the silence. "Very well, Mister Scott," the Vulcan responded at last. "All nonessential power has been suspended. Warp drive is also terminated; we have transferred to impulse engines." The captain paused, and when he spoke again, his voice was considerably quieter as well. "In addition, I suggest you seal off the Engineering section long enough to determine precisely who could have made such an error."

Scott felt his stomach hit the floor. "Ah . . . Captain," he said quietly, "the main suspect left Engineering about a minute ago—said he was going down tae the lounge to grab a bite tae eat."

"Indeed," the Vulcan's voice responded, sounding somewhat surprised. "I shall have Security detain him there. Upon completion of your repairs, Engineer Scott, please notify the bridge. Also, I request that you meet me in Sickbay following solution to the current problem. I wish to interview you and any technicians on duty during the incident."

Scott took a deep breath. It could've been worse. "Aye, Captain. Scott out." He looked at Donnelly again, saw the color drain from the young tech's face. He managed a smile before returning to the energy-flow monitoring board. "Don't worry, lad," he said amiably. "The captain doesna bite—and if annaone can get tae the bottom of this, he's the one tae do it."

Donnelly seemed skeptical, but nonetheless nodded. His eyes settled on the board, on the so-called "malfunction" readings. "Why would Reichert *do*

45

something like that, Mister Scott?" he asked at last.

Scotty felt the shiver dance along his backbone. "Now *that's* a question best left for the psyche specialists, lad. Why annaone would want tae blow up the ship—and themselves along with it—is beyond my ability to comprehend." He winked, feeling a little more at ease, and moved into the dimly lit corridor which would lead to the Jeffries tube. The damage had to be somewhere in that region. "Here, lad," he said, indicating a belt-attachment filled with intricate tools. "Hand me that flow-sensor kit." He hoisted himself up into the catwalk, accepting it from the young ensign's hands—which, the engineer noted, were trembling. "Now get yourself back over tae that board and give me a yell when those readings start tae stabilize."

Donnelly moved quickly, but chanced a look at Anderson as he returned to the main room. His partner's eyes were wide, disbelieving.

"Just how close did we come, Dave?" Anderson wondered once Scott had disappeared into the shadows and catacombs of engineering.

Donnelly shrugged, pretending nonchalance. "Don't ask," he said, eyes on the board. Within a few moments, the readings began to stabilize, to approach normal. "There, Mister Scott," he called into the communication panel. "That seems to be it."

Within another few minutes, Scott reappeared, a wide grin of relief playing on the rugged features. He walked over to Donnelly, slipped one arm warmly around his back. "Yae can tell your heart to start beating again, lad," he said. "Luckily our friend didn't have the experience to send us up in one big bang."

But he went to the flow-board, checking it and rechecking it himself . . . just to be sure.

On the bridge, Captain Spock rose and went to stand at the science station, looking briefly over First Officer Chekov's shoulder. For some reason, the computer facility beckoned him, calling him in a way which was scarcely natural; the gentle hum of the circuits and

46

microprocessors felt far more "right" than the harsh reality of the command chair. But he dismissed the illogical thought nearly as quickly as it presented itself. After being a starship captain in the Alliance for nearly seven years, now was a poor time to consider a major career alteration.

"All sensors monitoring nothing but empty space, Captain," Chekov provided automatically. "No Romulan vessels even near the edge of the Neutral Zone."

Spock nodded almost to himself. "And Mister Scott's present status with engine repairs?"

Chekov activated a series of controls, monitoring the engineering computers and comparing the information to ship's normal. "Matter/anti-matter energy flow now stable, sir," the first officer responded. "Engineer Scott signals that his repairs are now complete and that he is en route to Sickbay as per your orders."

"Very well, Commander Chekov," the Vulcan replied. "Notify Doctor McCoy that I shall be there presently." He turned and strode toward the doors; but before reaching the lift, his ears detected the faint whine on an incoming communication. He glanced at the communication panel, saw Uhura place the subspace decoding nodule in her ear, and waited. The standard morning's transmission had contained nothing out of the ordinary; if FleetCom was attempting to contact them now . . .

Presently, Uhura turned from the panel, automatically placing the nodule into the recording slot on the main board. From there, the message would be permanently inscribed into the *ShiKahr*'s records.

"Lieutenant?" Spock asked when the communications officer made no effort to relay the message. He noticed that the woman appeared shaken, eyes wide.

Uhura's brows furrowed as she met her commanding officer's eyes. She eyed the nodule carefully. "I . . . I'm not sure, sir," she responded at last. "That message—it *couldn't* have been correct."

The Vulcan moved to the communication panel instinctively. Something felt wrong. The dizziness was there again, but he fought it, drove it away with sheer willpower alone. "Precisely what was the message, Lieutenant?" he inquired, momentarily annoyed at having to ask a second time.

Uhura shook her head, glancing around the bridge. No heads turned; nothing seemed out of the ordinary. "It's on a priority code, Captain," she said quietly. "I think you'd better hear it yourself." Her eyes locked with the Vulcan's once more. *"Privately* might be best, sir."

A slanted brow rose. "Indeed?" But he trusted the communications officer implicitly. "Very well, Lieutenant Uhura. Have the message transferred to Doctor McCoy's private office and instruct Mister Scott that I shall meet with him in my quarters later this evening." He continued holding Uhura's gaze for a moment longer, wondering what could have brought such fear to her eyes. But he turned from the bridge and stepped into the waiting lift.

He would know soon enough.

Captain Spock entered Sickbay to find the lights already dimmed for night; approximately ten patients lay sleeping on the diagnostic beds, and save for the gentle hum of the medical computer, all was silent. He quickly passed by the beds, taking a moment to study the sleeping faces. Some he recognized, others were strangers; yet he experienced a peculiar affinity for each of them. A young female Rigelian lay peacefully on her side, and for an instant, the Vulcan wondered how she had risen to starship posting at such an early age. She could have been no more than nineteen Rigelian years of age. Curiously, the captain looked at the panel above her, mentally summoning a text-book accurate recollection of what her symptoms represented. The answer came almost without effort: hemoatrophia. Minor, he deduced, judging from the stabilized readings. She would soon recover; and for that, the captain was grateful. Regardless of all of Sarek's teachings, he still felt compassion—particularly for his crew, his ship, and for the few lifeforms he called friends. If Vulcan wished to consider him *T'kaul'ama* for that fall from logic, it was a sentence he would willingly accept.

He paused at the foot of the Rigelian's bed for only a moment longer, then moved on toward Leonard McCoy's office. But before reaching the door, it opened of its own accord and Lieutenant Christine Chapel stepped out, almost bumping into him in the darkened area.

"Oh!" she exclaimed, nonetheless careful to keep her voice lowered. "Captain Spock."

The Vulcan inclined his head. "Nurse Chapel," he replied formally. "I trust you have been well."

The nurse smiled warmly. "Yes, Captain. Thank you." She held out a mini-comp for the Vulcan's inspection. "Doctor McCoy has Ensign Reichert sedated at the moment. He was . . . quite violent when Security brought him in."

Spock nodded, studying the sparse information contained in the recording mechanism. Basically, it identified the patient, listing his symptoms as: paranoia, self-destructiveness and hallucinations. The Vulcan lifted a brow, then turned back to Chapel, unable to completely dismiss his own incident of the previous afternoon. "Nurse," he began, "have there been any . . . *additional* cases of . . . hallucinations?"

Chapel frowned as she considered the question. "No . . ." she finally replied. "Not directly, anyway." She indicated one of the diagnostic beds with a quick nod of her head. "The closest is Yeoman Devoran. She came in this afternoon, complaining of migraines and dizziness." Chapel laughed somewhat uneasily. "She also mentioned something about . . . well . . . seeing . . . ghosts."

"Ghosts, Nurse Chapel?"

The nurse shrugged. "She *did* ask me to keep it confidential, but . . . what with Reichert going a little crazy, I thought you might need to know."

49

Captain Spock nodded, glancing at Yeoman Devoran's sleeping form. He'd seen her only briefly, recognized her as being from Security Division. "She did not mention precisely what these . . . ghosts . . . looked like, did she, Nurse?"

Chapel shook her head, brows narrowing. "No . . . No she didn't." She paused, checking the readout above Devoran's head. "Doctor McCoy examined her completely, and wasn't able to find anything of a physical nature to account for the anomaly. He prescribed a mild tranquilizer and suggested she remain here for observation. I believe the doctor's also scheduled a full psyche exam first thing in the morning."

The Vulcan considered that—and realized it was precisely *his* reason for not having reported his own incident. If FleetCom heard rumors of a starship captain experiencing hallucinations . . . His half-human blood had already caused enough mayhem with the High Council; no point feeding prejudices.

He nodded curtly. "Thank you, Nurse. That will be all."

As Chapel turned to leave the Sickbay, the Vulcan strode to the doctor's inner office, waiting for a moment as he gazed quickly at Yeoman Devoran.

Reality wavered, but he chased the ghosts away with some silent incantation. Logic prevailed.

Doctor Leonard McCoy studied the readout above Reichert's head for the hundredth time, still not able to fully believe what every medical test confirmed: dual encephalograms—two distinctly different sets of brain waves. And even in the most pronounced cases of schizophrenia, McCoy had to admit that he'd never witnessed anything quite as bizarre . . . or impossible. It was as if Reichert's brain functioned on two different levels—each independent of the other.

His brows drew closer together, blue eyes squinting in thought as he looked down into the young man's face. The eyes which stared back at him were wild—trapped-animal wild and haunted; and even under the heavy sedation, the once-handsome features were twisted into a grimace which was both pitiable and frightening.

McCoy smiled warmly, ignoring the uncanny caterpillar-shiver which skittered up his spine. "Feeling any better now, Carl?"

Reichert merely stared at him, green eyes hardening dangerously. He did not speak.

Absently, McCoy reached out, touching the young ensign's arm in a reassuring gesture. "Don't worry, kid," he said. "We'll find an answer and have you out of here in no time." But even as he spoke the words, he wondered if they were a lie. In the entire history of the Alliance, no one had ever attempted to destroy a starship. For himself, McCoy wondered how this would affect the future of humans on board interstellar cruisers; the Vulcan High Council had been reluctant enough to accept Terrans in the first place . . . and something like this wasn't likely to go unnoticed.

But his attention was diverted as the gentle bell chimed on the sealed entrance to the security office.

"McCoy here," he responded automatically. "That you, Spock?"

"Affirmative, Doctor," the Vulcan's filtered voice responded.

Going to the small panel on the wall, McCoy keyed in the proper coded sequence which would open the door. He grinned broadly as the Vulcan entered. Despite the fact that he'd been on board nearly as long as the captain himself, he wondered if he would ever get used to the psyche games they always seemed to play. He looked at the Vulcan for a long moment, studying the familiar maroon command silks, the gold tie belt, and pants which fell to the top of knee-length black boots. Somehow, suddenly . . . it looked out of place—and he thought of Spock as a misplaced sheep in pirate's clothing. The only thing missing was a big gold earring in one pointed ear. Now *that* would be just about right! But he shook the image away, motioning toward a chair as the doors closed and sealed automatically behind the Vulcan.

"Before we begin, Doctor," Spock said, sitting gracefully on the edge of the chair, "I find it necessary to review a transmission from FleetCom."

McCoy nodded, easily detecting the tone of irritation in the deep voice. He also wondered why Spock was bothering to tell him. But he motioned generously toward the communication panel. "Help yourself, Spock," he said with a grin. "Care for a brandy?" he asked, proceeding to unlock the "medicine cabinet" and withdraw a dusty bottle.

The Vulcan's brow climbed as he thumbed the correct button on the communication panel. McCoy's nonchalant approach to any given situation never ceased to amaze him. Such complete adaptability. Within twenty-four hours, the doctor had treated at least fifteen patients—the majority for minor bruises and abrasions following the competition *tae kwan do* tournament in the gym; the ship was operating on minimal power due to the engineering incident; and an ensign—who now lay less than twenty feet away in a security-restricted area—had attempted to obliterate the entire vessel.

The Vulcan pondered that information, then slowly allowed the brow to resume its normal position. "Yes, thank you, Doctor," he conceded at last. "That would be appreciated."

McCoy stared at the Vulcan, then looked at the bottle in his hand. Very slowly, a wide grin manifested in the blue eyes. He hurried back to the cabinet and withdrew two fat-bellied snifters. Then, as an afterthought, he replaced the first bottle back on the shelf and grabbed another—slightly more dusty than its companion.

"When *you* condescend to take a drink, Spock," he explained filling the two glasses, "it's time to break out the good stuff. Vintage Antarean brandy," he boasted.

"Guaranteed to put hair on your chest and raise welts on women and children!"

The Vulcan studied the doctor curiously. "Precisely why would one wish to imbibe a substance which would essentially alter the individual's entire metabolism, Doctor?" he asked, but nonetheless accepted the glass which McCoy shoved in his direction.

McCoy shrugged. "Consider it a human weakness, Mister Spock," he replied, not noticing that he'd addressed his commanding officer by a less-than-fitting title for his rank. "Now what's this transmission all about? I thought we got FleetCom transmissions on morning shift."

The Vulcan nodded agreement. "Apparently," he replied, waiting for the computer to load and replay the message, "this is of some importance." But before he could further explain, the green light on the panel signaled readiness with two flashes and a gentle beeptone. The screen, however, remained blank as the message began.

"Admiral S't'kal to Alliance Starship *ShiKahr*," a very Vulcan voice intoned with almost mechanical precision. "As of this stardate, all Alliance vessels are hereby ordered to prepare for full operational battle readiness.

"After lengthy debate by Vulcan High Council and Human League of Planets, it is our joint decision to subdue any potentially dangerous invaders before hostilities arise. *ShiKahr* therefore ordered to continue mission at Neutral Zone, and await arrival of two sisterships. *ShiKahr* further instructed to stand ready as flagship for initial trespass into Romulan territory. Captain Spock, you are authorized to organize initial assault. Other Alliance captains ordered to obey your commands completely in this matter. Details of strategy and attack vessels to follow."

The voice ceased abruptly, but the small computer screen on McCoy's desk suddenly flickered to life, showing a series of graphs and grids—which, when viewed in perspective, Spock realized, represented an

53

intricate battle plan—one which called for deliberate invasion into a territory which had been outlined by Vulcan/Romulan treaty nearly a century ago.

The graphs continued to change very quickly, and the Vulcan could partially interpret the printed scramble-code line which ran along the bottom of the screen. When broken down into its millions of individual characters, the code would contain the details Admiral S't'kal had mentioned. Details for war.

He looked up, meeting McCoy's eyes, which were suddenly wide with something bordering closely on horror.

On the bed across the room, Reichert's body seemed to be wracked with a series of spasms . . . but when the Vulcan looked more closely, he realized—with an uncharacteristic chill—that the spasms were actually laughter.

Chapter Five

YEOMAN S'PARVA SLAPPED the mat, rolling as she fell and gaining her feet quickly. She rose on powerful back legs, and straightened to her full height of over six feet. The gold clip which had held her ears pinned back to the long manelike growth of hair clattered across the room, landing against the bulkhead. But the Katellan hardly seemed inconvenienced. Her coal-black eyes never wavered from her adversary as her thin lips curled into a smile which could have been seductive, could have been frightening. Sharp teeth glistened into a grin.

"Had enough, Chris?" S'Parva asked, instinctively remaining crouched in the defensive stance despite her opponent's weakened condition.

Breathing hard, Christine Chapel shook her head, cautiously circling the Katellan. The nurse made a quick grab for S'Parva's left leg, but the other woman stepped aside, brown fur shimmering in the hot white lights.

"Doctor's orders, S'Parva," Chapel said, trying the same move again and meeting with the same failure. "Leonard wants you to put in at least two hours of strenuous exercise in here every day for the next month." Absently, she heard herself gasping in contrast to S'Parva's easily controlled breathing, and wondered for a moment which of them was getting the best workout. She began circling faster, using her greater speed to compensate for the Katellan's increased bulk and power. Feigning first to one side, then to the other, her wide green eyes searched for an opening—an opening which didn't come. "Two hours a day," she gasped. "Until you're completely comfortable with two g's." She took another deep breath, watching the other woman's lithe body continue to evade her grasp in the heavy gravity. "Doctor's orders," she repeated, chest heaving almost painfully.

Unexpectedly, S'Parva lunged, ducked under the nurse, and brought her to the deck with little effort. The Katellan laughed, struggling to hold her writhing opponent to the mat. For a moment, success seemed imminent; but the nurse was more cunning and powerful than many human females. She slipped away, rolled aside, and would have gained her feet had it not been for the fact that the Katellan somersaulted across the mat in a quite natural movement and kicked her legs out from under her.

Christine landed heavily, with a thud, squarely on her posterior. The Katellan laughed again, seeing the confusion and very slight embarrassment in the nurse's eyes.

"Christine," S'Parva said, climbing to her feet and extending a helping hand, "Katella is a *three* g planet!" The easy laughter filled the room.

For a moment, Christine merely stared at the other woman—at the powerful muscles which ran the length of her body, at the long fur which formed a collar of sorts around the neckline of the workout clothes. McCoy was definitely going to hear about this. Physically, S'Parva could defeat anyone on board the *Shi-Kahr*. The workouts, therefore, obviously weren't intended for the Katellan. The nurse shook her head, brought her hands together in the universally accepted gesture of concession, then reached out to accept the furred hand which pulled her to her feet effortlessly.

"To resurrect an old Earth cliché, S'Parva," the nurse said with a sheepish grin, "I think I've been had."

S'Parva shrugged, called an official time-out period, then slipped one arm around her gasping opponent's waist and led her to the rest bench against the wall. Then, after retrieving the dislodged barrette and fastening the long ears back into a more convenient position, she quickly adjusted the controls just inside the sealed door. Gradually, slowly, gravity returned to Earth normal.

"Feeling better, Chris?" S'Parva asked, grabbing a towel from the bench and draping it around her neck. She took another, handed it to her partner, then sat down at the human's side.

The nurse shrugged, chasing away the nagging feeling of embarrassment. If she were out of shape, it was her own fault; and she'd long ago accepted the fact that McCoy never was one for a direct approach to any problem. She shook her head in mild disbelief, then let her head rest against the bulkhead as she began to laugh.

"I suppose it could've been a lot worse," she decided aloud.

S'Parva's whiskered brow rose onto a high canine forehead. "Oh?" she wondered, absently reaching out to massage the other woman's tense neck muscles.

Christine nodded, meeting the Katellan's confused expression, enjoying the warmth of the hands which were experts in the art of massage. "Oh, yes," she conceded with a laugh. "If the good doctor had *really* wanted to 'get' me, he could've set up this little workout charade with Captain Spock—under the pretense of only the gods know what!"

S'Parva's head tilted curiously to one side, accentuating her canine appearance. "Would he *do* that, Chris?" she asked incredulously.

For a moment, Christine found herself wondering . . . almost imagining. "No . . ." she said at last, experiencing a sense of melancholy she hadn't felt in years. A very faint, wistful smile replaced the reckless laughter of a moment before. At least it didn't hurt anymore. If she'd once felt something for the Vulcan which she'd labeled as love, that misplaced emotion had been replaced with respect—and the knowledge that whatever fantasies she had once entertained were not only illogical, but also impossible.

"No," she repeated unconsciously stretching her neck to one side as S'Parva's fingers probed deep into aching muscles. After the prolonged exposure to two g's, the now-normal gravity felt almost unreal, ethereal, and she allowed herself to drift. "There was a time, S'Parva," she relinquished, "that . . . well . . . a time when I didn't understand a lot of things about our illustrious pirate-captain."

S'Parva's hands continued massaging as a smile appeared on the thin face. "I think I know what you mean," she said quietly. "I've never met Captain Spock personally, but . . ." Her voice drifted into an almost embarrassed silence.

Christine looked up. "But . . . what?" she asked curiously, letting S'Parva's mischievous expression take shape on her own features. She felt her mind open to the Katellan in an easy and natural way, felt the gentle and curious telepathic aura which emanated from S'Parva.

"You . . . *cared* for him . . . didn't you, Chris?" S'Parva asked in a voice which was a tender contrast to the sheer bulk of the woman.

Christine looked away, suddenly uncomfortable. Despite the fact that her feelings for the captain had never been an easy secret, she wondered just how much S'Parva could psychically sense.

"That was a long time ago," she explained presently. "When I first came on board the *ShiKahr,* I thought . . . well . . . I thought I sensed a loneliness in Spock." She laughed wistfully. "And maybe I was naïve enough to believe I was the cure." She shrugged, not looking at the other woman. "But when

I finally understood what it means to *be* a Vulcan . . . that's when I understood that Spock can't allow himself to become too close to anyone."

But she wondered if that was really the answer. There had been moments when the Vulcan had been tender, even warm with her. But she consigned those times back into the past as the barely readable smile returned. At one time, she recalled, she'd finally opened up to McCoy about it—had told the doctor of her feelings, had even suggested that perhaps transferring to another ship in another galaxy would be the best thing for everyone involved. Fortunately, McCoy had talked her out of it, had even helped her lay her desperate feelings for the Vulcan to a more comfortable rest.

"I don't know what—or *who*—he's looking for out here, S'Parva," she continued after a long silence which reflected only the gentle and faraway hum of the engines. "But I hope he'll find it one day." She smiled, and finally allowed herself to meet S'Parva's eyes once again. In them, she read tenderness . . . and a definite sense of understanding. But as she continued gazing into the intense black eyes, she felt herself start to slip. She gasped, unconsciously grasping onto the sides of the plastiform rest bench.

For a moment, S'Parva merely looked at the other woman, then pulled her hands away, deep eyes going wide as an echoing gasp escaped her own throat.

"What's wrong, Chris?" she asked. But then the images came. "Don't tell me you've got it, too!" Telepathic overload.

Chapel shook her head, instinctively denying something which had plagued her twice earlier in the day. She managed a smile, took a deep breath, and forced the dizziness away. "It's . . . it's nothing, S'Parva." Yet she knew the Katellan could read her all too easily.

S'Parva shook her head violently, long ears trembling furiously. "Don't you see, Chris? When I was massaging your back. I've—we've *both* felt the same

59

thing. And I think I know what it is!" But she bit her lower lip in frustration. "Well, maybe not *what* it is, but . . ."

"It's nothing!" Chris repeated, surprised at the anger reflected in her tone. She felt red heat climb her neck, into her face, and chastised herself for not remembering sooner that S'Parva was a touch telepath as well as a directional sensitive.

"But it is, Christine," S'Parva corrected. "I've felt *exactly* the same thing—three times. Like I was . . . I dunno . . ." She shivered despite the heat of the room. "Like I was . . . slipping away from myself." Her voice lowered. "Like I was . . . losing any thread of sanity I ever had!" Impulsively, she rose from the bench, grabbing the other woman's arm and attempting to drag her toward the door. "Come with me down to the psyche lab," she pleaded. "I *know* there are *images* in there—but they pass by too quickly for the mind to record. If we can get some of them recorded on the vid-screen, maybe we can find an answer!"

Christine seemed dubious, then finally turned away. The vid-screen, for all its practical and medical uses, was still a humiliating experience. And despite the fact that S'Parva was right, the thought of four medical department heads—*and the captain*—psychoanalyzing her subconscious images caused her skin to crawl. *Nothing incriminating,* she thought. *Just damned embarrassing!* Images, yes. But . . . of what? *First Officer Spock?* She shivered. Easily enough explained—at least in her own case. *Straight out of the textbooks. Knock him down in rank a few points. Make him easier to attain.* The red heat crawled higher into her cheeks. No point dredging up restless—and unreachable—spirits. And the dizziness came again, refusing to leave her alone. She smiled to herself. It would be her secret . . . no matter what.

"Don't you see, Chris?" S'Parva interrupted. "It *could* be something important."

Christine smiled very gently, shook her head, and

grasped the Katellan's warm hand. "And it *could* be nothing," she countered. But she hesitated—wavering between S'Parva's obvious concern and her own need to protect herself emotionally. Something warned that she *should* agree to the tests . . . but another part of herself rebelled. "Just . . . give me a couple days to think it over," she said at last. "And if it's still happening then . . ."

Very slowly, S'Parva nodded, somehow understanding the nurse's unique situation without questioning it. She reached out, tentatively placing one supportive hand on the other woman's shoulder. "Yeah, sure, Chris," she agreed with a tender smile. "But . . . can we agree to . . . well . . . compare notes over those days? I'll tell you any images I get and you do the same for me?"

Christine nodded, knowing it was a promise she wouldn't keep. Working in the psyche lab as she did, S'Parva was dangerous. And if the Katellan wanted the Vulcan for herself . . . Anger flared, but she concealed it well as she rose to her feet. "Same time tomorrow?" she asked.

"Same time," S'Parva agreed—and suddenly found herself sprawling through the air to land on the practice mat in a disorderly heap of disheveled fur. Her eyes widened in surprise and disbelief.

Laughing, Christine lunged, legs wrapped tightly around the Katellan's thick torso. "In case you'd forgotten," she reminded her opponent, "we've still got another fifteen minutes to go in order to fill this prescription." She pushed her shoulder into the heavy chest, struggling to hold the Katellan down. Vertigo came, spiraled, then retreated. She tasted the anger again, felt the encroachment of a rival. For a single brief instant, she chastised herself for the unbidden emotions. Surely, she thought, she'd dealt with her feelings for Spock years ago. Yet now they returned with a vengeance . . . and a whispered promise inside her own mind. Someone who did not exist told her in a voice only she could hear that she would have the Vulcan . . . if only she did not tell.

"*Well*, Spock?" McCoy demanded, open palm slapping the top of the desk as he stared at the Vulcan. The captain had not moved from the chair all night, running computer program after program. Even Reichert had finally drifted into a fitful sleep.

At last, Spock looked up. "The transmission is indeed genuine, Doctor," he replied with what might have been a sigh. "The voice pattern is a precise match to samples of Admiral S't'kal's voice which are already on file in the central computer." He leaned back, meeting McCoy's angry, questioning eyes.

For a long time, McCoy just stood there, expression hard and cold. An eerie feeling had taken up residence in the pit of his stomach—a feeling which he recognized as fear. "What about confirmation?" he ventured hopelessly. "Nobody in their right mind would issue an order like that!"

He stomped restlessly over to the other side of the small room, trying to imagine how Spock could remain so utterly calm. "It's *got* to be a hoax, dammit, Spock! There's no other explanation."

Presently, the Vulcan rose, straightening the uniform tunic once again. But the gold sash remained in the chair from where he'd removed it the night before. Absently, he picked it up, tying it around his waist as he thought. But suddenly, an eyebrow climbed and he walked over to stand at McCoy's shoulder.

"Would you repeat what you just said, Doctor?" he requested.

McCoy's head turned rapidly in the Vulcan's direction. "What? That it's got to be a hoax?"

The Vulcan shook his head. "You formulated a hypothesis," he pointed out. "One which could well be the only explanation for the current course of events."

McCoy thought back, wishing his short-term memory was in better working order. But after a sleepless night and a suicide order, he reminded himself that he'd be doing well to remember his own name. But slowly, the words came back to him, and a smile appeared on his face. "That nobody in their right mind would give an order like that!" he recited, feeling vaguely like a child in kindergarten who had just enlightened the teacher. He glanced suspiciously at Reichert, grateful that the ensign was still asleep. "That would explain a lot, wouldn't it, Spock?" he asked, inclining his head in Reichert's direction.

The Vulcan nodded. "Indeed it would, Doctor," he replied. "If we assume that Ensign Reichert is not an isolated case, it may be possible to theorize that the two incidents are almost directly related."

McCoy's brows furrowed. "You mean to say that Admiral S't'kal *told* Reichert to destroy the ship?" He shook his head. "I can't believe that—"

"Not at all, Doctor," the Vulcan interrupted, arms now folded neatly across his chest in a posture which bespoke confidence. "However," he continued, "if we examine the basic intended result of each incident, I believe you will agree that there *is* a remarkable similarity."

McCoy thought about it, grateful that he'd chosen medicine as a career instead of espionage. "In other words," he reasoned, "both Reichert and S't'kal were trying to accomplish the same thing."

The Vulcan nodded. "Unfortunately," he said, "Admiral S't'kal is in a somewhat more advantageous position to implement his plan than Ensign Reichert."

McCoy's eyes widened again. "You're not serious about following those orders, are you, Spock?" he demanded.

"Disobeying a direct order from FleetCom will be a difficult task, Doctor," the Vulcan responded. "And yet it is obvious that we cannot permit Alliance forces to deliberately invade the Neutral Zone. The resultant war would obliterate any chance of peace for the next thousand years."

"But . . . what about those other starships, Spock?"

McCoy wondered. "If *you* fail to carry out those orders, you'll be court-martialed—and someone else will take command of the *ShiKahr*."

An eyebrow rose elegantly. "It will require at least six Vulcan standard days for those ships to reach the *ShiKahr*," he realized verbally. "In the meantime, Doctor, we must find some method of isolating the cause of this affliction. And not only must the cause be isolated, but a cure must be found."

McCoy paced over to the desk, flopping into the chair. It wasn't the first time Spock had asked him for a miracle—and he hoped it wouldn't be the last. He glanced first at Reichert, then at the Vulcan. At least he had a place to begin. Impulsively, he thumbed the communication panel. "Nurse Drew, get me four lab techs—equipped with mini-combscribers and portable brain scanners. Have them meet me in the medical briefing room in fifteen minutes."

"Affirmative, Doctor," came the filtered response.

Turning off the communication device, McCoy stared at the Vulcan for a long moment. "There's just one more thing before I officially get started on this, Spock," he said, rising from the desk and going to the Vulcan's side.

Spock waited.

"What about *you?*" McCoy asked pointedly. "You can't use your Vulcan physiology as a medical excuse this time. S't'kal's about as Vulcan as they come—and it's obviously affecting him."

The Vulcan turned away from the scrutinizing blue eyes. "I seem . . . able to control what few symptoms I have experienced, Doctor," he replied, voice clipped. "I believe your primary function should be one of isolating the anomaly within those who appear to be the most seriously affected." He strode toward the door, evading the hand which reached toward his arm. "If you will excuse me, I am due on the bridge."

But McCoy stepped in front of him before he could make his escape. "You haven't been altogether honest with me, have you, Spock?" he stated in the form of a question. "Symptoms?"

The Vulcan did not return the doctor's gaze as he stepped aside, pausing at the sealed doors for just a moment. "Doctor," he replied, irritation beginning to creep into the normally level voice, "you have your orders and I have mine—and while I must attempt to discover an acceptable way of ignoring mine, you do not have that same option."

McCoy's eyes widened and he bounced angrily on his toes. He'd never been told to mind his own business quite so formally. But before he could respond, the Vulcan had already slipped through the doors and into anonymity. But he'd hardly expected anything less from Spock.

He turned at last toward Reichert, only to see the other man's eyes suddenly spring open. The cold eyes followed Spock's exit and a dangerous smile broke out on thin lips.

" 'That he is mad, 'tis true: 'tis true 'tis pity; And pity 'tis 'tis true.' "

Reichert began to laugh again; that cold, uncontrolled laughter which sent eerie shivers dancing along McCoy's spine.

Chapter Six

COMMANDER TAZOL THREW himself angrily on the bed, slamming one heavy first into the pillow as he was forced to recall the events of the past week. A mission of glory—but for whom? The entire Romulan Fleet at his disposal . . . yet nothing had gone according to the Praetor's plans. He rolled onto his back, and an illegible cry tightened the muscles in his thick neck. Death would have been preferable to failure, he realized. He closed his eyes, letting the memory replay itself for the hundredth time. Slowly, almost with malice, the images filled his mind . . . images of the days so recently gone by. . . .

Tazol studied the printout of his orders as a devious smile came to his face. Turning in the command chair of the Romulan Flagship *Ravon,* he motioned his first officer over to his side with a quick nod of his head. "The Praetor sends greetings," he relayed. "Greetings and demands for the success of our mission."

A young Romulan female glanced briefly at the readout which the haughty Tazol dumped unceremoniously into her hand. "The mission is feasible, Commander?" she wondered, doubt punctuating her voice.

"It has already begun, Sarela," Tazol confirmed,

leaning back heavily in the black chair and propping one boot on the arm. "Our operatives in Federation territory were able to provide the Praetor with the information we will need to completely alter the history of this Federation." A cruel smile grew on the commander's lips. "And, subsequently, the *future* of the Romulan Empire."

Sarela studied her commander and her husband with open doubt revealed in wide black eyes. She did not like what she saw. As a commander, Tazol was a joke. And as a husband . . .

She let the thought drift into oblivion. The *Ravon* should have been hers; instead, she had received Tazol in marriage by her parents' arrangement. It was custom—a custom she had respected too long, but one she had come to despise over the six weeks they had been married. With an effort, she pushed the personal considerations to the back of her mind, meeting the harsh eyes defiantly.

"And how will this be accomplished, Commander?" she wondered, addressing the heavyset captain by rank rather than by the customary title adopted in Romulan marriage.

Tazol did not seem to notice, his eyes softening as he took a moment to study the lean form of the woman standing before him. "The Praetor has assigned two of the Empire's finest agents to this case," he explained. "They will bridge the time gap, return to Earth's past, and dispose of the sentimental pacifists who were instrumental in forming the basis for this . . . this *Federation* of theirs!" The word was a hiss of contempt. "And once that is accomplished," he added with a deceptively gentle smile, "the entire course of history in the galaxy will have been altered—allowing our Empire to claim the space, the planets and the resources which are rightfully ours."

Sarela continued to scan the computerized theories curiously. "In short, if our operatives are successful in murdering three old men, the entire Federation will never have existed at all?" Again, she heard doubt in her voice, wondered if Tazol noticed. As an officer of the Romulan Fleet for over nine years, she had learned that things were rarely as simple as they appeared on the computerized surface. She chanced a look at her husband, wondering if he possessed the rudimentary intelligence to be aware of those facts. Resentment crept in again when she recalled that his command posting had come as a gift from her own father more so than on any merit from Tazol.

"Once our operatives' mission is completed," Tazol said, "the universe will be ripe for Romulan dominion. By destroying the complacent fools who originally conceived a benevolent Federation, the history of the galaxy will be changed—weakened."

He looked up to the viewscreen which covered nearly three quarters of the front of the *Ravon*'s bridge, almost seeing the invisible line of confinement which marked the boundaries of the Neutral Zone. "No longer will our people be consigned to such a pitifully small area of space."

His eyes were distant, his words cold and deadly, and Sarela felt a chill climb the length of her spine. There had been no actual wars in the Empire for decades . . . but men like Tazol made it their business to remedy that situation.

"The problem lies not in the amount of space we possess, Tazol," she reminded him. "For there are an abundance of fertile worlds within our Empire. What matters," she continued, unable to hold the bitterness in her voice at bay, "is what one does with one's resources."

Tazol's face grew dark for a moment, eyes narrowing to threatening slits. "We were once a *conquering* race—and shall be again—when the Federation is erased from the memory of this galaxy forever! Only fools are farmers and shepherds; a Warrior need not concern himself with such mundane tasks. A Warrior's place," he continued angrily, "is to *take* what has been prepared for him—to eat the fattened animal, and leave fear in the land. Without the Federation and

Starfleet, there will be no one to stop us. We shall once again be that which destiny has chosen for us."

Sarela studied the man through coolly questioning eyes. "You recite rhetoric as well as any man, Tazol," she observed, the smile on her face almost glossing over the words of accusation. "But what is to prevent our Empire from being altered as well?" she asked, recalling previous attempts at time distortion. "If the work of our operatives will do this much damage to the Federation and their government, who is to say what it will do to the Empire?" She did not wait for an answer. "The Federation is nothing more than one minute grain of sand in a galaxy of sand. And Tazol," she pointed out emphatically, "science dictates that if one grain of sand is touched, all the sand moves, changes . . . distorts."

Tazol stared at the woman, then waved the argument aside with a gesture of his hand and a snort of dismissal. "You underestimate the mind of our Praetor, Lady," he replied. "Our entire fleet is now converging on this area of space—as close to the borders of this Neutral Zone as we dare." He eyed the screen once more, voice hardening as he spoke. "Once the Praetor gives the order, our operatives will be sent into Earth's past using a slingshot effect. And the Fleet will enter hyperspace to await the results."

He paused, thumbing a button on the arm of the chair. On the viewscreen, the star pattern disappeared to be replaced with a computer generated diagram of the Empire's boundaries. Seven blips showed on the readout, all moving slowly toward the *Ravon*.

"Once our Fleet achieves light-speed, we will be safe in a space which is not space at all. But of course you already know that, my dear," he continued in a condescending purr. A dark laugh separated his lips. "Your beauty occasionally causes me to forget that you are also a scientist." He reached out impulsively, slipping one arm around the woman's slim waist and drawing her to his side. "In the womb of hyperspace, any changes which might occur will not directly affect

69

any of our ships or those aboard them. And since we will carry the historical records of the entire Empire on board, any minor changes which may be caused to our history can easily be corrected once we re-enter normal space."

Sarela slipped free of the powerful arms which held her pinned to her husband's side. "Mistakes have been made before," she pointed out, ignoring the heads of the bridge crew which began to turn in their direction. "There are no guarantees, Tazol. None."

Leaning back in the chair, Tazol rubbed the light growth of beard, then shook his head in dismay. "As a scientist, it is logical that you should question these matters, Lady," he agreed. "But as a subject of the Praetor, you should remember that *his* mind is more capable of plotting galactic dominion than yours. The Empire's most brilliant scientists have worked on this plan for many seasons; there will be no mistake this time!"

As Sarela's eyes widened, she chanced a look at the *Ravon*'s young navigator—the man she would have selected for life-mate had she had the right to choose. In Rolash's eyes, she read hatred—hatred for Tazol, for the Empire, even for the Praetor. But she quickly looked away. Rolash was lost to her. She turned her attention back to the commander, the Warrior . . . the man she hated above all else.

"Even our Praetor has been guilty of error," she reminded the stranger to whom she was wed. "And his scientists are often employed in the art of speculation—especially if the Praetor pays them well to say what he wishes to hear." Her voice was oddly calm, cold, threatening. "And do not forget that the Praetor holds as little regard for individual life as you do yourself, Tazol. The Praetor is Romulan; that is his way. But *I* do not wish to become the casualty of an erroneous hypothesis," she stated flatly. "I, too, am Romulan, but my beliefs are not necessarily the beliefs of the Old Times. There comes a day when even the most powerful race must admit to itself that it has been defeated in battle. There is no dishonor in that, Tazol; it is nothing more than a fact. Our conquering days are over, husband; it is time to *build*—with what resources we possess."

A cold, gray laugh escaped Tazol's throat as he slipped to his feet in a surprisingly graceful movement. "Your pacifistic nature nauseates me, my fiery little animal!" he snarled. "And you are overlooking the fact that the Praetor himself will be aboard this vessel when we enter hyperspace! As ruler of our people, he will come to risk his life along with ours. He is not afraid of Death, Sarela, not afraid to die for the tradition of the Empire! His transport ship is on its way here now, and will be arriving within the day!" He leaned closer, a threatening black void covering his eyes. "I suggest you alter your way of thinking before he arrives, for you must certainly be aware of the fate of those who have shared your complacent beliefs in the past. The Praetor will not tolerate your weak views nor your efforts to sway the loyalty of this crew!"

Sarela's gaze hardened as she took a step nearer. "And who *is* the Praetor?" she asked pointedly. "Who is the man that hides behind a hooded robe? Has anyone ever seen him?" Without waiting for a response, she continued. "And those few who *have* seen him—his personal slaves and advisers—never leave his service. If they attempt to do so, they are dead before they reach the palace gates. You say that the Praetor's *ship* is en route here; of that I am certain. But how will you know that the man who boards this vessel is *really* the Praetor at all? How can you be certain that the man who comes here is not some impostor employed by the Praetor to lure the *Ravon* into a suicidal mission? How, Tazol?" she demanded. "How can you know these things? If the Praetor is as wise as you claim, he will not endanger his own life on nothing more than a computerized hypothesis!"

Tazol's face darkened with tangible rage which

twisted his features into an animalistic snarl. "You *will* be silent!" he commanded. "I shall not tolerate this blasphemy against the Empire!"

Sarela laughed gently, almost admonishingly. "Yes you will," she corrected. "For you do not possess the courage to silence me!" She met his eyes, testing his conviction, testing her own ground. "The Praetor would not be so foolish as to board this vessel in an attempt to avoid the paradoxes of time. He would sit back—safe within the walls of the Empireal palace—and wait for his fleet to do his bidding. And then—*only* then—would he step in to partake of the rewards. And Tazol," she said with a very gentle smile, "if there are no rewards, he will say that we acted alone—in a scheme to overthrow his authority and bring power to ourselves." She shook her head, lips growing tighter with anger. "We will be executed," she added matter-of-factly. "Not only you and I, but all who serve aboard the *Ravon* will die. Your Praetor would not allow us to live long enough to make it publicly known that *another* of his 'can't-fail' schemes had failed!"

A stray moment of horror which seemed to be circling the bridge found its way to Tazol's face. All heads were turned now, all eyes on him; and he suddenly realized that this fiery female *could* be correct. And something warned him that the crew of the *Ravon* might not support him in a critical situation which involved Sarela. She had been on the ship too long, had too many friends in anonymous places. He tasted indecision, fear, rage. "You will follow my orders, Sarela," he said at last. "I serve the Praetor! And the mere fact that you are my wife does not exempt you from that same duty!"

Sarela felt flame rise in her own eyes, but made no effort to disguise it. "And the fact that I am your wife does not automatically mark me as a fool either, Tazol!" she responded. "Our marriage was the mistaken bribe of my father!" She threw the computerized readouts into the vacant command chair. "These speculations are meaningless!" she spat out. "They are merely hypotheses based on the possible *success* of our agents in Earth's past. There are no provisions for *error*. No alternative plans have been formulated in the event that the operatives should fail—or if they are simply unable to alter the course of Terran history sufficiently. Not enough research has been done to know *how* the time flow will be affected. And as a scientist yourself, even *you* should realize that time alteration is never a certainty. There are too many variables, too many paradoxes—and any discrepancy spells failure!''

Striding back to the main computer console, she activated the controls which changed the viewscreen once again. "These are examples of a few of the mistakes your Praetor has made before, Tazol. Look at them—study them very carefully!

"Six seasons ago, we attempted to alter a single planet's history in the hopes of establishing a new form of government there which would be susceptible to the Praetor's rule. As a result of our tampering, the entire planet was laid to waste, the resources destroyed, and the people obliterated. No sheep to rule, Tazol," Sarela said quietly. "When our operatives created a flaw in the governmental system of that world's past history, they overlooked the fact that the *new* government was based solely on survival. Wars were the outcome. Disease. Ruin." She pointed at the top of the display, eyes hot with accusation.

"And when we attempted to change our own physical nature to render a stronger individual, we time-tampered with the genes of our ancestors! Again," she stressed with a frustrated gesture of her hands, "the results should be painfully obvious, Tazol. Nearly half the population of Romulus died as a direct result. Of course, the Praetor could *claim* that it worked; the Warriors who survived were indeed physically stronger. But as a whole, the experiment was nothing less than disastrous. By altering the genetic structure of our ancestors, the 'brilliant' scientists failed to take into account certain diseases to which our species *already* possessed an immunity. Once the genetic code was altered, that immunity no longer existed." She laughed bitterly, flipping the long, black hair back from her slender face. "No, Tazol. No experiment can *ever* be a complete success. For as long as there are uncharted variables, there will always be errors."

Tazol stared blankly at the screen. The implications were too frightening, too deadly . . . too obvious. "It will not happen this time!" he persisted, not knowing what else in the universe to say. "It *cannot* happen! We have learned from our errors—"

"Are you such a puppet that the suicidal tendencies of our species elude your comprehension?" Sarela interrupted. "You have stated that we were once a conquering race. Yes!" she agreed, indicating the viewscreen with a nod of her head as she moved to stand in front of the stunned commander. "And if you are not blinded by customs so ancient as to be oblique, you can see where that has gotten us. Greed, Tazol. Greed is the only motivating force behind any conquering race—and the Praetor is surely the most greedy man in the Empire. How many times has he sent entire starships to die on a whim, on a quest for some pretty trinket to adorn the palace walls?"

Tazol's face darkened as several members of the bridge crew murmured in agreement. "Your blasphemy against the Empire will not go unpunished, Sarela," he promised, wondering if it was a threat he could uphold. "I follow my orders; I honor my duty—even if that duty means death!"

But Sarela only laughed sarcastically. "A true son of the Praetor," she observed. "But keep in mind that I am not the only person aboard this vessel who does not wish to die in an insane attempt to rule a galaxy. History is on *my* side, Tazol—not the Praetor's. Whenever we have attempted to alter the time-flow in any manner, the results have never been as predicted. Or are you so intimidated by the Praetor that you would lay down your life on his whim alone? Would you fall obediently onto your sword to amuse him if he demanded it?

"Fear does not make a good commander, Tazol," she continued. "Especially if that fear is so deeply rooted that it blinds you to logical alternatives. It is easier to die a hero of the Empire than to live as one who opposes the Praetor's views—that is true. So go ahead," she entreated, indicating the viewscreen with one hand. "Go ahead and become another hero. Have your name added to the list of failures. It will make little difference in a thousand years—and you *will* die a hero, of that I assure you." She paused, lowering her voice to a deceptively gentle tone. "And neither your Praetor nor your wife shall mourn your passing, Tazol. You will be nothing more than a bad memory in the atoms of the galaxy."

Moving in to grasp the defiant woman by the arm, Tazol experienced fire in his blood. Sarela did indeed pose a threat—not only to his rank or his life, but to his pride. In the Warrior's tradition, he raised his hand high above her head, but stopped when Rolash turned threateningly toward him.

"Commander," Rolash interrupted coldly, "the Praetor's ship approaches. His crew demands docking coordinates."

Tazol wavered, looking first at the petite frame of his wife, than at the navigator, then at the viewscreen. After a moment of indecision, he shoved Sarela roughly aside. She could wait.

"Inform the Praetor of our position and prepare full honors for his arrival," he barked. He turned back to the woman, almost horrified by her calm eyes, her lack of fear. Indecision crept closer. *Who is the Praetor?*

"Transport vessel *T'Favaron* approaching docking coordinates," Rolash replied after a quick flurry of words into the ship-to-ship communication panel. He turned pale brown eyes back toward Tazol. "The Praetor will board in precisely twenty minutes."

Tazol surveyed the silent bridge, tasted fear in the

back of his throat. In the Empire, mutiny wasn't uncommon. "Any mention of this incident outside the bridge will be dealt with accordingly," he threatened, scanning the faces of the strangers who were his crew. Commanders had been known to disappear before— without trace or explanation. He had to maintain a front, a façade . . . a lie.

Gradually, all eyes returned to their panels, but Sarela slipped away from her husband's side once again. "Then you are as guilty as I," she pointed out, a smile finding its way to her face. "By not punishing me as required by the Warrior's tradition, you are as much a traitor to the ways of our ancestors as I am!" With a defiant glance, she turned and moved back to her own station. "I had hoped you would find enough mercy in you to kill me now, Tazol," she hissed. "For you cannot command me any more than you can command this vessel!"

"Silence!" Tazol demanded, staring blindly at the woman. "You will not speak of this again! Do you wish to bring the Praetor's wrath down on all of us?"

Sarela's eyes showed no intimidation as her lips gave way to a knowing smile. "Perhaps," she murmured, studying Tazol closely. "The horror in your eyes tells its own story. I may not have won my freedom from this marriage, but I have won a respect from you which you dare not revoke. You are fortunate that the Praetor will board our vessel in a few moments, for I would not hesitate to kill you, Tazol." She paused thoughtfully, and the smile grew to maturity. "And even your Warriors could not reach the bridge in time to save your worthless life."

The bridge fell silent as the commander turned toward the doors and strode away without responding. But . . . he couldn't help wondering if Sarela had been correct. What if it was just another impossible mission? *Who is the Praetor?* He shuddered.

With an effort, however, he slammed a heavy black door on the negative yammering in his head and moved into the lift—away from the bridge, away from

Sarela, away from the intangible danger. Duty and tradition took up a familiar droning chant in the Warrior's mind, and he found himself smiling by the time he reached the hangar deck. . . .

Slowly, the image faded, and Tazol sank back against the bed. It seemed years ago . . . centuries, in fact.

. . . And still he had not seen the Praetor.

Chapter Seven

ENSIGN KIRK STARED at his feet while trying not to let the nervousness he felt show on his face. Despite repeated efforts to avoid a confrontation with the *ShiKahr*'s Vulcan captain, he'd finally been trapped—quite efficiently and embarrassingly—by none other than Donner himself. It seemed to Kirk that the other ensign had taken remarkable pleasure in bodily dragging him to the lift and forcibly depositing him in the captain's quarters. Now he stood waiting. He'd heard a lot about Captain Spock—some good, some bad, all stern; he suspected he'd have little success attempting to explain his personal situation to the firm Vulcan commander.

The bruises on his face had been carefully concealed with medicinal makeup he'd stolen from the ship's store; but his left eye still ached, and his muscles were stiff and sore.

As he stood there pondering the floor, he could see the Vulcan methodically rustling through a stack of papers and computer tapes on the neatly arranged desk; and though Kirk had heard the usual scuttlebutt about some peculiar orders, he hadn't expected the captain to leave classified material so easily available. He looked more closely at the captain, remembering the dream of the night before; something—*someone*—shivered inside him.

"Ensign Kirk?" the deathly quiet voice asked after what felt like centuries. Still, the Vulcan did not look up.

"Reporting as ordered . . . Captain," Kirk returned, willing himself into a subordinate stance, which hurt almost as much as the bruises. It felt so out-of-place to be addressing the Vulcan in such a manner. The majority of his instructors at the Academy had been Vulcans; but there was something about this particular starship captain which defied conventional explanation. At the Academy—before the incident which had led to his dismissal from Command training—he'd gotten used to the quiet mannerisms, the lack of praise even when work was exceptional. But he sensed something more in this particular Vulcan—a fire beneath that coolly logical command pose. In a brief flash which had no explanation, Kirk suddenly saw their positions reversed. He was sitting on the other side of that big desk, wearing the familiar maroon silks of command . . . yet even that vision didn't quite hold true. His inner eye saw gold and blue, merging and twining together, forming a union and a rapport. A perfect balance upon which starships were run.

But reality slowly returned. That type of balance did not exist, Kirk told himself, blinking the absurd image away.

He waited in silence.

The Vulcan raised his head at last, studying Kirk carefully—and one brow suddenly shot up in surprise. *T'lema. He who walks in dreams.* For a long time, he continued holding the other man's gaze, feeling the moment solidify around him. There was no mistaking the intense hazel eyes, the almost defiant stance, the muscled body, the lock of errant hair which fell to the middle of the human's forehead. Yet he could see no sense of recognition in Kirk. The eyebrow slowly lowered as logic intervened. It was not impossible, the

79

Vulcan told himself, that he had merely seen a holograph of Kirk along with the other new transfer documents. It was equally as possible that he could have seen him on the FleetCom transmission tapes; Kirk was not unknown—especially following the incident at the Academy.

Still . . . there was something different; something which logic could not define. The young human ensign had been assigned to the *ShiKahr* when all other disciplinary measures had failed, and although Spock did not approve of the Talos Device—which had essentially deepened this human's problems—neither did he approve of drafting personnel to active starship duty against their wishes. Ship's safety could depend on the performance of any individual at any time, and since Kirk had no desire to be on the *ShiKahr*, it was nothing less than bureaucratic politics which had been instrumental in having the human assigned. Illogical at best.

To Spock, it was irrelevant that the young ensign had once been in Command training, but had lost the scholarship—and the personal interest—when a bizarre series of events had pointed the finger of guilt at him following the murder of Chief Instructor Sorek. Once convicted, Spock recalled, Kirk had been incarcerated for over a year, subjected to the Talos Device in an effort to discern the truth behind the murder, and finally shipped off to the Draft Academy once it became apparent that he either did not remember the night of the murder, or was too strongly disciplined to reveal the truth even under the harshest of methods. At any rate, Spock surmised, Starfleet must have considered him too valuable an asset to waste.

The Vulcan leaned back in the chair, continuing to observe the human's arrogant attitude . . . and the contrasting downtrodden expression.

"Ensign Kirk," he repeated presently, "you were scheduled to report for duty at 0800 hours on Monday morning, and at the same time for three subsequent days. Might I inquire as to why you did not deem it necessary to do so?"

Kirk's jaw tightened almost imperceptibly. "Captain Spock," he began, tone defensive and cold, "I'm sure you're aware that I don't want to be on this ship. And it's obvious that other members of your crew are just as opposed to this posting as I am myself." He raised his eyes, but chose a point above the Vulcan's head as a focal area. "I'm requesting a formal discharge immediately—dishonorable or otherwise; it's not important."

Spock heard the clipped tone of the human's voice, yet sensed something deeper. "Surely you realize, Ensign, that you were drafted into Starfleet because of your history of resistance to more conventional forms of discipline on Earth—combined with the fact that you were once in Command training yourself." He paused, eyes scrutinizing. "If you were to be discharged now—which is an impossibility under present circumstances—you would be sent to an Orion rehabilitation center for the rest of your life. And I assure you that you would find that far more degrading than any prejudices you might encounter on board this vessel."

Kirk shrugged with disinterest. "I'm not so sure about that," he said sharply, ignoring the urge to open himself to the compassion he heard in the familiar voice.

The Vulcan did not respond, then rose and paced the width of the quarters. He turned, studied the ensign through quizzical eyes, then returned and sat down in the chair once more. He looked closely at the human, and thought for a moment that he detected a hint of medicinal powder on one cheek. He dismissed it. Lighting could play tricks even on the most trained observer.

"Ensign," he said at last, "I will speak freely with you in the hopes of allowing you to comprehend the circumstances before you make an irrational decision which could adversely affect your entire future." He paused, brows furrowing. For a moment, time flip-flopped, then righted itself again. But for that single moment, he felt a rapport with this human, a knowledge that trust could be given . . . and received in return. Illogical under the circumstances, he thought. But nonetheless an accurate impression. "Other humans have been assigned to this vessel—men and women who did not initially wish to be here—yet all have eventually adjusted in one manner or another. Since you obviously attended the Academy with higher goals in mind at one time in your life—"

"That was six years ago," Kirk interrupted, still not looking at the man behind the desk. "Things were different then . . . *I* was different then." *I was different then.* There was a ring of truth in that. For an instant, Kirk felt as though he was listening to another person—a person he'd once known; maybe even a person he'd once been . . . or had wanted to be. He discarded the irrational thought, telling himself it was nothing more than lingering effects of the mind probe, the demon machine . . . the Talos Device.

Presently, the Vulcan indicated a vacant chair with a gesture of his hand. "Please be seated, Ensign," he entreated. The discussion was going to take longer than he'd originally intended, and though he certainly had more pressing matters than the attendance record of one single ensign, he found himself unable to dismiss the subject.

But the human shook his head. "I'd prefer to stand, sir." The proud flaring of the nostrils, the almost unconscious tension of broad shoulders.

The Vulcan noted it. "As you wish," he acknowledged. "At any rate, you have no doubt heard rumors concerning our current orders, Ensign?"

Kirk glanced sharply at the Vulcan. How did you answer a question like that? Admit it, and admit to being a ship-board gossip—to listening to scuttlebutt and receiving classified material. Deny it and get caught in a lie . . . worse yet. He wondered momentarily if the Vulcan was testing him, and managed a devious smile.

"If I heard that the entire Fleet had been diverted to transport Denebian slime worms to bait stores back on Earth, that wouldn't make it true, now would it?" he asked pointedly. "So, with all due respect, a rumor's only as good as the source."

Spock leaned forward, steepling his fingers in front of himself, elbows resting on the desk. His eyes darkened. Getting through to this stubborn human was going to take more time than he'd expected; and time, he reminded himself, was a scarce commodity. Within five days, two starships would be arriving at the Neutral Zone. And according to details contained in Admiral S't'kal's transmission, the attack on the Romulan Empire was scheduled to begin two days after that. He would have to come straight to the point.

"Ensign Kirk, you need not engage in the art of evasion with me—for I am not here to judge you. In truth, we may all be dead within a very short span of time—unless Doctor McCoy and I can find some solution to an unknown force which appears to be pushing the Alliance into undeclared war with the Romulans." He continued holding Kirk's gaze, almost compelling the human not to look away again. It was a difficult task.

Kirk fidgeted uncomfortably. "Why are you telling *me* this?" he asked at last.

The Vulcan rose, leaned across the desk, and came face to face with the human, almost surprised when the other man did not attempt to back away. "Because I am convinced that you are somehow . . . involved." The Vulcan's eyes closed, and he wished he were better with the Terran language. His statement sounded more like an accusation than a possible answer. "In other words, Ensign Kirk, I suspect you could prove to be a valuable asset to Doctor McCoy and myself."

Kirk squinted curiously. "Why?" he demanded.

The Vulcan sat back down, indicating the chair once more, surprised when Kirk relented and sank into it.

"I am familiar with your personal history, Ensign," the Vulcan explained. "And though it is now irrelevant that the Talos Device has been banned as a method of punishment, you need not fear it any longer." He paused, feeling an odd empathy with this human stranger. "However," he added, "you must understand that the Talos Device can also be used for the *benefit* of the Alliance—particularly in our present situation."

Kirk blinked, brows narrowing suspiciously. "What are you getting at, Captain?" he asked.

Leaning back in the chair, Spock studied the human for only a moment longer. "I require your assistance— yet I cannot directly order you to cooperate. Doctor McCoy has discovered that the . . . insanity . . . which appears to be spreading generally throughout the Alliance is based deep within the brain itself. In order to better understand the phenomena, we are accepting— on a volunteer basis—crewmen who are willing to submit to a complete vid-scan."

Kirk felt himself go cold inside. He turned away, refusing to meet the dark eyes which seemed to be almost pleading. "Forget it," he murmured to himself, suppressing the shiver which slid up his arms. "I've already had enough vid-scans to last a lifetime." And yet, in refusing the Vulcan, he experienced a deep sense of personal failure—as if he'd somehow disappointed a close friend.

The Vulcan remained silent for a very long time. "Very well," he responded at last. "The choice is yours alone, for as I stated, I shall not force you to cooperate." He paused, continuing only when it became obvious that the ensign had no intention of responding.

"It is on record that I do not approve of the Talos Device; it is a dangerous tool despite its reputed effectiveness." The Vulcan forced himself to remember that he'd dealt with men far more defiant than

Kirk, and he knew he could deal with this one if they could reach some type of understanding. But . . . the fear had to be obliterated first. And yet, men like Kirk didn't accept kindness easily—even when offered under a logical pretense. "If you are still troubled by the nightmares which are resultant from your previous experience with the Talos Device, I shall instruct Doctor McCoy to—"

"I don't have nightmares!" Kirk lied, voice rising defensively. He wondered what embarrassment there should be in knowing that the Vulcan could see right through him, but still it came. "I just don't enjoy having my brain picked like a goddamned fruit tree!"

The Vulcan leaned forward in the chair, choosing another angle. Time pressed forward. "Initially," he began, "you claimed to be innocent of the crime for which you were convicted; but later changed your plea to one of guilty. Why?"

Kirk said nothing, and as the Vulcan noted the blank expression on the ensign's face, he saw it slowly harden to one of stubbornness.

"Is your resentment of this posting due to the fact that you *are* innocent? To the fact that you feel you should perhaps be a commander rather than an ensign?" He knew he could not spare the human's feelings now—not if he wanted to approach the source of the problem. And yet, there was an emotion very close to pain related to what he was doing. Somewhere, buried and hidden beneath years of Vulcan discipline, there *was* pain. He closed his eyes for an instant, searching for the logical balance which suddenly seemed very far away.

"Does it really matter now, Captain?" Kirk demanded quietly. "And besides, what difference would it make anyway? I was convicted, wasn't I?" But he *didn't* remember the night Sorek had been murdered; he'd been too drunk from Finnegan's spiked-punch party to even remember walking across the grounds to the dormitory, much less whether or not he'd murdered his Vulcan instructor.

·"It is true that you were convicted," the captain agreed. "However," he pointed out, "conviction does not necessarily denote guilt." He was also aware that Kirk had already served a worse sentence than most men could endure. As a starship commander, he knew of the Talos Device; as a scientist on Vulcan, he'd once been foolish enough to test it on himself. The psychic nightmares which had resulted had been enough to make him demand that the Vulcan High Council ban use of the machine in all Alliance territory. After lengthy debate, the Council had agreed—but not in time to prevent its use on Kirk. For that, Spock felt a twinge of illogical guilt. He *should* have been there—Raising one eyebrow at the thought, he commanded himself back to reality.

"I have also been informed that your mind was resistant to Vegan thought probes and truth drugs which would, under normal circumstances, prove your guilt or verify your innocence." He hesitated, taking a deep breath as he noticed that Kirk actually appeared to be listening. It was a welcome change. "The psychiatrists assigned to your case could not understand the peculiar resistance, and you were convicted largely on circumstantial evidence as I recall."

Kirk shrugged noncommittally, masking the memory of the Talos Device with disinterest. "Kill anything you don't understand. Isn't that the law of nature?" He winced slightly when the muscles in his face tightened.

"No, Ensign, it is not," Spock countered, his voice unaccountably gentle. "It is, unfortunately, the law of many primitive cultures—but *not* the law of nature." He rose from the chair, looking more closely at the ensign's pale, drawn face. "And it is not permissible on board this vessel."

Taking a step nearer, he tilted his head as the very faint scent of makeup came to his nostrils. Absently, he reached out to touch the human's cheek for confirmation, but stopped when Kirk's eyes widened fearfully. The eyebrow climbed once more; Kirk's reaction was proof enough.

"Who is responsible for this?" Spock asked sternly.

Kirk turned away. "Nobody," he lied as the hot red color of embarrassment came to brighten his face. "I . . . I got drunk in my quarters and fell against the bulkhead in the dark." But he recognized it for the transparent lie it was. He glanced nervously at the door, and thought of running.

But the Vulcan moved to block his path, almost as if sensing the impending retreat. "Perhaps you would do better assigned to a nondrinking roommate, Ensign," he suggested casually. For a moment, he felt himself inadequate to deal with the delicate situation. Humans maintained such a fragile balance—a balance between pride and compromise, between anger and complacency, between truth and deception . . . between love and hatred.

"Donner has been troublesome to me in the past," he continued as if to himself, "and despite his abilities, I have considered transferring him planetside on more than one occasion." He looked at Kirk, wishing the human would meet his eyes. "I should have realized that his aggressive nature would eventually assert itself again." For an indefinable reason, he felt unnaturally protective of this human.

"It wasn't Donner, dammit!" Kirk exploded angrily. He felt the rage building silently behind his eyes—the same rage which had gotten him into brawls in the stagnant prisons on Terra, the same rage which always seemed to come at the worst possible times. "It was just my own clumsiness, that's all! And I don't want another roommate; I want a discharge!" Finally, he lifted fiery eyes, masking fear with a blink of fury. "Do I have to kill someone *else* to get thrown off this floating Alcatraz, or will you grant that request before I do, Captain Spock?"

Unprepared for the psychic outpouring which accompanied the verbal assault, Spock stepped back.

And yet, there was familiarity in the brief touch of minds. Even in anger, hatred . . . familiarity lived. He took a deep breath, steadied himself, and reburied his own sudden emotions somewhere beneath the mask of command. Recovering his composure, he moved back to the desk.

"Let us understand one another, Ensign Kirk," he began. "Threats pull no weight with me, and I shall not tolerate them." He paused for a moment, studying the angry denial in Kirk's expression. "Nor shall I tolerate the physical abuse of any member of this crew," he continued, tone considerably more gentle. "I am ordering you to tell me who is responsible for your injuries."

But Kirk remained mute and immovable. In his prison days, he'd learned what it meant to keep a confidence. "I'm responsible for my own problems," he stated at last. "And I don't need a keeper! Keep your half-breed sentimentalities to yourself, Spock!" He started toward the door, stopping only when he heard the auto-lock activated from somewhere behind him.

The Vulcan moved to stand between him and the door. *Half-breed*. The word hung somewhere outside reality.

"Very well," he murmured. "I will accept that as your answer for now. However," he continued, "I will also be advising the quartermaster to change your living accommodations; effective immediately."

Kirk felt the color drain from his face at the note of finality in the suddenly ominous voice. Now he'd really done it. Not only was he a weakling and a coward and a drug addict in Donner's eyes—but to be assigned new quarters for his own protection . . . He could already hear Donner's taunts, could feel the slap of the big man's open palm across his face—the type of slap one might administer to a disobedient animal. He looked up, desperation filling his eyes as he shoved pride in the background for one of the first times in his life.

"I—Captain Spock—I . . . apologize for my out-burst." But it hurt to apologize when it shouldn't have. Spock was different—"If you don't intend to discharge me, I'd like to stay where I am." He waited, listening to the pounding of his own heart.

Spock studied him coolly for a very long time. "I have already denied your discharge request, Ensign," he reminded Kirk. "And since you will not tell me who is responsible for your injuries, you leave me no alternative but to transfer you to other accommodations and alter your work-assignments as well." He paused briefly. "Despite what you may have heard about Starfleet duty or about me personally"—*half-breed!*—"you will discover that your life here can be rewarding—if you permit it to be." *And in the event any of us survive beyond the next week. . . .* He waited and, as expected, received no response other than a closing of the ensign's eyes in defeat. For an illogical moment, he found himself thinking of the future—with Kirk at his side. . . . Somehow, he told himself, he would find a way around S't'kal's orders. Somehow . . . they would live. "In the meantime," he said, drawing himself back to the problem at hand, "you are to report to Sickbay to have the full extent of your injuries determined and treated."

Hardened hazel eyes looked up at last. "I'd prefer not to, sir," he said in a voice which might have been defiant, might have been pleading.

"That is precisely why I am making it an order rather than a request, Ensign Kirk," Spock replied, using the authority which felt alien and unnatural. He turned away. "Dismissed."

For a long time, there was no sound. Then, after what seemed like empty hours, footsteps retreated. Carefully, the Vulcan glanced out the corner of one eye to watch the human go; and a thought crept into his mind which might have come from a dream he'd had a very long time ago.

I'd make one hell of a lousy ensign, Spock.

And though he'd never personally met Kirk before,

he was certain of one thing: The voice in his mind precisely matched that of the man who had just left his quarters.

He glanced at the chronometer. Sooner or later, the human would come around. He only hoped it wouldn't be too late. . . .

In the Psychology Lab, Leonard McCoy bounced nervously on his toes, waiting for the results of the day's last vid-scan. The young man on the table was unknown to the doctor personally, yet McCoy couldn't help feeling for him. The vid-scan, despite the fact that it was completely painless, was nonetheless an extremely personal thing. And though McCoy had always subscribed to the doctrine that anything an individual chose to keep sacred within the mind should be honored, he now began to fully appreciate the technology behind the instrument which had once been considered a potential chamber of psychiatric horrors.

On the screen above the patient's head, images were being recorded—precise video images of whatever stray thoughts and subconscious dreams or nightmares were traveling through the mind. In this case, McCoy thought, as with the majority of the other two hundred volunteers who had confessed to "mind slippage," it wasn't difficult to see the pattern. Mentally, McCoy sighed in relief; Lieutenant Christensen was the last. And with a sampling of over half the crew, the results should at least help in formulating a hypothesis.

Stored in the central medical computer were sample vid-scans of the crew—required by FleetCom as a prerequisite for any crewmember ranked yeoman or above. McCoy smiled to himself. In the "old days," it has been required of *all* Fleet personnel. But that was before humans had become standard operating equipment on vessels such as the *ShiKahr,* McCoy reflected, nonetheless thankful that the procedure was still practiced on a voluntary basis. And those records were now proving invaluable—as a control factor for the experiment if for nothing else. Compare and contrast.

He glanced at the man on the table. "Well, Christensen," he said with a grin, "the images you're generating on a *conscious* level are perfectly standard issue for a young man your age." He winked when the lieutenant laughed somewhat nervously.

"Nothing too heavy for you, Doc, I hope," Christensen replied, taking a deep breath and relaxing.

McCoy shook his head, thankful that the screen was always turned away from the patient's range of vision. If Christensen wanted to review his tape later, there would be no objections; but during the actual experiment, the doctor had learned that permitting the patient to watch the images while they were being recorded was vaguely akin to having a partner view a holotape while making love. Too many distractions to get the correct results.

He moved over to the diagnostic bed, resting his hand on the man's shoulder reassuringly. "I'm going to give you a shot of coenthal now, Dane," he explained. "It'll drop you down to an alpha level of sleep and give us a look at what's going on in the deeper levels of your mind. Okay with you?"

Christensen shrugged. "You're the doc, Doc," he agreed. "All I know is that if you people can find a cure for melancholy, I'm willing to do just about anything." He shuddered dramatically. "I think I'd much rather be phasered at point-blank range than go through another episode like yesterday." Warm brown eyes blinked at the memory. "Like . . . like falling through a hole into another version of a Lewis Carroll story—another whole world or something." He shuddered again. "Dark . . ."

McCoy smiled gently, then turned to prepare the hypo. "From what I've been hearing, you'd have to stand in line just to get a chance at the firing squad, kid." *Reassurance*, the doctor thought. *If they all know they're not the only one, maybe it'll slow the process. Safety in numbers* . . . At least it was a hopeful thought—one of the few he'd had in two days.

After a moment, he pressed the instrument against the man's arm and waited for the drug to take effect. Within thirty seconds the brown eyes drifted shut, and the readings slowly dropped. McCoy turned back to S'Parva, nodding. "Activate the monitor," he instructed. "If he starts getting in too deep, let me know and I'll bring him out of it."

S'Parva nodded, following the doctor's instructions. For a few moments, the screen over Christensen's head showed the usual images of resistance to drug-induced sleep. Subconscious figures representing the lieutenant and Sleep warred on a foggy battlefield. Sleep, a neuter magician, was clothed in black robes. He had no face, but a long sword dripping blood swung freely from his right arm. Christensen, nude and without a weapon, soon fell in battle.

Darkness filled the screen.

"Doctor McCoy?" S'Parva called, adjusting the controls for the widest possible scan.

McCoy turned in the Katellan's direction. He'd learned to recognize worry in the yeoman's tone. "Another negative scan, S'Parva?" he asked wearily.

S'Parva nodded, still gazing at the blank screen. "Nothing at all, Doctor," she responded. "All possible compensation already computed and implemented. Continuing negative response."

McCoy glanced at Christensen's sleeping form, then shook his head in dismay. Of the two hundred volunteers, thirteen had manufactured negative vid-scans under coenthal. The rest . . . varied. Images of an altered *ShiKahr*. A somewhat different FleetCom. And a golden-haired, golden-eyed captain. And though the images had always varied slightly there was no mistaking the definite similarities. It was a matter of interpretation, but the results were damned obvious. He looked at Christensen one last time, then quickly administered the drug which would restore the man to consciousness.

A stray thought coalesced into a theory, and he turned to S'Parva. "As soon as he's ambulatory, go ahead and release him. In the meantime, I'll be down in the captain's quarters." But his brows furrowed as he looked more closely at S'Parva. "How long have you been at this anyway?" he asked at last.

The Katellan shrugged, switching off the vid-scanner and moving to Christensen's side. Already he was beginning to awaken. "I forget," she replied finally, managing a smile for the doctor. "But I'd really like to stick it out till the end."

McCoy bounced on his toes. A stubborn Vulcan was bad enough—but S'Parva was, in many ways, the captain's equal. "Well, just don't fall apart on me now," he said with a smile. "I'm going to need your help when the computer spits out a theory on this thing."

"Any theories, Leonard?" S'Parva wondered.

McCoy's brows narrowed as he glanced at Christensen curiously. "Maybe," he conceded, rolling a computer tape over and over in his hand. "But it's still too early to tell." His eyes locked with the Katellan's. "Why don't you shut down the equipment, grab a few hours of sleep, and we'll go at it fresh in the morning." He glanced back at Christensen . . . and a shiver crawled down his spine. Like looking at Death himself. Still . . . no point starting a panic. No proof . . . *yet*.

He slipped into the corridor, then began to run toward a vacant lift.

Chapter Eight

COMMANDER TAZOL WAS not a patient man.

As the flagship *Ravon* emerged from hyperspace, approaching the Empire's central command post on Romulus, he tried to suppress the nervousness which had been building steadily in the pit of his stomach since the mission began. He wondered what they would find when the records of First History—the history which had existed *before* intervention into Earth's past—was compared to Second History—the altered history which existed now that the mission was completed.

Already, he could feel the beginnings of a most peculiar displacement as he tried to imagine what the Fleet could be facing if Sarela had been right—if the Empire was as drastically altered as the Federation was supposed to be. If she had been even remotely correct in her theories concerning alteration of the Empire, he wasn't at all certain he wanted to view the Second History records which would be available at Post One. Since the base itself could not be protected from those hypothetical changes, First History would have to be carefully compared with records of the Empire's "now-natural" Second History.

As the *Ravon* entered orbit, Tazol almost sighed in

relief; after Sarela's horror stories, he'd half expected to discover that the Empire itself no longer existed. But the familiar droning voice of Command Central provided orbiting coordinates, welcoming the Praetor's flagship back "home." At least that much was in his favor, and Tazol took the moment to pray to all Romulan gods that his wife had been in error.

Another matter which continued to plague Tazol, however, was that in the six standard days the Praetor had been aboard the *Ravon,* he had gotten only a glimpse of the legend—and that had been nothing more than a quick glance at a robed and hooded figure. It *could* have been anyone. Carefully surrounded by attendants, slaves and advisers, there was no way to determine who remained anonymous inside those black cloaks. And to add to Tazol's personal misery was the fact that the comparative analysis of First History to Second would require weeks to complete before conquest of Federation territory could even begin. For though alteration of the Federation should subsequently have resulted in the automatic alteration of Romulan territorial boundaries, the Praetor's scientists had pointed out that the paradoxes of time tampering would only open up the possibilities. Conquest—to suit the current needs of the Praetor—would still be required. Tazol scoffed aloud, rubbing a hand through his beard and cursing the intricacies.

It would be a long wait.

Temporarily resigning himself to his plight, he glanced at the young navigator. "Rolash, inform Command Post One that we require a direct tie-in from their main computer system to ours," he said, boredom highlighting his gruff tone and stabbing fiercely through ebony eyes. Mundane scientific duties were best left to mundane scientists; he wondered where Sarela had disappeared to. "But say nothing of the fact that our Fleet has been in hyperspace," he added as an afterthought. "We must not allow our true nature to be discovered until the historical data is analyzed on board this vessel."

Again, he paused, rubbing his chin thoughtfully. "If, after that analysis, we discover no major changes within the Empire, we will follow standard procedure." A devious smile came to his lips. "The Warriors are in need of a diversion, Rolash," he continued at last, "and I can think of no place better than the brothels of Tamsor."

The navigator's expression bordered dangerously on disgust. "Your orders shall be implemented, Commander," he acknowledged nonetheless. As his hands moved over the control panel, connecting the ship's computers in with the central system on Romulus, the bridge doors opened to reveal Sarela.

Without glancing at Tazol, Sarela moved to the science console, slipped into the chair, and inserted the decoding nodule into one neatly tapered ear as she studied the visual readout.

"Our operatives were marginally successful, Commander," she relinquished presently. But a look not unlike fear slowly came to dwell in wide black eyes. "However," she added, "certain changes *have* been affected in the governmental structure of our Empire."

Tazol felt his blood chill. Forcing himself to move at an unconcerned pace, he rose from the command chair and came to stand at his wife's side, gazing down at the data-feed and experiencing an emotion he recognized as anticipation slither through his stomach.

"Well?" he demanded.

"Apparently," Sarela began, "the operatives' success was limited at best. Starfleet does indeed exist . . . but not as before." She scanned the visual information as quickly as possible, allowing it to advance rapidly over the board. There would be ample time for the Praetor's scientists to analyze it in more detail later.

"One hundred years ago, calculating Romulan time," she recited, "our ships attacked a planet in the Eridani system—Vulcan. However," she added, "due to the fact that minimal research went into the nature of the Vulcans before this Second History attack, it was unknown that they were also a conquering species in their distant past.

"Though their violent tendencies had been curbed with logic and emotional temperance, the survival instinct remained intact. The Vulcans were the first race in Second History who were capable of withstanding the Empire's attack, their scientific knowledge having been in an advanced state at the time of our initial assault. After six months of battle, the Vulcans were successful in infiltrating our attacking forces and seizing control of several Romulan surveillance vessels." She paused, eyes locking with Tazol's fixed stare.

Slowly, the commander's expression mutated to one of denial. Yet he knew he could not dispute what was clearly written in the books of a history he had never experienced. This, then, was Second History.

"Is there more?" he barked, momentarily forgetting to play the role of arrogant disbeliever.

Sarela nodded, eyes returning to the small screen on her panel. "Though their own ships were larger than ours, Vulcan-built vessels were designed primarily for interplanetary travel rather than interstellar. However, they were quick to adapt Romulan stardrive and contact neighboring systems to aid on pushing back warships still being sent from our Empire."

She hesitated once again, holding one long finger over the control which would slow the data-feed. "A footnote to Second History reveals that the Praetor at that time *should* have made the decision to break off the attack on Vulcan and all systems in that quadrant. Instead, due to the nature of our species in combination with pressure from the Empire's Warriors who were obsessed with a desire for revenge, the Praetor allowed the attack to continue. The Vulcans were considered a serious threat," she continued, "as they were the only race we had discovered who could match our ferocity—and our intellect—in battle."

She glanced briefly at Tazol's face, noted the pale

coloration as she released her finger from the pause control. "Three of our Fleet's lightships were lured into Vulcan orbit by a computer synthesized distress signal—allegedly from one of our own ships. The lightships were attacked and . . . defeated," she emphasized. "With a total of seven vessels seized and five others nearly destroyed, the remainder of our Fleet returned home to the Empire."

Tazol took a moment to hope there was no more, yet the continuous stream of information across the screen shattered that illusion. He wondered fleetingly if his gods had deserted him . . . or if they, too, had been sacrificed somewhere in the crossroads of Time. He turned away. Anger turned to resentment. Resentment turned to fear. And fear transformed to desperation. In any History, it appeared that victory was not a luxury permitted to Romulans.

At last, Sarela continued. "At the time of our ships' return to the Empire, there had been no form of government on a galactic scale. However, shortly following our attack on Vulcan, their High Council established the groundwork for an Interstellar Alliance of Planets. The Vulcan High Council was also instrumental in the construction of the seven starships which comprise Starfleet as it still stands today." She paused for a moment, studying the board more closely. "Much of the information from that point forward is extremely limited—attributable to the fact that our intelligence operatives in Alliance territory are now more readily detected and their activities subsequently . . . halted."

Without waiting to hear the rest, Tazol returned to the sanctuary of his command chair, slumping angrily into it as he noted the eyes of the bridge crew slowly come to rest on him. "I suppose you find this information amusing, Sarela?" he accused hotly, looking for someone—anyone—other than himself to blame. He felt numb inside, cold . . . scared. He closed a heavy steel door on the thought; Warriors were not permitted to taste fear.

Turning in her chair, Sarela eyed her husband with open disdain. "I am still Romulan," she pointed out. "I find this information disturbing—for it seriously limits our operations in the future." She smiled gently. "But it is nothing less than I expected, if that is what you wish to know, Commander. And it is nothing less than our beloved Praetor *should* have foreseen."

She paused, eyes returning for a moment to the readout. "Even though the history of Earth was altered sufficiently to prevent Terra from establishing the United Federation of Planets, our operatives could do nothing to account for the pre-existing stability of other worlds—such as Vulcan and Organia—who would eventually have established a galactic government even without Earth's initial influence. *That* is how it happened in Second History," she stated flatly. "Though their Starfleet is now considerably smaller than before—approximately half its original size—it is now controlled largely by Vulcans. And in *both* histories, Tazol, even *you* must admit that the Vulcans are quite capable of being our equal in many ways."

Tazol's eyes never wavered as the fear left him to be replaced with cold determination. "But the Vulcans are benevolent fools!" he hissed, slamming a doubled fist down hard against the arm of the command chair. "The fire left their blood when they chose peace and logic over conquest! They *could* have stood by our side in battle against the weak—yet they became weak themselves, content with their computers and their *culture*." He spat the word out in hatred, grimacing as if biting into some unripened alien fruit. "They abandoned their Warrior rites for the boredom and servitude of peace!"

"Perhaps," Sarela conceded. "Yet the potential must always have existed for their ways of peace to change. Our time-tampering has made that change considerably more simple. The Vulcans are no longer the complacent and benevolent creatures from First History, Tazol," she pointed out, indicating the datafeed with a gesture of her hand. "They are now the

99

enemy—even more so than before—and an enemy who understands our nature perhaps better than we do ourselves." She glanced again at the readout, observing only minor structural changes within the Empire itself as the information continued to flow into the *Ravon*'s computer systems. "Our own borders are somewhat larger than before our operatives returned to Earth's past," she relayed, "but those borders *do* still exist. We are far from invincible—and only slightly better off than before."

She shook her head in frustration, the mane of black hair cascading down her slim back. "Surely you must understand that we have as little hope of defeating seven of their starships as we would have had with the original twelve!"

Defeatedly, Tazol searched for the legendary glimmer of hope which no longer seemed to exist in any universe. "Scan intelligence banks on the surface of Romulus," he commanded. "What are the military capabilities of the starships which exist within their Alliance now?"

After a flurry of hands over the controls, Sarela's eyes returned to the terminal. "Seven starships, varying only slightly in design from those of First History. Dilithium powered; warp ten maximum critical speed; warp seven maximum safe speed." Making a quick comparison to the facts she remembered from First History, she punched a series of buttons which produced a starship design display from both Histories on the viewscreen. For the most part, she recognized, they were identical.

"Phaser power and photon torpedo capacity precisely the same as before. Note: nonviolent security measures employed whenever possible. However, Second History reveals that the Vulcans do not hesitate to kill if necessary in order to protect planets within Alliance jurisdiction. There have apparently been incidents of Romulan vessels invading Alliance territory for over seventy years, but with only marginal success. Second History also indicates that our boundaries have remained unchanged for over forty standard years; and that both sides have recently signed a Treaty prohibiting violation of the Neutral Zone by either party. Essentially," she concluded, "we are facing precisely what we faced before—but now at the hands of the Vulcans—who are undoubtedly *capable* of far more treachery than their human counterparts from First History would have imagined possible."

Tazol grunted miserably, wondering if the Praetor would merely rip the command rank from his shoulder or have him tortured to death. It wasn't his personal fault . . . but the Praetor did not look kindly upon defeat. "Earth history?" he wondered, looking for even one angle which might shed some scrap of uplifting knowledge. *The Praetor will not allow us to live long enough to reveal that another of his "can't-fail" schemes has failed*. He tried to block the persistent thought.

"Earth history reveals that the most prominent changes occurred immediately following the assassination of Doctor Palmer and his two associates who would have formed the basis for the United Federation of Planets," Sarela replied presently. "Once those men were eliminated, Earth's history underwent a drastic change. The prospace exploration faction lost much of its status when Doctor Palmer 'disappeared,' leading certain key political figures to believe that he and his associates had fled into refuge to avoid 'embarrassing information' concerning a hoaxed contact with alien civilizations. Of course," she added, "it is believed that our operatives were responsible for that rumor; and that the Earth officials merely used it as an excuse to squelch what was then termed the revival of their space race." She skimmed the minor historical incidents quickly, then continued. "After several years, Earth began to exhaust its natural resources; its nations began fighting among themselves until the environment was almost totally destroyed.

"Vulcan scoutships established preliminary contact

with the existing Terran government sixty-five years ago—Second History time calculation—and Earth eventually joined the Alliance, being formally admitted five years following initial contact. By careful guidance, the Alliance was able to aid in reducing Earth's overpopulation, seeding several other Class M planets throughout the galaxy." She paused. "A footnote suggests that, as recompense for this aid, the Alliance instated a military draft of sorts. However, since humans displayed a remarkable adaptability to spacecraft conditions, the draft was mainly used as a tool to get social deviants off the planet. At any rate," she concluded, "there are now Terrans serving voluntarily aboard starships—many in high-ranking positions."

She glanced at Tazol, momentarily switching the screen off. "Essentially, Commander, our operatives were successful in what they were ordered to do," she pointed out. "They murdered the Terrans who would have formed the basis of the Federation. Yet regardless of the fact that the Federation as we knew it in First History was destroyed, an Alliance came into being in another manner. Earth played no part in its initial development . . . but that is now irrelevant. It *does* exist, Tazol."

Tazol continued staring straight ahead. One could not navigate through a paradox. "We are defeated once again," he whispered almost to himself.

Sarela considered the statement in silence. "It is said by the wise men of Romulus that history can never be artificially changed once it has already occurred naturally. Only minor incidents can be altered through time-tampering; and you must accept that Earth—one planet among millions—is indeed minor when compared to the galaxy itself. Though our operatives efficiently destroyed Earth's *role* in the Federation, they could not obliterate the concept itself. Its importance was too great, its memory too deeply embedded in the atoms of the universe."

Tazol's eyes rolled skyward in a gesture of long-suffering. "Your poetic explanations had best be saved for the Praetor," he muttered miserably, scanning the tired eyes of his bridge crew. "For I must now inform His Glory's attendants of our Empire's current status—and I do not believe he will find the information pleasing." He leaned back in the chair, wondering if it would be the last time. "However . . . he will not be so easily deterred; and I suspect he will wish to plan strategy before attacking the Alliance." It was a fleeting hope.

"Attack the Alliance?" Sarela repeated.

"It *is* our way as Romulans," Tazol reminded her. But he wondered if he would live long enough to see the attack. Bearers of bad tidings often met quick ends. And in that single moment, Tazol found himself wishing he'd never heard of the Empire, never seen the *Ravon*, never known what it meant to be a Romulan Warrior. Suddenly, the fields and the farms seemed the most appropriate place in all the worlds.

His eyes closed for a moment before he rose from the chair and turned away from the bridge. And yet . . . when he remembered the promise of power, it wasn't as difficult to swallow. And in a stray instant of unmitigated arrogance, he also realized that the Warriors of his own ship, his own clan, would surely be loyal to him . . . even if Sarela's officers or the Praetor were not. A faint smile threatened to break out on the round face, but he dutifully pushed it away.

"There is one other matter, Tazol," Sarela's voice interrupted as he reached the doors to the lift. "We are now displaced—as much as the rest of the galaxy and perhaps even more. Only those aboard our lightships will have any memory of First History at all—and we can no longer permit ourselves to respond to the things of our past. We must learn new ways—customs and behavior which are not a part of our natural memory."

Tazol turned red-rimmed, weary eyes in her direction. "What are you saying, wife?" he wondered. "I have no time or patience for your recitation of mourning."

Sarela stood, glancing around the bridge. "We are

103

not the same creatures who entered hyperspace while our operatives were in Earth's past. We are specters now, Tazol—ghosts of another place and time, relics of an Empire which no longer exists." There was a sadness in her wide brown eyes, reflected in her voice.

But Tazol only nodded. Already, he was beginning to realize that truth all too clearly. In the span of what had seemed only a moment in the dark embrace of hyperspace, all he had known had been painlessly obliterated . . . changed . . . subtly altered. And all for the sake of conquest—a word which sounded uncharacteristically bitter to his mind. He wondered if it had been remotely worth it . . . and when the rest of reality would begin to crumble.

And yet, he *was* a Warrior, loyal to the song of the sword. His grief for the past would not last long . . . and already he had the beginnings of a plan.

Outside the Praetor's assigned quarters, Commander Tazol paced restlessly, wondering when or *if* he would have an opportunity to meet the Romulan Praetor personally . . . or if he even wanted to. The nebulous figure had come aboard *his* ship, converted an entire Warrior deck for his personal use, yet still remained elusive and impossible to see. The Legend's attendants had taken the messages, along with a complete transcript of Second History comparisons into the massive stateroom hours ago—and had subsequently told Tazol to wait. As a Warrior, he grew weary of waiting; and as a man, he grew tired of playing hand servant to an inaccessible figurehead.

Another hour had come and gone, but at last the double doors slid apart to reveal two of the Praetor's advisers. Both were dressed in rich robes, carrying ceremonial jeweled daggers on silk belts and a disruptor tucked neatly at the top of black suede boots. For a moment, Tazol caught his mind wandering on three unrelated trains of thought.

First, it seemed illogical that the Praetor's voiced concerns always centered around the poverty of the

Romulan systems; yet his closest advisers wore the finest clothes and jewels. And the Palace, Tazol had heard, was nothing less than what some Terrans might term "heaven."

Secondly, Tazol had heard the usual rumors of the Praetor's personal slaves—lovely female trinkets to adorn the public arm of his throne and the private company of his bed. But during the entire time the Praetor had been on the *Ravon*, Tazol had observed only *male* scientific advisers and scribe-slaves—all of whom were young and unacceptably handsome.

And third, as far as anyone in the Empire knew, the current Praetor had produced no offspring to whom the title would be bequeathed upon his death. And if there were no male offspring, tradition was explicit: The new Praetor would be the one Warrior who could defeat all others in battle.

The Commander's lips curled into a devious smile as he began to see his own path a little more clearly.

But his reverie was interrupted as one of the advisers cleared his throat noisily, exuding an air of importance which Tazol found repulsive to acknowledge.

"The Praetor will grant personal audience to your science officer," the lithely muscled man stated without preamble. But his tone left no doubt as to the Praetor's displeasure with the information contained in the transcripts. "You will escort him here immediately, Commander Tazol."

Tazol felt a combination of anger, dread and embarrassment rise in the back of his tight throat. He tasted bile. Not only was *he* being used as a fetch-slave himself, but it now seemed that Sarela would be granted the one honor which had been denied to him since the Praetor came aboard. He opened his mouth to protest, then quickly clamped his lips together, remembering that argument would prove futile . . . or worse.

He inclined his head in the customary acknowledgment. "My scientific adviser is also my second in command . . . and my wife," he stated.

"Your personal affairs are of no concern to me or to our Praetor," the man returned without hesitation. "She will report here at once!"

As the shame of defeat rose to color Tazol's rugged face, he forced himself to respond with the correct salute. "It shall be done, Lord," he replied through painfully clenched teeth, then slid into the nearest lift chute before permitting his anger to reach maturity. Already, he could see the smug look on Sarela's face once she learned of her orders.

In a now-familiar moment of despair, he touched the sword at his side . . . and wondered what the almighty Praetor might think if the *Ravon*'s captain were found dead by his own hand.

But he dismissed the thought before becoming romantically enchanted with it, punching the button which would bring the lift back to the bridge. There was only one pleasant thought left alive in his mind: If heads were going to roll in memoriam to the Praetor's deceased plans of galactic dominion, perhaps that head would belong to the lovely Sarela . . . and not himself.

Chapter Nine

CAPTAIN SPOCK WAS alone in his quarters when the door buzzer demanded attention. He sighed to himself, unaccountably irritated at the interrupton into his private meditation regardless of the fact that he was technically on duty for another twenty minutes.

"Come," he acknowledged, then glanced up to see the ship's surgeon standing in the doorway. Rising, the Vulcan indicated a chair as the doctor entered.

"Well, Spock," McCoy began without preamble, "I'm aware that these findings should probably be referred directly to the science officer for immediate collation, but considering the circumstances, I thought I'd might as well come straight to the throne." He smiled wearily, sliding into the plush, black visitor's chair.

"Your tendency to exaggerate the powers of command can be most annoying, Doctor," the Vulcan replied, accepting the computer tape which McCoy proffered in his direction. "I presume you have completed the vid-scans of all the volunteers?"

McCoy nodded. "They're all on the tape, Spock," he explained, brows narrowing as the Vulcan inserted the raw information disk into the terminal on the desk. "So far, it's all hypothesis, but . . ." his voice trailed off.

"You have a theory?" the Vulcan wondered.

McCoy shrugged. "I dunno," he said at last. "Maybe I'm going a little crazy, too, but I'd swear the evidence I've compiled so far is pointing toward . . . well . . ." He threw up his hands, tasting hesitation. "I dunno," he repeated.

Spock's brows narrowed as he returned to the chair behind the desk. "Please come to the point if there is one, Doctor," he urged, voice harsher than usual. "Time is of the utmost importance."

McCoy swallowed hard. No point delaying making a fool of himself. "Well, it's starting to look as if there's no *real* scientific or medical cure for what's happening." He put one knuckle to his lip thoughtfully, then met the Vulcan's expectant gaze. "Dammit, Spock, if I didn't know better, I'd swear this whole thing is being caused by . . . by space itself!" But he waved his own statement aside with a quick, negative gesture. "Now I'll be the first to admit how crazy this sounds, but we've dealt with things of a similar nature before—the Tholians, for instance. Similar," he stressed, "but not quite the same. And with the Halkans," he added hopefully. "That parallel universe."

"Are you suggesting that we are slipping into an alternate dimensional plane, Doctor?" Spock interrupted, switching the tape scanner to the hold position.

McCoy glanced up sharply. "That's part of it," he confessed. "But I'm not sure even *that* would explain it this time, Captain. It's as if *we* don't belong in *this* universe—or as if this whole universe itself is somehow . . . alien to the mind." He managed a nervous laugh. "At least with the Tholians, the *ShiKahr* was slipping into a different universe—a pre-existing universe with physical results and measurable phenomena. And with the Halkan Mission: you, me, Uhura and Scotty just . . . *changed places* with our counterparts in the parallel universe. But now . . ." He fell silent.

The Vulcan leaned back in the chair, resting his

elbows on the arm and steepling his fingers neatly in front of his chest. "But now," he ventured, completing the doctor's sentence, "those counterparts no longer exist. The lifeforms appear to be pre-existing, yet this universe has been formed in some type of microcosm?"

McCoy glanced at the Vulcan. "Yes!" he exclaimed, surprised that the Vulcan could follow his reasoning when he wasn't sure he was following it himself. "That's exactly it, Spock! But the critical thing is—judging from the information we've monitored in those vid-scans, those counterparts of ourselves . . . of that universe itself . . . *did* exist at one time." But with that thought came another. "It's *we* who are the ghosts, Spock," he said, a shudder accompanying the peculiar consideration. "And based on what we've seen so far, I'd chance a guess that this insanity is eventually going to spread throughout the entire galaxy."

Spock considered that. "I agree," he said at last. "Yet attempting to recreate an entire universe—even assuming that the theory itself is plausible—is not something easily accomplished." He paused. "Nor will it be readily acceptable—particularly to the human mind."

"What are you getting at, Spock?" McCoy asked pointedly.

"The mind is only capable of accepting that which it can comprehend, Doctor," the Vulcan explained. "And though the parallel universe theory is now a commonly accepted fact, it is difficult for the mind to grasp the concept that no lifeform is utterly unique. As we discovered on the Halkan Mission, there are duplications—doppelgängers, if you will, with subtle or major differences. If we should attempt to persuade FleetCom that it is *this* universe which is unstable, I hardly believe the High Council would accept that information as fact. In any man's mind, Doctor, he is right; the right to life belongs to him alone. It is the law of individual survival—of a need to be unique."

"But if we *don't* do something," McCoy protested,

"I'd be willing to bet a year's pay that the problem will eventually . . . take care of itself. And that, Spock, is the law of nature! Just look at those orders from S't'kal! And even if we're successful in evading *those* orders, that's just the beginning. And it's no longer as simple as if we were just a danger to ourselves. Hell, Captain, with current technology, this entire *galaxy* could be lifeless within a year's time! Just on this ship alone, there have already been several cases of assault, personal threats . . . and Reichert's charade epitomizes it all!"

"Granted," the Vulcan agreed. "Yet I must ask you—as an individual lifeform theoretically unique unto yourself—would you be willing to essentially die to preserve a *concept* of universal stability?"

McCoy swallowed hard, but the answer was one he'd already had to consider. "I'll admit it's not a pleasant thought, Spock," he said quietly, "but it's even *less* pleasant to think of what happens if we're right and we don't do something." He leaned forward, elbows resting on the desk. "For the rest of our lives—however short that might be—we'd be living in a galactic asylum, complete with all the things humankind has finally started to rise above: war, disease, hunger, prejudice. . . ." He shook his head emphatically. "No, Spock, I'm not suicidal; but I'd also like to think that I'm not *selfish* enough to consider my own life more valuable than the lives—and the sanity—of an entire universe."

A very faint smile seemed to tug at the corners of the thin Vulcan lips. "I might have underestimated you, Doctor," the captain replied. But any amusement he may have felt quickly faded. "There is only one additional question I must put to you before proceeding further."

McCoy waited.

"Do you have a theory as to why only certain individuals appear to be affected by the madness?" the Vulcan asked presently.

"As a matter of fact," McCoy said with a grin, "I do. If—and I repeat *if* this dual universe theory is correct—then it stands to reason that a few things are always going to be the same." He shrugged. "Like with the Halkans, for instance: same people in both universes, same basic life-roles; just a different dimensional plane.

"But I'm starting to think that those people who *aren't* affected are playing the same role in *this* universe that they play in . . . in whatever universe they really belong to." He shook his head. "Hell, Spock, I'm a doctor, not a theoretical scientist, but I think you catch the general drift. Just using myself as an example, I'm probably not being affected because I'm a doctor in both places. Reichert, on the other hand . . ." He paused for a moment. "Reichert has the mental composition in *this* universe which made him an engineer's mate. But in *another* universe—the *'real'* universe, if you will—he could well be a businessman or a merchant, or even a pimp on Rigel! Who knows? But he's probably something completely different." He hesitated once again. "And yet," he continued at last, "the very molecules which determine how a mind operates are preset in the genetic code of the parents. And if that *code* remains the same in two different universes—yet the *environment* alters in the parallel universe, then it throws the brain out of kilter. The results: eventual insanity due to an inability to cope with change." He shrugged once more. "Or if you want to get downright psychiatric about it, it's the square peg and round hole theory: the mind rebels against anything which is essentially contrary to personal nature."

After a moment of silence, the Vulcan opened the top drawer of the desk, withdrawing a second computer tape. "In essence," he stated, "your theories confirm my own—and the theories of the ship's central research computers as well." He paused. "I have also taken the liberty of plotting a time curve—which, I

111

believe, will tell us precisely how long we have before the condition worsens beyond the point of repair."

McCoy's eyes widened as the Vulcan's words sank in. He stared blankly at the tape. "Why didn't you tell me this an hour ago, Spock?" he demanded, wondering if the Vulcan had merely wanted to see him squirm.

The captain rose, pacing the width of the quarters. And when he spoke again, his voice was very quiet, almost strained. "Since I myself am being . . . affected . . . by this apparent alteration, I did not feel I could trust my own theories exclusive of all others. I . . . wished to see if you and I, operating under different conditions, would reach the same conclusion and form the same hypotheses independently of one another."

McCoy felt himself soften toward the captain. It wasn't often that Spock admitted to *any* doubts, any weaknesses. "Then . . . I take it you've had . . . more problems?"

The Vulcan's eyes closed—almost painfully. "According to my calculations, Doctor," he replied, evading the direct question, "we have precisely fifteen Vulcan Standard Days before the insanity spreads beyond any chance of controlling or isolating its effects." He indicated the tape with a quick nod of his head. "During that time, we must endeavor to . . ."

"To what?" McCoy demanded, a moment of hopelessness creeping in to join with frustration. "Build a universe that none of us can even prove exists? And in fifteen days?" he laughed disbelievingly. "Hell, Spock, legend has it that the Earth was created in seven days! And now you're telling me that you and I—a Vulcan and a mere mortal—are going to construct an entire universe in two weeks!" Again came the sarcastic laugh. "No problem, Spock," he said reassuringly. "You handle the nebulaes and the quasars; I'll take care of the little things: like planets, suns, and weird personality quirks of trillions of lifeforms!"

The Vulcan lifted one admonishing brow. "If you can suggest some alternative, Doctor, I would be more than willing to entertain the idea."

McCoy rose from the chair, started to speak, then

settled for bouncing up and down on his toes as his lips tightened.

"If not," the Vulcan continued, "then I suggest you review the prepared tape at once. You will find computer confirmation of your theories in the recording, Doctor."

McCoy bit his lower lip in frustration, hard-pressed to ignore the icy Vulcan tone. "Right," he said at last, forcing calm on himself. "And I suggest you do the same with the vid-scan tape, Spock." He turned to leave, then abruptly changed his mind. "Oh—you'll notice that 13 out of the 198 tapes we ran show a negative scan under coenthal."

An eyebrow rose. "Explanation?"

McCoy felt Death peer over his shoulder. "It's purely speculation, of course, but . . . my personal theory is that those thirteen people have . . . already lived out their lives in whatever other universe there may be." He paused, thinking about that. "Which raises the question of morality—do we have the right to . . . sentence those people to death—when they've essentially been given another chance at life?"

For a long time, the Vulcan was silent. "Perhaps a more appropriate question would be: Do we have the right *not* to, considering all that is at stake?"

McCoy took a deep breath. "Either way, Spock, it's bartering lives." But he waved the argument aside, forcing himself to understand the Vulcan's situation; he was just relieved to be in his own shoes and not the captain's. "I know there's no easy answer," he said softly, "so don't feel compelled to find one. It's just one more angle to be considered."

The Vulcan's head inclined in acknowledgment as he glanced nervously at the desk chronometer. "I see," he murmured, returning to the chair and sitting down. He looked up, meeting McCoy's eyes. "Was there anything else, Doctor?"

McCoy shook his head. "Oh, yes," he suddenly remembered. "There *is* one other thing." He sat down once again. "That new ensign—Kirk?"

The Vulcan glanced sharply at the doctor.

"Well," McCoy drawled, grateful for the change of subject, "I talked to his new roommate yesterday afternoon—Jerry Richardson—and he said that he hasn't seen hide nor hair of Kirk since you had the quartermaster move the two of them in together." McCoy shrugged. "Maybe nothing," he said before the Vulcan could respond. "But once you take a look at those vid-scans, I think you'll understand why I'm a little . . . concerned about Kirk."

"Please explain," the Vulcan entreated, leaning forward curiously.

"I can't be sure, of course," the doctor replied hesitantly, "but Kirk *does* bear a remarkable resemblance to some of the images on that tape." He leaned back, biting his lip thoughtfully. "And I also found out that you ordered Kirk to report to Sickbay *last night*."

"He did not choose to do so," the Vulcan stated, not particularly surprised.

"Apparently not," McCoy confirmed. "But if you questioned him about it, he'd probably give you a lot of static about his ignoring an order being grounds for immediate discharge, and you wouldn't get much insight into the real problem." He paused. "But Kirk *did* come staggering into my office early this morning. And let me tell you, Captain, he looked like early death and plomik soup warmed over. At first, he wouldn't tell me what was wrong, wouldn't let anyone touch him—but then he started demanding lidacin."

"Lidacin?" Spock repeated quietly. "Why should he . . . ?" But then the answer came. Once under the influence of the powerful tranquilizer, the human would not dream; certain electrical impulses to the brain would be deadened; the slippage would not be as severe to the conscious mind. Far from a cure, but nonetheless an effective placebo. He looked at McCoy.

"In answer to your question," the doctor replied, "I didn't give it to him. But when I asked him to get on the table, he started backing up as if I'd just told him I was an ax murderer. It took me and four orderlies to get him down, and a double dose of coenthal to calm him down long enough to run a full exam." He paused. "When I got through with the tests, I found out that this kid's got some serious problems no one discovered before." He shook his head, slipping into a moment of thought. "I'd *love* to see a vid-scan on him, though I suspect he'd rather walk on hot coals than submit to *anything*."

Spock felt himself tense. Again, McCoy's suspicions about Kirk confirmed his own. The ensign *was* somehow important. "Precisely what type of . . . problems did you discover, Doctor?" he asked at last, struggling to keep his voice neutral.

McCoy's expression slowly transformed to a worried frown. "First of all, he's been addicted to lidacin for quite a while—and not the stuff we use on the ship, either. Don't ask me where he's been getting it, but he's been injecting himself with a ninety percent solution for at least six months. Hell, Spock, it's no wonder he's been acting like a zombie half the time."

Spock remained quiet for a moment. "I presume you will begin treatment of the addiction."

McCoy nodded. "Sure, but it'll take time," he reminded the Vulcan. "The main cure is abstinence—and that's not going to be easy on him, either. And while I don't personally approve of *anybody's* drug addiction, I approve of those Orion stitches-and-needles rehab colonies even less—which is where he'd end up if anyone other than you or me found out about this. But now . . ."

"I see," the Vulcan said softly, feeling a deep personal regret that the young ensign's life was such an apparent turmoil. The human *was* different, compelling . . . and somehow connected in a critical way to both universes. The Vulcan lifted an eyebrow in silent consideration. Perhaps Kirk was even the key to whatever answer existed. . . .

"The only course of action I can suggest," McCoy continued, calling the Vulcan back to reality, "is that we try to keep this under wraps—especially from men like Donner. If Kirk wants *out* of the Fleet as much as he claims, then he might go out of his way to make it known that he *is* a drug addict—just to get that discharge."

The Vulcan glanced up. "Apparently not," he countered, "or he certainly could have availed himself of that opportunity while still at the Academy waiting for active posting." He shook his head. "No . . . Ensign Kirk has chosen to be here; and I do not believe it is entirely by accident."

McCoy considered that. "In other words, you think he may be calling your bluff—trying to see how much he can get away with?"

"I am not certain," Spock replied, "for I have never understood the human capacity to say one thing when another thing entirely is desired."

McCoy grinned. "Like Brer Rabbit and the briar patch."

A look of confusion took shape on angular Vulcan features. "Brer Rabbit?"

But McCoy only laughed. "Never mind, Spock," he muttered. He sobered then, forcing himself back to more immediate problems. "The main thing right now is to get started on a treatment program."

"Begin immediately, Doctor," Spock instructed. In the back of his own mind, he realized he was taking a severe chance with his own career—and possibly the safety of the *ShiKahr*—based on a feeling alone. But transferring Kirk now would serve no useful purpose. *I'd make one hell of a lousy ensign, Spock.* The phantom words returned, spoken as clearly as if the man had been standing directly in front of him.

McCoy nodded almost to himself, noticing the distant stare in his captain's eyes. "I dunno," the doctor murmured. "Maybe I'm just looking for an answer under any rock—but there's something about him . . . something worth salvaging."

"Precisely what injuries did you find?" the captain asked presently.

116

McCoy scoffed. "He's been through a lot, Spock—most of it during the time he spent in prison on Earth. Several broken bones; all healed now. Scar tissue on the left lung from bronchial pneumonia—not terribly surprising, considering his weakened condition and prison living conditions. Lots of bruises," he added, "and a few lacerations." His tone darkened. "All fresh, I might add. But the physical injuries are just the tip of that proverbial iceberg."

"The Talos Device," Spock remarked, tone bordering on contempt.

"The Talos Device," McCoy confirmed. "That damned thing was used pretty extensively on him—so it's no mystery why he won't submit to a vid-scan." He shook his head once again. "And it's no wonder he was trying to pry lidacin out of me. He probably has nightmares left over from the Talos Device that would make a Klingon concentration camp look like a sixth-grade prayer retreat by comparison." He paused. "I've prescribed benzaprine orally for him—and that should curb the effects of the withdrawal within a few days." But his eyes darkened with concern. "The only problem is that he's going to have to come down to Sickbay every night to get the pills. I don't dare trust him with a bottle of the stuff; it'd be like candy next to the stuff he's been pumping into himself. He'd overdose in a day's time."

"Leave the medication with me," Spock suggested. At the very least, it would be an excuse to question the ensign further—and under a more gentle pretense. "Also, it would be too conspicuous if he were seen going to Sickbay every evening; even a man with Donner's limited intelligence would not have difficulty deducing the reason."

McCoy seemed dubious, but nodded. "I'll drop it off in a couple hours," he replied, rising from the chair. "Anything else, Spock?"

The Vulcan thought for a moment. "Negative, Doctor," he replied at last.

"Well," McCoy concluded, moving to the door.

"Since I've still got a few hours of correlation to do on this data, I'd better get back to my beads and rattles. . . ." For a moment, the doctor jolted internally. It seemed so natural . . . like a memory of a dream . . . Spock calling him a witch doctor . . . while someone else stood in the background suppressing a smile. He shivered, and wondered if he, too, was beginning to slip. Someone else. The third side of the triangle. Golden-haired, golden-eyed human. But before he could ponder it further, Spock rose to see him out.

The Vulcan studied the doctor. "I had always suspected that your medical practices were something less than scientific," he murmured, though he also felt an odd sense of déjà vu connected with McCoy's peculiar statement. He wondered briefly if it was McCoy who had always been at his side—and though that image brought a certain truth, he recognized that it was not entirely accurate. The images whisper-walked through his mind. Blue and gold. Warmth and companionship. Stolen moments when the firm Vulcan mask did not have to fit so tightly.

Somewhere, he told himself, he would find that reality again . . . or create it.

No sooner had the door closed behind McCoy than the communication panel beeped insistently. The Vulcan moved toward it, tense for no discernible reason.

"Spock here," he said, activating the device.

"Captain," Uhura's voice responded, "we've just received a transmission from FleetCom." Her voice sounded tense, confused. "Admiral S't'kal has ordered the *ShiKahr* to divert immediately to the Canusian star system." There was a momentary pause, then: "According to the transmission, we're supposed to pick up the Canusian ambassador for on-board Alliance affiliation negotiations with Canus Four."

The Vulcan sat down, eyeing the panel cautiously. Routine treaty negotiations in the middle of an undeclared war which was scheduled to begin in less than a week. An eyebrow rose. "Precisely how far distant is the Canusian system, Lieutenant?" he asked at last.

"Mister Chekov informs that Canus Four is only twelve light-years distant from our present position, Captain," Uhura responded.

For what felt like hours but was no more than fifteen seconds, the Vulcan considered his position. Obviously, he thought, the Canusian Mission was nothing more than another symptom of S't'kal's madness. And yet . . . the Vulcan realized that it *could* well serve to purchase time—provided he used the new orders to his advantage. If the *ShiKahr* were to be detained, perhaps S't'kal would at least postpone the trespass into Romulan territory. But . . . perhaps not.

"Very well, Lieutenant," the Vulcan replied at last. "Instruct the navigator to lay in a course for the Canusian system at maximum warp. Inform me once the *ShiKahr* has achieved planetary orbit."

For a moment, there was strained silence. Finally, Uhura's voice came over the panel on a sealed privacy channel. "Sir?" she asked in a hushed tone. "What about . . . the *other* orders?"

"Apparently, Uhura," the Vulcan replied, easily detecting the woman's concern, "Admiral S't'kal has decided that negotiating for peace with one world is of greater importance than beginning a war with an entire Empire. And . . . in this particular case, I believe he is correct."

Over the panel, Uhura laughed very gently. "Logical, Captain," she said quietly.

"Spock out." He turned off the communication device, leaned back in the chair, and took a deep breath. Hardly logical, he realized. But not unexpected. S't'kal was indeed quite mad . . . and soon, the Vulcan thought, he would not be alone in his madness.

It was late in the evening when the door buzzer sounded again, and though the Vulcan had long since abandoned the prospect of sleep, the grating tone was nonetheless annoying. He rose from the bed, only then realizing that he'd slipped into a state of light medita-

119

tion while planning the details for the scheduled meeting with the Canusian ambassador. He glanced at the chronometer: two A.M. The buzzer sounded again, more insistent . . . and more annoying.

"Come!" he said sharply, surprised at the harsh tone of his voice.

The door opened to reveal Ensign Kirk standing in the hall, bright hazel eyes flitting nervously back and forth from the corridor to the interior of the dimly lit room. He did not speak as he stepped inside, doors closing with a whoosh behind him.

The Vulcan studied him for a moment, quickly detecting the embarrassment hiding behind an outward expression of defiance. For the briefest of moments, the Vulcan wondered what in all possible worlds had brought the human to his doorstep at this hour of the night; but slowly memory returned, and he remembered the pills McCoy had left with him a few hours earlier. Without preamble, he reached into the second drawer of the desk, retrieved the bottle of benzaprine, and dumped two capsules into the palm of his hand, feeling unaccountably nervous in the human's presence. He proffered the pills in Kirk's direction, but still the ensign did not look up.

"Guess McCoy told you about my little . . . problem," the human muttered as if to himself. "But since when are the captain's quarters considered a dispensary?" He was angry at having the knowledge discovered by anyone—and especially embarrassed that the Vulcan commander had obviously been informed. But he felt his hard resolve start to weaken. He glanced up, meeting the Vulcan's eyes.

"The doctor informed me of your addiction to lidacin," the Vulcan confirmed presently. Kirk was such an enigma. He could never predict when the human would react with anger, when he would be embarrassed, when he would board himself up inside that stubborn wall and be completely unreadable. And the fact that he'd only met the ensign recently didn't aid the uncanny sensation of helplessness. "And in response to your second question," he continued, "I thought it would be better for all concerned if you came here rather than Sickbay." He paused, then took another risk. "You . . . obviously do not wish it publicly known that you are . . . experiencing difficulties, and I do not believe you sincerely wish to be transferred off this vessel." So, he thought to himself, this was poker.

Kirk looked up, started to deny it, then abandoned the pose with a deep sigh as he flopped, uninvited, into a convenient chair. "Mind if I sit down?" he asked after the fact.

A Vulcan eyebrow climbed high as the captain sank into his own chair. Bluff called. He waited mutely.

"Why do you care?" Kirk asked at last.

Spock glanced away. But the stakes were too high to permit intimidation to interfere with logic. "I have . . . discussed your case with Doctor McCoy," he began, wondering where the statement would eventually lead, "and have come to the conclusion that you are somehow . . . a critical factor in the survival of this . . . universe."

But Kirk laughed, startling him back to reality. "Now *that's* a heavy guilt trip, Captain," he said boldly. "I know the *ShiKahr*'s received some strange orders, but telling me that *I'm* a critical factor is taking psychiatry a bit far, isn't it?"

The Vulcan shivered, glancing forlornly across the room. "I can offer no logical explanation," he replied truthfully. "I can only state what I . . . *feel* . . . to be true." He forced himself to look up once more, demanded his eyes to remain locked with the human's. Somehow, he hadn't expected *this*. If *he* had been the intimidator before, it now seemed as if their positions were reversed; Kirk was questioning *him*. And yet . . . it felt right, normal, secure. He relented to intuition. "As I have informed you previously, there is a strong possibility that we shall not survive beyond this week. For the moment, it appears that we have, as you humans might call it, bought some time. Yet I shall not hesitate to point out to you—confidentially—that we are still not fully knowledgeable as to what we are facing nor how to . . . correct whatever damage has been done." He paused, wondering if he was making the correct decision. But holding back would accomplish nothing—and perhaps worse. He wondered what the human was thinking, what thoughts were traveling through the quick mind. "At any rate," he continued presently, "we have been diverted to the Canusian system." He held the intense eyes. "And I have tentatively scheduled you into the landing party."

Kirk's eyes widened. "Why?" he asked simply.

The Vulcan hesitated, steepling his fingers in front of him, wishing the action would accomplish the serenity for which it was designed. "Your early Academy records indicated that you were quite adept at diplomacy, Ensign," he replied, choosing a formal approach. "And since several members of the crew are temporarily . . . disabled . . . I find it necessary to utilize your services."

Kirk stared at the Vulcan, a smile slowly coming to the handsome face. "Suppose I refuse?" he asked pointedly.

The eyebrow rose once more. "In that event," the Vulcan replied, "I would have no alternative other than to expedite your immediate discharge from the Fleet." He paused. Poker indeed. "You would be transported to the space-port on Canus Four and eventually to an Orion colony," he bluffed. He leaned forward then, resting his elbows on the desk. "The decision is yours, Jim."

Kirk rose from the chair, shaking his head in mild disbelief. He turned away from the Vulcan, and felt a flare of the old anger. But it quickly faded as respect for the commander chased it away. "And what makes you think I wouldn't jump at the chance?" he wondered.

"You are not a fool, Ensign," the Vulcan responded. "I believe you are . . ." He hesitated, warring with feelings which suddenly welled in on him. "I believe you are . . . as displaced in your present role as I perceive you to be," he stated finally. "And that you . . ." But it wasn't easy to say; a lifetime of discipline and logic fought for survival. ". . . that you will . . . find the strength within yourself to . . . aid in this matter."

Kirk shook his head once again, then turned to face the Vulcan, wondering if it was even possible to trust again. He started to speak, then closed his mouth with the words still suspended in his throat. He took a deep breath. "All right," he conceded at last. And somehow, it didn't injure the fierce pride nor the stubborn ego as he'd half-expected it would. "For all the good it'll do, I'll go on the landing party."

The Vulcan nodded almost to himself. "Thank you," he murmured, recognizing the illogic in his words. "At our present speed, we shall be entering Canusian orbit early in the morning. Please report to the transporter room at 0800 hours."

Kirk nodded, feeling suddenly awkward as he noticed the two capsules of benzaprine on the Vulcan's desk. He turned toward the door.

"Ensign?"

He stopped, but did not face the Vulcan.

"Do you . . . ?" But his voice trailed into silence.

Kirk shook his head in silent negation of the unspoken question. "Tell Doc I flushed 'em down the john," he said quietly, and slipped into the corridor before the Vulcan could reply.

Once outside the captain's quarters, he leaned heavily against the bulkhead, eyes drifting shut. Someone else had made him say the things he'd said. Someone else had walked through his mind. Absently, he twisted the plain gold Academy ring on his left hand as he sank to the floor and began to tremble. Someone else . . . *I believe you are as displaced in your current role as I perceive you to be.*

He took a deep breath, running one hand down the smooth metal body of the ship. *She . . . silver woman-goddess*. It was time to change . . .

After a moment, he rose from the cool bulkhead, listening to the pleasant drone of the engines. Reality breathed . . . more easily now.

Kirk entered his newly assigned quarters silently, glancing about as he dragged the tunic over his head and flopped onto the bed, covering his face with one arm. Despite a prolonged walk in the ship's botanical garden, he found sleep elusive. And the conversation with the Vulcan, now that distance and time had intervened, left him confused. It wasn't easy to care again, not after what had happened the night Instructor Sorek died. His friends had deserted him without so much as a good-bye; but despite the fact that "every man for himself" had always been the unwritten rule of the Academy, bitterness continued to intrude whenever the memories threatened to surface. Yet now it appeared that someone who *should* have been a total stranger—and the ship's captain at that— was going out of his way to befriend him. But what disturbed the human most was that he *did* care . . . or someone inside him did.

With a deep sigh, he rolled to his feet, checking the chronometer to confirm that he was due in the transporter room in less than an hour. As he started into the bathroom to shower and dress, however, the doors opened to reveal his new roommate.

Richardson grinned as he stepped into the room. "Well," he said, looking curiously at Kirk, "did she finally throw you out?"

Caught off guard by the question, Kirk stopped. "Did *who* throw me out?" he asked cautiously.

Richardson shrugged, sitting on the edge of his own bed. "Whoever you've been sleeping with for the last two nights," he clarified, tugging off the regulation black boots and throwing them haphazardly into a corner. "You haven't been staying here," he added, "so I naturally assumed . . ." He winked conspiratorially.

Despite the man's presumptuous nature, Kirk found himself relaxing. Richardson was obviously nothing like Donner. "No," he muttered, " 'she' didn't throw me out." He turned toward the bathroom once again, then impulsively back to the other man. "I've just been keeping the plants company," he explained.

Richardson nodded absently as he discarded his uniform tunic and leaned back on the bed, staring at his wriggling toes. "Yeah," he said, "I used to go down there a lot when I was first assigned to the *ShiKahr*. It's always nice to take your girl someplace different—somewhere you don't have to be reminded that we're sitting on the biggest potential explosion in the galaxy." He shuddered over dramatically. "Hell, if that episode down in engineering had gone a different way, there'd be pieces of thee and me scattered from here to the Tholian Empire!"

Kirk smiled wistfully. "Then . . . it's not just rumor?" he asked, sitting down on the side of his own bed. At least Richardson seemed willing to talk shop and not ask a lot of embarrassing questions.

The other ensign shrugged. "I dunno," he said at last. "Everybody down in the psyche lab's been trying to keep it all quiet, but . . ." He grinned. "Word gets around."

Kirk smiled. "You work in the lab?" he asked conversationally.

"Yup," Richardson confirmed. " 'Fraid so."

Kirk's brows narrowed. "You sound positively overjoyed."

"Well," Richardson replied, stretching lazily, "right now we're involved in a vid-scan project—over half the crew altogether. Doc's been clam-mouthed about it, but it's not hard to figure out what's going on. Hell," he continued, "when two hundred people start forming lines outside the door, you can bet there's a reason."

"Any idea . . . what *kind* of reason?" Kirk prompted.

A smile came to Richardson's face. "Well, I'd like to think it's a fan club of mine—at least with the female population—but in this case, it seems to be an outbreak of paranoia or something." He winked again. "Security's been armed with butterfly nets and mounting pins, so I wouldn't worry too much, Jim."

Kirk laughed—the first genuine laugh he'd felt in months. "What about you?" he asked pointedly.

Richardson looked away, face suddenly darkening; for a moment Kirk wondered if he'd alienated his new roommate already. But the other ensign took a deep breath, rolling up onto one elbow, as a look of chagrin slowly crossed his features.

"I dunno," Richardson said at last. "I've felt a few twinges."

Kirk smiled reassuringly. "Such as?"

"Such as . . ." The other ensign laughed at some private memory. "Such as going up to the bridge the other day . . . doing things I couldn't explain."

Kirk waited.

At last, Richardson continued. "I just went up to the bridge as if I owned the place," he said.

"So?" Kirk asked. "What's so strange about that?" For some reason, Richardson seemed to belong on the bridge. Swing-shift. Relief.

"Nothing in itself," Richardson replied. "Everybody knows how to get there—even the people who aren't *supposed* to know!" He shrugged as if to dampen the memory. "But the weird thing was that I stumbled into the navigator's chair and started joking with Sulu as if it were the most normal thing in the world. Luckily," he groaned, "it was between duty shifts, so Captain Spock wasn't on the bridge yet. Everyone else must've thought I was just fooling around or something, but . . . I wasn't."

The chill which had been hanging above Kirk's head moved a little closer as he thought of his own reactions in the captain's quarters just a few hours previously. "It just seemed the natural thing to do," he surmised.

"Yeah," Richardson agreed with an embarrassed laugh. "And that's not all of it. When I looked at that panel, I knew every control, every maneuver this ship might make. And I've *never* been trained on navigational controls. I was interested in the soft sciences, the research angles; never went in for all the hardware and battle plans. But I swear, Jim, I *knew* all of it! I could've piloted this ship as well as Sulu—or maybe even Spock!"

"So what'd your vid-scan show?" Kirk asked curiously.

Richardson shrugged. "I . . . didn't take one," he said after a silent moment. He laughed—unconvincingly. "Don't ask me why, Jim, but . . . the thought of that machine telling every secret I own makes my skin crawl." His smile broadened. "And with S'Parva right there . . ."

Kirk grinned. "I think I know what you mean," he replied, easily detecting his roommate's fascination with the Katellan. But an idea slowly presented itself. "So . . . why don't you—in the name of science, of course," he said slyly, "find some way of getting S'Parva to do a telepathic link with you." He shrugged, feeling relaxed and comfortable with his new friend. "From what I've heard about Katellans, *that* should tell you as much as any vid-scan—and with half the embarrassment."

Richardson stared at Kirk, then blinked. "You're serious, aren't you?"

Kirk smiled. "Why not?" he asked. "You could tell her it's a control factor for the experiments—a more 'humanistic' approach to balance the technology of the vid-scan."

A wide, knowing grin slowly came to Richardson's face. "You know," he mused, "she might just go for it." He paused, rolling into an upright position and looking at the chronometer. "She'll be on First Shift duty call in less than an hour," he continued as if to himself. At last, he rose from the bed, stretching and yawning. "And it *is* a good idea, Jim—the control factor, I mean."

Kirk shrugged warmly. "Let me know how it goes," he ventured, getting up and heading toward the sonic shower. "I'd stick around to hold your hand, but I'm due in the transporter room in half an hour."

Richardson's brows narrowed. "Transporter room?" he repeated.

"Yeah," Kirk called from the bathroom, quickly dialing the correct comfort zone into the shower mechanism. After a few moments of the pleasantly stinging sonic waves, he opened the door and stepped out, walking back into the living area. He reached into the closet, withdrawing a red, silk uniform tunic.

But Richardson quickly came over, snatched the red shirt away and tossed it across the room. "Here," he said, digging deeper into the closet until he found a blue shirt. "Live a little—*and* a little longer, Jim," he urged.

Kirk's brows questioned.

And Richardson shrugged. "Let's just say that on *this* ship—or probably any other—you don't want to wear a red shirt on landing-party duty."

Kirk shook his head with a laugh . . . and quickly pulled the blue shirt over his head.

*   *   *

The landing party, consisting of five members, beamed down to the computer-specified coordinates only to discover themselves in a swampy area. Large trees resembling Earth cypress grew in abundance, and steam-demons rose off warm puddles like ghostly fingers reaching for the silver-gray sky. On the distant horizon, thunder spoke ominously, and an occasional flash of black-fingered lightning ripped its way through clouds.

Captain Spock observed their surroundings with an expression bordering on exasperation, then turned to survey the landing party. McCoy and Kirk stood to one side; and Donner—an unfortunate last-minute replacement for Alvarez—and Ambassador Selon of Vulcan waited on the other side. And were it not for the logical portion of his mind, Spock might have thought himself in a nightmare. A damp, musky smell drifted to his nostrils, and already he could feel the seepage of stagnant water leaking into his boots. In an almost human gesture, the Vulcan sighed.

The nightmare became considerably more vivid, however, when he began to sense that the landing party was being quite closely watched; even Ambassador Selon, who had been attached to the *ShiKahr* for three years, seemed nervous.

Spock took a step forward. "Tricorder readings, Ensign Kirk?"

Kirk glanced at the hand-held device, following closely at the captain's side. "Some sort of interference, Captain," he reported. "When we first beamed down, I was detecting humanoid lifeforms within a quarter of a mile; but the readings just suddenly shot off the scale. Possible effect of the storm."

The Vulcan nodded, but before he could even begin to draw his phaser as a precautionary measure, he discovered himself in the midst of a rain of spears and arrows which appeared from everywhere and nowhere. He vaguely remembered giving the order to disperse, and was peripherally aware of Donner's voice barking orders into the communicator for emergency beam-up.

The last thing he saw before he felt something sharp slide into his back with remarkable force was the familiar twinkling effect of the transporter yanking McCoy and Ambassador Selon back to the safety of the *ShiKahr*. Apparently, transporter circuits were being affected by the storm as well, he thought disjointedly. He could only hope that Donner, Kirk and himself would be next, for he doubted either of the humans would survive should they be captured by the tribal, warlike Canusian primitives. The one thing which didn't make sense, however, the Vulcan realized, was that the savages couldn't have known when and where the landing party was to beam down . . . unless . . .

Instinctively, Spock reached for the phaser as he felt himself falling. If he could hold off the attack until the transporter technician could recalibrate the controls . . .

Through vision blurred with increasing pain, he could see the primitives closing in—only six of them, he realized—three with spears trained on Donner, three with crude weapons leveled on Kirk.

Without knowing precisely why, the Vulcan slid the phaser into the lethal mode, rolled to his side in a wave of agony, and took careful aim, sending three of the savages to join their ancestors in oblivion.

"Jim!" he yelled as he saw the determined expression on Kirk's face. He didn't see that the human had already drawn his own phaser with surprising speed. "Jim!" Another flash of lightning—phaser blast.

The spears started falling again, like lethal rain from the sky.

It was his last conscious memory.

Chapter Ten

SARELA ENTERED THE Praetor's darkened quarters quietly, an armed guard on either side; and as she approached the high-backed chair from the rear, she could not avoid wondering what she would find in the face of the Praetor, what she would learn from the lips of a man revered even above the ancient gods. Tazol's anger had been pleasantly obvious when he'd informed her of the Praetor's demands for her presence and she knew that, whatever awaited her, it would be well worth the contempt and hatred she'd read in her husband's cold expression.

"The ship's scientific adviser, your holiness," one of the guards murmured as the party drew up to a halt behind the black chair which bore little resemblance to the palacial throne. "She is called Sarela."

Slowly, the chair turned until Sarela caught her first glimpse of the profile of a legend. But as the Praetor stood, her eyes widened in a moment of unconcealed surprise. The Praetor was only slightly taller than Sarela herself, and as the hood was lifted away from the shadowed face, the *Ravon*'s first officer found herself face to face with another woman. Her lips parted in astonishment, but she quickly remembered to lower her eyes in respect, bowing from the waist according to a tradition which she no longer respected, but followed out of habit alone.

"I am honored, my Lady," she murmured, too shocked to recall that she'd held nothing but contempt for the Praetor for years.

"Honored?" the robed woman remarked as her lips turned to a rueful smile. "You seem surprised." But she waved her argument aside with a quick gesture. "You shouldn't be," she added, her tone becoming more serious as she dismissed the guards with a nod of her head. With a quick flow of words, she summoned one of the slaves to her side, ordering wine for herself and Sarela, whom she addressed—surprisingly—as a guest.

Then, turning back to the ship's science officer, the Praetor studied her openly, accepting two glasses of blue Romulan ale from a well-muscled man. She handed one to Sarela.

Taking the glass slowly, Sarela remained silent for a very long time, willing her uncertainty away. "Forgive me, my Lady," she said at last, taking a sip of the wine to mask her confusion. "I was not aware . . ."

"That the Praetor might be female?" the other woman replied, a smile finding its way to her thin lips. Her dark eyes studied the color of the wine for a moment before raising the stemmed glass to her lips. "My father produced no male children," she explained presently, "and please rest assured that I have been through the customary training and preparation." Impulsively, she gestured toward a vacant chair. "Please," she continued warmly, "be comfortable with me. There is much to discuss."

Sarela moved into the chair, grateful for its solidity. For an instant, she found one of her own previous doubts creeping in. But logic alone dictated that, if the Praetor had wished to send an impostor, it would hardly be a woman. He would have sent some well-muscled Warrior with slightly higher than normal intelligence to carry off the pose. And with that knowledge,

Sarela felt one doubt leave her. But it was only one among many.

Setting the glass on the corner of a nearby desk, the Praetor removed the heavy black robes, revealing her body to be well developed and strong in appearance. The short uniform of the Fleet added to the lithe catlike musculature of her legs; and the sleeveless garment presented her as a powerful woman, not one accustomed to an easy life spent sitting dormant on a jeweled throne. Her face was thin and angular, but nonetheless attractive, with compelling black eyes accented with streaks of silver shadow-paint. She appeared to be approximately thirty-five seasons in age. Upswept brown hair accented the eyes—which, Sarela noted, were alight with knowledge and curiosity; and the thin curve of her lips bespoke a quality of humorous appreciation. The straight hair was pulled back from her face, then cascaded over her shoulders as it fell to midback, adding an air of femininity to the otherwise imposing physique.

"I will come to the point, Sarela," the Praetor began, returning to her chair and easing into it with one foot curled under the other leg. "Your views concerning the government of the Empire are not unknown to me."

As their eyes met, Sarela experienced a single moment of fear; no one questioned the Empire's politics and lived to tell of it. But she suddenly realized that she no longer cared; with a lifetime of marriage to Tazol ahead of her, command taken from her grasp by the same fool, and the displacement of time alteration forever embedded in her mind, she had little to lose.

"I am not ashamed of my views, my Lady," she stated, unconsciously raising her chin higher.

The Praetor studied her with remarkable curiosity. "Nor should you be," she replied. Her eyes closed as she leaned back in the chair and inhaled deeply. Honesty was something she could respect, and she smiled to herself. "Be advised that nothing said within this room is to go beyond these walls," she added. "And I must know that I command your trust."

Surprised at the Praetor's unorthodox approach, Sarela nodded. She had expected Death. "You have my word, Lady," she said, allowing herself a moment to think.

"And your trust?" the Praetor wondered with a lifted brow.

Glancing away, Sarela could not find it in herself to lie. She raised her eyes, steeling herself and wondering if the answer waiting on her tongue would mean her extermination. "Trust must be earned," she replied at last. "It is the way of our people—and a tradition which still holds true."

Surprisingly, anger did not spark in the Praetor's wide eyes. Instead, she retrieved the wineglass from the desk, sipping slowly at its contents.

"I am pleased," she said. "One who gives their trust unwisely often finds himself dead when the new sun rises." Again, she smiled. "In this room, you may address me as Thea. It is my given name, but one which must never be spoken outside these walls."

Unconsciously releasing the breath which had been suspended in her lungs, Sarela nodded. "Your anonymity is secure," she assured the other woman, relaxing despite her preconceived ideas concerning the Praetor. She was rapidly discovering that Thea was nothing like she'd expected, nothing resembling the rumors or even the legends. The woman seemed alive and vibrant, almost pleasant, definitely commanding.

The Praetor inclined her head toward the desk, upon which were stacked the computer transcripts of Second History. "I do not find this information surprising, Sarela," she revealed after a moment's hesitation. "It would have been foolish to expect anything different."

Sarela's brows climbed, reflecting her surprise at how closely the words echoed her own. In the background, she became aware of the two slaves moving about, and caught her eyes wandering to where the two men were apparently involved in some type of board game in the back of the oversized stateroom. She tried to dismiss the distraction, but her gaze continued to wander in their direction.

"Time tampering *can* be a useful tool," she responded, choosing a neutral approach. "Perhaps when its intricacies are more fully understood, the attempt can be made again."

Thea shook her head, then noted the other woman's obvious interest in the two preoccupied slaves. With a smile, she raised her right hand. "Tasme, Sekor," she called warmly. "Come sit with us."

As the two slaves quickly obeyed the command, Thea turned once again to Sarela. "Despite the Warrior's rumors," she explained, "my personal attendants are not mistreated." She smiled knowingly. "Some even . . . enjoy their duties," she added, her hand going absently to the long hair of one of the men as he sat on the floor by her chair. She petted him as one might stroke a kitten, fingers entwining gently in the sleek, black hair which tapered halfway down his back. With a nod of her head, she motioned the other slave to sit at Sarela's side, amused when she noted a flicker of embarrassment creep into the woman's eyes. "You needn't worry," she assured Sarela, "for as we have already agreed, nothing which transpires in this room becomes public knowledge. And, as you are no doubt beginning to discover, rumors are often only lies. Do not concern yourself with Tazol."

Not knowing what in all the worlds of Romulus to say or do, Sarela remained silent, not looking at the handsome slave who had been addressed as Sekor and now sat by her chair, resting his head on the arm. She chose a professional approach, mentally kicking herself for her obvious interest in the man's beauty a few moments before. "At any rate," she began, "we cannot be certain what will await us when we attack the Alliance, my Lady. Despite their reduced numbers, their starships are still more powerful than ours—and now carry a large complement of Vulcans."

135

Thea's brows climbed high on her forehead. "There is so much to consider, Sarela," she murmured, her tone somewhat weary. "But I assure you I have no intentions of attacking the Alliance." She paused, then reached across the desk, retrieving a stack of papers and computer tapes which she handed to Sarela. "The time-operatives were my father's idea," she explained. "But he died two seasons ago—long before their mission ever began." She glanced at the documents, leaning forward until they could easily share the same page. "But despite the Praetor's many powers, not even he—or she—can make decisions single-handedly which will affect the entire Empire. If no one else had known of the time-scheme when I became Praetor, I would have abandoned it without hesitation. However, too many of the Warriors had learned of it, and they would not have considered it 'dignified' to dismiss a scheme which would—theoretically—bring so much power to them." She paused, eyes growing momentarily distant. "We have failed with time alteration too many times in the past. However, now that it is done again, we must find a way to use it to our advantage."

Sarela looked blankly at the other woman. "I do not understand, my Lady," she replied. The documents which Thea had produced seemed to be nothing more than handwritten lines, some of which were in a dialect meaningless to her.

"There comes a time when even an entire race must change," Thea explained. "But our people have always been a Warrior people, and no effort has been made to alter that sad truth. The papers you now hold in your hands are taken from the Vulcan Tenets of Discipline, handed down from the time of Surak in their Ancient Days." She paused, black eyes searching Sarela's face as she leaned back in her own chair.

Sarela's eyes widened. "I have heard of them, but I did not know they truly existed," she murmured. "It was said to be only another legend."

Thea smiled wistfully. "A legend only because my

father's father did not permit these documents to be viewed by anyone, including his closest advisers." She paused for a moment. "You see, Sarela, even in First History, the Romulans and the Vulcans were not unknown to one another. Legend has it that we are, in fact, quite closely related. According to my father's notes, which I discovered upon his death, these Tenets of Discipline were stolen from the Vulcans during the time of Surak himself—by an early band of our space-faring ancestors." She shrugged. "Thousands of seasons ago," she conceded, "yet the explanation seems to be a logical one. And, at any rate, as Second History has rendered our own past—we *can* now change. The alterations in the Empire itself are minor—mostly centering in the past—a past which stemmed from battle with the Vulcans a hundred seasons ago. We were defeated—forced to accept that defeat. And as a result, we were compelled to accept aid from the Vulcans for a short period of time. My advisers have studied Second History carefully, and I have been informed that our people *now*—in this displaced timeline—are decidedly more complacent than ever before. In essence, they are susceptible to change, Sarela—the people, like you and I, grow weary of war and poverty."

Sarela studied the other woman carefully. "But *can* we change?" she wondered intently. "Even the fragments of tapes I viewed on the bridge showed our Second History to be no less violent than First," she added. "And I do not understand what these words on parchment can possibly do to alter an entire civilization."

Thea tilted her head, slumping down in the chair to place her feet on the desk. "The Tenets of Discipline are blasphemous to the way of the Warriors," she said calmly, "but nonetheless valid if we wish to survive. Surak was apparently born 'out of time' in both Histories. He saw beyond the need for battle, just as you and I see beyond that desire for fleeting glory. At first, even *he* could not understand what he was doing.

Eventually, however, his people began to listen to his views—but only when it became obvious that they had no other alternative. It was a choice between peace among themselves or eventual annihilation as a race."

Sarela nodded quietly to herself. "The Vulcans were once a violent race," she recalled. "As much or more so than we are ourselves."

"But they listened to reason, Sarela," Thea repeated. "Just as our people must learn to do."

For a moment, Sarela found herself wondering if it was possible. She remembered a time in the past when the Warriors had even revolted against the Praetor—a time when there had been no wars in the Empire for twenty seasons, and the bloodlust had flared once again in men such as Tazol. And she recognized that a Warrior without war or hope of war was a dangerous creature. "Our Empire is large, my Lady," she pointed out cautiously. "And even the word of the Praetor is sometimes questioned. Your armies at the palace will stand by your side. But if the Fleet and the Warriors oppose you . . ." Her voice trailed off.

"The time will come," Thea replied evasively, "when not even the Fleet can stand against us, Sarela." She paused, looking absently at the slave at her feet. "When that time arrives, I may see fit to give the Empire an heir to the title I now hold . . . but not until then." With a heavy sigh, her eyes closed. "Our children are taught the sword before they are taught to read or write. I will not bring a son into the Empire only to see him die a fool."

Sarela listened to the morose words in silence. "Then your reasons for permitting the time operatives to complete their mission are . . . personal?" she stated as a question. "You hoped to be able to alter the Empire's historical structure sufficiently to allow peace among our people, peace with the Alliance?"

Thea nodded, then held her hands up in a gesture of frustration. "But we must first *force* the Alliance to hear us, just as we must compel our own people to listen to the words which saved the Vulcans from themselves." She paused. "It will not be easy, for men such as Tazol and the Warriors do not wish to see these changes." She sighed. "As Praetor, they will hear my words . . . but as a woman who must maintain anonymity, they will be inclined to dismiss them." She smiled wistfully. "As you pointed out, Sarela, even the Praetor's word is sometimes questioned; and from your own experience, you have learned that the Warriors are often given precedence over the builders of our society."

Sarela's eyes darkened. "But it has always been the way of our people that women are equal to the Warriors. Indeed, many women have *been* Warriors, even Fleet Captains on our ships of conquest."

Thea studied Sarela carefully. "But a woman has never before been Praetor—and those who have tried did not live long enough to make their mark on the Empire. The Warriors are fools, Sarela. It is easy enough for them to play their games of conquest, permitting women to join them in battle, while secretly abhorring the fact that we are quite often their mental superior." She smiled once again.

"That is somewhat of an understatement, my Lady," Sarela said with amusement.

Thea laughed lightly, a deep sensuous sound. "That is the one thing our ancestors accomplished when they tampered with the genes of those who preceded us. By creating a stronger male Warrior, they failed to account for certain genes and chromosomes which determine mental capabilities. It is no wonder that the majority of commanders in the Fleet are female; the Warriors are physically superior, that is true . . . but most are incapable of intricate reasoning."

Sarela smiled ruefully, but a cold, silver chill slowly climbed her spine. "But therein lies the problem, my Lady," she said. "They *are* physically stronger, and they would not hesitate to kill anything which threatens their way of life—including the Praetor—especially if they consider the Praetor vulnerable."

Thea nodded quietly. "It is a possibility," she conceded. "My guards will protect us, but even all the forces of the palace will not be able to stand against the Fleet for long. The dichotomy between the Warriors and the rest of our people is too great. That is one reason why my anonymity must be carefully guarded. My father was cautious, and for that I am grateful to him. He made it understood within the palace that I was to be granted complete rule as Praetor upon his death; and my advisers and attendants have never questioned that authority. I have given them no reason to do so," she quickly added. "And I was once the commander of a flagship while my father still lived." She smiled. "Perhaps it was his way of testing me— and perhaps I even failed that test in many ways. But he never permitted it to be known that I was his daughter. He told the Empire only that there was an heir to the throne . . . and the Warriors naturally assumed that his heir would be a son."

"Then your father must have known that you would eventually try to change the Empire," Sarela surmised.

Thea's brows furrowed. "Perhaps," she conceded. "And perhaps that is his legacy of punishment."

Sarela looked questioningly at the other woman.

"He was embittered when I was born," Thea explained. "He could father no more children, and had produced no previous offspring. Perhaps he even believed that on the day I came to power I would be foolish enough to reveal my true identity." She smiled. "I believe that, when he sent me out to command his flagship, he did not think I would return." Again, she paused. "But nonetheless, I must have proven myself to him in some way, for he provided me with the protection I needed. And so long as my views appeared to mirror the Warriors' wishes, even they have accepted me as Praetor. It is the fact that my views are now something less than traditional which places me— and you, now that you know who I am—in danger."

"Then we must take care when presenting the Tenets to the Empire," Sarela suggested. "No one must know—at least not immediately—that the Praetor is female." She knew now that her own gender was what had robbed her of command. Once Tazol, a Warrior of her father's camp, had been chosen as her life-mate, it was a convenient excuse to instate him in a high position within the Fleet. She felt the anger rise in her veins when she realized that she had been right in her previous assumptions: Tazol was hardly fit for command of a garbage truck. He was nothing more than her father's puppet, her father's heroic gesture to the Warriors . . . and perhaps even her father's slap in the face. In many ways, she suddenly realized how much she had in common with Thea.

"To a Warrior," Thea said sadly, "conquest is the only means of survival." She shook her head very gently. "Try to imagine telling Tazol that we should make peace with the Alliance. He views peace only as a cemetery filled with the bones of our enemies. He comprehends nothing else . . . and neither do the other Warriors."

Sarela sank back in the chair, absently lifting the wine goblet to her lips. "There is another matter," she said guardedly.

Thea glanced up, eyes questioning.

"If the Vulcans are as perceptive as we believe them to be," Sarela proceeded, "it will not be long before they discover that their universe has been altered." She paused, remembering her own First History. "And as you well know, their tradition of dignity and duty will not permit them to allow Second History to remain. They will do everything in their power to reinstate the past as it was before our agents were sent into Earth's history."

Impulsively, Thea rose from the chair, paced the width of the room, then turned sharply. "I have already considered that aspect to some extent," she revealed. "Which is why we must contact the Alliance immediately. My studies of Second History point out the fact that the Vulcans have not yet discovered the physics of time travel whatsoever; it exists only in theory to them, or in the form of infrequent accidents over which they possess no control. They have never been able to bridge the time-gap at will—which operates in our favor." She paused, putting one hand thoughtfully to her chin. "We must make certain they do not discover the *cause* of their displacement before we have the opportunity to meet with them. And . . . it is suggested by my scientific advisers that, even if the Alliance *does* eventually succeed in re-creating First History, certain effects of Second History will still remain intact."

Again, Sarela looked questioningly at the other woman. "The intricacies of time alteration are indeed paradoxical," she murmured.

"In effect, Sarela," Thea explained, "First History still exists in the molecular memory of this universe. It is—or *was*—a physical reality, the reality which *would* have been had we not sent our operatives into Earth's past. That First History reality cannot be erased, no matter how successful our operatives were. As you say, someone within the Alliance will eventually discover what has happened, and will indeed attempt to correct it. I do not know if that can be accomplished, but for the moment it is irrelevant. What is important is that we move quickly. Since the mind can reach beyond the physical boundaries of *any* universe, we must contact the Alliance before they discover that we are responsible for what has transpired." She paused. "In essence, certain individuals will exist in both universes—as well as in a host of other universes and alternate dimensional planes. And since *Second* History, now that it has been *created,* is no less physically real than First . . . it, too, will remain forever locked in the memory of the entire universal concept." She hesitated once more, brows furrowing with the attempt to explain.

"In other words," Sarela surmised, "we must attempt to make peace with the Alliance—with specific *people* in the Alliance—relying on the theory that, whether Second History remains intact or not, that peace will still remain."

Thea nodded very slowly. "Not precisely accurate, but essentially correct. I do not know if *any* peace we make now will withstand the test of time itself. We must hope, however remote that hope is, that they do *not* discover our tampering at all. But since that is, granted, too much to expect, we must rely on my advisers' word that those who exist in both First and Second History will retain at least partial memory of both universes. In other words, since our ships were in hyperspace at the time of our operatives' work, we know both Histories—one from experience, the other from computer tapes. At this point, the men and women aboard our light-ships are the only beings who retain both sets of knowledge. However, if the Alliance is eventually successful in setting the time-flow right again, those who are instrumental in doing so— those people who actually *do* it—will retain at least partial memory of both Histories, since they will have had physical reality and consciousness in both time-lines."

"I see," Sarela mused. "But . . . which is to be done first? Do we present the Tenets of Discipline to the Romulan people *before* contacting the Alliance, and hope that the Warriors will listen? It does not seem a likely possibility," she added logically. "And if we attempt to contact the Alliance first—without giving our people an *opportunity* to hear the words of peace first, they will surely believe that we are attempting to betray the Empire."

A smile came to Thea's lips as she moved back to the chair and sat down, her hand returning to the slave's head. "I have not abandoned *all* my Romulan instincts, Sarela," she replied elusively. "Certain star-ships and Alliance personnel are not unknown to me, and subterfuge is often a necessity if we are to gain what we seek."

Sarela's eyes focused on the Praetor's hand, which

was stroking the slave's hair in gentle contrast to the cunning words. "How may I aid you, Lady?" she asked, finally releasing her own doubts and reaching out to touch the shoulder of the young slave who sat at her feet.

Laughing from deep in her throat, Thea curled into a more comfortable position in the large chair. "We shall contact the Alliance first," she said, "and the rest will take care of itself. Tazol is not foolish enough to prevent my transport ship from leaving this vessel. He needn't know precisely where we are going, and he will hardly attempt to stop even his wife if she is in the company of the Praetor!"

Sarela returned the laugh, becoming more and more interested. She no longer cared about Tazol, no longer cared *what* he would think.

"At any rate," Thea continued, "it has come to my attention that the VSS *ShiKahr* has been monitored in the vicinity of the Neutral Zone. That ship will be our destination," she continued knowingly. Her eyes grew distant. "In First History, there were two officers aboard that ship—then known as the USS *Enterprise*—who were once devious enough to trick an Empire Fleet Captain into practically handing them our cloaking device." She avoided mentioning that *she* had been that Fleet Captain. "And while you are correct in your assumption that the Alliance might not listen to mere words from the mouth of a Romulan, there is a wedge which can be used against those two officers which will *force* them to help us." She smiled to herself.

Sarela returned the smile with one of her own. The cloaking device incident was not unknown to her, and even she had heard of the two Starfleet officers to whom Thea was referring. "What shall we do, Lady?" she inquired.

"All we need do is . . . kidnap . . . either one of them," Thea replied without hesitation, "and the other would do anything in his power to retrieve his friend—

even to the point of negotiating with us." She smiled gently. "And the Alliance, unlike the Empire, grants great power to its starship commanders. If a workable peace treaty can be signed by one of their captains, that treaty is then binding to the entire Alliance."

Sarela considered that. "They trust their officers highly," she surmised.

Thea nodded. "Would that I had known that years ago," she murmured to herself. But she quickly pulled her mind back to reality. "At any rate," she continued, "there is a certain Vulcan who will prove invaluable to us."

Sarela smiled at the simplistic beauty of the plan, daring to think that it had a certain potential. She raised a questioning eyebrow, however. "What is to prevent them from attacking your ship the moment we are detected on their sensors?" she wondered hypothetically.

"The Vulcans are basically a benevolent race," the Praetor reminded Sarela. "They will not attack a vessel which appears to be in distress—even if it is a Romulan vessel. And once we are safely aboard their ship, I have a plan which will insure the Vulcan's attention for as long as necessary to begin formal negotiations."

Sarela sank back in her own chair, her hand absently stroking the slave's smooth shoulder as she spoke. "Tazol will be dark with rage when he discovers what has happened," she remarked, feeling an odd moment of joy at the thought. "And if peace *can* eventually be established, even he will not dare lead the Warriors in an attack against the palace—for he would know that the Alliance would defend Romulus just as it defends any of its own worlds." She laughed lightly, delighted with the idea of her husband's reaction. "He will become useless—even more so than he already is!"

"Fools like Tazol are easily replaced," the Praetor responded as she eyed the young man at Sarela's feet. "And if we are cautious, he will know nothing of our plan until it is too late for him to do anything to prevent it." She sobered suddenly. "Do I have your trust now?" she asked.

Sarela's eyes spoke for her as their gazes locked. "Our views mirror one another, Lady," she replied. "I would welcome an opportunity to stand with you in this endeavor."

The Praetor rose, going to stand directly in front of the other woman as a smile found its way to her lips. "It has also come to my attention that you are somewhat . . . displeased with your father's choice for lifemate," she stated deviously.

"Tazol is a thoughtless child," Sarela replied, "but he *is* my father's choice." She wondered fleetingly why her personal life should be of interest to the Praetor . . . until a single phrase came back to her: *No one ever leaves the Praetor's personal service.* Thea would not be likely to permit her to return to her former life; she already had seen too much. A chill climbed her back, but she ignored its implications.

Thea studied the other woman for a very long time. At last, she reached down, taking the slave at Sarela's legs by the hand and drawing him to his feet. "As a gesture of friendship and a token of my own trust," she said, eyeing the treasured slave appreciatively, "I give Sekor to you until you reach your decision regarding a proper life-mate."

Sarela's eyes widened. "Only the Praetor is permitted to *choose* a life-mate!" she remembered incredulously, almost oblivious to the fact that Thea continued to hold the man's hand out to her freely.

An easy chuckle slipped past the Praetor's throat. "I thought we had agreed that the time for change has come to the Empire," she remarked. "I can even have Tazol executed if it would make this gift easier to accept." She paused as she caught a glimpse of insight into Sarela's hesitation. "Would it be any simpler if you considered how many times *men* have given *women* as gifts? It is no different, Sarela. He is yours . . . if you wish him."

For a moment, Sarela could not respond, until she suddenly caught herself laughing. "As a gesture of friendship . . . and trust," she murmured, mirroring the Praetor's words, "I accept."

She slowly grasped the slave's outstretched hand, surprised at how relaxed the man appeared, how unconcerned he was to be handed over as a gift, almost a bribe. But she knew he was far from a bribe; and it was easy to guess by the easy twinkle in Sekor's eye that he knew it as well. She took a deep breath, accepting her attraction to his beauty.

"But it isn't necessary to kill Tazol," she added, feeling a burden lift from her shoulders when she realized she was now free of him forever. "He is, after all, just a mindless child—not responsible for his actions. Let him live . . . if you wish it."

Thea's brows furrowed slightly. "Mercy?" she teased. "You, a Romulan, bred to revenge and tradition, show mercy to a man whom you despise?"

But Sarela only smiled. "Not mercy, Lady," she corrected. "Pity."

Chapter Eleven

THE VULCAN AWOKE, and noticed without emotion that the pain in his back had all but paralyzed him. He tried to force weighted eyelids apart, but to no avail. Scents drifted to his nostrils, and he breathed deeply. Antiseptic. Clean. Noises of gentle footsteps.

"Take it easy, Spock," a familiar voice murmured as he struggled to move.

Delirium crept closer, its black hands creating a mutation of reality.

"J-Jim?" he whispered, his voice coming out as little more than a painful gasp. Breathing, he discovered, was quite painful. But as reality slowly returned, he wondered why he should be addressing the young ensign as "Jim," and precisely why he should think that Kirk, of all people, would be leaning over him. And yet, as with so many things, it seemed natural, familiar . . . as if it had happened that way countless times before.

"It's McCoy," the voice explained. "Just take it easy for a while, Spock."

Sinking back on the bed, the Vulcan felt a moment of disappointment mingle with confusion. "The landing party?'' he asked, battling a demon of pain. "Are they . . . ?" He opened his eyes at last, wincing at the bright light which stabbed sensitive pupils.

McCoy nodded, but the Vulcan could see that the usual sparkle was absent from the blue eyes.

"Everyone's safe, Spock—except Donner," the doctor said, knowing that attempting to delude the Vulcan into quiescence would prove futile. "He was already dead when we beamed aboard." His voice was gentle, soothing; yet he knew there was nothing he could say to ease the guilt Spock would feel. "We've got him in the cryogenic chamber for now," he added. "I can't do anything for him here, but maybe the doctors at Starbase Ten will be able to help."

Spock's eyes drifted shut once again. Despite his personal disapproval of the ensign's bigotry and violence, he had no desire to see the man dead; and he wondered if he'd made the wrong decision in allowing him to be part of the landing party to begin with. But still . . . too many crewmen unable to function . . . too many incidents of slippage . . . Death would have claimed someone, regardless.

"And the others?" he demanded, teeth clenching with agony as he attempted to speak.

"Selon took a spear in the behind when he turned to run," McCoy said through the tunnel of darkness. "He won't be sitting down for a while, but nothing too serious. Doctor M'Benga's patching him up right now."

Spock nodded, then struggled to rise on one elbow, stopping only when the doctor's hand pushed him gently back down.

"Kirk?" the Vulcan asked, feeling something related to horror slice through him. The last conscious thought . . . Kirk . . . "What about . . . Jim?" The pain moved a little closer, threatening to take him back to blackness.

"Not a scratch," McCoy's distant voice said reassuringly.

Chapter Twelve

THE PRAETOR PACED across her quarters restlessly. "The *Ravon* will be leaving Romulus orbit and returning to the border of the Neutral Zone within a day," she said quietly. "At that time, we must make our move."

Sarela nodded. They had been over the intricate scheme at least ten times, and still she wondered if it could be as simple as Thea made it sound.

"In essence, Lady," Sarela stated, "this Vulcan . . . this starship captain . . . will present the Tenets of Discipline to our people in your stead?"

"Yes," Thea confirmed. "Now that my advisers have completed their study of Second History, and have confirmed that Spock is indeed captain of the *ShiKahr,* there are no more details to be considered. Since no one knows who the Praetor really is, and since Vulcan and Romulan external physiology are almost identical, there will be no arousal of suspicion when he makes the presentation to the governors of Romulus and the Warriors' representatives." A smile came to her lips. "And I do not believe the Warriors will be foolish enough to initiate the Rite of Challenge immediately. They will require time—to choose their Champion and take the customary vote of Tribal

Kings. And *that*," she concluded, "will give us the time we need."

"And by tricking the Vulcan into posing as the Praetor," Sarela reasoned, "we will *also* be trapping him into negotiations for peace and trade treaties with the Empire?"

"Essentially," Thea agreed. "For once Spock enters Romulan space of his own free will—which he *will* do—he will be compelled to exonerate himself of espionage charges in the eyes of his Fleet Command." Her brows narrowed thoughtfully. "In essence, he will be coerced into doing as we wish—for he will be unable to return to his Alliance without arousing suspicion on himself otherwise. Yet if he can provide a workable treaty of peace and *fair trade*—the one thing which is seriously lacking in Second History—his own neck will be spared and we will have what we want as well. No one is harmed; and both parties benefit equally."

Sarela put the writing stylus aside. "Suppose he simply refuses?"

Thea smiled knowingly. "He will not refuse, my friend," she promised. She lowered herself into a nearby chair. "James Kirk," she stated simply, curling long legs underneath herself. "Kidnap James Kirk, keep him from the Vulcan *long* enough . . . and Spock will do anything in his power to get him back safely, Sarela.

"In addition," Thea continued, "my communications specialists have recently intercepted a routine transmission from the *ShiKahr*. It seems they were informing their Fleet Commander of a mission in the Canus system—a mission which apparently did not go according to plan. The details were sparse . . . yet I had the impression that their vessel was somehow . . . *lured* into the Canusian system under false pretense. Odd," she mused. "But at any rate, my translators have learned that the great and powerful Captain Spock was injured in this little escapade—and that his treasured human is still at his side even in this alien universe." Her eyes grew distant. "In any reality, it seems, there are constants—random elements of Fate which dictate certain relationships no matter what the circumstances or universal changes."

"Then . . . by using James Kirk as a method to blackmail the Vulcan into accepting our terms," Sarela stated, "you will then be able to manipulate him into making the presentation and standing against any challenging Warrior?"

Thea nodded. "We have already had to admit that the males of our species are physically stronger, Sarela," she said. "And though I would welcome a chance to meet a Warrior in battle, I am not arrogant enough to deceive myself into believing I would be the victor. On the other hand, the Vulcan should have no difficulty in defeating whatever Champion the Warriors may choose." But a very Romulan smile suddenly parted thin lips. "And no matter *what* the outcome," she continued, "the payment of the Vulcan's personal debt to me is long overdue. His actions aboard a Romulan flagship in First History *earned* him a sentence of death. Yet what I propose, my friend, is a far better price than even that! I shall also force him into specific agreements regarding trade routes for Romulan Merchant vessels. Our systems will no longer be poor, Sarela . . . and though my old friend Spock will suffer a certain humiliation, he will learn to do our bidding."

Sarela lifted one slanted brow. "Then . . . you do not intend to let him go, do you?"

A laugh slipped past the Praetor's throat.

Chapter Thirteen

THE VULCAN AWOKE to the sensation of pain—someone slapping him repeatedly across the face. Hard strokes which did not relent.

He turned back toward pleasant darkness and dreams. Pain was easily ignored.

But the tormentor did not cease. Another slap. More powerful. Another. Again.

His eyes opened, refused to focus, and anger flared unexpectedly in the center of his chest. His hand shot out, grasped the offending intruder, and flung him roughly away. Slowly, normal vision returned.

"Well, Spock," McCoy said, picking himself up off the floor. "It's about time you came out of that healing trance! I thought I was going to have to bring in the heavy artillery!"

Eyes wide, the Vulcan steadied himself, only then realizing that he'd been moved to a high-backed recovery chair in Sickbay. Through the clear divider screen, nurses and orderlies hurried about their duties; and he was grateful that all seemed oblivious to his presence. He took a deep breath, somehow amazed that life still flowed through him. An eyebrow rose as composure returned.

"Forgive me, Doctor," he murmured. "I did not realize . . ."

McCoy smiled, rubbing one wrist. "As long as you're among the living, I think I can live with a broken arm." But the blue eyes darkened.

"Ship's present status?" Spock asked, rising to his feet. He frowned at himself. A pressure bandage wound itself around his chest, just under the sternum, and as he stood a moment of dizziness threatened to drag him back down. He fought. "Precisely . . . how long was I in the healing state, Doctor?"

McCoy moved to the Vulcan's side. "You weren't out that long," he replied. "About eighteen hours altogether from the time we beamed up." He paused, studying his captain's unsteady stance. "The spear nicked your left lung, but no serious damage. But what was starting to worry *me*," the doctor continued, "was that you didn't seem to *want* to come out of the trance." He shrugged. "Can't say that I blame you . . . considering what's been going on around here."

The Vulcan stepped away from the doctor, forcing himself to stand steadily on legs which threatened to buckle. "Explain," he demanded.

"Well, for starters," McCoy began with a sigh, "the whole Canusian Mission was just a . . . *ruse*." He laughed nervously. "From what Chekov told me, there is no Canusian Ambassador—at least not in the sense we were lead to believe. The whole damned thing was a setup—apparently by S't'kal himself." McCoy frowned. "But when Chekov contacted Fleet-Com this morning to tell them about the incident, S't'kal denied the whole thing—said the *ShiKahr* was never ordered into the Canusian system at all. First the Romulan orders—and now this. I don't think we need any more confirmation of our suspicions. S't'kal's mad as a hatter, Spock—but the question is how to get him out of power before he single-handedly wipes out every starship in the Fleet!"

The Vulcan considered the information in momentary silence. "I presume Mister Chekov brought it to the admiral's attention that we do have a recording of his previous orders in the ship's computers?"

McCoy shrugged. "I'm a doctor," he grumbled, "not a carrier pigeon. But you know Chekov. I don't think he'd let S't'kal pull the wool over his eyes—and certainly not without a good fight."

"And our present situation?" the Vulcan asked, reaching for the clean uniform which waited on the foot of the bed.

"We're right back where we started from," McCoy replied. *"Literally.* S't'kal really must have blown a Vulcan fuse over the Canusian incident—ordered the ship back to the Neutral Zone at maximum warp . . . and that's where we're sitting right now."

The Vulcan nodded to himself, then met McCoy's eyes as he walked purposefully toward the wall communication panel. He quickly pulled the tunic over his head, then depressed a button on the panel.

"Chekov here."

"This is Captain Spock," the Vulcan replied. "Present location?"

"Three-point-two light-years from the border of the Neutral Zone, Captain," the first officer responded. "Cruising at Warp One; awaiting arrival of VSS *T'Ruda* and sistership as per Admiral S't'kal's orders."

The Vulcan took a deep breath, mentally reviewing the time-curve of the insanity's progression. Studies had proven that the "slippage" would continue at an increasing rate, growing more pronounced with every moment that the *cause* was not isolated and corrected. After precisely fifteen-point-two-five days, the Vulcan recalled, utter madness would result in over half the population of the Alliance—irreversible madness. If uncorrected within that time . . . He let the thought trail off, realizing the illogic of dwelling on it. Three days wasted already—two on the Canusian Mission, another in Sickbay. And even at maximum warp, Starbase Ten and Admiral S't'kal were a minimum of fourteen days away. But an eyebrow rose as a plan of action slowly presented itself.

"Mister Chekov," he said into the panel. "Compute last recorded position of the *T'Ruda*. Based on that computation, what is minimum traveling startime back to Starbase Ten?"

In the background, the Vulcan became aware of McCoy standing at his shoulder. He turned to see questioning blue eyes widen in disbelief.

"What are you planning, Spock?" the doctor demanded. "Because if it's what I *think* it is—"

"In this particular case, Doctor, there are no viable alternatives," the Vulcan replied, grabbing the black pants and pulling them on despite the pain in his back and chest. "And as you yourself have pointed out, Admiral S't'kal must be stopped until some specific plan of action can be devised."

The doctor bounced angrily on his toes. "There *is* no course of action, Spock!" he said harshly. "Can't you get it through your thick Vulcan head that you can't—"

"Captain?" Chekov's calm voice interrupted.

Spock continued staring into the doctor's accusing eyes.

"Proceed, Mister Chekov."

"According to our computations, Captain," the first officer replied, "the VSS *T'Ruda* is four Standard days away from our current location and, assuming they were to turn back immediately, it would take them approximately nine days to reach Starbase Ten."

"You *can't* be serious, Spock!" McCoy said, grabbing the Vulcan by one arm.

The Vulcan merely looked at the doctor's hand, then stepped away from the offending grasp. "Mister Chekov, have Lieutenant Uhura establish contact with the *T'Ruda*'s commanding officer."

He switched off the communication device, turning back to McCoy's hardened expression. The doctor had positioned himself between Spock and the exit.

"Please, Doctor," the Vulcan said, "do not inject yourself into a confrontation with me; for every moment we waste seriously jeopardizes our chances of success."

McCoy stared mutely at the Vulcan, anger building to desperation in hot blue eyes. "You're as crazy as S't'kal!" he accused, throwing up his hands in defeat.

A Vulcan brow rose beneath sleek black bangs. "Perhaps you are correct," Spock murmured as if to himself. He quickly pulled on the black knee-length boots, then turned toward the door. "If you will excuse me, Doctor, I am due on the bridge."

Forcing himself to relax, Jerry Richardson sank back against the head of the oversized bed. On the other side, Yeoman S'Parva mirrored his actions, a wide grin spreading across her canine features.

"What's the matter, Jerry?" she asked. "Afraid I'll bite?"

Richardson laughed, unprepared for humor. He glanced around the lab, trying to ignore the fact that conditions were something less than ideal. On the other side of the privacy divider, two technicians would be monitoring heartrate, blood pressure, respiration, electroencephalograms and various other critical bodily functions during the experimental telepathic link. He felt himself blush all the way down to his toenails, then chastised himself for his own nervousness. But despite the dual-universe rumors which had been making the rounds, and regardless of the fact that the experiment could well shed some light on an apparently grim subject, he found relaxation impossible.

"Let's just say I never *really* believed you'd agree to this," he replied at last.

Across the bed, S'Parva shrugged. "You forget that Katellans aren't Vulcans," she reminded him. "Telepathy is the main form of communication on Katella—and not at all unpleasant.''

Richardson swallowed. *That's what I'm afraid of!* he said to himself. But he managed a smile. "Is there anything we have to do first?'' he asked. "Take out the garbage, walk the cat . . . get married?''

Laughing, S'Parva shook her head. "All you have to do is let me come into your mind,'' she replied. "The rest'll be easy.'' She propped herself up on one elbow, meeting the ensign's expectant gaze. "And presuming there *is* something out of sync, it shouldn't make any difference to the higher consciousness. I'll be . . . acting as a guide mainly,'' she continued, "helping you follow any images you receive.'' She looked over her head. "And all of it will be automatically recorded on the vid-scanner for analysis.''

Richardson frowned thoughtfully. "So . . . theoretically, the mind will just slip back into its natural . . . universe.'' He wanted to laugh, to cry, to do anything at all to break the sudden tension. "I *could,*'' he ventured, "find myself sweeping the men's room at the bus station!''

The Katellan winked. "Or working as an Orion slave trader,'' she suggested as an alternative.

The human sighed deeply, grateful that S'Parva had taken the time to explain the current theories to him. But the idea of an entirely different universe . . . He shuddered. "Okay,'' he conceded at last. "In the name of science, let's get on with it.'' *In the name of science.* He made a mental note to strangle his roommate at the next possible opportunity.

After a moment, S'Parva nodded toward the technician who was waiting just outside the privacy divider. The young lieutenant disappeared, and the lights dimmed to night normal.

In the darkness, Richardson breathed deeply, feeling the Katellan's soft-furred hand slide into his own, fingers entwining reassuringly. He was peripherally aware of the hum of medical monitoring equipment, and of the gentle surge of psychic warmth which he

159

felt from his partner. He smiled to himself . . . and reality slowly spun out of focus as their minds joined.

Curved corridors swam into being. Familiar . . . yet different. He chose a well-lighted one, walked down it slowly, stopping in front of a well-known door and glancing up to see the nameplate.

LIEUTENANT JEREMY J. RICHARDSON

Part of him blinked disbelievingly. *Lieutenant?*

Go into the room, Jerry, S'Parva's distant voice urged.

He stared at the door, wondering what he would find on the other side. Himself?

Go ahead, S'Parva whispered. *It can't hurt you. . . .*

He took a deep breath, heard it in stereo. For an instant, he felt something walk through him, pass through his soul. He wondered fleetingly if it was Lieutenant Richardson. He shivered, feeling out of place. A phantom hand reached out, touched the door, verified solidity and reality.

But before he could enter the room, footsteps sounded gently on the deck behind him. He turned, startled, and felt himself slip deeper into the illusion which was far more "real" than anything he'd encountered in days.

"Morning, Captain," he said before his conscious mind which was still somewhere in an alternate reality could stop him. "The night crew had a little poker party up on the bridge, so just ignore the stale beer and peanuts in your chair."

Hazel eyes sparkled warmly, and a man in a gold command tunic winked. "Sure, Jerry," the captain agreed with a grin. "But I'll have to tell Lieutenant Masters that you won't be able to keep that date I set up for you—since you'll be too busy down in the brig."

Richardson laughed, yawning. "Night, sir," he said. "Or good morning."

The captain continued on down the corridor as Richardson slipped through the double doors without a second thought. Inside, he tugged off the shirt, sat on the edge of the bed, and removed the black boots.

It was comfortable, he thought, not knowing precisely what he was comparing "it" to.

But he leaned back on the bed and closed tired brown eyes.

He would stay.

"Jerry?"

Cold water splashed on his face.

"Jerry, open your eyes! For chrissake, open your eyes!"

He rolled away, disappointed. The room changed. The bed was no longer soft. "Go 'way," he muttered miserably.

Someone pulled him into a sitting position, hands rubbed briskly across his neck and shoulders. A feminine voice coaxed him back to reality.

It hurt.

Lieutenant . . . bridge posting . . . best ship in the Fleet.

"Go 'way!" Anger now. Resentment.

"Jerry, I'm coming into your mind again," S'Parva's voice informed him in a tone which left no room for argument. "I'm going to pull you back." But she was in a tunnel somewhere.

No . . . "No . . ."

Something slid warmly into his mind, caressing him, holding him, comforting him in soft brown arms. He moved toward it, sensing protection. For a moment, he tasted the flavor of peace. *Home . . .*

But as quickly as the feeling of solace came, it was pulled away, ripped from him—gently, if possible. He moaned aloud.

Stop fighting me, Jerry, a tender voice whispered. *You can't stay . . . at least not now. Your body can't exist without your mind . . . not on two different planes. You have to come back.*

161

He felt himself breathe, wondered why it felt unnatural. *Home . . . ?*

Yes, S'Parva said gently. *But you can't stay. We need you here, Jerry. Follow me back into the light. . . .*

He sighed to himself, and slipped away from the man on the bed. Like levitation, he thought consciously. Or astral travel . . . Lieutenant Richardson would have to wait . . . for a while.

His eyes opened, back on the *ShiKahr*.

"Jim," he murmured. "Captain Kirk!"

The command chair rose around his slim frame, surrounding him with an ever-increasing feeling of responsibility and weariness. An eyebrow rose. Illogical consideration. But Time pressed forward. Time . . . hot and red and lethal. Time . . .

"Status report, Mister Sulu?"

"Nothing out of the ordinary at the moment, Captain," the helmsman responded. "Sensors were picking up a blip of some sort earlier," he added, "but it faded almost as quickly as it appeared." He glanced toward Chekov.

"Just the normal instrument fluctuations now, Captain," Chekov provided. "Apparently, the blip was just an . . . unusual sensor malfunction. We're checking into the matter, but no miscalibration of sensors currently detected."

Spock nodded to himself. "Spatial scan?"

"Normal," Chekov replied; but an expression of confusion slowly grew on his features as he eyed the viewscreen. "Surely the Romulans would not violate the Neutral Zone with the *ShiKahr* in the vicinity; their instruments are undoubtedly capable of detecting us, sir."

Spock leaned forward, studying the familiar star pattern. "The Romulans have never been noted for their integrity nor their predictability, Mister Chekov," he pointed out. "And their cloaking device would aid greatly in getting a small vessel well inside Alliance

162

territory before their presence could be detected." He glanced at Uhura. "We still have to wait until the blip is identified," he decided aloud. "Contact the *T'Ruda*, and have their commander hold his present location until further notice."

"Aye, Captain," Uhura responded.

With a dubious look, Spock rose from the chair, going to the science station. "As a precautionary measure, Mister Chekov, run a full security check on *all* ship's sensor equipment. If that generates negative findings, begin an immediate sonar scan to detect anything large enough to be a vessel within five light-years."

The first officer stared mutely at the captain. "Sonar scan, sir?" he repeated incredulously. "That'll take days!"

"Not if you begin at once, Commander," the Vulcan countered. "And the time will be considerably short-ened if you enlist the aid of off-duty personnel in Auxiliary Control. The complete scan should require no more than forty-eight hours." But internally, he grimaced. Two days . . .

The Vulcan turned from the bridge, heading toward the lift doors; but before he could reach them, the communication panel buzzed noisily.

"Uhura?" McCoy's voice said. "Is Spock up there?"

"This is Spock," the Vulcan replied, stepping over to the speaker.

"Spock, I need to see you down in Sickbay right away. Ensign Richardson and Yeoman S'Parva just handed me the results of a private research project, and I think you might be interested in them. Also," the doctor added, "this concerns Ensign Kirk. Unfortu-nately, the quartermaster hasn't been able to find him. He's not in his quarters, not listed on any duty shift, and the computer indicates that he hasn't used his identification chip for meals since the Canusian inci-dent."

The Vulcan felt himself go cold inside, only then

consciously realizing that he hadn't seen Kirk in over a day. Odd . . . he hadn't sensed anything wrong. But with that thought came another. He hadn't sensed *anything*. An eyebrow rose, and a cold phantom which he recognized as himself took a step closer.

"I shall attempt to locate Ensign Kirk myself, Doctor," he said at last. "If my search is successful, I will meet you in your office later this evening."

"Well . . . don't take too long, Spock," the doctor replied after a momentary hesitation. "If you can't find him within a couple of hours, get down here anyway."

Irritation crept closer, threatened to mutate into anger. "Of course, *Captain* McCoy," he replied, and headed for the lift once again, unaware of the astonished stares which followed him.

Chapter Fourteen

As SHIP'S NIGHT fell, the Vulcan walked down the long corridor which would lead to the ship's botanical gardens; but as he reached the double doors, he stopped. A sudden wave of dizziness and disorientation swept over him, and blood sang in his ears. He took a deep breath. Something had drawn him here, he realized disjointedly. Something . . . human. After a momentary battle, the dizziness passed; and, forcing his hand to move, he depressed the button which would open the doors.

Ship's night was everywhere, and the pseudo-sunset colors on the garden's dome gave an ethereal glow to the odd variety of plants, trees and flowering vines which climbed the walls, completing the illusion of a small forest. He entered into silence, but a quick survey of his surroundings left him illogically disappointed. The room appeared empty.

He turned to leave, recalling McCoy's insistence,

but stopped when his ears detected a faint sound of movement no more than a few yards away. His eyes traveled back to the doors, warring between Time and duty; but slowly his gaze returned to the central portion of the gardens. He'd heard of other starships becoming inhabited by certain animals which sentimental human crewmen smuggled aboard during planetfall, and he couldn't help wondering if some rodent or cat had taken up residence on board the *ShiKahr*.

Choosing a path which would lead to the source of the noise, he made his way past to dense foliage until he reached the garden's center. Six large trees grew in a circle, their branches cascading to the ground like dark veils of mourning. In contrast to the eerie sight, the scent of fresh earth and flowers came to the Vulcan's nostrils, and he inhaled deeply, wondering how long it had been since he'd experienced the inner peace which had once been a natural state of being.

Shoving the melancholy thought to the back of his mind, he simply stood there, pointedly ignoring Time and galaxies as the lighting grew progressively dimmer. At last, only a luminescent purple haze remained. For a moment, the colors took his mind back to Vulcan—to childhood days when the red sun had slid beneath a distant horizon, and golden sands had begun to cool beneath his bare feet.

Vulcan! He turned from the image. Starfleet had indeed been the only solution; and except for unbidden moments of retrospection, he had—he thought—succeeded in divorcing himself from the past altogether. But here, with only the plants to share private memories, perhaps it was safe to think of what he'd left behind. He realized that his nerves had been something less than perfect recently . . . and a few more minutes could not matter so very much.

In many ways, Spock accepted that he was no longer Vulcan at all; that culture and heritage had been stripped from him too many years before—when the marriage to T'Pring had terminated in disastrous mental disharmony.

He felt the sting of embarrassment return to darken his face, despite the fact that it was now years later. But his mother's human blood had been too strong, and the emotional traits which had been bequeathed to him in her genes had condemned him to spend the remainder of his life as a drifter . . . an outcast. Amanda could not be blamed for that, he realized logically . . . yet even Sarek had seemed pleased to see him go.

And, at the very least, he was free of T'Pring— an unfaithful creature who had held nothing but contempt for his mixed blood and distasteful human emotions.

T'kona . . . Go from this place alone. That's what T'Pau had ordered when T'Pring demanded formal severance of the bond. *Leave Vulcan. Do not come back. T'kona, Spock . . .*

Less than Vulcan . . . other than human. No choice but to obey T'Pau's command.

And Vulcan was gone.

He was drawn from his disturbing melancholy, however, as he heard the sound again—a distinct rustling of leaves less than twenty feet away. With an arched brow, he moved closer to the circle of trees, parted their branches quietly, and peered into cool lavender darkness. It took a moment for even his keen eyes to adjust, but he was soon able to discern the lone figure on the ground. At first, the logical portion of his mind asked if someone had been injured, or had fainted from the humid heat of the gardens. It was only when he looked closer that he remembered why he had come here to begin with: Kirk.

Quietly, carefully, he edged closer, kneeling by the man on the ground.

Dressed in civilian clothing, the human had drawn himself into a fetal position, and was clutching his chest tightly in sleep. Apparently, the Vulcan surmised, Kirk had fallen asleep in the afternnon "sun" of the gardens. But even in repose, the ensign appeared tired and troubled, almost to the point of mental and physical exhaustion.

Telling himself it was purely professional concern, knowing otherwise, Spock studied the sleeping man openly, not surprised to see several scars and bruises. But in those minor injuries—apparently a combination of Donner's rowdiness and the Canusian incident— Spock observed much more. For an instant, he was in Sickbay, standing over this human as he'd done a hundred times before. Kirk had been injured during planetfall (again); McCoy was working frantically to save his life (again); and Spock knew he must be there when his companion awakened (if indeed he ever did).

Wrenching himself free of the memory which wasn't a memory at all, the Vulcan leaned back to sit on the ground. But as he sat there, alone despite the human's presence, a sudden simplicity of vision presented itself. A few moments before, he had accepted that he was no longer Vulcan; and the concept that ancient doctrine and taboos would prevent his helping the young ensign severed whatever strand had tied him to his own heritage. With the cool rapport of a meld, he could stop the human's nightmares, erase the lingering mental anguish from the Talos Device . . . fill emptiness with purpose.

And perhaps there would be other answers as well. The mind knew no limits. And any universe—no matter how small or large—could dwell inside one thought.

T'lema . . . he who walks in dreams.

No . . . Kirk was no stranger to his mind.

Dizziness swayed the Vulcan's hand. Logic fought . . . and lost. Before permitting himself the luxury of altering his decision, he initiated the mind meld.

Kirk tensed instinctively in his sleep, from the mental thread which gently entered his mind. But as he became aware of his true surroundings, his eyes snapped open, a gasp of surprise slipping past his control when he saw the Vulcan commander leaning over him.

For a moment, Spock did not move. And as their eyes met in near-darkness, the Vulcan thought he detected the same sense of recognition in Kirk that he had experienced within himself. For the briefest of instants, reality had altered.

Not moving, Kirk took a deep breath. "What are you doing?" he asked pointedly, tone neither accusing nor encouraging.

The Vulcan began breathing again, and hesitantly withdrew the initial strand of the fragile link. He did not have a logical answer; yet his suspicions were confirmed. He *did* know Kirk . . . or would know him in some alien future. In the mind, the Time-mistress had no authority, the Reality Keeper was lost. And Kirk's reaction alone proved *something*. Logically, *Ensign* Kirk would have responded with outrage, the Vulcan thought. But the utterly calm human exterior left him confused.

"I . . . sensed that you were troubled by . . .

dreams," he stated, schooling his voice to its calmest level. "Please forgive me," he added, annoyed by words which became more clipped and difficult as he continued. "I did not intend to . . . intrude."

Surprisingly, the enigmatic human only stretched out on the ground. "Since I'm already considered to be crazy by the majority of people on this ship," he began, "maybe it won't be too difficult to say what I'm thinking for a change." He smiled wistfully, wondering where his anger had disappeared to. "Then you can haul me down to Sickbay and have me fitted for one of those jackets that tie in the back."

A curious brow arched. It was the first time Spock could recall the ensign displaying any sense of humor at all. "Please explain."

Kirk didn't move from his reclining position as he began nervously twisting the gold ring on his left hand. His eyes settled on the ceiling, on the purples and muted blacks and the foggy humidity which was shedding dew-tears on the mossy ground.

"Right now," he began, "I feel just about as phoney as that sunset." Somehow, it was easier to share his thoughts with the Vulcan than he'd expected. Briefly, he wondered how far the meld had gone while he was asleep, but . . . no. It was something else which had thrown their lives together. "I don't know myself anymore," he added matter-of-factly, "but I *do* know you." He turned, studying the angular face of his commanding officer.

The Vulcan's expression softened as he held himself open to Kirk's visual inspection. "Would you consider me a madman if I informed you that I reflect your thoughts?" he asked.

Kirk propped himself up on one elbow, looked cautiously at the Vulcan, then abruptly abandoned the pose of disinterest. "I talked to a couple of people down in the psyche lab," he confessed at last. "Gossip has it that the *ShiKahr*'s been swept into some sort of alternate universe."

The Vulcan remained silent, watching Kirk twist the gold band. "That is one theory," he relinquished, wondering where the conversation was leading.

For a very long time, Kirk continued to stare at the captain; but his expression slowly hardened to one of bitterness.

"What made you save me instead of Donner down on Canus Four, Captain?" he asked. Disjointedly, he cursed himself for the sudden anger; yet it came anyway. Another blessing of the Talos Device. "Or was it an accident that you just *happened* to go out of your way to kill the savages who were closer to me?" He didn't wait for an answer. "Donner's little friends were directly in your line of fire, Captain," he continued. "Yet you deliberately let him die. Why?"

The Vulcan blinked, surprised by the chameleonlike change in the human. He glanced away, suddenly uncomfortable. It was a question he'd asked himself constantly since the incident. It was a question to which there was—again—no logical answer. "I . . . calculated that there would be ample time for a second shot," he responded. "Donner was more experienced in planetfall." *Liar!* his mind screamed. *Unfit for Vulcan. Unfit for Command. Liar!* "Unfortunately, my calculations were incorrect." He steeled himself, told himself to be silent, but to no avail. "It was a command decision," he added, battling another wave of dizziness and disorientation.

Kirk muttered to himself, then looked straight into the Vulcan's eyes. "*Logically,*" he said, "you *should* have saved Donner. He belonged here. He . . . *wanted* his life." Darkness crept into his cheeks.

One eyebrow arched as the Vulcan attempted to

mask his own sudden emotions with the appropriate air of command. "And you do not want yours?" he asked. It was dangerous territory.

Kirk shrugged. "That's not what I meant," he snapped, turning away from scrutinizing eyes which stripped away the charades. He forced himself to speak more calmly. "All I know is that Donner had more of a . . . *right* to life than I do." He bit his lower lip painfully. "Look, Captain," he said at last, "whether you saved my life by accident or by choice doesn't matter." He paused, hating the part of himself which had broken free to the surface. "But you might've done both of us a favor if you hadn't!" He avoided looking at the Vulcan; it hurt to care. "This . . . this isn't right," he insisted. "I don't know what *is* right, but it isn't this! It's as if we're all going through the motions of something we can't even begin to understand!"

The Vulcan flinched inwardly despite his cool exterior, appalled that any living creature could hold such little regard for its own life. It *did* matter—if not to Kirk, then to him.

"If you are familiar with the dual universe theory," he began, feeling his own muscles tense, "then you are aware that your assumptions may well be correct. There is every possibility that your alternate life is completely different from that which you are currently experiencing. And if a way can be discovered to reinstate—"

"Stop it!" Kirk hissed, damning himself for the threatening emotions which were starting to build again. Hope was the worst of all. Misplaced, hopeless hope. "You've *got* what you want, *Captain* Spock!" he said hotly, unable to control the anger. "You've got everything *anybody* could ever want, so why should I believe you're in any hurry to change things?" Hardened hazel eyes locked with stunned ebony ones. "You've got your precious ship and your pious logic and your goddamned supremacy to keep *you* happy. And I've got my *life!*" He spat the word out in disgust. "Well, you can have both, sir!" he continued, climbing to his feet in an uncontrollable wave of fury. "You can take the whole damned mess and—"

But before he could complete the sentence, he found himself falling to the ground, thrown by the Vulcan's arms. Lethal anger flared in the human's eyes as he fell painfully into the dirt.

"Understand *one* thing, Human," a rough whisper commanded harshly. "On this ship, your life *does* belong to me! If I choose to spare it, that is a choice by which you are bound!" He saw a single instant of fear and disbelief in the wide, hazel eyes, but that glimpse was enough. The madness covered him, claiming him. "I grow weary of your self-pity, Kirk. And Time, in *this* universe, shall not wait for you to outgrow your childish bitterness!"

In the back of his sane mind, a logical Vulcan voice requested an answer as to what had brought his anger to the surface with such a vengeance. But the madman ignored it.

Fierce hatred flared on Kirk's proud features. "So why don't you just transfer me off this ship and out of your hair?" He suggested.

But the Vulcan merely shook his head as something tore free inside him.

T'kona . . . He had nothing left to prove—not to Vulcan, not to himself. Vulcan was a word without meaning, a port in which he was never to be welcomed again.

Something dangerously resembling a smile came to his lips.

"No," he stated very gently, sensing another wave of fear flash through the human. "No . . . I shall not make it so simple for you, Kirk." He shook his head, an eerie laugh parting lips which had never laughed before. "It is time to stop running!"

Suddenly a look of horror crossed Kirk's face. He could sense Spock trying to infiltrate his mind. "You wouldn't dare . . ."

"In *this* universe," he replied, "you are *wrong,* James Kirk!" At which point he infused himself into the human's mind.

Kirk tensed against the unexpected dizziness which swirled through his thoughts and clouded reality. His eyes closed, and he did not notice when the gold Academy ring slipped from his finger and lodged in the loose sand. It was just another part of the past . . . gone.

He took a deep breath, tired of fighting, and surrendered to the pleasant vertigo which accompanied the meld. Somewhere, a Vulcan stranger-friend removed the layers of fear and hesitation; and for an instant, Kirk tasted regret . . . regret over what his actions had obviously cost the captain. It *could* have been different, he thought. It *should* have been different. But the Vulcan took the pain away, too—the pain of the past, of memories which were somehow unreal and unimportant.

At last, Kirk opened his mind's eye. The terrain was familiar . . . and deep in the primal darkness of the mind, a man he recognized as himself was waiting. . . .

*   *   *

Edith . . . a warm face, compassionate eyes.

And love. His arms went around her; but some-
where in the back of his mind, Kirk knew he was
saying good-bye.

Nebulous territory, the mind.

His eyes scanned the night sky of a filthy city
somewhere on Old Earth. Edith or the stars . . . Edith
or the Enterprise. *Captain's decision . . . command*
decision. But it did *hurt. Again. She. Silver woman*
goddess. She. The decision was premade when the
universe itself was created.

The ghost of Edith slipped away, leaving his arms
empty.

Miramanee . . . priestess of a forgotten race. Mira-
manee . . . wife. Peace here . . . except for the dreams
and the faces in them. One dark and angular. One
blue-eyed and curious. His eyes searched the face of
the Indian-goddess. Gentle, beautiful wife-for-a-sea-
son. But there was guilt . . . guilt of cheating on a
long-established mistress. She demanded *more than*
simple tools and ancient gods. She demanded *all . . . a*
price.

Miramanee stepped aside.

Other faces . . . some forgotten, some well-remem-
bered. Deela, Ruth, Rayna (Forget the pain, Jim.
Forget).

He turned toward the Source.

"Congratulations, Captain Kirk," *Admiral Komack*
said, pumping his hand vigorously. "She's all yours
for the next five-year mission. Take good care of her."
The admiral laughed. "Treat her like a wife—only
better."

Trembling, Kirk nodded. She. Silver flesh and
blood and bone. Starship. A love-affair not to be

taken lightly. A responsibility not to be handled alone.

Warm, dark eyes entered reality.

Spock?

The syllable echoed in his mind. Blood-brother among the stars. The other half of the whole. The other part of the Trinity. The only other person She *would accept in his life.*

Yes, Jim, *a deep mind-voice said shakily.* I . . . believe we have indeed found our answers. . . .

Kirk swallowed. But . . . is it real?

The answer was enough. It is all that *is* real, Jim.

But the new reality rejected Kirk, sending him back down a long tunnel of darkness. Yet there was no pain. He could go back, he told himself. He *would* go back to her.

Somewhere, in a distant alien reality, he heard himself start to breathe again. Thoughts of birth came to his mind . . . thoughts of coming into a cruel world.

On the *ShiKahr,* James Kirk opened his eyes to see the Vulcan regarding him with an unreadable expression.

One eyebrow slid beneath disheveled black bangs as Spock shook his head, then looked away, angular face darkening.

"I . . ." The Vulcan stood suddenly, turned away as the full memory of what he had done returned.

"Wait," Kirk's voice commanded quietly.

The Vulcan stopped, but did not look at the other man.

Kirk climbed slowly to his feet, brows narrowing as he pondered Spock's tense frame. For a moment, he could think of nothing to say . . . but he forced himself to remember what he'd seen in the meld, forced himself to rely on the man who commanded starships. *Ensign* Kirk retreated respectfully.

"Spock?"

"You must forgive me, Ensign," the captain stated flatly. "I . . . am obviously not myself. This . . . *incident* . . . must be reported at once." A forced meld, regardless of impact or reason . . . it was wrong. He started to walk away, suddenly recognizing his own insanity for what it was. Blood murmured hot against his ears.

Kirk only laughed.

Spock eyed him carefully.

"Why?" the human asked. "How can you regret proving to me that there *is* something worth living for?" He didn't wait for an answer. "If that other universe *is* real," he ventured, "then you had every right to do what you did." Reality wavered, fighting the transformation, but he held on, using the Vulcan's downtrodden eyes as a focal point.

But Spock merely shook his head. "There is a danger," he stated.

Kirk tensed. "What?" he demanded.

Giving in to the human for a moment, a Vulcan eyebrow rose as he met the ensign's eyes. Now he understood the bitterness . . . now he knew how much Kirk had lost. And his own losses, he reflected, seemed minor by comparison.

"There is a danger that we may not be able to . . . get back," Spock said at last. "A danger of becoming . . . permanently entrapped in *this* universe." His eyes closed painfully. The emotions were too close to the surface; and he began to recognize the additional danger as well . . . the danger within himself. "In the event that should happen," he continued, using the sound of his voice as a reminder of reality, "our minds will not . . . *accept* this reality into which we have been thrust."

Kirk swallowed with difficulty. A few moments ago,

it had seemed so easy . . . so right. "How long do we have?" he asked.

The Vulcan glanced away. "Less than eleven days," he replied truthfully. "And there is not enough data— at the present time—to know where to begin effecting repairs."

Kirk considered that and all the implications. If there were no way to re-create that other reality, it was over. All of it. He looked away before the thought could transmit itself to the Vulcan. Something in him refused to accept defeat; something stronger than Ensign Kirk demanded a chance . . . a right to the life he had once known.

"Then we'll *make* a way," he said, wondering what special control he thought he possessed over the universe.

The Vulcan nodded silently, easily sensing the determination—and the desperation—in this peculiar ensign-captain. "The ship's computers are working on possible theories," he ventured. "And if a way can be discovered before time itself intervenes . . ."

The sentence trailed off, and Kirk thought he saw the Vulcan tremble. For an instant, the hopelessness reasserted itself, but he tried to drive it away. "We've faced worse, Spock," he said, wondering where the words were coming from, wondering what he was referring to. "Something has to come along."

The Vulcan shook his head, started to respond, but was cut short when a hidden communication speaker chirped noisily. He felt himself jolt in surprise and anger.

"Captain Spock?" Uhura's voice said questioningly.

But the Vulcan made no immediate move to respond. His eyes remained locked with Kirk's.

At last, the human smiled, taking a deep breath as

some unspoken message passed between them. "Duty calls . . . Captain," he said with a grin.

Very slowly, the Vulcan nodded. "Indeed . . . Captain," he replied.

After another moment, he moved to a nearby stone bench, sank down onto it and activated the wrist communicator. "Spock here."

"Captain," Uhura responded, "the VSS *T'Ruda* is signaling us; requesting your presence on the bridge."

The Vulcan glanced at Kirk . . . and let the moment fade after taking a deep breath. There were still unanswered questions . . . but for now his priorities were clear. If only he could hold on long enough, keep insanity at bay . . .

He let the thought go back into darkness. "On my way, Lieutenant," he said at last, switching off the communication device as he turned back to the human. He stood . . . on legs which seemed unsteady and weak.

"If there's anything I can do to help," Kirk offered, letting the sentence trail off.

Spock nodded, and started to walk away; but he stopped suddenly. "Perhaps there is, Ensign," he said quietly. "I believe Doctor McCoy is expecting both of us in Sickbay for review of some new information concerning the dual universe theory. Perhaps you could see to the doctor's needs while I speak with the *T'Ruda*'s commander." And, the Vulcan realized, it would keep McCoy off *his* back for a few more minutes.

Kirk nodded, then gave a mock salute, trying not to think of what would happen if they were wrong, if they were unable to make the changes soon enough. Already, he'd felt twinges of the madness . . . of an insanity worse than Death itself. And it was easy to see the toll it was taking on Spock. The Vulcan appeared tired, drained . . . almost frightened beneath the layers of command.

But he laid those images aside. The universe had always obeyed his commands before, he reminded himself. And Time was like an old friend . . . one he'd tricked too often in the past.

Chapter Fifteen

CAPTAIN SPOCK LOWERED himself into the command chair, dark eyes focused on the central viewscreen. The stars of the Romulan Empire spread a band of gold across the sky, but he found no beauty in it. Instead, he felt his own brand of insanity take a step nearer. It called him by name, whispering promises that could never be fulfilled. He found himself wanting . . . needing. Blood sang through his ears, a song of sirens and the hot red sands of Vulcan. His mind slipped into the rhythm of blood, the call of home . . . but a home which no longer seemed to exist in *any* universe.

"Communication coming in now, Captain," Uhura said, breaking into his reverie. "Switching to audio-visual transmission mode."

Leaning back in the chair, the Vulcan waited, absently drumming his fingers on the side of the chair. He glanced around the bridge, at the expectant eyes of the crew. They had been briefed, he reflected, but did they truly understand what they were facing? Time itself had become a viable entity, pressing forward, demanding precedence above all else. He took a deep breath, attempting to battle the increasing impatience. But when the picture finally shimmered to light on the screen, he felt himself relaxing just a little.

"Captain Spock!" the *T'Ruda*'s commander said cordially. "It's been a long time!"

The Vulcan inclined his head in greeting. "Indeed," he murmured in surprise. *"Captain Pike?"*

The human nodded, a wide grin spreading across handsome features. "Your recommendation had a lot to do with it, Spock," he said warmly. "But I'll save the thanks for when we get together in person." But the bright blue eyes darkened ominously. "I . . . take it you people got the word from FleetCom?"

"Yes," Spock said simply, nonetheless relieved that it was his former first officer and friend who now commanded the *T'Ruda*. Perhaps it would make matters somewhat easier. "After discussion with the *Shi-Kahr*'s senior officers, I am forced to state that Admiral S't'kal's orders seem somewhat . . . peculiar."

Pike nodded. "Yeah," he conceded with a heavy sigh. "At first we thought it was somebody's idea of a bad joke; but the orders are confirmed as genuine." He laughed weakly. "Can't say that I like the idea of initiating an unnecessary war, but . . . I'm assuming FleetCom has reasons they aren't making known." His voice trailed off momentarily. "Spock . . . tell me *one* thing. Have your people been having any unusual problems over there?"

An eyebrow rose as the Vulcan studied his old friend. "Please specify," he requested. There was no margin for error.

"Well," Pike responded, "we've had several incidents of crewmen doing . . . odd things. Hell, one of the shuttles was stolen right off the hangar deck—and the problem wasn't detected until too late for us to get a tractor beam on it. Luckily, we weren't too far from Base Ten when it happened, and I got word that the lunatic who hijacked it ended up back at Com Headquarters. But that's just part of it," the human continued. "There've been other things, too. Lots of schizophrenia, according to my chief medical officer. Nothing he's been able to pinpoint scientifically yet, but . . ." Again, there was a long pause. "We're working with a skeleton crew, Spock—right down to the bare bones. And if we're going off into the Neutral Zone—uninvited, if you take my meaning—we're taking one hell of a chance. I've informed S't'kal of our situation, but he just keeps repeating his previous orders. I don't think he's taking me seriously when I tell him we're down to nothing over here!"

The Vulcan took a deep breath. "Commander Pike?" he said gently.

The human's eyes darkened to a frown. "What is it, Spock?"

For a long moment, the Vulcan was silent. Mutiny did not come easily . . . and the blip was still unexplained. He pressed a button on the side of the chair which would automatically scramble the transmission into code, then retranslate it into language on the *T'Ruda*.

"Captain Pike," he said, "what I am going to tell you is something which will require your personal consideration as well as professional. It is not a matter to be taken lightly."

Pike nodded. "Anything you suggest has to be an improvement over our present situation, Spock," he said at last. "Whatever you need or want, don't hesitate to ask."

Spock took a deep breath. "You must return to Starbase Ten at once, Captain," he stated without preamble. "For on board this vessel, we have irrefutable proof that Admiral S't'kal is experiencing the effects of a condition which has rendered him functionally insane. He must be stopped." He paused, looking closely at his former first officer. "Have you yourself experienced any . . . peculiarities?" he asked pointedly.

Pike shook his head. "I've been just fine, Spock," he said. "But do you realize what you're suggesting? I can't just walk into the Base and tell S't'kal to relinquish his authority."

"Please, Chris," Spock interrupted, feeling another press of Time, "hear me out. The peculiarities you have encountered on the *T'Ruda* are symptoms of an even greater . . . dilemma. It is *not* confined to starships or starbases; indeed, I cannot be certain that it is confined to this galaxy."

"What're you talking about, Spock?" Pike asked slowly. "And don't get me wrong. We've put together a few theories on our own—which is what I wanted to talk about in the first place—but we'd vetoed a lot of them as too crazy to even consider. Care to extrapolate?"

Across thousands of light-years, the Vulcan held Pike's expectant gaze. "At present time," he began, "we have approximately eleven Standard days in which to correct an apparent . . . malfunction in this universe itself. Currently, we are unable to formulate a workable hypothesis as to what has *caused* this malfunction; yet the symptoms and the eventual results are easily computed. In essence, our research has proven beyond a reasonable doubt that this very universe is some distorted reflection of another—and it is the *other* universe from which our true reality stems." He paused, motioning to Uhura. "I am instructing my communications officer to transmit a complete duplication of our research programs directly to your central library computer. If, after your science officer has analyzed the material, you do not find yourself in agreement with my conclusions, I shall surrender my position as captain at once, leaving command of this vessel to First Officer Chekov."

Again, he paused, noting that Uhura had already keyed the information into a coded transmission.

"Since it is also a fact that only certain individuals are affected by the madness," the Vulcan continued, "it is clear that someone such as yourself must replace S't'kal at once. Though that shall not solve the entire problem, it will keep further incidents to a minimum until a more permanent solution can be implemented."

Pike stared mutely at his old captain for a very long time; and Spock thought the human would simply

184

terminate the transmission altogether. Finally, however, a very faint smile came to Pike's lips.

"It's an alternate dimensional plane, isn't it, Spock?" he asked at last, slapping one hand down across the arm of the command chair. "I heard about the Halkan incident a couple years ago—and that's been part of the basis for our own research. I dunno if we can *add* anything to your conclusions, but I know damned well we won't disagree with them!"

The Vulcan nodded, allowing himself the luxury of breathing again. "And the *S'Tasmeen*'s commander?" he asked. "What are Captain Benedict's views on the current situation?"

"The *S'Tasmeen*'s a day behind us, Spock," Pike provided. "And you don't have to worry about Benedict. She's had as many troubles over there as we've had on the *T'Ruda*. Personally, I think she'd stand in line to get a crack at S't'kal. Between the two of us, we've been working on the dual universe theory around the clock. Unfortunately, there don't seem to be any clear-cut answers. About the only thing I can add to what you've already told me is that Captain Benedict's research points to the possibility that whatever caused this . . . alteration, for lack of a better word, had to be one specific incident. Something technological as opposed to natural phenomena."

"Then it is possible to surmise that the alteration has been done by a specific party for a specific purpose," the Vulcan stated.

"That's the gist of it," Pike confirmed. "Don't know what good it does us at this point, but it's worth considering. Unfortunately," he added, "Benedict's theories are also going along the lines that this incident had to be based in the past history of one specific world. But since *we* haven't developed time-travel yet, we'd might as well say that the cause was the fall of the Roman Empire. It's easy enough to see where the Romans went wrong, but not quite so easy to go back and correct it."

"Indeed," the Vulcan replied. But a stray thought whispered through his mind. Certain cultures *did* have time-travel abilities. Perhaps S't'kal *did* know more than he was telling . . . yet starting a war with the Romulan Empire hardly seemed a viable solution. "If you will excuse me, Captain Pike," he said presently, "I must return to my research. Please inform me once you have reached your decision regarding our . . . interim solution."

But Pike only laughed. "There's no decision to it, Spock," he said. "And I know I can speak for Captain Benedict, too. S't'kal has to be yanked off that throne of his—and we're the only ships close enough to do it. We can get back to Starbase Ten without arousing too much suspicion anyway—just by saying that the main warp engines are out of balance. That'll buy us some time. And general rumor has it that S't'kal's been getting a lot of static from unaffiliated worlds in Alliance territory already." He smiled. "Word has a tendency to get around fast—especially when it's classified top secret." He paused for a moment. "What're your people going to be doing in the meantime?"

"I have a certain theory regarding the specific cause of the alteration," the Vulcan replied. "Also, there *is* a hypothetical formula for using ship's power to create a time warp. Unfortunately," he added, "that theory has never been tested—and even in the event it should be found workable, we do not know where to begin looking. If my suspicions are correct, however, there may be an alternative to random chance."

Pike nodded. "Well, since time seems to be a scarce commodity, I'll leave that end of it up to you." Again, the blue eyes softened. "Take care, Spock," he said. "Pike out."

The screen went blank, but the Vulcan did not immediately look away. Presently, the stars returned . . . alien stars. Cold. Stars of the enemy. He thought of the blip which had been detected earlier.

His blood sang.

* * *

Ensign James Kirk entered Sickbay to find Jerry slouched into a recovery chair in one corner. His head rested squarely in his hands, and a faint purring snore seemed to erupt from the chair. S'Parva lay sprawled on the floor of McCoy's office, head neatly tucked between well-groomed brown paws; and the doctor sat lazily at the desk, feet propped haphazardly on one corner of a mess.

"Well," McCoy grumbled, glancing at the chronometer, "it's about time you showed up." He looked expectantly over Kirk's shoulder. "Isn't the captain with you?"

Kirk shook his head, unabashedly grabbed an unoccupied chair, and dragged it over to the desk, winking at his roommate when Richardson opened sleepy eyes.

"Captain Spock was called to the bridge," he explained. "He asked me to relay any information." Suddenly, he felt confident again, sure of himself. "So, in the words of the poet, what's up, Doc?"

McCoy's face tightened to a disbelieving frown as he slid his feet under the desk and slapped the arm of the chair in one swift movement. "If that Vulcan's not half crazy, I'll eat my shingle!" He eyed Kirk curiously. "And you seem awfully chipper, Kirk," he observed. "Care to tell me why?"

But the ensign only shook his head, a smile coming to light hazel eyes. "Let's just say I've got a reason to be," he replied evasively.

From the corner, Richardson groaned. "I'll say," he muttered, stretching his arms above his head and yawning deeply. "Talk about rapid promotion!" A deep sigh parted his lips.

Kirk's brows narrowed. "What do you mean, Jerry?" he asked, feeling a shiver crawl up his back.

Richardson shrugged, nodding quickly toward McCoy. "I'll let Doc explain it, Jim," he said. "Remember that link you suggested I do with S'Parva?"

Kirk nodded. "I remember," he said, glancing over to where the Katellan was starting to awaken. She

187

stretched lazily, arching a long back and neck and finally sitting up. He turned to Richardson. "What about it?"

"Well," McCoy said, "from what we can tell from their link, Kirk, you could figure very prominently in some major changes around here." He inserted the holo-tape into the desk scanner, adjusting the controls, then leaned back to wait as he studied the human. "At this point," he added, "I don't know what the hell we're going to *do* with the information, but I suppose there's no harm in your seeing it. And *then*," he stressed, "maybe you'll give in to a vid-scan."

Kirk shrugged. At this point, he thought, he'd probably do just about anything. *She* was alive in his blood again. "Maybe," he conceded, glancing at Richardson. His roommate appeared downright nervous. "Jerry?"

"Just look at the tape, Jim," Richardson replied with a gentle smile. "Consider it a graduation present."

Once the tape had been played, Kirk leaned back in the chair. Despite the meld with Spock, it was nonetheless disturbing—and uplifting—to see it in living holographic color. And at the very least, it was tangible confirmation.

He looked expectantly at McCoy.

"Don't ask *me* to explain it, Kirk!" the surgeon said quietly. "I'm a doctor, not a film critic." He paused, blue eyes scrutinizing the ensign. "You have anything to say about it?"

Kirk took a deep breath. "Only that it . . . feels right," he ventured, allowing himself to relax in McCoy's presence. In many ways, the doctor was almost as familiar as Spock; the only thing missing was the customary glass of brandy. He thought about the meld, but avoided mentioning it. There was something which seemed to demand privacy . . . something in the Vulcan's demeanor when they'd parted in the gardens. He rose from the chair, reaching automatically for the

188

tape. "I'll drop this off at the captain's quarters," he volunteered.

But McCoy's hand grabbed his wrist. "Not so fast," he said, rising from the chair to face the ensign. "If I know you—which I suspect I do—it'll be like pulling teeth from a Gorn to get you back in here once you leave. How about that vid-scan?"

Kirk glanced nervously at the chronometer, and allowed the cunning starship commander to slip out. He pulled the tape from the machine, slipping easily from McCoy's grasp. He chose his most charming smile. "Captain Spock *did* want this information as soon as possible," he pointed out with a wink. "What's the matter, Doc? Don't you trust me?"

McCoy bounced on his toes. "No," he stated flatly. "I do not." But he smiled anyway, taking a deep breath as Kirk stuffed the tape into the pocket of a ragged flannel shirt. The doctor observed the remnants of leaves and dirt on the ensign's clothes, but he merely tucked the details into a safe corner of his mind as Kirk disappeared into the hall.

"Well," Richardson yawned, "I guess I'll have to get another roommate. Royalty beds down on the officers' deck." He turned to S'Parva. "Whatta you doin' tonight, sweetheart?"

The Katellan shrugged. "Not much," she said with a wink to McCoy. "What'd you have in mind, Romeo?"

Bluff called, Richardson gulped.

McCoy shook his head in mild amazement.

Captain Spock lay back on the bed, but the meditative state eluded him. And he knew now, beyond any reasonable doubt, that his own deadline had been shortened. *Pon farr.* Another symptom of the universe's insanity, he thought. It had merely come for him in this manner . . . the one manner which he could not hope to escape. Logic alone was useless. He glanced over to the nightstand, dark eyes scanning the computer tape which Kirk had dropped off an hour before. Answers, yes. Even truth. But . . . for what? Without a way to go back in time and correct the cause, they were trapped. And that, he realized, was the *ultimate* truth.

For himself, it wouldn't matter; for without a bond-mate, the blood fever would insure his own death within a week. An eyebrow rose. Time had set a most efficient trap, he mused. Even if he *could* return to Vulcan, there was no one there for him, no one with whom he could establish even a temporary bond. And the thought of attempting to mate with a soul-healer left him cold. No . . . Vulcan was still not the answer.

But before he could ponder it further, the communication panel by the bed chirped noisily for his attention. He inhaled sharply, the sound seeming far louder than usual, far more irritating than necessary. Rolling onto one elbow, he depressed the response button.

"Spock here," he acknowledged wearily.

"Aye, Captain," came the reply, "this is Mister Scott on the bridge." The engineer paused and there was a mumble of rapid conversation in the background. "I think ye might want tae come up here right away, sir. Sonar scans have located that blip again—and it's definitely a ship of some sort. Probably a transport vessel of some description, but we've got no further details yet."

Spock was already on his feet, reaching for the clean uniform shirt which he'd efficiently laid out before going to bed. "On my way, Mister Scott," he confirmed, and headed for the door after arranging the rest of the uniform neatly in place.

As he strode down the corridor to the lift, however, he couldn't help noticing the empty spot by his side . . . a place which, in another place and time, would have been filled with Kirk.

He ignored it as best he could, trying not to think too closely about what he'd seen in the human's mind. For if the blip turned out to be a Romulan cruiser, the entire matter could be rendered academic. As Captain Pike had pointed out, word had a tendency to get around; and if the Romulans had somehow intercepted S't'kal's orders . . . He let the thought fall from his mind, hoping he could find the same cunning in himself that his captain from that other surreal universe had possessed naturally.

Settling into the command chair, Spock attempted to ignore his own increasing pressures. The blood in his ears was a constant roar, a never-ending phantom whispering suggestions. He slammed a door on it.

"Status report, Mister Chekov," he demanded, voice coming out harsher than intended.

"Last sensor contact with the blip occurred precisely seven minutes ago, Captain," the first officer provided, glancing into the hooded scanner. "At that time, we were able to verify that it's a ship of some type. Too small to be a battle cruiser," he continued, "but definitely too large and clearly defined to be an asteroid or other space debris. We also detected power emanations from the vessel, but they weren't of sufficient duration to determine source of power." The Russian glanced up, meeting his captain's eyes. "They're playing with us, sir."

The Vulcan leaned forward on the edge of the chair, eyes scanning the viewscreen despite the fact that he would see nothing visible. "Spatial scan?" he asked.

"We've been running that scan since we first detected the blip again, Captain," Chekov stated. "Whatever that ship is, she's fast—fast enough to evade our sensors."

Suppressing a frustrated sigh, the Vulcan rose from the chair, turning impulsively to the communication panel. "Lieutenant Uhura, open all hailing frequencies in the event they wish to establish contact."

"Aye, sir," Uhura responded, flipping the series of controls required to broadcast universal friendship codes on all channels. "Negative response, Captain," she continued presently. "If anyone's out there, they're refusing reception."

"Keep trying, Lieutenant," Spock instructed, moving back to the command chair. He sat down quickly as a wave of unexpected nausea washed over him. He felt himself pale, and hoped no one else noticed. "If it is a Romulan vessel, they obviously came here for a purpose and will eventually state their demands."

"Yes, sir," Uhura acknowledged, replacing the nodule in her ear. "Captain?" she said. "I *am* picking up a faint transmission on our T-channel now."

"On audio, Uhura," the Vulcan requested.

As Uhura worked the controls, a seemingly recorded message filtered through the bridge, broken occasionally by loud bursts of static. "This is the Scoutship *T'Favaron,*" a female voice intoned mechanically. "We have become separated from Mothership *Ravon,* and believe ourselves to have drifted into Alliance territory. Sensors distorted, power failing. Any Romulan vessels receiving this transmission, please respond directly to computer."

Spock listened to the coded message carefully, annoyed that it took the *ShiKahr*'s computers a full three seconds to translate the difficult Romulan coding.

"We are using our cloak to prevent detection by Alliance vessels," the message continued weakly, "but our power begins to wane. Supplies running low, fuel nearly exhausted. Please respond."

Spock waited. It *could* be a trick, he reminded himself firmly. And yet . . . it could also be the one answer he needed. An eyebrow climbed high.

"We have them pinpointed now, Captain," Chekov said suddenly. "Their ship appears to be a Scout-class Romulan transport vessel; only light armaments registering on our sensors."

The Vulcan hesitated for only a moment longer. "Put a tractor beam on that vessel, Mister Scott," he instructed. "Bring them into the hangar deck." He pressed a button on the arm of the command chair. "Full security detachment to the hangar deck," he said into the panel. "Condition: yellow alert."

Chapter Sixteen

ONCE THE HANGAR deck was pressurized and the indicator light showed green on the panel outside the door, Captain Spock nodded to the six Vulcan security guards who would precede him into the giant room.

"Segon," he said, addressing the chief security officer, "use utmost caution. But under no circumstances are any of the passengers to be harmed. If they are armed, disarm them quickly, but take no aggressive action. We do not wish to fuel Admiral S't'kal's cause if this vessel has trespassed into Alliance territory by accident."

But something in the back of his mind warned that it was no accident. His own words came back to him. *I cannot be certain that it is confined to this galaxy. Or to the Alliance,* he added, a sudden thought presenting itself. Indeed, the Romulans' arrival appeared quite timely.

As the hangar deck doors slowly opened, the Vulcan's eyes narrowed to study the alien ship which he discovered to be strikingly familiar in configuration to an Alliance shuttle. The major differences being the highly colorful paintings of a bird of prey and the domelike bubble which sat atop the small craft. The vessel rested on two podlike runners; presently a surface door slid back, a ramp extending to compensate for the four-foot elevation off the deck.

Surrounded by the security team, Spock watched the vessel closely as the doors separated to reveal two Romulan women attired in the familiar Fleet uniforms of the Empire. The insignias on their arms revealed one to be a counterpart of an Alliance lieutenant; the other was apparently a sub-commander—the Empire's version of a starship first officer. One eyebrow rose as the Vulcan stepped closer, coming to a halt at the base of the ramp.

Inclining his head in formal greeting, he studied the women carefully, suppressing an uncanny sense of déjà vu as he met the dark eyes of the lieutenant. The well-sculptured alien features seemed familiar, haunting . . . like a face in a dream. But he put the thought aside.

"I am Captain Spock," he stated, noting that they carried no weapons. "You have been taken aboard the VSS *ShiKahr*."

The sub-commander's eyes scanned the hangar deck with obvious interest. "I am called Sarela," she replied hesitantly. "Second in command of the Romulan flagship *Ravon*." She wondered if the Praetor had made a wise move in deciding to reveal their true names, deleting only the fact that Thea happened to be the leader of the entire Romulan system. She nodded toward the other woman. "This is Thea," she added, "our ship's science adviser."

As the security team formed a tight circle around the group which encompassed Spock and the two Romulans, the Vulcan nodded formally. "Though you will be officially debriefed in the morning, there are a few questions I must ask of you now." When he received no negative response, he continued. "What was the nature of your mission at the time your vessel became separated from the *Ravon*?" He began walking, indicating the hangar deck doors with a quick gesture. "And why did your ship venture so far into Alliance

194

territory? Surely your sensors were capable of discerning your location."

Sarela fell into step beside the Vulcan as they began walking; Thea assumed the correct supportive stance by her side. "What is to be done with us?" she demanded, pointedly ignoring the questions. "Alliance ways are not unknown to our people, and you will gain no secrets through torture or mind probes." She raised her chin defiantly, playing the role to the hilt.

Stopping, the Vulcan turned to study the women carefully. He noticed matter-of-factly that Thea seemed to be deliberately avoiding his gaze. "Whatever you may have been told regarding Alliance procedure is, no doubt, considerably exaggerated. You will not be harmed, regardless of your intent when you crossed the Neutral Zone. You will be turned over to the authorities at the nearest Starbase, and the officials shall decide what is to be done with you at that time. Most likely," he elaborated, "you will be questioned—without the use of torture—then returned to your Empire via long-range transporter."

Sarela began walking again, exchanging glances with Thea as they kept pace with the Vulcan. "Very well," she conceded. "Though I do not necessarily accept your words as truth, I will speak freely with you."

As they entered the long corridor leading to the turbolift, she squared her shoulders. Apparently Thea's advisers had known their work well, for the Vulcan had responded as predicted throughout the brief exchange.

"The *T'Favaron*'s mission was to scout the surface of Kavol—a planet well within the Romulan system," Thea relinquished, speaking for the first time. "We were a party of seven," she continued, staring straight ahead, "but our numbers were diminished to only Sarela and me."

Spock took it all in silently; it corresponded roughly with what he knew of Romulan procedures. "What became of the rest of your party?" he asked as the two women were ushered into the lift, followed closely by himself and three of the guards.

"We do not know," Thea responded, her voice distant. "They were to take readings of the planet's geography, collect mineral and soil samples in preparation for colonization, then return to the *T'Favaron* within two days. When the third day did not bring them back, Sarela and I initiated a search for them on our own." She paused, staring absently at the peculiar insignia on the Vulcan's chest as she spoke. "At that time, we were already overdue to rendezvous with the *Ravon*. Unknown to us, however, an ion storm had swept our mothership off course. When she returned to retrieve our shuttle, her commander no doubt believed us to have been destroyed in the storm. Our own engines had been rendered temporarily inactive due to the atmospheric disturbances created by ion particles; and we were unable to achieve orbit or effect repairs on our communications equipment until well after the *Ravon* had proceeded on to her next mission."

As the lift slowed to a halt, Spock stepped out onto Deck Three. It wasn't an impossible story, and he recalled that an ion storm had indeed been monitored within Romulan territory only a few days previously. If they were lying, they had researched it well. He glanced at Thea once again, caught her watching him. For a moment, there seemed to be something he should say to her, something he should remember . . . but the thought quickly abandoned him as he began to walk.

After a moment, he drew to a halt in front of double doors, turning once again to the peculiar Romulan woman. "Until more suitable quarters can be arranged, you will share these accommodations," he stated flatly. He avoided mentioning that he had no intention of splitting them up; if they were together behind one set of doors, guarding them would be considerably less risky. "Be advised that your room will be guarded at all times," he continued, "and that you will not be permitted outside these quarters unless accompanied by myself or my first officer."

Thea laughed aloud, entering the darkened room and pointedly reaching for the light switch. It was exactly where she knew it would be, precisely where Second History diagrams had said it would be, and she found herself relaxing a little more as the role slipped easily into place.

"You fear us?" she asked. "You, a Vulcan, tremble with terror at the sight of two Romulan women?"

"Hardly," the Vulcan returned, his tone cold. "But history has proven your treacherous nature; and considering previous incidents in this sector, I do not intend to take unnecessary chances. You will be held here, in technical custody, until Command dictates further orders." Despite their apparent harmlessness, the Vulcan felt a very human feeling creep into the pit of his stomach. He thought of Time again . . . and reality. Alliance espionage had verified that the Romulans did indeed possess certain time-travel capabilities; and if the truth could be discovered . . .

"You will be questioned further in the morning," he stated, drawing himself back to his own reality. "In the meantime, should you require food or drink, it will be brought to you on request." He stepped into the room, indicating a panel by the door.

"So far," Sarela remarked, "you have kept your word concerning our well-being." She glanced appreciatively at the large room. "But we shall see how honorable your Alliance truly is once we reach this Starbase of yours."

Declining comment, Spock stepped back into the hall, uncannily aware of the dark eyes which followed him. He turned, brows narrowing suspiciously as he studied Thea. She held his gaze for a moment, then quickly glanced away. But the moment was enough, the Vulcan thought to himself. And there was an unverbalized message somewhere in her eyes.

With a quick nod toward the guard, the Vulcan

stepped back, allowing the doors to close. "I shall be in my quarters until morning, Lieutenant Segon," he said in clipped Vulcan dialect. "If our guests require anything before then, have Mister Chekov attend to it."

Segon nodded, assuming his position directly in front of the door.

But as Spock walked slowly down the corridor back to the lift, he felt himself start to relax. Illogical under the circumstances, he thought . . . but perhaps the Romulans were more of a blessing than an accidental curse.

Jim Kirk was goaded awake by the sound of an unusually large insect buzzing persistently in his ear. As his eyes opened, he fought the now-normal disorientation, realizing that the sound came from a somewhat more conventional source. Rolling to his feet with a groan, he noticed that Richardson was completely oblivious to the door buzzer due to the pillow covering his head.

With a wistful smile in his roommate's direction and a muttered curse at whoever dared to be on the other side of the door, he moved to the panel on the desk, depressing the button which would release the lock mechanism.

"Come," he said.

The door opened to reveal two security guards, dressed in the red attire of Vulcan security. "The captain requests both of you to come to the central briefing room immediately," the taller of the two stated without preamble as they moved into the room and flipped on the lights.

Kirk blinked at the sudden stab of white fluorescents, staring numbly at the two men in a moment of stunned disbelief. Suspicion warred with hope; perhaps Spock had uncovered some vital piece of information related to the time displacement theory. Trying to shake the cobwebs of sleep from his mind, he said nothing; then, after a long silence, nodded his agreement.

"Yeah, sure," he managed, stretching and yawning and attempting to ignore the tingle of intuitive suspicion which stood his hair on end. "Tell him we'll be there as soon as we're dressed."

The two guards looked at one another, but did not move. "We were ordered to . . . escort you," the second man replied.

Kirk shrugged. "Suit yourself," he said casually. But his mind was far from at ease. He moved to Richardson's bed, nudging his roommate with the side of his bare foot. "C'mon, Jerry," he said miserably. "The military is exercising its God-given right to drag us out of bed at three in the morning."

Richardson didn't move.

"Get up!" Kirk continued, nudging him a second time.

Richardson moaned sleepily, rolling onto his back when Kirk finally yanked the pillow away. Shielding his eyes from the lights with one muscular arm, he groaned. "Huh? What're you talking about, Jim?" He dragged himself to wakefulness at last, glancing up to see the two guards standing inside the door. "What the hell?" he exclaimed, bolting to his feet. "Is it a red alert or something?" He remembered something about the Condition Yellow, but that had been canceled hours ago. And he also realized that the two guards didn't look like any of Segon's usual monkeys. Still . . . he passed it off to the fact that the Red Shirts seemed to come and go far more quickly than anyone else.

"What's going on?" he demanded, stumbling across the room and digging through a stack of disheveled clothes.

Kirk smiled, but his eyes were guarded as he pulled the tunic over his head and began struggling into the uniform pants and boots. "According to our friends, Captain Spock wants us down in the briefing room." He realized that it would have been considerably easier for the Vulcan to summon them with the intercom, but rank had its share of privileges . . . among them the right to send messengers to take the brunt of complaints when awakening someone from a sound sleep.

Once dressed, Jerry turned. "Well, fellas, what's this all about?" he asked, bending down to zip his left boot and almost toppling over in the process. Only Kirk's extended hand caught him automatically before he fell.

"Our orders are to bring you to the briefing room," the tall one replied stiffly. "I have no other information."

Jerry shrugged, glancing at Kirk's guarded expression. "Hell, Jim," he mused, "escorts no less!" He noticed that his roommate also seemed to be taking his time about getting dressed, and wondered if Kirk was receiving the same psychic warning that he was himself. The day's events had left him shaken, a trifle paranoid, extremely disoriented . . . and he couldn't recall a time when Spock had sent armed guards to escort *ShiKahr* crewmembers to some place as mundane as the briefing room.

Kirk's sidelong glance confirmed it.

Moving to the door, Kirk eyed the two guards suspiciously, then cast a warning look in Richardson's direction.

"Oh!" he said, snapping his fingers as if in recollection. "I don't mean to insult you two—especially since you probably outrank me by at least a couple months—but what with all the uproar over the Canusian crisis and all the new personnel on board the *ShiKahr*, Captain's orders say we have to follow procedure." He noticed Jerry's supportive but confused expression, and smiled his most charming smile when he saw a look of unmitigated horror appear in the tall guard's eyes for just a moment. "I don't suppose you'd mind giving me the computer code-sequence for

200

the day, would you? Just following orders, boys," he added apologetically, and winked.

The two guards stared at one another blankly. "I . . . the sequence has slipped my mind," one of them muttered. "Tasme, do you recall the code?"

The other guard shook his head. "I came on duty less than an hour ago," he hedged. But his tone hardened as he turned back to Kirk. "It is irrelevant, Ensign!" he hissed, his tone hardly that of a coolly logical Vulcan. "You will come with us immediately. Captain Spock does not like to be kept waiting." He grabbed the human roughly by one arm, shoving him through the door and completely obliterating any remaining doubts in Kirk's mind.

Kirk planted his feet firmly when he saw the other guard seize Richardson in the same manner. "Maybe so," he replied, his voice surprisingly calm until he brought his elbow hard into the man's ribs. "But I've got a feeling he'd like Romulans aboard the *ShiKahr* even less!"

With the guard momentarily doubled over, he wrenched free of the hand which still held his arm, and lashed out at the man's face. In the background, he was peripherally aware of Richardson moving in on the second man, and of the battle which ensued. He realized disjointedly that they would have little hope of defeating the Romulans in hand to hand combat; physiology simply wasn't in their favor, and he hardly expected a fair fight . . . nor did he intend to offer one.

With a brutal lunge, he succeeded in knocking the taller Romulan to the ground; but out of the corner of his eye, he saw the other grab Richardson's wrist and twist the human's arm up hard behind his back. Kirk's heart sank, and he winced when he heard the snap and his roommate's muffled gasp of pain.

The last thing Kirk remembered was seeing the one called Tasme pull a Romulan disruptor from the back of a utility belt. A high shrill sound filled the room . . . and blue lightning escorted him down into oblivion.

"Now we must take them both!" Tasme complained, shouldering the unconscious burden and glancing down the deserted night corridor.

"No!" Sekor argued. "The Praetor's orders were to bring Kirk!"

"Do not be a fool, my friend," Tasme protested. "The other one can identify us too easily. If we are not able to get off this vessel, he would know who we are!"

With a sigh, Sekor bowed his head in acknowledgment of defeat. "I shall never understand our mistress, Tasme," he stated, lifting Richardson's limp form and following the other man down the hall toward the transporter room.

Tasme laughed lightly. "But would you choose another life for yourself?" he asked pointedly.

Sekor only shook his head as a smile lit his eyes. "I am content to do our Lady's bidding," he murmured as they drew to a halt at the end of the hall. "The rewards far outweigh the tribulations . . . even in moments such as these!"

Sobering, Tasme depressed the control panel which would allow access to the room. "We must return to the *Ravon* immediately," he stated. "From there, our Lady wishes Kirk transported to an uninhabited world in the Romulan star system. . . . He let the sentence trail off, stepped into the transporter room, and heaved a sigh of relief. The room was empty.

Thea lounged comfortably in the high-backed chair, one elbow resting on the briefing room table. Black eyes scanned the room, going first to Sarela, then to McCoy, Scott and finally Spock.

"So you see, Captain," she said quietly, "your alternatives are limited. If you wish to see Ensigns Kirk and Richardson again, you *must* do as I request."

Hardened Vulcan eyes locked with cunning Romulan ones; but he had to respect the sorceress. She had planned it well. "You realize, of course, that I could order a complete vid-scan of yourself and your companion." But he was already learning to hate poker. "And neither of you should deceive yourselves into believing that your minds could withhold the information."

Thea laughed gently. "Once again, you have underestimated the mind of a Romulan, Spock," she said. "Neither Sarela nor myself *know* precisely where your friend is being held; for it was simple enough to predict that you would resort to those methods." She shook her head, long hair falling across her shoulders as a smile came to her lips. "The choice is yours, Captain," she continued. "Accept my words as truth—accept *me* as a Praetor who grows weary of harmful tradition and stagnation—and you shall have your . . . reward." She paused, eyes hardening. "But should you refuse me . . . you will never see James Kirk again."

The anger moved closer as Spock's hands tightened on the arm of the chair. Dizziness drove forward, sending waves of heat and nausea through him. He took a deep breath, eyes closing for a moment as he fought to recapture a control which had already been lost. Vulcan . . . the final curse. The ultimate irony. A biological madness for which no scientific cure existed. But as his eyes opened and he looked at Thea, a sudden simplistic truth came to him. She was, he realized, his only hope—a passport into the Romulan Empire . . . where time-travel was a reality.

"I shall require time to consult with my senior officers," he said, eyes traveling from McCoy to Scott. "You will be returned to your quarters and informed of our decision within two hours."

Thea's head inclined in acknowledgment. "Very well," she conceded. "If you agree to come with me—to present the Tenets of Discipline to the governors—we must leave as soon as possible. There is a Tribunal

203

meeting in less than a week on Romulus; and it is there that we must make our move."

The Vulcan considered it. For himself, a week would be too long; the drive of the blood fever would destroy mind and body long before then. But for the universe . . . if he could somehow discover the Romulans' secret to Time, perhaps there would be some alternative. Mentally, he reviewed the time-curve. Less than ten days remaining. But it was, he realized, the only choice available.

With a quick nod toward the guards, he rose respectfully as Thea and Sarela were ushered from the room. Then, turning back to the *ShiKahr*'s senior officers, he took a deep breath.

"Suggestions, gentlemen?"

McCoy paced angrily across the width of his inner office, blue eyes hard and cold as he whirled on the Vulcan. "I don't give *half* a damn about *what* those Romulans told you, Spock!" he steamed. "You can't go traipsing off into the Empire and get away with it! The Alliance'll have your head the minute you get back here—*if* you get back!"

The Vulcan leaned back in the chair. "There would appear to be no alternative, Doctor," he stated flatly. "As we discussed in the briefing room, the Romulans are the only known society to possess time-travel physics; and if my suspicions are correct, it is entirely possible that it is they who are responsible for the time alteration which has taken place."

McCoy bounced on his toes as he came to a halt in front of the *ShiKahr*'s commanding officer. "Do you have any idea what S't'kal would say about your little scheme?" he demanded hotly.

"By your own admission, Admiral S't'kal is not sane; his opinions, therefore, are irrelevant."

A human hand slammed hard against the top of the desk, less than five feet from the Vulcan. "Blast you and your logic, Spock!" the doctor snapped. "You can't honestly *believe* that Thea is the Romulan Praetor!"

Spock listened to the doctor's continued tirade with a patience which surprised even him. "Again, by your own admission, the readings taken during her debriefing indicate that she is, in fact, relaying the truth." He paused, meeting McCoy's steel-cold eyes. "And since you can provide no evidence to support your emotionally-based theory that she is lying, I am forced to consider the possibility that she is not."

The red heat of anger rose in McCoy's face. "They're blackmailing you, dammit!" he shouted. "And do you have any idea of what could happen if you go off into the Empire waving a bunch of pacifistic documents under the Warriors' noses? It'll be like a red flag to a herd of bulls!"

The Vulcan's brow arched. "Doctor, it is rapidly becoming my impression that you were not listening during the debriefing. Both Mister Chekov and Mister Scott have come to the conclusion that Thea's plan could well work to *our* benefit. And keep in mind that what we *agree* to do inside the Empire need not coincide with what we actually accomplish."

McCoy shook his head, started to respond, then met the commander's eyes. "What did you just say?" But he waved the question aside. "If I'm reading you correctly, you're telling me that—not only are you planning on handing yourself over into enemy territory—but you're also working on some hare-brained scheme to trick Thea!" He threw up his hands in a gesture of defeat. "If I didn't know better—which I *don't*, at this point, Spock—I'd swear you've got a deathwish!"

The Vulcan took a deep breath. "Do you have any alternative suggestions?" he asked.

Again, McCoy bounced angrily on his toes. "No," he said simply. "I do not. But I do have questions, Spock—questions which you'd better ask yourself! For one thing—not that it matters now—but how *did*

Thea get Kirk and Richardson off the ship? I thought you scanned their vessel when it was hanging out there in space, and that she and Sarela were the only two on board."

"I *did* scan the *T'Favaron,* Doctor," Spock admitted, finally becoming impatient despite himself. "Apparently, her slaves were smuggled aboard in a drug-induced state of hybernation. They did not register as lifeforms, and therefore were not detected. When the vessel was brought aboard the *ShiKahr,* Thea had time to administer the counteragent which would revive them. Once the security detachment left the hangar deck, they fled. And, considering Romulan counter-intelligence, it is hardly surprising that they were attired in Alliance security uniforms. By the time the incident came to anyone's attention, Kirk and Richardson were already gone—beamed back to the Romulan mothership."

McCoy scoffed miserably. But he knew it had been an honest mistake. Even Spock couldn't second-guess everything; and whether the captain would admit it or not, it had been a simple case of human error in a Vulcan. "So . . . what *do* you plan to do, Spock?" he demanded at last.

The Vulcan rose, began to pace. "That will depend largely on Thea," he said quietly. "Provided I can elude her scrutiny, there is a distinct possibility that I shall be able to tie into the Romulan computer system and verify precisely what damage has been done—and where to correct it."

The blue eyes widened. "Just like that?" he replied disbelievingly. "She's just going to give you easy access to all the Empire's records and you're going to single-handedly solve all the problems of the universe. Poppycock!" he continued angrily. "What you're *going* to do is get yourself killed or stranded—and I'm not sure there's much difference where the Romulans are concerned."

But the Vulcan shook his head in silent negation. "The fact that Thea deliberately and premeditatedly

206

kidnapped Ensign Kirk is in itself a confession of their guilt," he reasoned aloud. "For, as you have been forced to realize, Kirk *is* a vital link between this universe and the alternate timeline to which we truly belong. Thea obviously knows that as well, and is using it to her advantage." He paused. "What she apparently does *not* suspect is that we are aware of the time alteration."

McCoy remained silent for a moment, then sank wearily into a chair, leaning his head against the wall. "You're basing a mighty big venture on very little evidence, Spock," he pointed out. "Sure, I'll be the first to admit that Kirk is awfully peculiar—even familiar!—but it's difficult to believe that his kidnapping had anything to do with a Romulan plot to alter the entire history of the galaxy. That's pressing it a little far, isn't it?"

"Perhaps, Doctor," the Vulcan conceded. "Since my own . . . evidence . . . is purely of a subjective nature, it is difficult to be certain. However," he quickly added, "the synchronicities are fascinating. And, as we have agreed, our alternatives are limited." He studied the doctor's expression for a moment, then abandoned the hope of attempting to keep the details completely to himself. "In another universe, Doctor, James Kirk was a starship commander—captain of *this* vessel in altered form. And while accepting the fact that Thea is *also* familiar to me, I am forced to consider the possibility that I have had some altercation with *her* in the other universe as well. She is, quite probably, the one key which could unlock the doors to both universes."

McCoy shook his head, hand gripping the arm of the chair. "You're taking one hell of a chance, Spock," he argued. "But that's nothing new in this business, I suppose." With a sigh, he leaned back until the chair rocked up on two legs. "But the question is, Spock, *can* you do anything about it in the time we have left?"

The Vulcan considered that. "Essentially, if we do not act soon, research has shown that the molecular structure of this *new* universe will begin to shift—will mold permanently to complement the structure as it exists after the time alteration. It is much the same as many of your early medical transplants," he continued. "When a new organ is placed in the body, there is a period of time during which the body will either accept or reject the foreign organ. Time alteration—in this case—is working on the same theory, yet on a much larger scale. If we envision this new universe as the body, and ourselves as the foreign organs, perhaps the connection will become clearer. And," he stressed, "in this particular case, the 'body' has already begun to reject what is alien to it."

McCoy looked dubious. "I'm with you so far," he said haltingly. "Go on."

"It is as if we are occupying physical space which is molecularly alien to our minds, Doctor," the Vulcan continued. "However, in many ways, we are experiencing a reverse rejection. It seems that the organ—our physical and mental beings—is rejecting the body. And after a while, both organisms will become diseased. The diseased organ and the diseased body will continue to exist—but as individual units. And as the time-wound begins to heal, we will be unable to recreate what *must* be. The two units—organ and body—will become one gigantic diseased structure which is incapable of surviving."

McCoy rubbed one eyebrow thoughtfully. "I see what you mean, Spock," he conceded. "But it's still a big risk." But he let that angle go. "And there's something else," he said at last. "Your acting abilities leave a lot to be desired. How can you expect to pull off a pose as the Romulan Praetor when you can't even fool *me*?"

The Vulcan glanced away. "What do you mean, Doctor?" he asked cautiously, walls snapping firmly into place.

"Well," McCoy drawled, eyeing the Vulcan closely, "it doesn't take a trained eye to notice that you've been grouchy as an old bear in hibernation for the last week—not to mention that you've been off your feed for longer than that—not to mention that you haven't been sleeping regularly—not to mention that your bodily function readings have been erratic since before the incident on Canus Four. . . ." He let his voice trail off, then lowered the anvil. "Now if I was a suspicious man—which we both know I *am*—I'd say you were either sick or . . . well . . . entering the early stages of *pon farr.*"

The Vulcan's eyes closed painfully. The displacement, the time-distortion . . . and as he had just explained, his body and mind were rejecting the new universe in the most dreaded of fashions.

"It is a possibility," he confessed presently, voice barely a whisper. "However, I still have enough time to do what must be done in the Empire before my own condition becomes . . . acute." He stared numbly at the floor.

Pulling a hand-held scanner from the top of the desk, McCoy ran it close to the Vulcan, almost surprised when Spock made no effort to protest. "And what happens when it *does* become critical?" he asked, temper rising again when he remembered that the Vulcan was unbonded.

The Vulcan steeled himself. "If I am able to reconstruct the universe as it *must* be," he ventured, "the problem will most likely disappear. Since it is based on the physiology of my *current* history—and not on the physiology of the other, *correct* timeline, there is every possibility that it will—"

"Spock!" McCoy interrupted angrily. "Between the 'ifs' and the 'maybes,' you're going to get yourself killed! Well here's another one for you: *maybe* you're wrong! What then?"

Coal-black eyes hardened as Spock met the doctor's accusing stare. "In that event," he replied stiffly, "I shall die." He turned toward the door, stopping only when McCoy's hand closed unexpectedly on his arm, forcing him to turn around. He hadn't seen the doctor even rise from the chair. . . .

209

"Now you listen to me, you stubborn Vulcan!" McCoy began, eyes blazing human fire. "Whether you care to admit it or not, I *am* a doctor. And while I may not be able to cure you of your biology, I *can* treat some of the symptoms! And I'll be damned if you go charging off into the Neutral Zone without *me!* Try it and you'll find yourself slapped down with a medical restraining action so fast it'll make your logical Vulcan head do cartwheels! Try it!" he dared. "If the ship's doctor—meaning me—relieves you of command, not even those muscle-apes from Security will back you up!"

The Vulcan's eyes traveled to the hand which constricted on his arm and held him immobile. "If that is your formal request to . . . accompany me into the Neutral Zone, Doctor," he managed, holding the anger at bay, "I would be . . . grateful to accept." If nothing else, perhaps the persistent human would be able to slow the condition's progress, buy more time.

McCoy stared mutely at the Vulcan, a very faint smile hinting at the corners of his lips. "Well . . . why didn't you just say so in the first place?" he muttered. He bounced happily on his toes, but a sudden thought came to him. "Er . . . Spock? Just how do you intend to explain me to the Romulans once we get inside the Empire? Blue eyes and wavy hair don't exactly fill their bill."

The Vulcan studied him curiously. "There are various human offshoots in the Empire," he remembered. "You will be my . . . personal attendant. However," he added, forcing a lightness of mood which came with difficulty, "the Romulans have another word for it."

McCoy felt his face redden, but was too relieved to give a damn about pride. If Spock was agreeing to let him go, he could survive being called a slave.

At last, the Vulcan turned to leave, slipping into the corridor and leaving McCoy alone.

The doctor shrugged, trying to chase away the uncanny sense of displacement which replaced the Vulcan's presence. "*You* won't live it down either, *Master*

Spock," he muttered once the captain was conveniently out of hearing distance. *But let's just hope I can keep you alive long enough to worry about dignity. You stubborn, pigheaded, crazy, illogical Vulcan! Just don't die on me now—not this close to a home I don't even remember but seem to want. Just don't die on me now, Spock. . . .*

Alone in his quarters, Spock discovered sleep elusive. Somewhere, a stranger whom he recognized as himself walked deserted corridors . . . alone . . . yet not alone. He thought of Kirk, and mentally reached out to the human, attempting to verify . . . what?

An eyebrow rose. *Jim?*

For a brief instant, he thought he felt an answering echo; yet it faded as quickly as it came. He took a deep breath which came out as a sign. But at the very least, the human was alive. That much was certain, and the telepathic link between them had survived the transformation of a universe. And somehow, even Thea had recognized his price.

In a fleeting moment, he wondered what Alliance Command would say when—*if*—they learned of his agreement to Thea's scheme. Even if peace and trade treaties did eventually result from it, it would hardly matter. If he were able to reconstruct the original timeflow, it would completely erase everything he had known . . . including S't'kal and FleetCom. Technically, therefore, since the Alliance would no longer exist, he did not require their permission.

His eyes closed . . . but dreams quickly intruded.

Somewhere, a drummer pounded tightly stretched skins; and Madness—a faceless entity with hot red eyes—danced naked in a dry lake-bed, demanding human sacrifice.

The fever claimed him, wrapping him in ember-hot arms for the night.

Chapter Seventeen

KIRK'S EYES OPENED to the sensation of water dripping on his face. Dragging himself back to consciousness, he raised one hand to his forehead, fighting the dizziness and pain which rose in his stomach as he tried to move. Reality refused to focus.

"Spock?"

"Juliet?" another familiar voice said as Kirk became aware of a supportive hand on his shoulder. "Sorry to disappoint you, Jim," Richardson added, words coming as if through a tunnel, "but it's just Prince Charming without his Cinderella. And on *this* hunk of rock, I don't think there's even an ugly stepsister."

Struggling to sit up, Kirk leaned heavily on Richardson for support, grabbed the wet cloth from the other ensign's hand, and rubbed it briskly across his face. After a moment, his eyes opened, scanning the desolate terrain, and he found himself suppressing a groan of dismay.

Jagged rocks reached toward a pale yellow horizon on all sides; and skeletal trees with black-fingered branches dotted the alien landscape. The ground was relatively soft, consisting of muted brown sand and a smattering of tiny clear crystal-pebbles vaguely resembling diamonds. As the blue sun sank low on the horizon, the clear rocks glistened, giving the illusion of a sea of shiny stones. Overhead, somewhere high among the rock buttress, a spring gurgled noisily, sounding like a muted whisper of children's voices.

At last, Kirk met his roommate's eyes. "I feel like a person who just swallowed a bottle of rubbing alcohol," he muttered, wishing his head would clear. "What the hell happened?"

Richardson shrugged absently, then winced at the stab of pain which ran through one arm. "Close range disruptor stun," he surmised. "That was a good try you made back on the ship. Too bad it didn't work."

Forcing himself to remember the turn of events, Kirk breathed deeply. "Not exactly standard issue Security people," he recalled.

Richardson grunted, leaning up against the outcropping of rock, shielding his eyes from the sun with one hand. "Our little friends left a pile of survival gear over there," he continued, jerking his head toward a mound of green canvas packs resting against the base of the buttress. "But since I flunked basic tent-building in survival school, I thought I'd wait around for some help in setting up housekeeping." He paused. "I hope you read Romulan cookbooks, Kirk."

Kirk managed a smile, glancing to where the gear had been haphazardly dropped to the ground. "I don't suppose they decided to stay for dinner," he surmised.

Richardson shook his head. "They did ask me to relay their humblest apologies, but I had the impression they were in a bit of a hurry to get back." Gradually, he sobered. "I was barely awake myself, Jim," he explained. "But I did hear one of them summon a Romulan cruiser for beam-up, so I'd assume we're not in the Alliance anymore." His eyes narrowed curiously. "Still . . . if they'd wanted to knock us off completely, they wouldn't have left that stack of junk for us to play with."

Kirk nodded to himself. "Dead hostages don't command a very high price on the open market," he said quietly. Then, looking at Richardson, a frown came to his face. "C'mon," he urged, putting his own misery in the background. "Let's see what we can do about that arm."

Without waiting for an answer, he stripped off the uniform tunic, struggled with the sleeves, then grunted appreciatively when the fabric finally ripped. His eyes scanned the horizon carefully as he sought something to use as a splint. Finding a nearby tree with low-hanging branches, he stood—a little too quickly, he discovered, as the desertlike world shifted and spun out of focus. He took a deep breath, waved Richardson's unspoken protest aside with a quick gesture, and edged over to where the skinny tree had poked its way through the rocks and was growing at a crooked angle. Bracing himself with one foot, he lifted the other leg, drew back at the knee and kicked.

With a startled snap, the tree severed almost at the base. After picking it up and breaking the main branch to an appropriate length, Kirk turned to see a puzzled and worried expression take shape on Richardson's face. He returned to his friend's side, took the man's wrist in one hand, and slowly extended the arm to its correct position, grimacing as he felt the ligaments straighten.

"This is to pay you back for all the dirty clothes you left all over my bed!" he said, trying to refocus Richardson's attention.

Richardson winced. "It's not broken," he said matter-of-factly, "but it *will* be if you keep that up!"

Kirk managed a laugh, looking at the alien landscape once again. "Any idea where we are?"

"Well, at first glance," Richardson began with a mock-professional air, "I'd be willing to bet that we're not in Oz." He flinched when Kirk began fitting the branch to the arm. "But if you'll look out that window on your left, you'll see that we're now passing over the—ouch!—Golden Gate Bridge. On your right, you'll see the Pacific Ocean. That tiny speck is a lifeboat, containing your captain and crew. And if you'll further observe—ouch, dammit!—you'll see that the left wing is on fire." He grinned warmly. "Use your imagination, Kirk," he urged. "And don't pinch the stewardess."

Kirk laughed lightly, using strips of the dismembered uniform to tie his handiwork in place. "Better?"

Richardson grimaced. "Do Gorns fly?"

After another moment, Kirk finished the splint, rose to his feet, and brushed loose sand from his knees. "Let's see what our hosts left to eat," he said, going quickly to the pile of survival gear and dragging the two largest bundles over to where his roommate waited. He began digging through the first pack, pulling out an assortment of ration bars (labeled in Romulan dialect); instruments which appeared to be for cutting and digging, presumably to use in search of food; and finally, a standard Alliance-issue medi-kit.

"Efficient little bastards, weren't they," Richardson said, leaning forward to survey the contents of the bag.

But Kirk didn't answer. His eyes remained locked on the contents of the medi-kit . . . and the two full ampules of lidacin. He took a deep breath, then glanced at Richardson out the corner of one eye.

"How's the pain in the arm, Jerry?" he asked at last, also noting the diluted coenthal and another painkilling substance which was marked with the universal symbol for morphine.

"Manageable," Richardson decided. "Save the stuff for later." But his brows furrowed as he studied Kirk's face. "Do you . . . remember anything that happened while you were unconscious?" he asked presently.

Kirk felt a chill climb along his spine. "No," he replied. "Why?"

"Well, when you started coming around, you kept calling for Spock." An easy grin came to the ensign's face. "Now in itself, that may not seem so strange. He *is* the captain: fearless leader, bold ruler, god among mortals, et cetera and so on and so forth. But that's not what caught my attention." He laughed reassuringly at Kirk's confused expression. "Maybe it

215

doesn't mean anything, and maybe it does," he continued, "but you kept asking Spock about the *Enterprise*. You kept asking him if the *Enterprise* was safe."

Kirk felt something change inside himself, a moment of nonreality, a moment of elation . . . and finally, the bitterness and the loss. "I . . . the *Enterprise* . . ." He rolled the word off his tongue, comparing the sound with the feelings which accompanied it. Warm. Secure. Home.

But for a moment, *Ensign* Kirk resurfaced. Never to touch her. Never to know her. Never to *have* her. "I don't know," he snapped angrily. "Probably just another bad dream." He wondered why he was becoming defensive again, why he felt so helpless and alone. The lidacin stared up at him from the medi-kit, but he turned away before the illusion could tempt him further. "It's nothing, Jerry. Just forget it!"

"Whoa!" Richardson remarked, eyes widening. "Are you *sure* about that, Jim?" he asked, wriggling around until he could lean comfortably against the rock-face. "And even if *you* are, I'm not. I saw it in S'Parva's mind, too—during the link—and I'm convinced that it's something important. Think, dammit!"

Kirk rose, started to run, then abruptly sank to the ground once again. *Enterprise* . . . It was just a word, he told himself. Meaningless. Obscure. But *that,* he realized, was the real lie. With a conscious effort, he chased the bitter ensign-reflection back into the mind shadows, trying to remember more details of the meld he'd done with Spock. *She. Enterprise . . . She.* At last, the pieces fell into place like laser-carved puzzle segments. He took a deep breath.

"It's . . . *she's* . . . the ship," he said at last.

Richardson remained silent for a moment, warm brown eyes darkening thoughtfully. *"Your* ship," he added finally, reaching out to touch Kirk's arm in a gesture of reassurance. "S'Parva and I saw it, too . . . we just didn't have a name for it."

For a moment, *Ensign* Kirk rebelled, slamming against the heavy walls which *Captain* Kirk had placed around him. But it was a losing battle. Hazel eyes drifted shut. "Am I a fool to believe that?" he asked, as much of himself as of Richardson. "Or . . . is it really possible?"

Richardson shivered slightly as a chilly wind whistled through the rock-face, playing alto to the soprano whispers of the spring overhead. "All I know is what I *feel*," he replied. "And I *feel* like *that's* where we belong. The rest of it," he continued with an embittered laugh, "is the illusion, Jim."

Kirk turned slowly, eyes instinctively scanning the late afternoon sky. "Well," he said, not daring to dwell on the silver-warm image, "we're not going to do anybody any good sitting *here*." He rose from the ground, began untying the second bundle of survival gear, and found the small two-man dome-tent.

"Want some help?" Richardson asked, crawling over to Kirk's side on his knees.

"I'll handle the tent," Kirk suggested, spreading the numerous canvas strips and support poles onto the ground. "You see what you can find to eat."

Richardson sat cross-legged on the ground. "I'm a lousy cook," he complained. "And I'm more concerned about how we're going to get *out* of here. At least in sixth grade, you always knew Mom and Dad would come back at the end of a miserable week. But I don't think our little friends have any such intentions—at least not immediately."

After laying out the tent, locating the stakes and driving them into the ground, Kirk sat down facing his roommate. "Well, our choices are limited to building a spacecraft out of rocks and branches, or just sprouting wings and flying." He grimaced. "Care to hazard a guess at our chances?"

Richardson winked. "We may be *physically* stuck here," he conceded, "but there's nothing to keep us from *thinking* our way out." He leaned back on the ground, pillowing his head on his good arm. "Since the telepathic link with S'Parva was done just yesterday, her mind should already be receptive to mine; and if I can establish a directional link, we may be able to let her know we're here . . . wherever 'here' is."

Kirk grunted amiably. "I'll set up the tent," he repeated, meticulously joining two poles together to form the basic structure of the alien contraption. "You see what you can find to eat."

"Suit yourself," Richardson agreed, not moving from his place on the ground. "But if I were you, I'd try to establish a link with Spock. If the images I saw in the link with S'Parva are even remotely correct, you might be able to get through to him telepathically. When I was *Lieutenant* Richardson, I had the strong impression that you and Spock belong together *there,* too. Besides, what've you got to lose but your sanity?" he asked with a smile.

Kirk felt himself open up a little as he connected the pole to the snap-tight canvas body of the tent. "If that's the case, I've got *nothing* to lose," he decided. He glanced over his shoulder, confirming what the chilly breeze suggested. In a few more moments it would be dark. "Okay," he said. "I'll try the telepathic link with Spock just as soon as we get camp set up. But it won't do much good to send a message only to have him rescue two frozen corpses, Jerry."

Still, Richardson didn't move, eyes alight with mischief as Kirk hoisted the tent into position. "Now that that's taken care of, what's for dinner, Juliet?" he asked.

Kirk stared mutely at the other ensign, then leaned back, resting on his heels. "How'd you like me to break your other arm?" he asked pointedly.

At last, Richardson rose, strode over to last bundle of survival gear, and popped open the snaps. He peered inside. "Well," he said miserably, "we've got a choice between *T'krouma* and *S'latami.*" He shrugged. "And since the Romulans didn't condescend to put pictures on the cans, there's no way of knowing *what* the hell we'd be eating!"

Kirk managed a laugh as he secured the final lock-tight mechanisms at the proper height on the poles.

When completed, a pale blue dome wavered and breathed on the alien landscape like some misplaced animal. After grabbing the tent-pack and withdrawing two well-insulated sleeping bags, he crawled inside.

"I'll pass," he decided as Richardson crawled through the small opening and zipped the "door" shut behind him.

The other ensign grinned. "You're not as crazy as I thought," he said, wriggling carefully into one sleeping bag. He took a deep breath, eyes closing. "You gonna do it?"

In the near-darkness, Kirk glanced at his roommate, letting the images fill his mind. "Yeah," he muttered, feeling reality waver. Already, he could sense another presence; and as his eyes drifted shut, he gave in to the pleasant warmth which accompanied it. *Trinity* . . . *She* . . . Dark, angular features took shape in his mind's eye, and he began to project outward.

Neutral Zone . . . desert world . . . blue sun . . .

Chapter Eighteen

McCoy EYED THE Vulcan curiously. Somehow, the long black robes and hood seemed natural on Spock, and the doctor found himself suppressing a smile as they walked across the hangar deck and boarded the *T'Favaron*. His medical check on the *ShiKahr*'s captain that morning, however, left him troubled. Blood pressure elevated; glandular hyperactivity; emotional stress. Even with the drugs he'd administered to slow the condition's progress, there was no way to know how long the Vulcan could hold on.

As they entered the small craft and assumed their positions along the wall, the doctor exchanged glances with S'Parva. He knew the Katellan didn't trust their Romulan hosts any more than he did himself; and it had been an uphill struggle convincing Thea to permit S'Parva to come along. Only Spock's insistence that the Katellan was his personal guard had finally swayed the Praetor . . . but McCoy suspected that the lie had been about as transparent as glass.

With a sigh, he settled into the chair, surprised to discover that the *T'Favaron*'s interior was almost identical to an Alliance shuttle. Six passenger seats lined one wall; the other side contained a fold-down bed and emergency medical equipment. And other than the black interior walls and unrecognizable symbols, McCoy could almost make himself believe he was transporting down to some harmless planet for a few days of R & R.

"Once we reach the *Ravon*," Thea's voice said, interrupting his reverie, "you will be escorted to my quarters-deck immediately. Since no one on board that vessel knows the Praetor's true identity, it will not appear odd." She smiled in Spock's direction as she slid gracefully into the command chair. "Do not look so grieved, Captain," she intoned as long fingers activated the controls which would bring the engines to life. "If we are successful in our attempts, you need never see me again once you return to your Alliance."

One eyebrow arched beneath a hood which cast black shadows across the Vulcan's face. "It is not your presence which troubles me, Thea," he replied coldly. "It is the fact that you have resorted to tactics befitting your species which causes me to question your true motives." He paused, wrestling the unbidden emotions back under control. "I shall not underestimate your cunning again."

Thea smiled as the *T'Favaron* began rotating toward the hangar deck doors. The viewscreen followed the ship's rotation, until finally the distant stars of the Romulan Empire came into view.

"You have not underestimated me, Spock," Thea countered, testing the thrusters and finally easing the small craft through the opening and into the black void. "You have merely been forced to admit that, in this particular game, I hold all the high cards."

"If you speak of Ensign Richardson and Ensign Kirk," the Vulcan returned, "then *you* have underestimated *me*. It is not solely on their behalf that I am agreeing to your scheme." He ignored the warning glance from McCoy.

Thea nodded absently, waiting until the *T'Favaron* had cleared the mammoth starship, then boosting power until the whine of the engines filled the cabin.

221

"Then it *is* a myth that Vulcans do not lie," she remarked to Sarela. "But no matter. Tasme and Sekor have informed me of their safe transport to a planet well inside our Empire—a planet with ample food and water to support them for a *very* long time . . . if necessary."

Spock contained his reaction as the ship maneuvered its way clear of the *ShiKahr*. After a moment, Thea's hands moved over the controls once again. There was an instant of engine silence as the power went momentarily off the scale; the viewscreen erupted into a brilliant pattern of light as the vessel achieved warp speed.

That, Spock realized disjointedly, was one distinct difference between an Alliance shuttle and the *T'Favaron*. But when he remembered who owned this particular craft, he wasn't surprised. Thea could command anything she wanted . . . and he realized with a sigh that his mere presence was sufficient proof of her authority.

During the course of the two-hour flight, Thea and Sarela explained once again what would be expected of him. Once the *Ravon* reached Romulus, the pseudo-Praetor would be taken to the palace, briefed on the importance and idiosyncracies of each of the Romulan governors, and prepared for the Tribunal meeting. At that meeting, Thea explained, the Tenets of Discipline would be read and explained; questions would be answered; and, if necessary, arguments would be entertained from the Warriors' two representatives. At the conclusion of the meeting, the Praetor would return to anonymity and the Tenets would be placed in the hands of the governors, where the doctrine contained within the strict laws of discipline would be presented to the individual worlds of the Empire.

Spock took it in quietly, asking questions only when necessary. But his mind was scarcely on the charade. Instead, he concentrated on Thea—on her strengths and weaknesses. If he could learn precisely what had been done to alter the timeflow, it might be subsequently possible to discover what must be done to remedy the situation. But escaping her scrutiny was not likely to be easy.

At last, as if out of nowhere, the *Ravon* appeared, its protective invisibility cloak lowering as the *T'Favaron* approached. Despite the chipped paint on the underside and battle scars from numerous phaser strikes, it was still an impressive sight, hanging in space just barely within the boundaries of the Neutral Zone.

Turning in her chair as the docking computers went on automatic, Thea smiled. "Do you feel soiled to be in the territory of your enemy, Captain Spock?" she asked of the Vulcan. "Or will even you admit to the excitement—and the changes—which you are about to create?"

Spock studied Thea carefully, noting absently that she was attempting to bait him into an emotional confrontation. "I am a Vulcan," he replied stiffly. "Excitement is alien to me."

"Indeed a myth, Lady," Sarela replied with a wistful smile. "He lies as well as any Romulan in the Empire!"

But as Thea continued to study the Vulcan's hardened expression, the cold dark eyes, she felt something inside herself soften. At one time, their positions had been reversed . . . and now *she* could almost feel sorry for *him*, could almost consider being gentle with him. But she turned her back on the alien thought.

"Come," she murmured once the docking maneuver was complete and the *T'Favaron*'s doors slid open onto the *Ravon*'s hangar deck. "The Praetor should see his finest flagship."

"Well, Spock?" McCoy grumbled impatiently, standing over the Vulcan's shoulder. Thea and Sarela had left over an hour before, under the pretense of going to Sarela's quarters to retrieve all personal belongings; but the doctor hardly expected them to remain absent forever.

Dark eyes slowly lifted from the computer terminal

223

in their assigned quarters. "There is indeed information concerning time displacement," Spock confirmed. "Apparently the Romulans have attempted it several times. Unfortunately," he added, "securing all pertinent information from this terminal would appear to be impossible." He paused. "Thea no doubt suspected we would avail ourselves of the terminal; yet she also knew we would be unable to find anything of value."

The doctor bounced angrily on his toes, glancing at S'Parva out the corner of his eye. "Can't you break through the programming?" he asked pointedly. "After all, you've said yourself that the computer systems here aren't *that* different from those on the *ShiKahr*."

S'Parva moved forward, still finding it difficult to maneuver gracefully on two legs, but nonetheless resigned to it. "It would be a relatively simple matter to break into the computer's programming, Leonard," she said to the doctor, "*if* we knew where the main system was located. Since the break-in can only be accomplished from the central or auxiliary banks, and since those systems are located in another area of this vessel, I do not see an immediate solution. This," she indicated, "is nothing more than an information retrieval terminal—but in order to get the data we need, we would have to know precisely what programs to call up."

She leaned forward, studying the small terminal over the Vulcan's shoulder, one ear accidentally slipping free of the clip which had held it in place. It tickled the captain's neck unnoticed, until she saw the Vulcan lean back in the chair and look up at her. With a gentle smile, she shrugged, then reclasped the ear firmly into place. "Sorry, sir," she murmured.

An eyebrow rose as the Vulcan checked the desk chronometer. "I am scheduled to make a routine inspection tour of this vessel in approximately one hour," he began. "Thea feels it would be wise to begin the masquerade while still aboard the *Ravon*, since Commander Tazol holds considerable prestige with the other Warriors. Undoubtedly," he continued, "Thea and Sarela will accompany me on the tour, and the two of you will remain here under guard." As an idea began to take shape, he turned to S'Parva. "The door-guards know who we are," he pointed out, "for they serve the Praetor personally. However," he added, "once the tour of the *Ravon* begins, even Thea will be forced to acknowledge me in the role she has assigned to me. Since she will be posing as a mere adviser, she will not be able to question my requests without placing suspicion on herself. And since it is apparently common for the Praetor to be seen in the company of his personal slaves and guards, it should not appear unusual if I request the doctor's presence after the tour is in progress."

S'Parva smiled to reveal sharp white teeth as the plan became clearer. "When the guards open the doors to escort Leonard out," she said, easily picking up on the captain's plan, "it should be easy enough to escape." She scratched her whiskers thoughtfully. "If I can telepathically disrupt their thought patterns— make them *believe* we're actually going *on* the tour, the illusion itself should be enough. They'll *think* we're right there at their sides; and while they're *really* only escorting Leonard to join you on the tour, I should be able to find an unoccupied computer access chamber and retrieve the necessary information. I'll get back here; and by the time you and Thea return, every-thing'll be normal again."

The Vulcan nodded quietly. "Since Thea has ap-parently taken over this entire deck for her personal use, it should not be difficult for you to move about freely. The majority of her advisers and slaves will be part of the tour party, and therefore occupied." He activated the small terminal once again, eyes intent on the screen. "According to these diagrams, there is an access chamber approximately a hundred yards down the corridor from our present location."

S'Parva took a deep breath. "Just keep them occu-pied for an hour and I'll have the schematics of the whole damned Romulan system!" she said confidently.

For a moment, Spock felt himself relaxing, and allowed his eyes to close. Yet he was still painfully aware of the time elements, the numerous deadlines, and the rapid progression of his own shameful condition. Already, he had felt the telltale signs of mental lethargy; and now, more than ever, he could ill afford imperfection. One mistake, he reminded himself, and it would be all over.

But his eyes sprang open suddenly as he felt the hiss of a hypo against his shoulder. He turned to see McCoy regarding him curiously, standing a safe distance away as he replaced the offending instrument into the medi-kit.

"Precisely what was that, Doctor?" he asked coldly.

McCoy's brows rose as the familiar nervousness and worry returned. "Just a little something to keep you on your feet during the tour, Spock," he replied, his voice unaccountably gentle. "Whether you believe me or not, you're on the verge of collapse!"

The Vulcan's eyes closed as he mentally returned to his own problems, pointedly ignoring the doctor's intrusion. "I assure you," he stated, "I am quite well at this point."

McCoy studied the hand-held scanner which he'd been running close to the Vulcan's body. "You'd better let *me* be the judge of that," he replied, his chin setting firmly. He glanced out the corner of his eye, noting that S'Parva had curled up on the foot of the bed and appeared to be almost asleep. He leaned closer. "You're going to have to do *something* soon, Spock," he warned. "And short of the obvious, I'm at a loss! These drugs aren't going to keep you going indefinitely; your biology's just too strong!"

The Vulcan's hands closed into fists underneath the table. "I am well aware of that, Doctor," he returned, voice deeper and more dangerous than usual. "I suggest you work on your own acting abilities and leave my personal affairs to me!"

Stepping back, the doctor shook his head in dismay and disbelief. "I've never seen any man as stubbornly set against something that's supposed to be *enjoyable,* Spock!" he said to himself. "And you can't convince *me* that there wasn't *someone* on the *ShiKahr* who could've . . . well . . ." He let the sentence trail off, face reddening. "Hell, half the crew's been trying to find the lock-code to your quarters for years!" The anger welled up again—anger at stubbornness, pride, Vulcan dignity. "Dammit, Spock!" he swore, grabbing the chair and swirling the captain around to face him. "What's so terribly *wrong* with letting someone help you? Or do you just *like* being a martyr to Vulcan?"

Before he could move, Spock rose from the chair, powerful hands seizing him by the arms and roughly hurling him aside. Black eyes glistened like daggers.

"Your prying ceases to amuse me, Doctor!" the Vulcan hissed, taking a threatening step toward where McCoy had landed awkwardly against the wall. "And if you cannot confine your inquisitions to your laboratory, I may well find a reason to terminate your usefulness!"

McCoy blinked, staring into the haunted eyes of an animal. For an instant, the old stubbornness rose in the back of his throat, but he quickly clamped down on the angry response. He managed an unfelt smile, realizing that he'd finally found the Vulcan's limits.

"Sorry, Spock," he murmured, carefully edging away from the Vulcan's range. He took a deep breath. "I . . . guess I . . . pushed too far."

Without response, the Vulcan turned away, walked through the open archway into another part of the quarters, and would have doubtlessly slammed the door had it not slid shut behind him.

McCoy glanced nervously at S'Parva's stunned expression.

"He's no good to us dead, Leonard," the Katellan

said gently. "Don't blame yourself for trying to talk some sense into him."

But McCoy slammed one fist into the other palm. "Sense, S'Parva?" he echoed. "You can't talk sense into a crazy man!" His own eyes darkened thoughtfully. "Maybe the only chance *is* to drive him over the edge. . . ."

The tour lasted precisely forever; and by the time the "Praetor" had completed the routine inspection of the bridge, engineering level and shuttle hangar deck, Spock found himself growing increasingly impatient. His eyes locked with Thea's for a moment, then quickly glanced away.

"I request the attendance of my personal slave, T'Lennard," he said in unbroken Romulan dialect, speaking to the *Ravon*'s commander—a little spiked toad of a man who had been dutifully groveling and scraping for well over an hour.

"I shall bring him personally, my Lord," Tazol replied, bowing from the waist.

But the Vulcan shook his head, annoyed at the black hood which hampered peripheral vision and added to the intense heat in his neck. "Negative," he responded sternly. "Merely summon my quarters and have T'Lennard escorted here by my guards."

Tazol bowed again. "Yes, Lord," he said stiffly, eyes lowering in respect as he moved toward a communication outlet on the wall.

But Thea stepped forward, eyes narrowing suspiciously then lowering as she addressed the Vulcan. "If the Praetor grows fatigued, perhaps the tour should be postponed until a more suitable time."

The Vulcan watched as Tazol stepped out of hearing distance, then met Thea's penetrating gaze. "If the Praetor does not trust her pawn," he countered levelly, "perhaps another should be selected, Thea." He paused, tone softening. "I . . . merely need . . . medication," he stated.

Thea's face darkened, but she harnessed her reaction quickly. "Should you be lying, you will need more than medication," she replied. But as Tazol returned to the tour party, she manufactured a smile.

"The guards will bring T'Lennard at once, my Lord," the *Ravon*'s commander said with the traditional Romulan salute. "Is there anything else my Praetor requires before proceeding to the Warrior's gaming deck?"

The Vulcan shook his head, started down the corridor once again, then stopped when the whine of an alien communication device erupted from the nearby wall. After excusing himself with exaggerated apologies, Tazol stepped over to the device, speaking for a long time in hushed tones. At last, however, he returned to the group, his expression dark and unreadable.

"My apologies, Lord," he said quietly. "Apparently, there has been some disturbance on Romulus." He looked up, addressing the shadowed face of the Vulcan pseudo-Praetor. "Details are sparse, yet it seems that the governor of Romulus has . . . gone mad." He bowed respectfully once again, as if to diminish the news. "Without direct summons, Governor T'Rouln attempted to gain entry to the palace. He . . . had several Warriors with him, my Lord," the commander continued shakily, "and there was bloodshed on the palace grounds."

In Thea's eyes, the Vulcan read a moment of horror, of confusion, of disbelief. Also, he saw a truth. She had not encountered the madness until now. An eyebrow rose.

"Did T'Rouln give any reason for his attempted seige, Commander?" Spock asked.

"According to Commander Tavor at the palace, the governor believed he had . . . received a summons from the Ancient Ones," Tazol murmured, laughing nervously at the absurd explanation. "He stated that his mission was to tear down the palace walls, sell the riches within . . . and bequeath the proceedings to the people of Romulus." He paused, looking at his boots

229

when he spoke again. "Commander Tavor sends his regrets, my Lord, with the news that Governor T'Rouln was killed during the battle."

Thea's brows rose, but she carefully turned to the Vulcan. "As your adviser, my Lord, I point out that we must return to the palace at once. It will be necessary to appoint a new governor immediately."

Spock nodded, glanced inconspicuously at the wrist chronometer, then turned back to the *Ravon*'s commander. "We will complete the tour quickly, Captain Tazol," he said. "Notify your bridge crew at once; have them lay in a course for Romulus at maximum speed."

Tazol bowed again. "Yes, Lord," he replied, and returned to the communication outlet.

"Well done, your Excellency," Thea said, keeping her eyes on Tazol's back nonetheless. "You impress even me." With one hand, she motioned Sarela closer. "Verify the information through my private channel to Tavor," she instructed the other woman. "While I do not believe Tazol is brilliant enough to manufacture such a lie, it is nevertheless wise to be well-informed."

The Vulcan stared blankly at Thea as Sarela walked away, surprised that the Praetor had not been aware of the madness long before now. For an instant, he found himself wanting to merely explain the situation to her, present her with the evidence uncovered on the *Shi-Kahr*, and rely on whatever integrity she possessed. But the consideration quickly left him. Without coming directly to the point—without telling her how much he already knew about the time-tampering—there would be no way to guarantee her reaction. And angered, she could have the truth extracted forcibly. With the rapid progression of the *pon farr*, there would be no way, the Vulcan realized, to prevent himself from revealing whatever she wished to know should she order a vid-scan. He watched the real Praetor carefully as she stepped aside, conferring with Sarela on one side of the corridor.

230

But the Vulcan's attention was diverted as the lift doors at the end of the hall opened, and two guards escorted McCoy toward the tour party. Dressed in elaborate Romulan slave attire, the doctor appeared vaguely ridiculous. Flowing silk robes tapered to the floor in splashes of bright colors; and the ornate gold collar around the human's neck shed an air of mystique to the normally reserved surgeon.

As McCoy approached, face red, he bowed. "You requested this slave's company, Lord?" he asked in faltering Romulan which was laced with a distinctive Southern accent.

The Vulcan inclined his head in acknowledgment.

"I . . . am in need of medication," he murmured, his eyes going instinctively to Thea's as she returned and stood close at his side. For a moment, he was sorry he had chosen that particular excuse, but resigned himself to the consequences.

McCoy's brows narrowed as he took a step forward, careful to speak in quiet tones. "What about Tazol and the guards?" he wondered. "I didn't exactly have room to strap on a medi-kit; and with the blasted garb, the colors clashed like hell!"

But Thea's eyes clouded suspiciously. "Then . . . you are genuinely ill," she surmised, scrutinizing the Vulcan. She shook her head in frustration. "We shall terminate the tour and return to quarters at once. Sarela has informed me that the incident at the palace was genuine; and while I have no immediate explanation, it is obvious that Tazol will become suspicious should we continue with the charade of an inspection."

Looking guardedly at McCoy, the Vulcan nodded. "Very well," he conceded, slipping back into the role of Praetor as he summoned Tazol over with a quick gesture. "I grow weary of waiting, Commander," he said. "This flagship is obviously in fit condition; and I see no need to proceed further."

Tazol's face darkened, but he bowed nonetheless. "As you wish, my Lord," he murmured. "The *Ravon* is setting course for Romulus; we shall attain orbit within twenty-one hours at our present speed."

The hooded figure inclined his head in acknowledgment. "Dismissed, Commander Tazol. Carry on with your duties."

Nodding curtly, Tazol quickly slithered into the nearest lift, leaving the corridor empty save for Spock, McCoy, Sarela, Thea and the two guards.

But as the Vulcan turned to Thea, it was to confront questioning eyes.

"What is the nature of your illness?" she demanded quietly. "For obviously it is a condition which your doctor seems unable to treat adequately."

But before the Vulcan could respond, McCoy stepped forward, nearly tripping over the long robes. "Now listen here!" he began defensively. "I may agree to parade around like a goddamned Christmas tree in this costume of yours, and I may even agree to risk life and limb by walking into your Empire, but I'll be damned if I'm going to stand here and listen to you practicing medicine without a license!" He cast a sidelong warning glance in the Vulcan's direction. "Captain Spock was injured during a routine planetfall last week; he's taking antibiotics to combat infection—and when he doesn't get treatment on time, he manifests symptoms of fever! So you leave the doctoring to me, your royal Highness!"

But Thea only laughed at the doctor's tirade. At first, she found herself doubting his word; but when she remembered the intercepted transmission of a few days before, the story fell temporarily into place.

"Very well," she conceded, leading the way back to the lift with Sarela close at her side. "But if his condition worsens, Doctor, you may rest assured that blame will fall squarely onto *your* shoulders."

McCoy bit back the sarcastic comment waiting on his tongue and followed the tour party into the lift. But as his eyes scanned the Vulcan, he shivered inside.

Even beneath the hood, the darkened features were those of a trapped animal . . . an animal dangerous with its madness.

With Sarela and Thea asleep for the night, Spock studied the tapes which S'Parva had provided; and though the information was vast, consisting of several hundred hours of reading, there was no mistaking the fact that Thea had been directly involved. And yet, going back into Earth's past to *stop* the Romulan operatives would not be as simple as stepping through some mystical portal of Time. He would need a ship; and stealing something as conspicuous as a Romulan cruiser would not be easy, particularly with Thea monitoring him at all times once they reached Romulus. She had made passing comment on Governor T'Rouln's attack on the palace, the Vulcan recalled; yet she had either not connected the governor's actions with the madness which was spreading throughout the galaxy . . . or she was, quite simply, pretending to ignore it.

But he glanced back down at the computer readout of the time-warp physics. In order to break the barrier between time and space, he would have to take a ship as close to the sun as possible, relying on the strength of the engines to pull the vessel free of the incredible gravity once a speed surpassing Warp Seventeen was achieved. That speed alone might be enough to rip a ship to shreds, Spock thought; the structural stress should, logically, be so incredible that the vessel would disintegrate. But apparently, something in the peculiar physics of faster-than-light travel caused an object moving at Warp Seventeen or greater to expand, to achieve infinite mass and thereby avoid destruction. In essence, the ship became *part* of time, and could navigate through the eons as well as navigating through physical space. To the Vulcan, it was only an untested theory; but to the Romulans, it was obviously a fact.

Once free of the sun's gravitational pull, the snapping effect would hurl the vessel to even greater speeds, until finally the time-flow would snap into reverse. He was both surprised and somewhat annoyed to discover that it was a matter of physics. In theory, at least, it appeared simple.

But as he felt the tensions mounting in his own body once again, he wondered if the entire ordeal would be rendered academic. Despite the fact that the *pon farr* was attributable to the insanity of time displacement, he could no longer control its effects. A quick glance around the huge room confirmed that McCoy and S'Parva were already asleep, each curled onto an elaborate Romulan half-bed with brightly colored comforters.

The Vulcan took a deep breath, staring at his own neatly made bed. His legs trembled as he stood, but he moved carefully, using the wall for support as he stripped off the black robes and sat on the edge of the bed to remove the boots. After another moment, he lay down, closed his eyes and drifted into red darkness. Fire whispered, licking hungry tongue-flames over his body. Sleep did not come for a long time. But dreams were quick to intrude.

. . . Neutral Zone . . . desert world . . . blue sun.

It was an alien landscape, scattered with rocks, towering boulders, and a few scraggly bushes which had survived the harsh terrain. Deepening shadows lengthened, grew, coalesced into total darkness. Overhead, the clear night sky was strewn with thousands of curious eyes, shining in intriguing patterns and constellations . . . none familiar.

In the midst of the darkness, there was a voice—distant at first, then closer. It spoke one syllable repeatedly. The syllable, too, was a recognized sound, an arrangement of consonants and vowels which held meaning.

234

Spock . . . Spock?
The stars grew brighter.
Jim . . . Jim? *He reached for it.*
For a moment, the stars took them.
But gradually, the stars began to fade . . . and were lost somewhere in the silver-gray sky of an alien morning.

The Vulcan awoke, almost expecting to see the familiar face leaning over him, smiling some lopsided mischievous smile. But as reality returned, logic pointed out that it had been nothing more than a dream.

And yet . . . the star pattern remained in the Vulcan's mind; and the phantom voice whispered in his ear, calling his name repeatedly. With a lifted brow, he rose from the bed, careful not to awaken McCoy or S'Parva with his quick movements toward the computer console.

The drummer sounded in his ears, a symphony of thunder. But he made it to the chair, slumped into it, and activated the terminal. After finding the correct mode, he stared at the screen for what felt like hours. At first, the star patterns of the Romulan Empire were nothing more than alien configurations of light. But when he continued his search through the files, viewing the stars as they appeared from various planets in the Empire, he suddenly understood the meaning of the dream. It was Kirk's distress beacon, Kirk's way of letting him know where he and Richardson were located.

At last, as he continued rapidly thumbing the switch which would advance the program, he came to the diagram of the star patterns as viewed from Remus, sister-world of the Romulan governmental planet. And there, almost like a smile, appeared the precise constellation which had filled his dream.

Neutral Zone . . . desert world . . . blue sun . . .

As he sat there pondering the simplicity of the message, Spock felt the first glimmer of hope he'd experienced in a long time. But when he turned, preparing to dress for the day's events, it was to see S'Parva leaning quietly over his shoulder once again.

Another time, he could have responded with a lifted brow or questioning glance; but with the dream still etched in his mind, the fever burning brighter than stars in his blood, and the knowledge that they would soon reach the Praetor's palace, his eyes widened as a gasp slipped past his waning control.

S'Parva eyed the screen, however, almost oblivious to the Vulcan's uncharacteristic nervousness. Her whiskers twitched. "I saw the constellation in my mind, too, Commander," she murmured. "They've made contact, but . . . without a ship, there's no way to get to them."

But the Katellan's voice came through a distant tunnel. A sound like an ocean began to roar, and long fingers of hot darkness reached into the Vulcan's mind, tugging him down into unconsciousness. For a brief instant, surprise registered on angular features.

Greedy hands covered his eyes, caressing reality with fire. He fell.

Chapter Nineteen

WITH A GASP, Kirk awoke, hands constricting on some invisible demon which had crept into the tent during the night and now attempted to strangle his very life away. Movement was impossible, and hot dry air stabbed his throat as he tried to breathe.

"Whoa! Wake up, Jim!" a distant voice commanded insistently.

Hands closed on his shoulders—gentle, reassuring hands of a friend. He inhaled sharply, his eyes focused, and he found himself face to face with Richardson. Glancing suspiciously around the tent, he felt paranoia as he tried to sit up; but the twisted sleeping bag constricted across his chest and arms, throwing him back at the ground.

Quickly, Richardson unzipped the restrictive gear, hoisting Kirk into a sitting position. Brown eyes narrowed with concern. "That must've been one hell of a dream, Jim," he remarked, crawling over to the "door" and throwing back the two main flaps. "When I went out to take a better look at our predicament, you were sleeping like a little crumb grabber.

After a moment, Kirk laughed wearily, wiping sweat from his forehead. "So much for mind links," he muttered to himself. But his eyes darkened as he recalled what he'd seen . . . what he'd *felt* during the "dream." Putting one hand to his brow, he forced himself to breathe at a normal rate; but the air which filled his lungs was searing, parched with the sharp scents of the desert.

With an effort, he dragged himself to his feet, staggered outside, and stared at the terrain once again. Even with the pale blue sun low on the morning horizon, heat-monkeys had already started to dance among the rocks. And within another two hours, Kirk realized, the inferno would be directly overhead. Wiping beads of sweat from his upper lip, he turned to find Richardson at his side.

"The spring's large enough to cool off in," the other ensign suggested, shielding his eyes from the sun with the splinted arm. "And I thought I saw a few scrawny fish in a pool up there," he continued, jerking his head toward the crevice which led up to the spring's source. "But you'll have to bait the hook," he added matter-of-factly.

Kirk grimaced, walked over to the edge of the rock-face and lowered himself to the ground, looking up at Richardson's puzzled expression. "How about you?" he asked pointedly, unable to shake the dreamlike quality. "Any luck with contacting S'Parva?"

Richardson shrugged, still standing. "I felt *something,*" he said quietly. "But I'm not sure. . . ." The sentence trailed off. "Hey, c'mon, Jim," he said, easily detecting the other man's anxiety. "There's no point sitting here having a stroke." He reached down, grabbed Kirk's arm, and pulled him to his feet. "Let's shed a few clothes and see what we can do about staying alive. If *that* works, we can get back to work on the telepathic links after breakfast." He grinned reassuringly. "No point burning out your brain, either," he pointed out.

Without waiting for an answer, Richardson stripped

off the uniform tunic; and Kirk noticed with a smile that his roommate had already cut a ring around the sleeve. It remained, like some reminder of a life they'd once known. He watched as Richardson began climbing up through the rocks, and finally forced himself to follow.

After a silent five-minute trek which left sweat-beads standing at attention on his chest and face, he found himself in a natural rock "room" of sorts. On three sides, smooth white boulders stretched approximately four feet into the air; and on the third side, the rock had been worn smooth. Water cascaded noisily down the far side of the buttress, forming a winding narrow stream which stretched off toward the afternoon horizon. Heat-demons practiced eerie rituals along the river bank; and from his current elevation, Kirk could discern that the end of the desert was nowhere in sight. He sighed to himself, then turned back to his immediate surroundings. In the center of the rocky walls, approximately twelve feet in diameter, a stream of crystal-clear water gurgled up to form a pool. In the pool itself, several large rocks jutted upward; and Kirk realized that they could, if necessary, simply wait out the heat of the day sitting in cold water.

"What'd I tell ya?" Richardson asked with a grin as he tiptoed carefully over the slippery rocks, sat down on the edge, then lowered himself in, water lapping up around his neck. He splashed playfully in Kirk's direction.

Staring down at the tempting water, Kirk grinned. "Well," he said, stripping off his shirt, "I guess it's a damned sight better than roasting!" He felt a trickle of sweat run down his spine.

But as he slid into the cold spring, letting the waters close over his head, he suddenly understood that the heat was within himself; the spring provided no real relief. Holding his breath, he sank lower into the pool, letting the absolute silence lull him along. But the link wasn't broken, he realized abruptly. And something was terribly wrong.

Kicking his way upward, he broke the surface, grabbing quickly onto the rocky edge for support. His head pounded ominously, and he did not look at Richardson.

Beneath the cold water, his body shivered . . . but the taste of Fire and Death filled his mind.

Chapter Twenty

McCoy shook his head, pacing across the quarters and staring at the Vulcan who remained unconscious on the bed. Color gone, breathing shallow, blood-pressure almost nonexistent; defeatedly, McCoy slammed his fist against the wall as his eyes sought S'Parva's.

"There's nothing more I can do for him," he murmured, trying to make himself accept that unacceptable statement. He cared for the Vulcan—perhaps more than professional ethics should have permitted—and the knowledge that all the galaxy's medical skills couldn't help left him angry.

"If the Romulans discover this, Doctor," S'Parva said quietly, "they will soon realize that our commander is not who he is claiming to be. If Tazol begins to suspect . . ." Her voice trailed off. "Though they are physiologically similar, Romulans do not undergo the time of mating. . . ."

"Tazol need not know," a deep female voice intoned from the doorway of the large room.

McCoy whirled about to see Thea standing just inside the quarters, her own eyes fixed on the unconscious Vulcan. Anger flared again. "How long have you been standing there eavesdropping?" he demanded harshly.

"Long enough to receive confirmation of my suspicions, Doctor," the Romulan woman replied. She met the physician's wary eyes. "Can you help him?" she asked pointedly.

McCoy bounced on his toes. "If I could help him," he snapped, "I wouldn't be standing here!" He tried to shove his own emotions into the background, but found they wouldn't leave him alone. "And just what do you propose to do now?" he demanded. "Shove Spock into the nearest disposal unit and find someone *else* to pawn off as the Praetor?" He didn't wait for a response. "If you can't handle your own responsibilities," he accused, taking a step nearer to the woman and staring down at her through hot blue eyes, "then you've got no business even *being* the Praetor! Hell," he added, finding the Judas-goat he needed, "it would suit *me* fine if the Warriors *did* overthrow your glorious rule and you right along with it!"

"Do not forget, Doctor McCoy," Thea interrupted levelly, "that I am quite capable of snapping your spinal cord should you provoke me sufficiently." She held the damning gaze steadily. "And you may rest assured that I have suspected the nature of Captain Spock's illness for quite some time." She smiled gently in S'Parva's direction. "Your assumption that Romulans do not undergo *pon farr* is essentially correct," she stated. "However, despite mutations which have occurred in both species since our biological paths forked several million years ago, even certain Romulans *are* telepathically . . . receptive to this . . . condition."

McCoy's brows knotted as he struggled to hold his temper at bay. For himself, he didn't particularly care if Thea *did* break his neck; but for Spock's sake, he forced himself to listen. "Can *you* help him?" he demanded.

Thea stepped away from the doctor without responding and went to kneel by the Vulcan's bed. With one hand, she gathered the limp fingers in her own, entwining them. The other hand moved to the fevered brow in a motion not unlike a caress.

"Leave us," she commanded. "There *are* Romulan methods of reaching into the mind of one such as your stubborn captain; but I shall not employ them to satisfy your curiosity." She glanced up. "Leave us," she repeated.

Bur McCoy moved forward defensively. "Not a chance," he countered. "Spock's *my* patient, and I'm not in the habit of leaving an unconscious man at the mercy of the enemy!"

Thea's eyes turned cold as she faced the doctor, slowly removing her hand from the Vulcan's forehead. As the physical contact was broken, the captain moved restlessly, reaching out blindly for the phantom hand.

"Then you condemn him to death with your petty professional jealousy," she pointed out. "Do you deny that you are unable to help him?"

Refusing to budge, McCoy shook his head. "If I can't save his life *now,* then I *can* administer a drug which will put his body in a state of hibernation."

Thea smiled wistfully. "An effort to stall the inevitable at best," she deduced, her eyes closing for a moment. "No . . . I cannot permit that. Time will not stand still, Doctor; and I need your commander at the palace tomorrow." She rose from the floor, moving to the desk and activating a communication panel. A moment later, Tasme and Sekor entered the room. "You will both go with my personal attendants," she instructed McCoy. "And you will not disturb me again until I send for you. If I require your medical services when Spock regains consciousness, I will send for you."

McCoy stared at the two slaves; but despite his personal wish to remain at the Vulcan's side, he had already been forced to admit his own helplessness. Perhaps Thea *did* know a way. . . .

Fleetingly, he turned from the Vulcan. "C'mon,

S'Parva," he muttered, following the two slaves out of the room. "Let's leave the witch doctor to her rituals!"

But Thea only smiled as she knelt once again by the Vulcan's side, taking his hand in her own. "Sometimes witch doctors can provide a cure which medical men would find impossible," she murmured to McCoy's retreating back. Once they were gone, she glanced at the Vulcan once again, studying his face openly.

Lined with pain, he was nonetheless a desirable—and useful—creature. "But you *will* live," she whispered to herself. "I cannot permit you to die, for no one else can do what you must do once we reach the palace." She waited for only a moment longer, then turned her full attention on the Vulcan as she brought her hand to his face, seeking the neural centers into the mind.

For a moment, there was rejection, but she swept it aside with a single thought.

"You belong to us now, Spock," she intoned in the ancient ritual. "You belong to me. . . ."

Spock's mind opened to ponder blackness. At the end of what appeared to be a long corridor, a single light shone through. But gradually, the light split into two distinctive halves. One was pale . . . distant; the other held an immediacy which could not be ignored. He moved toward it, feeling heavy and surreal, weighted down by some forgotten burden which continued to burn its way through him.

As he came closer to the second light, he saw that it had a name, an identity. Thea.

His mind fought; she must not know, must not see the plan in his thoughts. She must not see that his charade was nothing more than a charade within a charade.

With an impossible effort, he tore himself free of the link, black eyes opening to study the Romulan woman leaning over him. For a moment, he wondered if he had already slipped into Death, if this was some fleet-

244

ing illusion left over from life. For another instant, he wondered if the field-density between the two universes had already closed; and he himself was quite mad.

Thea.

He tried to speak, but the word hung suspended in his throat until he understood precisely what was happening. She had come—uninvited—into his mind, had sought out the last remaining ember of life, and had artificially sustained that spark with her own strength, wrestling him back from the eager arms of death. There had been no time for her to travel beyond superficial layers of consciousness, the Vulcan realized, allowing his mind to relax. His eyes closed, safe in the knowledge that his plan was still known only to himself. Perhaps she'd bought a few more hours of time. . . .

But he soon became aware of the gentle hand which caressed his forehead, smoothing damp hair back from his face. He tried to pull away from the enticing touch, but she grasped his hand in midair, forcing him to meet her eyes.

"Without my assistance, you will die, Spock," she informed him, her voice coming as if from a great distance.

He wrestled away from the words . . . but found himself too physically weak to move. She had broken his resistance, he realized with a flare of anger, had soothed the logical portion of his mind into something bordering dangerously on acceptance . . . even desire. He remained taut and unyielding. "You do not understand, Thea," he replied, voice escaping as little more than a whisper. "Our minds . . . are not . . . not enough alike. . . . No bond . . ." His head moved restlessly on the pillow as he struggled to form coherent syllables. "Cannot establish a link . . . not enough time. . . ." He drifted into silence, darkness moving closer. Still, he could feel the strand of her mind brushing against his own, refusing to deliver him into unconsciousness.

"At last, you *have* underestimated me, brave Captain," Thea replied, her hand drifting down to soothe the tight muscles in the Vulcan's back. "But no matter. A temporary link *already* exists; even you must admit to feeling something. . . ." She paused, then gently turned his face toward hers. "Look at me and tell me to go; and I will follow your orders."

The Vulcan's eyes clenched tightly shut, and he realized with a certain horror that she was right. He had been a fool not to recognize her seductive nature before. In the madness of *pon farr,* he *did* want her. But in a last attempt to serve logic, he shook his head violently, trying to sever the link without success.

"I . . . I cannot, Thea! It is a decision to be made for life . . . and I cannot stay with you!" He felt the shame and despair building in his throat, drove it away with an effort which hurt more than he would have thought possible. She was Romulan. She was the enemy.

. . . She was the only logical alternative.

"Sshhh," she replied, soothing the damp forehead once again. "In the Empire no one speaks of forevers. There is only *now* . . . and the link we share is temporary. But for as long as you remain here, your mind is twin to my own. Come," she murmured, slipping her arms around his back and drawing him to her with remarkable strength. "As a creature sworn to the ways of Surak, you must realize that your own death would be illogical. It would accomplish nothing—other than, perhaps, to redeem your precious dignity." But despite the biting truth, there was no malice in her voice.

"I admire you for your conviction, Spock," she whispered, her lips tracing a line down the Vulcan's neck despite his continued resistance. "And now you must learn to admire yourself." She paused as some of the resistance slowly ebbed away. Eventually, she knew he would recognize her for who she was—a woman of his past, an enemy who had promised to make a place for him years ago. "We have met before," she added, trying to soften the psychic cries which slammed against her own mind. They faded

246

slowly, quietly . . . until she knew there was no more hesitation left. "In another time and place, perhaps we would have chosen this freely. . . ."

Painfully, the Vulcan opened his eyes, staring through the red haze of fever to study the face which was poised less than an inch from his own. For a moment, he could almost believe her. And he knew now that he *did* find her compelling, mentally stimulating . . . physically intriguing. And yet, logic dictated that those feelings were present simply because of his own shameful condition. He took a deep breath, letting the pain take him.

"I do not . . . do not know you," he lied to himself.

"Then you will," Thea promised. "And perhaps one day you may be able to forgive me for saving your life in this manner." Her words drifted away as she leaned down to kiss the parched lips, placing her hand once again on the side of his face. As the link deepened, however, she could no longer hold herself in the role of savior. She succumbed to *his* needs, *his* thoughts, *his* desires. "I have almost forgiven you for the incident with the cloaking device," she whispered. "Perhaps you can be as generous someday."

Unable to deny the raging inferno in body and mind, Spock slumped weakly into enemy arms. If he was to live, he told himself, this may be his sole alternative. But . . . even if he could forgive Thea, he did not know if he could ever forgive *himself* for the imperative of *pon farr* which left no choice but to respond.

Clenching his mind tightly, he turned to the time phantom, trying not to let the salty fever-tears slip free.

Chapter Twenty-one

THE OVERVIEW OF the palace was no less spectacular than the Vulcan had expected; and though he found himself still anxious and nervous in Thea's presence, he knew that she was the sole reason he had survived. As the *T'Favaron* circled low over the palace, he glanced down at the high stone walls and glowing force fields; inside the gates, row upon row of Romulan soldiers stood at attention, preparing to herald their Praetor's return.

As the *T'Favaron* finally entered the landing pattern, Spock surveyed the various entrances to the huge quadrangle, mentally choreographing every possible escape. But even with the electrified iron bars which covered all doors leading into the palace itself, he suspected his main problem would be in finding his way to the outside at all. The palace was a maze of corridors, designed to be impassable by anyone who hadn't spent a lifetime learning the routes, secret passages and dead ends. But nonetheless, as he glanced at Thea, he realized he had one distinct advantage. Through the tenuous link with the Romulan, he could discern certain facts—among them what route she would take herself in the event she ever found it necessary to flee the palace walls.

As the ship touched down, engines purring to silence, Sarela rose from the command chair, exchanging glances with Thea before rising from the console. "Commander Tavor signals that the armies await inspection, my Lady," she said presently, "and that all is well within the palace."

Thea nodded, then turned to inspect the ceremonial robes which the Vulcan now wore. Her head tilted curiously as she stared into the dark, faceless entity behind the veils.

"An impressive sight, Spock," she said nonchalantly, feeling the now-constant resistance to the link as he rose to his feet and accompanied her to the surface doors. McCoy, S'Parva, and the rest of the slaves and advisers followed close behind.

Not surprised by the Vulcan's continuing silence, Thea smiled. "Since the Praetor acquires many new slaves, your being seen with Sarela and myself will not appear unusual to the soldiers. Should anyone question you, simply state that we are newly captured possessions." She paused, tone sobering. "Walk quickly through the soldiers, acknowledge no one other than the army's officers. Once we are safely inside the palace, Tavor will see to your safety personally."

"Tavor?" the Vulcan questioned, remembering the name.

"The head of the army," Thea explained. "He knows my plans well—and he will know who you really are. We contacted him from the *Ravon* long before we came aboard your starship; and he has agreed to protect you from men such as Tazol." She shook her head gently. "But do not permit yourself to believe he will follow your orders over mine simply because you wear the robes. The army follows *his* commands; and should you be foolish enough to attempt to wield the power of your attire, you will not live long enough to bid farewell to your two friends."

The Vulcan straightened, muscles taut. "If I am injured," he stated logically, "your plans are ruined.

And since it is obvious in your mind that you have no intention of ever releasing me or these two officers, I see no logical reason to proceed."

But a light came to Thea's eyes as she continued to study the hardened figure before her. "There *is* one thing which will hold your tongue forever in place if necessary," she reminded the Vulcan. "Your own blood still surges with hopes of accomplishing the impossible. You cannot deny that your mind houses some plan to defeat me. Your heritage and your honor will keep you alive long enough to do what must be done—for you cannot deny that you have stolen part of the truth from my own mind."

"Now wait a minute!" McCoy interrupted, taking a step forward. "I thought you said we were going to be released once this harebrained scheme of yours was finished!"

Turning to meet the accusing eyes, Thea inclined her head in acknowledgment. "And you trusted the word of a Romulan?" she asked pointedly. "Surely you realize that I cannot permit you to take proof of my true identity back to your Alliance. Even if peace results from this, there will always be those among my people who will not willingly abide by it. And while that may be true in *any* case, I must know that I have the freedom to move among the people of the Empire without my identity being discovered."

McCoy's face reddened with anger. "Then what's the point?" he demanded. "If you come charging into the Alliance, kidnap two starship officers and *demand* to make peace—but still hold us hostage for the rest of our lives—what makes you think anyone's going to believe your promises? The Alliance won't sign a treaty as long as you're holding us here against our will!"

"Perhaps not," Thea acknowledged, "but that is a chance I must take. If it becomes necessary to barter flesh with your Alliance, your presence will be a useful wedge. And even your officials will understand that returning the three of you would be a risk which the Praetor cannot take. The Alliance will make peace for the galaxy, Doctor. Three starship crewmembers will be considered a price well-paid.''

McCoy remained silent, too stunned to reply. He forced himself to remember that Spock had a plan, forced himself to remember there was something more important to fight for. If the Vulcan was successful in re-creating that other timeline, it would all be rendered academic. And the tapes the Vulcan had stolen from the *Ravon* had proven it possible. But as he stood there studying the robed and hooded figure, he couldn't help wondering what had really happened between Spock and Thea . . . if the Vulcan had made some unspoken bargain with the devil.

Once Spock and his party were ushered to separate quarters, Thea made her way down the long maze of corridors which would lead to Tavor's private office. Gargoyle eyes stared down with hollow smiles from the high stone ceiling, and thin streams of smoke poured from the nostrils of dragon-headed statues which lined the private corridor.

As she came to General Tavor's door, she took a deep breath, then quickly entered, using the passkey attached to her belt. Once inside the room, she found the handsome young man lounging comfortably in a plush chair behind the carved wood desk. Ornate tapestries hung from ceiling to floor, and the thick maroon carpet sank pleasantly beneath Thea's feet as she crossed the room. In one corner of the room, a divan made of overstuffed black velvet sat before a gently burning fireplace. She looked away.

"Tavor," Thea said, inclining her head gently and taking a moment to appreciate the heavy musculature of her general. "The journey was tedious; and I am grateful to be home in the palace again." She smiled, going to the desk and pouring a glass of vintage ale. As she looked at Tavor, her eyes grew lighter. "I have missed you, my old friend," she murmured. "But . . . tell me . . . what has happened to T'Rouln?"

Leaning back in the chair, Tavor did not return the Praetor's smile. Instead, he propped booted feet on the corner of the desk, then reached up to unfasten the frog-closure of the thick brown cape. It fell to the floor unnoticed as the deep brown eyes went dark.

"Governor T'Rouln was once a friend, my Lady," Tavor replied, a hint of regret hiding behind the efficient tone. "We played together as children." He paused. "Yet the man who attempted to storm the palace gates bore no resemblance to the Warrior I once knew."

Taking a sip of the blue ale, Thea slid into a nearby chair, curling one leg underneath the other. "I regret his death, Tavor," she murmured, staring absently at the light reflecting from the general's shoulder-length black hair. "Yet . . . it seems that he was indeed . . . mad?"

Tavor nodded gently. "Perhaps," he conceded. "But there have been other incidents as well." He paused, expression shifting to one of suspicion. "As of this afternoon, I received word of several similar incidents throughout the Empire. On Kalora Six, riots broke out when Governor S'Limou single-handedly authorized the release of several political prisoners." His tone darkened. "As with T'Rouln, there was no explanation for this unauthorized action." A sigh parted thin Romulan lips. "There are others, my friend . . . too numerous to mention."

Thea set the ale aside; Tavor so rarely expressed emotion, yet the weariness seemed to emanate from the powerful frame and disciplined mind. "What else?" she asked, feeling a sudden chill slide up her back as she remembered something she'd sensed in Spock's mind during the initial link.

Insanity . . . two weeks to build a universe . . . or see one die. . . .

At first she'd tried to pass it off as another symptom of the *pon farr*—the Vulcan's *own* insanity, his own deadline. But as she recalled the transmission which had been intercepted from the *ShiKahr* several days before, her eyes widened. Her own words to Sarela came back to her. *I had the impression that their vessel was somehow . . .* lured *into the Canusian system under false pretense. Odd . . .*

She held back the sudden fear which came with the realization of the coincidence. "You said there were other incidents, Tavor," she prompted.

"Indeed," the general replied. "I was . . . forced to kill four of my own soldiers this afternoon, my Lady," he said very quietly. "While I was performing the routine inspection of the troups in preparation for your return, one man attempted to assassinate my chief lieutenant. A fight broke out . . . and four men were left dead." He shook his head. "According to our medical advisers, autopsy showed symptoms of massive disruptions in the cerebral cortex—as if the brain of each man had been somehow . . . shorted out." He hesitated for a moment. "And while I have not yet received medical information on Governor T'Rouln, I suspect the findings will be the same."

Thea rose from her chair, heading automatically toward the door. But before leaving, the turned to face Tavor once again, her eyes softening. "I shall question the Vulcan further," she explained. "Perhaps he knows something of value."

But Tavor merely stared at the Praetor as he rose and went to stand close at her side. "He . . . intrigues you, doesn't he, Thea?" he asked.

For a long moment, the woman did not respond. "He is a tool, my old friend," she said at last, finding herself unable to meet the questioning dark eyes.

"But he *does* stir your blood," Tavor surmised without accusation.

Biting the inside of her lip, Thea reached out, touching the young man gently on the arm. At last, she looked up, then quickly glanced away. "Yes," she whispered, wondering why she should feel so utterly guilty because of that confession. "And for that I *am* sorry." She paused, wrestling with unfamiliar feelings. "If I once believed I could divorce myself from his . . . hold on me . . . I was a fool, Tavor." She looked up once again, then reached out to caress the expectant features. But as the general turned away, her hand fell slowly back to her side.

"I will wait, my Lady," he murmured. "And I will protect your chosen companion with the same fervor I have reserved for you."

For a moment, Thea merely stared at the man's back, then reached out once again, turning him to face her. At one time, she had respected Tavor as a cunning Warrior. At another time, she had loved him. But as she opened her mouth to respond, she found nothing to say, nothing to eradicate the sudden pain which rose in her own mind. Very gently, she ran one hand down the length of the general's neck.

"If it will make this any easier for either of us, my friend," she said softly, "you may rest assured that the Vulcan's feelings for me do not exist as you may imagine them. And . . . as with any living creature, I do not expect I shall be able to dwell long within a void of aloneness." She felt her face darken with a combination of shame and regret. "I . . . would be honored . . . to know that you will wait."

Tavor took a deep breath, then nodded. "Time grows short, my Lady," he said, his tone returning to that of the professional adviser. "The remaining governors will soon be arriving at the palace gates."

With a tender smile, Thea nodded . . . and forced herself to turn away from the dark eyes which wanted her.

Once inside the Praetor's lavish living quarters, Spock found himself contemplating the evening ahead. He glanced at the ornate clock: less than four hours until the Tribunal. But as his eyes scanned the room, he permitted himself a moment to relax. In many ways, Thea's private sector of the palace was much the same as the House of Sarek.

Black velvet curtains completely covered one wall; and then opened, the Vulcan discovered a tremendous plate glass window which overlooked a small pond. On the horizon, the blue sun of Romulus was setting, casting long shadows across the room. Against one wall, an elaborate desk made of solid silver faced into the spacious living area; an overstuffed sofa of blue velvet rested in the center of the room; and various marble statues representing the Ancient Ones of Romulus were stationed like sentinels by the carved wooden doors. Through another exit, closer to the back of the living area, was the bedroom.

But as he sat on the sofa, considering his own predicament and pondering the fact that less than eight days remained, he knew instinctively that he was alone within himself. S'Parva and McCoy had been quickly ushered to separate quarters—through a long maze of corridors and passageways which would be impossible to retrace; and Thea had made it clear that they would not be reunited until after the Tribunal meeting.

As if on cue, the two carved doors which lead into the corridor swung open, and Thea stepped quickly into the room. Dressed now in casual Romulan attire, her face seemed brighter, and even Spock could not deny the fact that she was indeed compelling.

He turned away from the thought, taking a step closer as he attempted to dismiss the uneasiness which had become his constant companion.

With a nod of her head, Thea moved to stand directly in front of the Vulcan, surveying the soft brown tunic he now wore. The robes were draped neatly over the chair at the desk, and she glanced at the black reminders of responsibility only briefly.

"Tonight we shall alter the course of two entire civilizations, Spock," she stated almost to herself. She continued observing him in silence for a moment. "I regret that it was necessary to deceive you into this scheme," she continued at last. "But . . . since you must realize that escape from the palace is impossible, can you not acknowledge that there *are* other alternatives?" She paused, then went to sit on the end of the tufted sofa. "Stay with me," she said as casually as if asking nothing more important than the time of day. "After tonight—with the governors acknowledging you as Praetor—there will be nothing we cannot do."

Spock's eyes closed; and despite the personal approach, he nonetheless wondered if she was attempting to bait him. "You know that I cannot stay, Thea," he stated. But he noticed that he'd automatically gone to sit by her side. "What we both *are* forbids me to make any other decision—and you have already stated that forevers are not discussed in this Empire."

Biting her lower lip, Thea laughed gently . . . almost sarcastically. "Then we are still nothing more than enemies," she deduced. "Nothing more than two opposing factions, each sworn to our separate duty. Is that all?" But she shook her head. "No, don't answer that. Neither of us needs to hear what is already obvious, what is written in your eyes." She hesitated for a moment, her tone becoming more professional as she spoke again. "I know that you are not foolish, Spock. And I would be deluding myself to believe that you are not aware of what has happened in this universe." She glanced away, her eyes distant and unreadable.

The Vulcan remained silent, then raised one brow. "I am aware of the time displacement," he confessed.

Thea nodded to herself. "I saw your plans in your mind while you slept, Spock," she informed him, steeling herself. "But suppose you should fail in this unspoken plan to steal a ship and attempt to correct the damage? Are you aware that your success in that undertaking would result in your own destruction?"

"I am aware of the consequences," Spock stated levelly. Somehow, he wasn't surprised to learn that she'd second-guessed him once again.

"Are you?" Thea countered, suddenly angry. "Do you really understand? If you are successful in going back in time to prevent my operatives from altering the time-flow, you will be killing yourself! You are as much a part of *this* universe *now* as your alternate self is a part of the other. You cannot go back in time, destroy my operatives, and hope to simply step back into your alternate life! For if the time-flow is corrected—if First History is reinstated—the person you are in Second History will vanish!"

The Vulcan nodded once more. "I am prepared to accept that possibility." But it was a thought which had plagued him from the beginning. "However," he added, "should I choose my life as I know it *now* over what I know to be correct, I am no less than a murderer. If I choose to stay with you and make no attempt to correct the damage which has been done, I condemn an entire universe to extinction."

Thea sighed deeply, leaning back on the sofa and resting her head against the Vulcan's unresponsive arm. "You will die," she stated simply, stressing each syllable in an effort to make herself believe it. "The moment you step back into time and stop the operatives from destroying the roots of the Federation, you will no longer exist. History will revert to what it was before—with you and I on opposite sides of a galaxy."

The Vulcan was silent for a long moment. "And if I proceed with your plan to present the Tenets of Discipline to the governors tonight, only to later go back in time and intervene in your operatives' mission, the Tenets will have limited effects at best. Had your advisers been more thorough in their investigation of the long-term effects of time alteration, they would have understood that the changes your operatives have caused cannot withstand the strain of the universe itself. Already, the minds of those born in Second History are seeking to return to their natural environment. Eventually, if something is not done to correct the damage, we will *all* die, Thea." He paused thoughtfully. "The universe is not molecularly stable to the point of being able to tolerate the type of

257

displacement which has resulted from your scheme to conquer the galaxy."

"My *father's* scheme," Thea corrected, her tone tired and weary. She looked closely at the Vulcan, wondering if it was just another plot. But when she remembered what Tavor had said moments before, she felt the anxiety build in her stomach. "If what you are saying is true," she mused, "then you are dead either way." She paused, feeling the sting of truth in her own statement.

"There are alternatives to death," Spock pointed out, sensing her weariness. "And while I do not know what would occur should you choose that alternative, I assure you that it does exist."

Leaning forward on the couch, Thea allowed her eyes to meet the Vulcan's. "What is your alternative, Spock?" she wondered, already understanding that there was little she would not do to keep him alive, to keep him by her side.

"Join me," he returned without hesitation. "Since you are a product of First History, logic dictates that you can exist freely in either environment."

Turning away, the woman stood, took a few steps, then stopped. "Join *you?*" she repeated with a bitter laugh. "After everything I have done to bring you *here,* you ask me to join you in a plan which would mean your extinction?"

"You already know that the structure of this Second History universe cannot endure," the Vulcan countered, rising to stand directly behind the Praetor. "And even if you do not join me, it shall not matter within a few more days." He paused. "Ask your scientific advisers. Tell them to seek hypotheses from your computers. You will find that there are less than eight days remaining in which to correct this situation. If we do not act before then, it will be too late, Thea. The time-wound will heal; and we will all become trapped in a madness for which there is no cure."

"No!" Thea protested, whirling angrily about. "That is impossible!" But she knew it wasn't. "The

258

people of Second History have no other memories! The people they are *now* is all they know!" She clenched her eyes tightly shut.

"Hardly," the Vulcan stated calmly, grasping her by the shoulder and turning her to face him. "The science of the mind is a science not easily understood. It seems that thoughts and memories transcend even the dimensions between time or universes. And in your Empire and my Alliance, the minds of those from Second History will fold in on themselves. The mind will ultimately seek to re-create its native environment— even if the only manner to accomplish that would be permanent disassociation with *this* reality. Everything will stop, Thea—all that you know." He made no effort to conceal the extent of his knowledge now; anything she wanted to know, Thea could doubtlessly attain through the link.

"And what do I profit by joining you?" Thea wondered. "Even if I believed you—what would *I* gain by helping you go back in time?"

The Vulcan turned away, slipping into her mind as if to somehow soothe the psychic pain which emanated from the Romulan. "I have nothing to offer," he replied, feeling an illogical sting of sorrow in that statement. "If I could . . ."

For a long time, Thea did not move. Then, carefully, she reached out and rested one hand on the Vulcan's shoulder. "There is one thing which you can still offer to me," she said gently. "I believe you know what that is."

Looking into the dark eyes, the Vulcan shook his head. "How can I stay with you if I no longer exist?" he asked, easily reading the thought. "If I am successful in stopping the operatives, I cannot even offer myself as hostage."

"Then stay with me *there!*" Thea countered, damning herself for his magnetism. "Stay with me on this past Earth—this planet which is reputed to be so beautiful in the spring! I have nothing to return to here," she added. "If the universe is righted once again, I am no better off than before. The Empire will be the same as it was in First History. My people will continue to die within the confines of the Neutral Zone while your Federation flourishes!"

With a gentle softening of the eyes, the Vulcan shook his head. "And yet you know that you cannot abandon them, Thea," he pointed out. "If you assist me, when you return to First History, you alone will have memories of what has transpired in both realities."

"Stop it!" Thea protested, unwilling to hear the rest. "You cannot say that I will be the only one to remember—even if I should join you! When *you* return to First History—"

"I will no longer exist," the Vulcan said gently. "You have stated that yourself, and know it to be true."

Thea bit down hard on her lip, trying to concentrate on theories which suddenly seemed far too complex for any mind to conceive. "Then . . . if you are successful in intercepting my operatives, you have no intention of even attempting to return here . . . to this point in time," she murmured almost to herself.

"I *cannot* return, Thea," Spock replied. "For once the timeline is corrected, the Spock of Second History will no longer exist."

Forcing herself to consider the unspeakable possibility, Thea reached out to grasp both the Vulcan's hands in her own. "Then what will become of you?" she asked, damning the answer before it came.

"If I am successful," the Vulcan replied, making no effort to withdraw his hands from hers, "it will not matter. The life I seek—the life which must be for my alternate self in First History—will automatically be re-created. Whatever happens to the person I am *now* is irrelevant—for he is nothing more than a specter."

"It is not irrelevant!" Thea argued. "How can you—a Vulcan—do this? How can you plan to go into Earth's past, knowing that you are committing suicide as a result?"

"It is not only my own life, Thea," Spock reasoned, "but the lives of billions of others as well. If I am successful, anyone who accompanies me into Earth's past will not be able to return to the future—except you, if you choose to join me. As I have stated, you are a product of First History—therefore immune to the paradoxes of time travel. However, you must consider those who are *not* immune—the lives which would be lost to madness in the Empire as well as the Alliance." He shook his head very gently. "I cannot permit my personal wishes to stand in the way of what *must* be . . . and I do not believe you can either."

Turning away, the Vulcan was silent for a long moment. "There is a possibility that I will simply vanish the moment the operatives' mission is foiled," he continued presently, attempting to ignore the horror he read in Thea's eyes. It would be too easy to allow her to sway him, he realized . . . to easy to slip into some "logical" madness which dictated that she was correct.

"And if you're wrong?" Thea asked at last. Not really wanting an answer, she waved her hand in a gesture of dismissal, and turned away. But after a moment, she faced the Vulcan once more, a sense of hopelessness permeating her voice as she spoke. "Can you not accept that, this time, you have lost to me, Spock?"

"Defeat comes only when there are no further alternatives, Thea," the Vulcan replied. "And—this time—there are still choices." He held her gaze steadily. "Why must it be a contest?" he asked, struggling to keep emotion at bay and logic in the foreground. "If you truly seek peace, can we not work together?"

"If working together means that I gain your death as a by-product, you must already be mad to think I would accept!" she snapped. "And surely you realize that I have chosen you for reasons other than to masquerade as the Praetor!" She walked away, going to stand at the edge of the huge silver desk. Angrily, she slammed one hand down across the flat surface, eyes narrowing dangerously. "There is no man in this Empire for whom I would risk the things I have risked on your behalf, Spock," she continued. "You alone can stand at my side as equal." She forced herself to look at him, to hold the cold black eyes. "Will you have me say that to you outright? Will you force me to abandon Romulan pride and tell you that I have chosen you for *myself* as well as for my mission? If so, then I say it to you now—without shame and without pride." She felt the sting of alien tears, but blinked them back before they could fall. "I *need* you. The Empire needs you. . . . What more can there be?"

"James Kirk," the Vulcan murmured without hesitation. "And all the others like him who would never be content with the life your time alteration has thrust upon them." He wrestled with the human blood which had stirred to life in his veins. "I admire you as a leader; I respect you as a Romulan." But without giving her a chance to respond to what might have appeared a weakening of his position, he continued. "However, I would hardly be able to respect my decision should I agree to stay with you here—now— in this place and time. You must understand that, if my link with James Kirk has transcended even the gulf of space and time, my first responsibility is—and apparently always has been—to him and to the *Enterprise*." It was just a word, just a collection of consonants and vowels . . . yet it held inexplicable meaning.

"If we were both Romulan," he continued, exploring his own feelings cautiously, "I would be . . . honored . . . to accept what you offer. But we are not even of the same universe, you and I." He shook his head as the unbidden sadness stabbed a little deeper, as regret slowly chipped away at the Vulcan armor. "We do not belong together, Thea—not here, not in that other universe. You *must* accept that," he persisted, attempting to be gentle with words which came with difficulty. "We are of two separate realities . . . and always will be."

Looking up into the dark eyes, Thea did not respond. Whatever she did or did not do, she would lose him. Whether he simply faded out of existence or went mad, there would be no future together. She was, she realized, looking into the eyes of a phantom created by an old man's greed for galactic dominion. Her father had been a fool . . . and once again had bequeathed her the sorrow. She turned toward the double doors.

"I must speak with my advisers," she stated, her voice suddenly cold and clipped as she accepted the fact that she could not hope to keep him.

Spock shook his head gently as he moved up behind the Romulan and touched one arm tentatively. "If you help me, Thea, you will be able to take the knowledge you have gained in Second History and apply it once the timeline is corrected. We *can* make peace, but not here." He looked over her shoulder, then allowed one cheek to rest on the top of her head. With the link still open between them, her loss was difficult to ignore; and regardless of the professional distance between them, he could not help but feel . . . something. Less than Vulcan, less than human, he thought. Hovering somewhere in limbo between the two. And if he were to die, a moment of tenderness was a luxury he could afford.

"Once the timeline is righted," he continued, "it is likely that the Spock who *does* exist in First History will maintain certain memories of *this* reality, too. Second History has happened—it *is* happening—and the evidence points to the fact that the higher consciousness cannot forget anything which has happened to it." He paused, absently running one hand down the length of her arm. "And if my alternate self *does* remember, Thea, you can go to him. If he does not, *make* him remember. You will have knowledge of both Histories, as well as the telepathic skills. And you must use those tools to form peace between our two peoples in a universe where it can endure."

Trembling, Thea nodded almost imperceptibly, then

moved away until the Vulcan's hand fell to his side. "What guarantee do I have?" she asked at last. "What promise can a phantom make which will withstand the distance between universes?"

Spock considered that. "You have my word," he promised at last. "And *his*. Since the other Spock is a reflection of myself, he cannot completely turn away from you. He will listen to your views, and will even help you present them to the Alliance as it will exist in First History. Make him remember, Thea," he repeated fervently. "It is the only alternative either of us have."

Turning, she looked into the Vulcan's eyes. "You are asking me to take you on a journey through time, destroy the Empire's achievements—questionable though they may be—and see a universe die as a result. And yet, despite this madness, I cannot find it in myself to deny you that opportunity."

Spock started to respond, but she waved his words aside with a quick gesture, bringing one hand to the firm chest until she could feel the gentle thrum of the Vulcan heart. "I do not wish to lose you," she confessed, "but neither do I wish to keep you here if you could never give yourself to me without mourning what you have lost in a universe which you have never seen." She turned away, feeling the weight of responsibility settle once again on her shoulders.

"If my advisers can show me any evidence to support your claims, perhaps I will consider helping you. If not . . ." Her voice trailed off. "If not, then you will be free to return to the *ShiKahr*. You are more easily replaced than you might imagine, Spock," she continued. She heard the sting in her words, yet knew she had to put the walls back in place. She had to become the Praetor again . . . if for no longer than to leave the room.

"But there is one thing, Spock," she continued as her hand settled on the doorknob, "one thing which you will never be able to forget. In any universe, in any time, there will come a day . . . a night spent alone,

264

lonely . . . when you will regret losing the rapport between you and me."

The Vulcan's eyes closed painfully. "I am aware of that," he whispered, the words echoing strangely in his ears. "I do regret it now . . . and shall perhaps regret it in that other universe, too." He reached out, but touched only empty space as Thea pulled away.

She nodded curtly as the mask of authority dropped firmly into place. "So do I, Spock," she murmured, slipping into the hall. "So do I. . . ."

Alone, Thea walked down one long corridor, made a series of turns, and finally came to a dead end in the maze. In the deepest part of the cul-de-sac, an iron statue portraying a horned demon stood with outstretched arms. Hollow eyes glowed with the eternal fire of Romulus, and red smoke poured out between long black fangs. The demon had smiled forever . . . almost gloating.

Impulsively, Thea sank to the cold stone floor, absently touching the cloven hooves of the beast. Her eyes closed. As a child, she had often prayed to Bettatan'ru—had asked the demon-Lord for a suitable mate, a handsome Warrior to stand at her side, a man to be honored and to give honor in return. She looked into the black eyes now, and felt herself harden inside.

"Even you, my childhood friend," she mused. "Even you have abandoned us and returned to your steamy heaven." A laugh parted her lips as she glanced down the empty, darkened hall.

The beast's eyes glowed, but Thea laughed again.

"Have I angered you with sacrilege?" she wondered, a hint of bitterness creeping into her tone. "Or are you nothing more than deaf stone and metal?" She shook her head, thinking about the confrontation with the Vulcan. "It is logical that *he* would choose the path he has chosen. But when even the Ancient Ones turn their backs, Bettatan'ru . . . I must question my loyalties. . . ." Her voice drifted away as she rose from the floor, feeling very much like the little girl in her

265

father's palace who had often sneaked into the forbidden Corridor of the Beast.

"Strike me dead," she invited, staring into the hot red eyes of Romulan passion. "For if you do not . . . I shall assume that your powers are gone—that you are nothing more than the cheap iron from which my ancestors forged you!"

She waited.

The beast's eyes glowed.

And after a moment, Thea turned her back on the demon-Lord. She walked away, choosing the corridor which would lead to the central computer facility.

She did not look over her shoulder . . . and the beast did not intervene.

After what seemed like hours, the doors opened once again into the Praetor's living quarters. Thea entered slowly, now cloaked in the black robes of her title, but with the hood lowered to reveal her face.

"I have spoken with my advisers," she said, not meeting the Vulcan's expectant gaze. "And unfortunately they find themselves in agreement with your calculations." She paused, her tone more gentle when she spoke again. "There have been several . . . incidents in the Empire as well as in your Alliance," she murmured. "And . . . it seems that very little time remains." At last, she looked into the deep black eyes. "Why did you not tell me of this deadline sooner, Spock?"

The Vulcan studied her closely. "Would you have believed me?" he asked pointedly.

She glanced quickly away. "I have also been informed by my advisers that the Warriors are not likely to permit you to go into Earth's past should they learn of your plan. Already, Tazol has called a conference of the Tribal kings." She smiled fleetingly. "Not unusual in itself, but I do not believe it is difficult to guess his reason. He undoubtedly suspects—and I have no doubt that he will eventually gather enough of the

Warriors together and attack the palace. There is no time to continue with the charade now."

The Vulcan lowered himself to the sofa as Thea took a chair across the room. For some reason, it still hurt to hear the bitterness in her voice . . . and to remember the gentleness he'd seen in her mind during the *pon farr*. But he drove the intruding thoughts away. "We must move quickly," he stated. "What decision have you reached?"

Thea rose, began to pace. "I have decided to help you," she said at last. "You, Sarela and I will take the *T'Favaron* into Earth's past." She met his eyes steadily and came to stand before him. "Since my advisers have also informed me that your existence will be terminated once you intercept my operatives," she continued coldly, "I find myself quite eager to begin." She transformed the alien emotion of love into the familiar sensation of anger and responsibility—feelings she well knew how to handle. "I was a fool, Spock," she added. "A fool to believe I could be anything more than what I am—a Romulan. I accept that now, just as I accept that the Empire cannot permit itself to die as a result of my father's erroneous scheme."

"Are you abandoning the possibility of eventual peace between the Empire and the Alliance?" Spock asked. He tried to reach out with the link, but it suddenly seemed as distant and unreachable as that other universe.

"We are a warrior race," Thea recited, her eyes brighter than usual. "Perhaps it is not meant to be any other way in any universe, Spock."

The Vulcan noted that she didn't specifically answer the question. "There are others who must accompany us on the voyage, Thea," he said guardedly.

"James Kirk," Thea reasoned, tone bordering on contempt. She leaned closer. "When I met you before—in that other timeline—I knew then that he was something special to you." She paused for just a moment. "Can he be worth what you are doing,

Spock? Can any one man be worth an entire universe?"

The Vulcan's response was direct and without hesitation. "Yes. And you must realize that my reasons go beyond James Kirk. We have already discussed them; your advisers have confirmed them. In less than one Standard week, madness will spread throughout your Empire, Thea. That is the one fact you cannot deny."

A smile came to the Praetor's lips. "Perhaps," she said casually. "But I shall always wonder if you lied— if James Kirk is even deeper in your blood than Vulcan!" She waved her hand in dismissal. "But no matter. We have no time to argue loyalties. If we are to attempt this mission of yours, we must be on our way at once—before Tazol and his men move against the palace." She hesitated for just a moment. "Your other friends—the doctor and the female Katellan—will remain in the company of my personal guards." She smiled once again. "I would be foolish to relinquish *all* my high cards; and if you are wrong about this, your lies will purchase their death."

The Vulcan knew he needn't worry about being wrong; and was almost grateful that McCoy and S'Parva would be spared the transition. They would simply step back into their other lives in one fashion or another.

"Even if I am successful," he stated, "Tazol will still know what has happened. He is a product of First History, and will not be changed once that timeline resumes. If he resists your authority now, he will continue to do so in First History as well."

Thea shook her head in mild disbelief. "Can it matter to you?" she asked. "At any rate, do not concern yourself with what happens once we leave the palace—for neither you nor I shall ever return."

A questioning brow rose at the note of finality in her statement. "And where will you go, Thea?" he inquired. "I do not believe you will relinquish the title of Praetor so easily."

With a smile, the woman nodded. "In your universe, it is said that rank possesses certain advantages. The same is true here. Even if I cannot hope to withstand a full-scale attack on the palace, I *can* purchase retaliatory power once I return from Earth's past. My closest advisers have already transported onto three of our Fleet ships, and are preparing to offer power and wealth to the officers in return for helping defeat Tazol and his men. Once clearly implicated in the plot to overthrow the Praetor, Tazol can be executed. In the meantime," she continued, "I have ordered the palace grounds evacuated. When the fool attacks in the name of tradition and honor, he will attack nothing more than empty walls."

"Very well," the Vulcan murmured. "However, if you wish to maintain any hope of establishing peace with the Alliance—the Federation," he corrected, "we must take James Kirk into Earth's past as well. Even though my alternate self will retain certain memories of what has transpired in Second History, his word alone will not be sufficient. You will need Kirk's influence as well."

"The influence of a man who is responsible for taking you from me?" Thea asked with a lifted brow. Her eyes darkened as she turned away. "Very well," she agreed at last, as her own logic intervened. "However, keep in mind that you will both be under my surveillance. And any attempt to do any more or less than what I direct will result not only in your own death, but his as well."

The Vulcan inclined his head in agreement. At the very least, he would be with the peculiar human to face the nonexistence which would surely result if they were successful in destroying the Romulan time-operatives.

"I am prepared, Thea," he stated, not permitting himself the luxury of considering it further. It would be too easy to alter his decision. Here, he had life, command of a starship . . . and the promise of a future

Chapter Twenty-two

KIRK WAS AWAKENED from a comparatively sound sleep by the persistent whine of what could have been a shuttle's engines had he not been in the middle of a desert wilderness. As his eyes opened lazily, he discovered Richardson already sitting up, peering through the window-flap of the tiny tent.

"You may not believe this, Juliet," Richardson stated, "but that's either the cavalry coming over the hill, or else our little paradise is being invaded by the Martians."

Kirk bolted upright, threw back the tent flaps, and found himself staring at the alien craft which was slowly making its way toward the campsight at an altitude of less than a hundred feet. "There aren't any Martians, Jerry," he reminded his roommate. He crawled outside, Richardson close behind. "From the looks of it, I'd say it's probably a Romulan shuttle of some sort."

Richardson glanced sharply at Kirk. "Well," he sighed, standing up and offering his strong arm to assist Kirk to his feet. "Whatever it is, we won't have much luck hiding from it. . . ." He let the sentence trail off as he began walking toward where the machine was settling to the ground in a relatively flat area approximately fifty yards away.

Kirk felt a moment of something like elation as he looked up to the sky, his eyes settling on the smiling constellation which was directly overhead. He reached out tentatively with his mind, feeling his heart quicken when he touched a surprisingly familiar presence. He stared at the craft, then back to the stars, a smile slowly finding its way to his face.

"It's Spock," he murmured to himself as he grabbed Jerry's arm and headed toward the alien spacecraft. "I think room service finally got our message."

As the engines died down to a gentle purr, Kirk stood staring at the shuttle, trying to imagine what the *ShiKahr*'s Vulcan captain would be doing aboard an enemy vessel. But something stirred in the back of his mind, and he knew that Spock hadn't defected, that his loyalty was still above suspicion. He waited, exchanging expectant glances with Richardson.

After another minute, the two surface doors slid apart, a ramp extending to the ground. The interior light of the craft revealed a black silhouette in the doorway, but to Kirk even that shadowy figure was immediately recognizable. He felt a moment of disbelief, and discovered that he'd been holding his breath.
Spock?

I am here, Jim, the familiar mind-voice responded as the slim figure descended the ramp and came to stand with the two stunned ensigns.

Once away from the blinding interior light of the craft, Kirk felt his jaw go slack as he looked into the fathomless black eyes which seemed to reflect starlight. "Spock?" he repeated.

"Yes, Ensign," the Vulcan responded with a gentle half-smile as he read the relief and warmth in the human's eyes. "I was able to perceive your thoughts quite some time ago. Unfortunately . . . I did not have the ability to come for you until now." In that moment, he felt his own doubts slowly leave him to be replaced with the contentment he'd sensed through the tenuous link. But he turned his eyes on Richardson, glancing disapprovingly at the splinted arm with one quizzical brow.

With a grin, Richardson shrugged. "Would you believe me if I told you that a beautiful nymph rose out of that spring up there and broke my arm when I called her 'Juliet'?" he asked.

"Hardly," the Vulcan responded. "However," he added, "we do not have much time." He inclined his head toward the *T'Favaron*. "There is much to explain, and we must be on our way."

Kirk felt his stomach knot, but held back his own queries for the moment. "Just tell me one thing, Spock," he said as they neared the craft. "Were we . . . were we right about the time alteration theory?"

The Vulcan nodded, erasing Kirk's fears with a simple gesture. "We were correct, Jim," he confirmed, his tone nevertheless sad for a reason Kirk couldn't pinpoint. Spock glanced once again at Richardson. "I will attend to your injuries aboard the Praetor's vessel," he said. "If you will both accompany me . . ."

"Whoa!" Jerry protested, stopping in his tracks. "The *Praetor's* ship?"

"For the moment, Mister Richardson," Spock said evenly, "the Praetor is our only ally. Please follow me. As I have stated, time is of the utmost importance."

Kirk exchanged questioning looks with Richardson, then slowly followed the Vulcan up the ramp and into the brightly lit interior of the *T'Favaron*.

Once Spock had explained precisely how he had come to be so deeply involved with theoretical enemies, Kirk found himself relaxing just a little. But he noticed that Thea seemed to be going out of her way to avoid him; and he couldn't help but wonder if she bore some grudge he was not personally aware of.

But with Jerry sleeping on the medical cot, and the two Romulan women occupied with piloting the ship, he discovered himself alone with the Vulcan. If what Spock suggested was true, he knew they would both be facing something not unlike death; and despite his problems of the past, Kirk did not wish to die.

"How do you know you can trust those two, Spock?" he asked in a whisper. "How do you know they won't just ditch *all* of us on some back-water planet and leave us there to rot?"

The Vulcan shook his head. "They cannot afford to do so, Jim," he explained. "If they do not permit us to do what must be done in Earth's past, then they condemn their entire Empire to eventual and permanent madness. And, as a conquering race, insanity would hardly be profitable to them." He paused for a moment, then forced himself to meet Kirk's eyes. "Also, I believe I can trust Thea because of . . . other incidents," he murmured. But the words came with more difficulty than he'd imagined.

Kirk's brows furrowed as he looked up from the floor. "Such as?" he wondered, not immediately detecting the Vulcan's hesitation.

Looking away, Spock's eyes scanned the view screen, the cold void of space. "She . . . saved my life," he stated at last, hoping that would be enough.

Kirk smiled as he remembered the mind-fever he'd felt himself. Without explanation, it had vanished . . . and as he glanced at Thea, the reason became clearer. "As long as you're alive," he said, "let's assume we can trust them. What now?"

"That," the Vulcan replied with a seeming sigh of relief, "will be up to Thea. She has agreed to assist us only in getting back through time, but has made it clear that any further plans will be our own."

Kirk nodded quietly. But no matter how he looked at it, it all came back to one simple thing: nonexistence for himself, for Jerry . . . and for Spock. He bit the inside of his lip in silence. "I guess I've still got a little of the coward in me, Spock," he confessed, then shook his head in negation of his own impulsive statement. "It's not that I'm afraid to die. I think that's been on my mind ever since the ordeal at the Academy. But . . . ."

Spock's eyes closed as he realized how closely those thoughts paralleled his own. "I know," he barely whispered. "We both claim to want that other timeline, those lives which seem far more real than our current reality. And yet . . . it is a paradox. For once time is set straight, the people we are *now* will no longer exist . . . and I occasionally find myself not wishing to give this up."

Kirk nodded to himself, then managed a weak smile. "Am I selfish to want both?" he wondered. "I seem to remember a friend telling me that I needed someone to look up to." He grinned, then laughed lightly. "Don't ask me where that thought originated, because I honestly don't know. But . . . regardless of all the problems when I first came aboard the *ShiKahr,* I *do* look up to you now . . . and I think I'm afraid of losing that." He shrugged, trying to shake off the heaviness which had settled on his shoulders. "I don't even know what or who I am in that other timeline . . . much less whether or not I was happy. And right now . . . it comes down to the fact that I'm not . . . *sure* about anything." He smiled once again. "Another dilemma, eh, Spock?"

The Vulcan remained silent for a long time, head tilting curiously as he studied the human's indirect approach. "In any timeline, I know that you will be as unique as you are now . . . and I believe you will find your happiness."

Kirk stared at the floor, then laughed somewhat sarcastically. "Hell, Spock," he managed, "in *this* universe, I've never commanded anything bigger than a bath-tub fleet. The thought of a starship . . ."

Spock sought something reassuring to say. Within another thirty minutes, the *T'Favaron* would reach maximum velocity as it fell toward the sun . . . and then there would be no turning back. It was now or never. He closed his eyes, relying on something he'd seen in the human's mind—an uncanny ability to turn even the most tense situations into humor. "Then perhaps you would be well advised, Jim," he suggested, "to think of the *Enterprise* as a rubber duck, and the galaxy as a slightly larger tub."

Kirk looked up, jaw falling with disbelief until he observed the warm twinkle in the Vulcan's eyes. He laughed aloud. "It's called a rubber *ducky,* Spock!" he corrected. "A rubber *ducky.*"

The Vulcan's head inclined in agreement, maintaining dignity to the last. "As you wish . . . Captain Kirk," he conceded.

As the blue orb of the Romulan sun filled the screen, Thea turned in the command chair, scanning first Spock then Kirk. As she looked at the human, she wondered what special qualities he possessed which could apparently control even the most stubborn of Vulcans, what special aura he had which made him belong at Spock's side in any universe.

"When we emerge from hyperspace," she began, forcing a professional detachment on herself, "we will be in orbit over Earth." She turned to Sarela.

The other woman studied a readout on the computer terminal, then focused her attention on Kirk and the Vulcan. "By Earth standard time, the year will be 2097—approximately six hours before the conference which would have brought about the groundwork for the United Federation of Planets." She paused. "The Praetor's advisers have informed us that the operatives will already be in San Francisco when we arrive."

Thea's eyes continued to watch the Vulcan's reaction closely despite her feigned disinterest. Once the ship reached Earth, she would never see him again; but she turned her back on the thought. "At any rate," she said, ignoring the illogical feeling of loss, "the three of you will be taken to a secluded area a few miles from where my operatives will make their attack. Since even we do not know *precisely* what occurred on that day, it will be up to you to devise a plan to stop them." She smiled wistfully, almost arrogantly, not intending to make it any easier for the Vulcan than necessary. "If you are successful, First History will automatically reinstate itself. But if you fail . . ." Her voice drifted off. "Should you fail," she continued at last, "my operatives will certainly kill you. Either way," she added, "you shall not be returning to this timeline or this universe. For even if my operatives are unable to destroy you, I have no intention of bringing any of you back into the Empire. The *T'Favaron* will leave Earth shortly after you are released there . . . and we shall not meet again."

The Vulcan lifted one brow at the hardened bitterness in her voice. "If we are successful," he reasoned, "we will all simply return to the lives we held in First History. Return transportation is not necessary."

Thea smiled. "Success may not be as simple as you imagine," she pointed out. "You forget that you will be attempting to stop two of my most highly trained operatives from doing what, to them, is a pleasure. They are programmed to kill; and they will not permit themselves to be destroyed without a struggle." She laughed lightly. "They are, in my father's estimation, quite indestructible."

Kirk glanced at the Vulcan, but maintained the outward pose of self-assuredness as he saw the guarded expression in his friend's eyes.

"Am I to presume," Spock replied, "that your operatives are something more than human or even Romulan?"

"I am surprised you hadn't deduced that before, Spock," Thea stated sharply. "My father may have been a fool, but he was also the Praetor. He would hardly send flesh-and-blood men to undertake such an important task." She met the Vulcan's eyes head-on. "They are what you might term androids, my fearless captain. And they have but one purpose to their programming." She turned casually back to the control panel once again. "However," she mused, "in a few moments, it will all be rendered problematical. Do you wish to change your decision, Spock?" she asked pointedly, glancing over her shoulder. "Do you wish to admit that not even you and your brave human friend can defeat the Empire's most technologically advanced creations?"

"You might be surprised," Kirk muttered to himself. For a moment, he felt *Captain* Kirk reassert himself, felt the tingle of excitement a starship commander would feel when faced with the impossible. He squared his shoulders, rose from the chair, and began to pace down the aisle of the narrow craft. "In fact," he bluffed, "you've just made it infinitely simpler."

Thea's eyes widened suspiciously. "In what way?" she demanded, activating the controls which would release the ship into free-fall toward the sun.

Kirk shrugged, casting a knowing glance at the Vulcan. "Machines aren't capable of independent thought," he reminded her, trying to figure out what in all the worlds he was doing. "And if they can't reason," he continued with remarkable conviction, "they may be even less efficient than those flesh-and-blood men for which you hold such little regard." He smiled to himself, satisfied. "And as you probably know, *machines* have a nasty tendency to break down at the most inopportune moments. . . ."

Thea smiled as she studied the challenging expression in the bright eyes. "It is indeed a pity you were not born Romulan, Kirk," she replied. "The Empire could use men like you."

"The Empire *uses* everyone, Thea," he returned coldly. "Including you."

Both brows climbed high on the Praetor's forehead.

278

"Whether you believe me or not, James," she returned, "I *do* hope you are successful. For if you are, we shall surely meet again in that other universe . . . and perhaps I will be able to prove to you that my views hardly reflect those of the Empire you have known previously. And if not in peace," she mused, "perhaps we would be fortunate enough to meet in battle." She smiled, then turned when Sarela touched her shoulder.

The other woman indicated the panel with a quick motion. "We approach the designated coordinates to navigate an elliptical path around the sun, my Lady," she explained. "If we are to continue with this mission, we must do so now. If we move any closer to the sun without achieving light-speed, the ship will begin to heat, and the gravitational forces will crush us."

"Very well," Thea replied, her eyes lingering on Kirk for just a moment before she returned her attention to the controls. "Since our two allies seem so willing to die, let us oblige them. . . ."

The blue and green sphere completely filled the screen when the scream of the *T'Favaron*'s engines finally died down. For a moment, as Spock glanced at the Earth, he was almost surprised that they had survived.

"We will begin descent to the planet's surface immediately," Sarela said. "Our cloaking device will prevent detection on their crude radar systems, and we will make planet-fall approximately two miles from the point where our operatives will strike."

Thea inclined her head in acknowledgment, then operated the controls which would activate the invisibility cloak and drop the ship into the atmosphere. She wouldn't allow herself to look at the Vulcan. That part of her life—and his—was over.

Kirk glanced nervously at Richardson. "How's the arm?" he asked, needing something to say to break the silence as they waited outside the *T'Favaron* in a small clearing among giant redwoods.

Jerry shrugged, flexing it carefully. Without the splint to which he'd grown accustomed, he found movement awkward but bearable. "Still a little sore," he confessed, "but better." He grinned nervously. "What's keeping Spock?" he grumbled at last.

Kirk shook his head, kicking at the rocky ground. "I dunno. . . ."

Inside the small craft, Thea turned to survey the Vulcan one last time. Dressed now in contemporary Earth attire, he appeared vulnerable, and she felt her hard resolve soften just a little. With Sarela checking the *T'Favaron*'s engines in the back of the ship, she knew they were alone. "I do not wish to lose you," she said truthfully, "but I have come to understand that one cannot commit oneself to an illusion, Spock."

The Vulcan studied the tender expression on the face of his old enemy . . . his former lover-of-a-sort. "Sometimes," he responded very gently, "illusions are far more enduring and pleasant than reality." He held the dark eyes. "And reality is little more than a grand illusion itself—especially where you and I are concerned." He paused, trying to decide if it was gratitude or something else which made him linger. "Perhaps . . . if we *could* choose our destinies . . ." His voice drifted away.

Turning from him, Thea bit her lower lip. It hurt more than she'd expected, more than should have been permissible. "Please don't say it," she murmured. "Promises from an illusion are scarcely relevant."

The Vulcan nodded to himself, glancing through the open doors to see the sun slowly sinking beneath a cloudy autumn horizon. It was his last sunset, he realized disjointedly, the last time his eyes would ever see the greens and blues and reds and golds of Earth . . . or any other world. In less than six hours, he would be nothing more than a memory in the atoms of the universe.

He turned abruptly toward the double doors, toward the ramp, toward his own destiny, and did not look back.

"Spock?" A gentle plea.

He stopped, but did not turn.

An unseen hand touched his shoulder, and a final moment of warmth passed through the link. "If I could choose," Thea's voice whispered, "perhaps I would indeed choose illusion. . . ."

But her hand fell away, leaving them both alone.

Chapter Twenty-three

In SILENCE, SPOCK, Kirk and Richardson made their way into the outskirts of the city. A gentle patter of rain had started to fall, and as they moved down the steamy gray sidewalks, occasionally passing by pedestrians and bikers, Kirk felt himself shiver. He glanced briefly at the Vulcan, noticing that his friend had carefully pulled a wool hat down to cover the irrefutably pointed ears. Spock seemed unusually silent, but the human tried to pass it off to the tension they were all starting to feel in a very tangible way. Overhead, the sky had turned slate-gray, blending almost perfectly with the ancient architecture of the old city. At last, after what seemed like hours, the Vulcan stopped, glancing up at a modern high-rise hotel which seemed vaguely out of place in the conglomeration of slanted roofs and cobblestone streets.

"From what I was able to discern through Romulan computer records of the event," the Vulcan stated, breaking the ominous silence, "the three officials who are to be assassinated will be holding a preliminary conference in this building this evening." He paused. "It was during that meeting, according to Second History, that Doctor Palmer and his two associates . . . disappeared."

"How did they die?" Richardson asked, pulling the

bulky knit sweater, which Thea had provided, tighter around his chest as a brisk wind whipped through an open alley.

"That," the Vulcan replied, "is where the records are sparse. We know only that they were not seen after the meeting. However," he added, "I believe we can assume that the operatives would have found some method to dispose of any evidence. Also, their methods of execution were apparently sophisticated, since Second History reveals that the operatives were never captured."

Kirk nodded to himself. "Which means there's at least a billion and one possibilities, Spock," he observed. "And six hours isn't enough time to figure out which one is the right one in time to prevent it."

The Vulcan studied his human companion carefully. The rain had stopped, and the strong breeze had already started to dry the damp golden hair. "Alternatives?"

Kirk shrugged. "Well, since we know that it happened *during* the meeting, we have to find some way to be *in* on that meeting. The Romulans are obviously going to be designed to appear human—since Earth hasn't had any contact with alien civilizations at this point. But even if they *look* human on the surface, if we can get into that meeting, it shouldn't be difficult to spot them."

Richardson groaned. "I seriously doubt they'll be eating nuts and bolts for an appetizer, Jim," he pointed out.

Kirk glanced at the Vulcan as a smile grew on his lips. "I've got a plan, Spock," he added, quickening his pace toward the hotel as he grabbed the Vulcan by the elbow and fairly dragged him along. "It's a long shot, but . . . I think I've got a role for you that'll make your charade as the Praetor look like the sixth-grade Christmas play by comparison!"

Once inside the lobby of the massive hotel, the conference room was easy enough to locate, Kirk

283

discovered. And other than occasional glances from well-dressed businessmen, their presence scarcely seemed to be noticed. Making his way down a long hall which led to the banquet facilities, Kirk felt himself breathing a little easier.

Making one last turn into a more secluded area of the hotel, he found what he'd sought. The Starlight Ballroom rested at the end of one plushly carpeted hall; two sets of doors stood open, and various officials from numerous governmental bodies seemed to be arriving in a continuous flow. Glancing over his shoulder, Kirk motioned the Vulcan into a small corridor which apparently led into the kitchen area. Then, with Richardson at his side, the human walked boldly up to the first set of doors, and peered inside. One long table had been set with approximately thirty chairs; ornate floral arrangements ran the length of the table, and a large globe of the Earth as viewed from space rested in the center of the arrangement. Intricately carved candle holders held white candles; and with the dim lighting, the table seemed to glow with importance.

As he stood there, staring into the empty room, he soon became aware of Doctor Palmer and his associates. They seemed to stand out in the crowd, the human noticed with a grimace, as he observed several finely clothed men and women cloistering at the end of the hall less than twenty feet away. Under any other circumstances, Palmer could have been just another face in another crowd; but as Kirk looked at the man, he suddenly understood the importance of one individual dressed in a casual business suit. In Palmer's unspoken words, Kirk realized, his own future rested.

After a few moments, the crowd began drifting into the room; there was a scuffle of chairs, a murmur of hushed conversation . . . and absolutely no one who even vaguely resembled a Romulan. He studied the faces carefully, yet nothing seemed out of the ordinary. Any one of those thirty milling figures *could* be an assassin . . . or none of them. Yet something like a sixth sense warned Kirk that his hunches had paid off in the past. He glanced over his shoulder, and found Richardson engaged in mundane conversation with a stately woman who, Kirk realized, was old enough to be the ensign's mother. But at least no one seemed to object to their presence in the hall. Within another few moments, the woman smiled gently, blushed appropriately when Richardson kissed her hand, then disappeared into the banquet room. A porter came to the doors, kicked the support guards away, and allowed the last few guests to enter.

He glanced at Kirk. "Are you gentlemen part of Doctor Palmer's party?" he asked politely.

Kirk shook his head with a smile as Jerry rejoined him. "We're waiting for someone," he said casually, motioning to a nearby guest elevator.

The porter nodded with exaggerated courtesy, then quickly disappeared.

Kirk turned to Richardson, then sank down onto the plush courtesy divan against one wall. He took a deep breath. "I think we can safely assume that our little friends are inside," he stated. "We'll give it another five minutes—just long enough for things to settle down in there—and then we'll make our move."

Jerry took a deep breath, glancing around the now-empty hall. "You sure about this, Jim?" he asked.

Kirk shook his head with a lopsided grin. "Not at all," he confessed, then motioned around the corner. Presently, Spock stepped out into the corridor, one brow raising questioningly.

Kirk waited, hand poised on the doorknob. He closed his eyes for a single moment, inhaled, then turned the knob and entered the crowded room with a purposeful stride. Spock and Richardson followed close behind.

At the unexpected entry, the man Kirk recognized as Palmer stopped in midsentence, his weathered face tightening with curiosity and a faint hint of irritation as he studied the three intruders. "Gentlemen?" he asked, maintaining the dignified pose despite the accusing expression. "Is there some mistake here?"

Kirk smiled reassuringly as he moved to the doctor's side at the head of the table. All eyes were on him. "Please pardon the interruption, ladies and gentlemen," he began confidently, scanning the curious eyes which stared at him from the long table, "but since this meeting centers on the possibility of contacting other intelligent life in the galaxy, I thought you might be interested in something I have to show you."

His eyes turned to the Vulcan, who was still clad in the woven hat, then nodded to Richardson as all eyes followed his gaze. In a single movement, the Vulcan reached up, removed the hat, and raised his eyes to the crowd as the slanted ears and undeniably alien features were revealed.

At first, there was a moment of hushed astonishment, a few disbelieving laughs, and a general aura of shock. Kirk's eyes traveled quickly over the crowd, noting that everyone in the room was staring at the Vulcan with wide-eyed wonder—with two obvious exceptions. Those two, however, had already risen from their seats on opposite sides of the table, their faces cold and expressionless. He saw one of them raise a hand, and something metal glistened in the palm.

In one quick flurry of movement, Kirk whirled about, tripped the stunned Doctor Palmer, and sent him sprawling to the floor—out of the line of fire when a silent weapon hurled its death charge into the air. Spock had been right; it wasn't a conventional weapon. In a moment of out-of-sync disjointedness, he saw the small cartridge hit the wall behind where Palmer had been standing just a moment before. The capsule disintegrated on impact, and a green fluid oozed down the wall.

Poison—undoubtedly undetectable once in the bloodstream—and undoubtedly a poison for which there were no antidotes on Earth. The operatives had probably intended to make their silent move sometime during the meeting itself; and, at the very worst, the

286

cause of death would have been listed as coronary arrest or massive stroke. The weapon was held in the palm of the hand, barely larger than a coin, and could be discharged repeatedly during an apparently innocent movement such as a wave of the hand.

For an instant, time stood still; but the crowd quickly began dispersing as reality returned. People ran to the exits; and Kirk noticed abstractly that Palmer and his two associates had ducked out a back entrance which lead into a kitchen area—where they would hopefully be safe until the melee was over.

He saw the Vulcan move in on one of the operatives instantaneously, the hard fist lashing out to send the pseudo-man to the ground. But the satisfaction faded when he turned to see the expression of horror on Richardson's face. In a single instant, he knew that his roommate had been hit by one of the cartridges, and he felt himself go cold inside as it all came home. They had come here to die, or simply to go back into nonexistence . . . but now that it was actually happening, *Ensign* Kirk discovered himself all but paralyzed with resentment and something bordering on terror. Disjointedly, he realized that these two alien machines were responsible for the whole thing—his out of place life, the surreal universe to which he had belonged . . . and now for the death of his friend.

Turning his anger on the operatives, he forced himself to move, lunging across the table toward the second android. In the sudden confusion, most of the guests were already gone, and the few which remained were beginning to run toward the door, some tripping and falling, then quickly regaining their footing. As if in a film, Kirk heard the muffled shouts, the shuffling, and the sense of panic which permeated the air. In another moment, his ears detected the horrible hiss of the weapon's discharge once again, as the operative fighting Spock began firing several rounds in a circular motion, obviously aiming for the direction of Palmer.

By the time Kirk's shoulder impacted with his own android's stomach, however, the room was clear except for Spock, Richardson and the two machines.

With difficulty, Kirk wrenched his gaze away from Richardson, and managed to bring the Romulan machine to the floor. But he knew he would have little hope of defeating a mechanism in hand-to-hand combat. Desperately, he grabbed for one of the chairs which had been overturned in the panic, and brought it down across the Romulan's head. But instead of lapsing into unconsciousness as a human would have done, the operative merely rolled to its side, its expression never changing as it kicked Kirk's feet from under him and brought him down. The chair splintered, raining jagged wood.

Kirk grabbed in slow motion for the mechanical throat, then forced himself to remember that his usual street tactics would be of little value now. His eyes scanned the floor; and a bittersweet satisfaction settled in his stomach when his gaze settled on one of the candleholders which had been knocked askew. He grabbed it frantically before the operative could get a firm grip on him. Then, rolling quickly to his feet, the human backed up as the machine advanced, its cold blue eyes never wavering. When the android stood less than a foot away, looking down at Kirk as if in victory, the human lashed out with the crude weapon, driving the point of the candle holder deep inside the glass eye. The mechanism reacted only by stumbling back one step, then advancing again, using the visual sensor in the other eye to sight its target. Somewhere, it had lost the weapon it originally carried, and relied on its own strength now, moving in on the human once again.

Kirk doubted that the device would be foolish enough to repeat the same mistake twice, and he waited until it loomed over him, its six-foot frame blocking all other sight. Every instinct told Kirk to kick, to go for the vulnerable areas as he'd done in the past; but he realized that this machine had no weak points . . . other than its numerous sensors.

He could easily see where his first attack had all but obliterated the one eye; and if the mechanism could be permanently blinded, it would hardly be able to complete its mission. At the very worst, it would wander around aimlessly until its power source was exhausted.

As he saw the mechanical arm rise above his head in slow motion, he feigned to the right, then deliberately rolled to the floor, slipping between the machine's long legs and coming up behind it before it could turn. With a grunt of pain as one leg kicked him a glancing blow, Kirk picked up the dismembered chair, wrenched one sharp wooden leg free, and used it as a club to beat the insane machine back. Then, continuing to battle the flailing arms, he drove it toward the table, his thrusts laying several layers of pseudo-skin open to reveal nothing more than a bloodless mass of what faintly resembled human flesh. As it fell to the floor, apparently disoriented by the battering which clouded its sensors, Kirk turned the sharp end of the chair leg toward its midsection, leaned into the thrust with all his strength, and drove it deep inside the mechanical assassin.

Though the expression on the operative's face never altered, there was a sound of what might have been mistaken for pain in a human. But the last shred of logic informed Kirk that it was nothing more than the advanced gears and sensor mechanisms grinding to their final halt, nothing more than the programming banks being destroyed once and for all.

He continued leaning into the chair leg with his own weight, however, feeling the sting of angry tears in his eyes. It was too late . . . too late for Jerry, maybe for any of them. He'd seen Palmer escape, yet he couldn't help wondering how long it would be before someone else came bursting into the room to discover the evidence.

As he felt the last twitch of movement from the alien machine, he forced himself to stand on shaky legs, turning to see Spock observing him from across the room. The second operative was in a similar state of disarray on the floor, but the Vulcan's cold gaze held no sense of victory. The warm, secret smile was absent.

Kirk felt his mind chill in denial when he saw the single drop of green blood on the long-sleeved shirt. Perfectly clean and round, he knew without daring to ask that the Vulcan had been hit with one of the poison cartridges too. He stopped breathing, felt time stand still, fold back on itself, then start forward again. For a moment, he thought he would find himself in another universe right there; but something stabilized as he continued to stare numbly at his companion. "Spock?" he murmured, his legs unable to move well enough to bridge the short distance between them. "Spock! No!"

The Vulcan shook his head. "There is still time, Jim," he responded, his voice somehow weaker than Kirk remembered it. "We must move quickly, however, for I do not know how long I can . . . can . . ." His words faltered and he swayed slightly.

"Spock!" Kirk gasped, moving a step closer as the horror climbed inside his mind with tangible force.

The Vulcan raised his hand, motioning Kirk back. "We must . . . destroy the operatives completely, Jim," he explained, knowing he could not permit himself the luxury of going to Kirk now. He reached into the folds of the loose-fitting shirt, withdrawing a Romulan disruptor.

Kirk's eyes widened as he stared at the weapon. "Spock . . . why didn't you just . . . why didn't you use that to begin with?" he demanded, feeling a surge of anger as he realized that it would have spared the Vulcan's life. "Why?" he persisted.

The Vulcan's eyes warmed as they met Kirk's, and he methodically set the weapon to its widest disintegration beam. "Despite the fact that Thea gave me this to destroy her operatives, I could not . . . find it in myself to be so gentle. . . ." He swayed once again, then glanced briefly at Richardson, who had slumped to the floor. His eyes were closed, face pallid, breathing shallow. In another moment, the Vulcan realized, he would be dead, and he felt the forbidden emotions swell in him once more. But it no longer mattered. "I could not deny you the victory over the men who have made us what we are, Jim," he explained, his voice weary. "I could not . . ." His words slipped away.

Kirk felt the tightness in his throat, the sting in his eyes. He looked at the two dismembered machines on the floor, then turned back to the Vulcan, suddenly understanding why Spock had chosen that course of action. It was, Kirk realized, Spock's way of letting the defiant Ensign Kirk emerge victorious just once—the Vulcan's way of allowing *him* to reconstruct the very universe they had lost. He smiled wistfully, then went to retrieve the disruptor from trembling hands. Without a second thought, he turned the weapon on the machine he had battled and pulled the trigger.

A bright flash of blue lightning filled the room, enveloping the still figure for a moment; and when only a dark shadow remained on the floor, Kirk knew it was over. Then, still holding his own emotions at bay, he turned the device on the second machine, repeating the action mercilessly. It wasn't killing, he told himself. A machine had never lived to begin with . . . and he wondered if *he* had either.

When it was finished, he turned back to the Vulcan, slipping the weapon into his own shirt. In another moment . . . it would be over for them, too. He looked once at Jerry, then moved to the young man's side and placed one hand on the whitened face. There was no life there. And soon, Kirk realized, he would follow.

He rose, his eyes fastened on the still form of his roommate . . . and very slowly, he saw reality start to dissolve. In an instant, only empty space remained where Richardson's body had been. Kirk swallowed the sudden pain in his throat, trying not to mourn for a phantom . . . but it wasn't easy. *Romeo* . . . he thought sadly, realizing that poison had perhaps been a fitting end. The tears tried to come, but he refused to acknowledge them.

"C'mon, Spock," he murmured, taking his companion's arm and forcing the captain to lean on him as he made his way toward the open doors. "I don't want to be here when the authorities show up. . . ."

The Vulcan accepted Kirk's support without resistance, grateful for the warmth and security as the cold hand of Morpheus came a little closer.

When they reached the hall, it was still deserted. Apparently, Kirk surmised, the confusion was still too recent for the place to be swarming with police, hotel officials and curious onlookers. His only satisfaction was in the knowledge that there would be nothing to find when they did arrive.

He led the Vulcan to the nearby elevator, stepped inside the waiting car, and pressed the button which would lead to the roof. There, he thought mournfully, they would be able to see the stars. . . .

The Bay was calm and quiet as Kirk looked down, still supporting the Vulcan with his own waning strength. "How long, Spock?" he asked, his voice surprisingly calm with acceptance. "How long before we . . . ?"

Spock shook his head, eyes closing. "I do not know, Jim," he whispered. The poison, he knew, had already taken its toll. He slumped to the gravel floor of the roof, not surprised to hear the human slide down by his side. For a moment, he tried to go over the details . . . not that it would matter, he reminded himself, but they seemed nonetheless important.

The worst that would happen, he understood, would be that Doctor Palmer and his associates would have a large mystery to explain . . . and no evidence to support their claims.

He let it go, turning his attention to Kirk instead. For a moment, he felt the dizziness; but this time, he realized, it wasn't because of the poison. With the operatives destroyed and his own death imminent, First History was struggling to reassert itself.

"I . . . do not believe the end will be painful, Jim," he stated logically.

Kirk smiled wistfully at the Vulcan's peculiar train of thought, but didn't respond.

The Vulcan sighed deeply, glancing up at the stars once again. "Are you sorry to leave this particular life?" he wondered philosophically.

"No . . . I'm not, Spock," he said, suddenly realizing the truth in that statement. He too felt the dizziness, the disorientation, the unreality. "If this had happened six years ago, I might've been sorry . . . but I feel like I've gained something . . . like I've found something that was missing back at the Academy. . . ."

The Vulcan nodded, noticing without alarm that his legs were numb, his arms growing cold and distant as if they were no longer attached to his body. There wasn't much time . . . but that no longer seemed important. He had found his contentment as well. "Then come with me," he murmured. He inclined his head toward the black night sky.

Spock began the meld. Kirk knew they were dying, perhaps only to be resurrected in another universe, another time . . . a distant reality. But it felt safe, secure . . . right. *She* would be waiting, he told himself.

Chapter Twenty-four

"WELL, CAPTAIN," McCoy drawled, leaning back lazily in the oversized black chair, "I haven't had a chance to talk to many people this morning, but from what I can tell so far, the dreams have all but stopped." He frowned, however, as the blue eyes studied Kirk curiously. "All except for you, Richardson and Spock," he added darkly.

Kirk's brows furrowed as he considered his own peculiar dreams of the previous evening. Slipping away . . . going home . . . lost. "You're right, Bones," he agreed momentarily. "But the dreams I had last night weren't anything like the ones previously." He shook his head with a sheepish grin then brushed the memories aside. "Hell," he added, "two nights ago, it seemed like half the crew was having paranoid nightmares. Now—all of a sudden—it's stopped. . . . Why?"

McCoy shrugged. "For what it's worth, Jim, I've got a prescription."

Kirk looked up expectantly. "Unless it gets worse," McCoy explained, "just let it go." He put one hand to his face, thoughtfully biting one knuckle in silence for a long time. "Dreams are funny things, Jim. Some philosophers even say they're like windows into another dimension . . . and if that's true, I don't want to press my luck this time!"

Curious hazel eyes questioned the doctor. "What do you mean, Bones?" Kirk asked, realizing that he'd been feeling precisely the same hesitation. When he'd awakened that morning, he'd wanted nothing more than to climb out of bed, slither into the shower, and run as far away from that pillow as possible.

"Well . . ." The doctor paused. "If the dreams *I* had last night are any indicator of another reality," he continued, "then I'd personally opt to stick *this* one out for the duration!" He grinned warmly. "And if you could've seen yourself through my eyes in that dream, I think you might agree . . . *Ensign* Kirk."

The captain felt himself go cold despite the fact that his friend was obviously ribbing him about something in a fleeting dream. But what unnerved him was that he had also dreamed of being an ensign, a phantom . . . a somewhat less than flattering reflection of the man he now was. He shuddered internally. "Then . . . you think we should just wait it out and see if it starts to happen again?"

McCoy nodded. "Killing time is a hobby, Jim," he stated warmly. "Whether you do it by playing chess with Spock or chasing nightmares really doesn't matter." He shrugged. "Two days ago, I might not have said that. But now . . ." His voice drifted into silence, his eyes distant. "Just leave it alone, Jim," he stressed. "Or, if it really bothers you, talk to Spock about it." He frowned. "I'm convinced that tight-lipped Vulcan knows something, but I'll be damned if he's going to tell *me* what it is! When I tried to talk to him this morning as a follow-up, he slipped through my fingers like the proverbial greased sehlat. Still the same old Spock: evasive and stubborn right down to that thick Vulcan core."

Kirk smiled wistfully, catching just a glimpse of his own dream as he rose from the chair. "Aren't all starship captains, Bones?" he asked, and walked through the doors before the doctor could reply.

For some unidentifiable reason, Kirk found himself not wanting to go to the bridge. Duty shift was still thirty minutes away and, deciding that he had ample time, he chose a secondary lift which would lead to the deepest levels of the massive starship. He let his mind wander, trying to recapture the threads of an elusive memory as he made his way toward the garden.

As the lift doors opened onto the lower deck, he stepped out and walked slowly down the long, empty corridor, welcoming the humid air which wafted out as he went inside. With a deep sigh and a secret smile, he selected a path and, without knowing why, began striding purposefully toward the center of the garden.

For a moment, it seemed that he stepped outside himself, and a strong sense of déjà vu teased his nostrils in the crisp "morning" air. Briefly, he reminded himself that the paperwork on his desk was anything but finished; yet despite the routine patrol with no shore leave in sight, his mind wasn't on petty details and personnel transfers. He sighed, remembering the morning's orders from Starfleet Command. According to Komack, the Romulan Praetor had personally requested new treaty negotiations—breaking a silence which had lasted for nearly five years. But what unnerved him was the fact that he hadn't been particularly surprised when he'd finally learned Komack's reasoning behind the extended patrol. It seemed a natural progression. And, he reminded himself, Komack would probably ask for his help in the negotiations, considering his previous contact with Romulan society. And if the treaties could be renegotiated to benefit both sides, he knew it would be well worth the interminable wait at the border of the Neutral Zone.

He turned his mind momentarily away from the responsibilities of command, allowing himself the luxury of relaxing . . . even if for only a moment. As he walked along the path, he stopped frequently, almost expecting to see someone else in the garden; and the déjà vu whispered through his mind again. The uncanny sensation lingered, goading him until he reached the circle of trees and sank down onto one of the weathered stone benches.

He remained there for a long time, pondering the way the sand shifted and moved beneath his boots, the way the thin sheen of dew disappeared from multicolored leaves as the pseudo-sun climbed higher in the surreal sky. But as he continued to stare at the ground, his eyes caught the glint of metal just underneath his left foot. Curious, he leaned down, brushed the loose sand aside with a certain reverence, and picked up the gold ring which had edged its way beneath a fallen leaf.

Holding it in his hand, he studied the simple design carefully, turning the band over and over until he noticed the carved initials inside. The ring seemed familiar, almost ghostly, and for a moment he was hesitant to look too closely at the inscription. But his inborn curiosity asserted itself, and he tilted the band up to the light. J.T.K.—LUCK WALKS WITH YOU.

He felt a chill climb the length of his spine, and was momentarily tempted to bury the relic back in the ground as one might attempt to inter a spirit of the past; to pretend he hadn't known what the inscription said before he'd tempted fate and read it. The message was clear; its origins undeniable. Upon entering command courses at the Academy, each new pupil received the ring as a token of luck. Usually, the ring would be purchased by a close relative, a mate or friend.

But he turned away from the absurd thought which attempted to slip into his mind. He had no patent on those initials, he told himself. The ring could belong to anyone. But something else informed him that this wasn't the first time he'd seen the phantom band,

298

wasn't the first time he'd held it in his hands . . . or the first time he'd slipped it easily onto his fourth finger.

As he continued to stare at it, not breathing, he felt the dream fragments take a step closer, threatening to reveal the truth before he was ready to hear it. He turned from the memories.

"Captain?"

With a start, Kirk jerked his head upright, gasping as if he'd been caught in some heinous crime. And yet, he wasn't terribly surprised to see his first officer standing a few feet away.

"I did not intend to startle you, Captain," the Vulcan apologized, noting Kirk's uncommon nervousness. "Please forgive the intrusion."

Kirk managed a sheepish grin, then motioned his friend to share the bench. As the first officer complied, Kirk slipped the ring from his finger, clutching it in the palm of his hand, though he suspected Spock's keen eyes had already seen it.

"What brings you down to the bowels this early in the morning, Spock?" he asked, attempting to mask his own inexplicable guilt with curiosity.

The Vulcan studied Kirk compassionately. "I thought perhaps I would find you here, Captain," he replied. "Doctor McCoy has informed me that the dreams appear to be dissipating." He paused. "However, the doctor also made it clear that you did dream last evening. I . . . believe he was concerned."

Kirk shrugged. If anyone else had questioned him, he might have been angry; but the Vulcan's casual approach warmed him. "Guess I'm just a diehard, Spock," he said lightly, turning the ring over in his hand without realizing it. He looked up. "Bones also mentioned that you eluded his professional grasp again. Any particular reason, or are you just keeping in practice?"

One eyebrow arched as a moment of pleasant surprise peeked through the firm control. But Spock quickly regained his composure. "I . . . wished to discuss the matter with you before fueling the doctor's curiosity," he stated.

Kirk nodded with a gentle smile. "What is it, Spock?" he asked.

The Vulcan glanced away for just a moment, then took a deep breath. "In my dream last night, I . . . sensed that you and I were . . . engaged in a meld when . . ." The sentence trailed off. He'd watched Kirk die in that dream, watched him fade to nothingness. And despite the fact that he had accompanied him on the journey, he still found it difficult to conceive of his friend's death.

Kirk met the dark eyes steadily. "You dreamed that you and I were linked in a meld when we died," he said, completing the sentence and surprised himself when he didn't flinch from the memory.

One long brow climbed beneath neatly combed bangs in a moment of surprise. "Indeed," Spock murmured.

Kirk smiled fleetingly. "It's all right, Spock," he assured his friend. "I wouldn't have mentioned it either, except that . . . I've had a feeling ever since I woke up that something . . . *happened*. I want to say something happened *last night;* but I'm not sure how that works." He shrugged almost in frustration. "I know this might sound illogical, Spock," he confessed, "but I feel like I've been asleep for thirty years!" He laughed, trying to break the tension which had settled in the air. "Now if I'd been out on shore leave all night, that wouldn't be so strange. But I went to bed early and woke up with one hell of a hangover this morning!"

The Vulcan nodded, then absently checked the wrist chronometer. He glanced curiously at Kirk. "Perhaps it would be wise to discuss the matter in more detail later this evening," he suggested. "Since we are both due on the bridge . . ." He let the sentence trail off, unfinished.

Kirk nodded, grateful that Spock recognized his need for time, his need to re-establish himself. For a moment, he wondered precisely what that was supposed to mean. He'd only been off duty for a little over twelve hours; but it seemed like years, centuries . . . perhaps longer.

He rose from the bench, slipping the ring onto the fourth finger, almost without thinking about it.

Settling into the command chair, Kirk found his mind wandering. He glanced occasionally at Spock's back, trying to imagine what particular research project held the first officer's attention this time. He'd suspected for years that the Vulcan's eyes remained glued to the hooded scanner simply because it made him appear busy when he was, in fact, irrefutably bored. He smiled to himself, trying to picture the Vulcan reading *Alice in Wonderland* in machine language, or perhaps watching some ancient *Tom and Jerry* cartoon to amuse himself.

As he sat there watching the Vulcan and gazing at the unchanging star pattern on the viewscreen, his attention was diverted when the doors opened onto the bridge, revealing Lieutenant Richardson. For a moment, Kirk thought that the young man seemed different, not quite as naïve and innocent as the captain had originally pegged him. But as the lieutenant made his way to the navigator's chair and slumped behind the controls with an exaggerated sigh, Kirk knew it was the same man who was beginning to gain quite a reputation as the ship's resident Romeo.

"What's the matter, Jerry?" Sulu asked, interrupting the silence with a smile. "Been out tomcattin' again?"

Richardson shrugged, checking the controls, then leaned back in the chair. "Nothing so dramatic," he complained with an overacted sigh. He leaned closer to the helmsman, unaware of Kirk's curious scrutiny.

"Dreams again," he grumbled. He gave a manufactured shudder.

Kirk felt himself stiffen, unconsciously leaning closer.

"You'll get over it," Sulu was saying. "Chekov'll be back on first shift in a week, then you can go back to sleeping in again." He smiled. "Just boredom, my friend," he added reassuringly. "So far, you're the only one I know of who had rotten dreams last night. And hell, I almost envy you. The rest of us seem to be settling back into the old routine of doldrum."

"I could use a little doldrum," Richardson remarked with a grin, indicating the star pattern with a nod of his head. "Even that painting out there seems like nirvana in comparison to what I remember of last night!" He set his eyes to the screen, then gave up the pose of interest, leaning closer to Sulu in a conspiratorial manner. "There's only one redeeming quality to nightmares," he confessed in a hushed tone. "The Praetor has gorgeous . . ." He let the sentence trail off, his hands forming into an hourglass with a somewhat exaggerated top.

Sulu elbowed the other lieutenant, glancing nervously over his shoulder.

Kirk managed to avert his eyes before being caught in the distasteful act of eavesdropping.

"In case you hadn't noticed," Sulu muttered, "the Big Man's on the bridge! And besides, I thought you had your eye on S'Parva this week."

Jerry shrugged, slipping back into the old routine. "There's no such thing as too much of a good thing, Sulu," he replied. "I have to play the field, let the galaxy know I'm out here. I have to give more than one woman a chance for true and lasting happiness."

Sulu's eyes rolled as he shook his head. "One of these days, Jerry, one of those innumerable women is going to take you up on the offer. And if my suspicions are correct, you won't know what in all the galaxy to do about it!"

Jerry shrugged. "True," he confessed with a groan.

In the Vulcan's quarters, Kirk sat slowly on the ornate meditation pillows, his eyes scanning the dimly lit room. Against one wall, the Watcher held the Fire of Vulcan, his demonlike appearance somehow soothing. A faint scent of incense drifted through the room, and Kirk was pulled from his reverie as the first officer returned to the living area.

Without speaking, the Vulcan lowered himself to sit at Kirk's side, then allowed the cool mask to drop. Somehow, it seemed cumbersome, unnecessary. "Jim," he began carefully, "I have given the matter further consideration, and I . . . believe there may be a way to discover the meaning of these dreams." He looked into the eyes of the Watcher, choosing a neutral focal point. "I do not know if what I suggest will work, but it is a method to discern what reality—if any—these visions possess."

Kirk studied the Vulcan's slightly nervous demeanor. "You know me, Spock," he said gently. "I'll try anything twice."

"Twice?" the Vulcan repeated.

Kirk nodded. "I have to be sure if I like it or not," he explained. But he quickly sobered. "What d'you have in mind?"

The Vulcan glanced away for just a moment. "A meld," he said at last. "Again, I can offer no guarantees; and if you do not wish to—"

"I didn't say that, Spock," the human interrupted with a gentle smile. "I *do* want to try it. And even if the whole thing turns out to be nothing more than a mind-game, I still want to know."

The Vulcan nodded very slowly, but did not respond.

Kirk managed a smile, feeling suddenly awkward but anxious. "Last chance to throw me out, Spock," he offered quietly.

But the Vulcan shook his head as the decision became clear. *It is time to stop running . . . for both of us.* An eyebrow rose at the unusual train of thought, but he made no effort to block the implications. "I believe the only answers we will ever have are within ourselves, Jim."

Kirk let himself relax, not expecting the meld so quickly, but determined to go through with it anyway.

For a moment there was only the surreal quality associated with the meld.

And then, somewhere, in a universe locked away from reality, a Vulcan commander and his human friend demanded recognition.

Chapter Twenty-five

KIRK STARED AT the floor for a very long time after the meld was dissolved. Even the Watcher had gone to sleep; his flames had quieted to embers, and the faraway hum of the *Enterprise*'s massive engines was the only sound. He found himself unable to speak, to think, or even to breathe at a normal rate. Willing himself back to the present, he shook his head, looking up into the dark eyes.

"Did . . . did *any* of it really happen, Spock?" he asked. He'd seen everything that other Kirk had experienced, everything that other Spock had experienced, and he now found himself shaken, troubled . . . irrefutably guilty.

Studying Kirk carefully, an eyebrow rose as the Vulcan lounged wearily against the thick black pillows, resting his head against the bulkhead. "We can never be certain, Jim," he stated. "There is no proof other than what we have shared in the meld; and that is, of course, purely subjective."

Kirk sighed to himself, studying his folded hands for a long time. But his eyes widened as he finally noticed the gold band on his fourth finger. "The ring!" he exclaimed, slipping it from his hand and presenting it to the Vulcan. "I—*he*—was wearing it when he first came aboard the *ShiKahr,* Spock!" He replayed the images from the meld through his mind, seeing it in a slow-motion panorama, seeing even the minute detail of the ring falling from the young ensign's finger to land in the precise location where he'd discovered it that morning. He swallowed hard, and wondered if that alternate self had deliberately left it for him to find.

The Vulcan turned the plain gold band over in his hand several times, finally glancing at the inscription. When his eyes returned to Kirk's, they were distant. "Are you certain, Jim?" he asked. "It could be . . ." But he knew it wasn't a coincidence. It fit Kirk's hand perfectly . . . as if it belonged there.

"I'm *sure,* Spock," the human replied. Again, he turned to the meld, but even though it had been dissolved only moments before, certain aspects were already dimming, growing more distant and obscure. *There is an energy field between the two universes.* The words came back to him; and he wondered if some part of that other Kirk and Spock still existed in disjointed, ethereal form, if they walked the corridors like ghosts in a last moment attempt to prove that they had lived and breathed and existed. "I don't know what the ring meant to him personally," he murmured, "but I *do* know that it was important."

The Vulcan leaned forward, genuine curiosity lighting the angular features. "Starfleet would hardly accept a ring as sound evidence of alteration of the universe, Jim," he pointed out logically. "And . . ." His voice trailed off. "I am not certain we should inform Command at all."

Kirk glanced up sharply, remembering the morning's message from Starbase—and its sudden relevance to what he'd witnessed in the meld. If Thea was serious about forming peaceful relations between the Empire and the Federation, it would only be a matter of time before she *did* seek them out. "Why not?" he wondered.

"Starfleet Command is, unfortunately, run by what

you might term 'desk-bound paper-pushers,' Captain,'' Spock replied. "Without hard evidence, they would not be inclined to believe us." He paused. "And in that event, we would both find ourselves enduring a series of physical and mental examinations which would make Doctor McCoy's beads and rattles seem most enjoyable by comparison."

Kirk smiled to himself, knowing it was a bridge they would simply have to cross when they came to it. But he wasn't about to let the Vulcan get off that easily either. A devious smile lit the hazel eyes. "And you're also afraid Komack might not appreciate the fact that your counterpart got a little carried away by the Romulan Praetor," he jabbed devilishly. "Don't worry, Spock," he continued with exaggerated seriousness. "I agree. And your little secret's safe with me." He shook his head in manufactured disbelief, ignoring the twin brows which slid up to hide beneath the long bangs. "But if Thea was a product of First History to begin with, she'll have the memories, too—even more so than you or I." He paused dramatically. "And there's another matter, Spock," he added, tone deepening progressively.

The Vulcan waited, knowing his friend was teasing him; but it was still difficult to believe that he had succumbed to the persuasive powers of the enemy . . . in *any* universe. He turned away from the thought, finding it distasteful to the logical portion of his mind.

"What other matter?" he asked innocently.

"Well," Kirk said with a grin, "if Thea *does* have the memories, and if we *do* eventually end up participating in treaty negotiations . . . you *could* find yourself being the center of attention for a long time to come, Mister Spock!"

The Vulcan stared at Kirk. "I do not understand, Captain."

Kirk shrugged with seeming nonchalance. "You *could* be the first person in Federation history to be sued by the Romulan Praetor!"

The eyebrow climbed. "Captain!" the Vulcan responded with an exaggerated air of sourness. "Need I remind you that I am not responsible for my counterpart's actions? Starfleet could hardly hold me accountable for—"

Kirk laughed, reaching out to slap his companion lightly on the back. "Just plead the Fifth, Spock," he suggested.

Spock's jaw went slack with genuine disbelief, but he knew it was the only way either of them would be able to accept the scope of what had transpired. Remembering an ancient human proverb, he found some small comfort in the knowledge that Kirk was obviously laughing to keep from crying.

"Really, Captain," he said in the customary banter, "I am due on the bridge in less than five hours. I believe a period of rest is required by regulations."

Kirk nodded, standing up and moving toward the door. He felt the lingering warmth of the meld, and settled into it. But he turned to meet his friend's eyes one last time. "Thanks, Spock," he said gently, thinking for a moment of Ensign Kirk. "From both of us."

Epilogue

IT WAS LATE in ship's night when Kirk found himself in the lift which would lead to the lower levels of the *Enterprise*. Without understanding why, he knew he had to go to the gardens once again. *There is an energy field between the two universes*. And it worked both ways, he reminded himself. Soon, the time-door would be closing forever, separating him from a man very much like himself and a Vulcan very much like his own first officer.

As he entered into the surrealistic moonlit setting, he thought for a moment that he sensed another presence. It did not frighten him; instead, a feeling of warmth and familiarity lingered. He followed it, unconsciously walking faster toward the center of the garden and the old stone bench.

Parting the cascading branches, he slipped inside the circle of trees with a reverence, going to sit on the cold concrete slab which was moist with dew. For a long time, he remained there, utterly still, waiting for someone or something he couldn't quite define. A few times, there was a warmth by his side, almost as if an unseen hand touched him gently on the shoulder. But when he turned, only the darkness and the eerie sensation of loss remained.

He glanced down at his hand, caught himself absently twisting the gold ring on his fourth finger. Then, in a moment of dawning comprehension, he understood precisely why he had come here. There was one last tie to be severed. . . . One last duty to be performed.

Taking a deep breath and closing his eyes, he slipped the ring from his hand, held it for just a moment, then let it slip to the ground where he had first discovered it. For an instant, there was a sadness which seemed to wash in on him from everywhere and nowhere; but when he felt the surreal hand touch him on the arm once again, his suspicions were confirmed. The ring had been an offering—from one part of himself to another—and now the time had come to return it as freely as it had been given.

He opened his eyes to see the band lying on the cold ground at his feet; yet he dared not pick it up again. It belonged to a different man, another reality; and he wondered if, given the same circumstances, he would have been able to do what Ensign Kirk had done. The ring stared up at him . . . and without understanding how he knew, he also realized that it would not be there when morning came. Feeling a combination of joy and sorrow, he studied the serene surroundings, trying to catch just a glimpse of an illusion, trying to see a ghostly phantom which had once been himself.

There was nothing . . . other than the persistent knowledge that he was not alone.

For an instant, he felt like an intruder; but that thought departed when a gentle thread seemed to enter his mind for just a moment. He did not know if the warmth came from his alternate self, or from the Vulcan who had befriended that young ensign. Or, he decided, perhaps there was no real difference.

He rose slowly, and walked to the edge of the circle of trees, turning to see the glint of metal in the loose sand. In another moment . . .

310

But it was a moment he could not share, an instant out of time reserved for someone else. He had his own life now.

" 'Luck walks with you,' " he murmured, stepping back onto the garden path without a backward glance. Whoever they were, they had found their peace, had made their own reality . . . and, without selfishness or regret, they'd given him back his own.